The HUSTINGS
A FAMILY WEB

D. L. Gollnitz

ARCHWAY
PUBLISHING

Archway Publishing books may be ordered through booksellers or by contacting:

Archway Publishing
1663 Liberty Drive
Bloomington, IN 47403
www.archwaypublishing.com
1 (888) 242-5904

Because of the dynamic nature of the Internet, any web addresses or
links contained in this book may have changed since publication and
may no longer be valid. The views expressed in this work are solely those
of the author and do not necessarily reflect the views of the publisher,
and the publisher hereby disclaims any responsibility for them.

Any people depicted in stock imagery provided by Getty Images are
models, and such images are being used for illustrative purposes only.
Certain stock imagery © Getty Images.

Scripture taken from the King James Version of the Bible.

ISBN: 978-1-4808-8191-4 (sc)
ISBN: 978-1-4808-8193-8 (hc)
ISBN: 978-1-4808-8192-1 (e)

Library of Congress Control Number: 2019913742

Print information available on the last page.

Archway Publishing rev. date: 9/25/2019

This work is dedicated to my husband, Bill.

Stories originate in recesses of the mind. No one can account for strange plot development when a writer allows a character to lead the way.

CONTENTS

Chapter
ONE

NOVEMBER 1945: A CHILD ARRIVES

Nurses were scurrying in all directions. The baby's heartbeat was irregular. Emma's blood pressure dropped radically as she hemorrhaged on the delivery table.

It had been twenty-three long hours of fear and anxiety for Robert Husting. His wife struggled for her life behind those big hospital-gray double doors. Emma, just out of his reach. Maybe forever.

Robert tried to be strong, but the looks on the faces of those who hurried past him were not encouraging. Reaching out to stop one of the nurses as she moved past him, he realized his own needs were not important to her at the moment. Feeling helpless, he slumped away and returned to the hard, green chair, letting his head fall into his hands as his elbows rested on his knees.

The dark gray business suit and crisply starched white shirt were showing his fatigue. Crumpled sleeves, a loosened tie, and beads of sweat on his forehead spoke to Robert's state of mind. Staring at his highly polished black wingtip shoes, his vision blurred with emotion and fatigue. Thoughts of his beautiful Emma flooded him.

Her glowing skin, beautiful dark hair, and black-brown eyes were outward signs of her vibrant personality. Emma filled a room the moment she entered. She'd always dressed fashionably, even in the last few months of pregnancy. Just three days ago, they had dined with friends at the posh Wilmington Dinner Club. Emma sparkled with her nails and hair in perfect order, wearing a pale yellow suit that had been tailored to her tiny pregnant body. Dinner conversation had been easy and pleasant. There were no signs of problems with her pregnancy, and Emma kept up her normal routine. Until yesterday.

Yesterday. The beginning of a new way of life for Robert.

"Mr. Husting, I'd like you to meet your new baby daughter!"

Robert raised his head slowly, unsure if he had heard correctly.

"My … my what?"

"Open your arms. Here you go. Meet your new baby daughter."

Without knowing what he was doing, Robert held a bundle of pink.

"Where is Emma?"

"The doctor will be with you shortly. I'm sorry, Mr. Husting."

The nurse walked away, leaving Robert in the waiting room with nothing but a baby.

Juggling the little body in his arms, he stood up and called out. "Wait—where's Emma? What am I supposed to do with this baby?"

Before Robert could put all the pieces together, Dr. Evans appeared. Bloodstains were splattered on the front of his surgical scrubs. His white shoes were dotted with red and brown. A surgical mask dangled around his neck. He stood solemnly, staring at the little life resting in Robert's arms. "A beautiful little girl, isn't she? Congratulations, Mr. Husting."

"I need to see Emma." Robert shifted his weight from one foot to the other, his head swinging back and forth as he searched the doctor's face for answers.

"We did all that we could, Mr. Husting. I'm sorry."

"All that you could … what does that mean? Where's Emma?"

"I'm sorry. The bleeding was extensive. We did everything we could. She slipped away from us, but we were able to save the baby. You have a beautiful little girl," he said.

Stepping closer, Dr. Evans put a hand on Robert's shoulder. "A nurse will be here soon to take the baby to the nursery. Under these conditions, we like to let the father hold his child. You know, it's like giving a little bit of hope for the future. I'm sorry." Dr. Evans turned and walked away, his shoulders hanging low.

Robert stood stunned. His knees felt weak, and the weight of this tiny thing was greater than he would have ever expected. With two steps backward, he fell into the green chair. This time, he let his head fall back against the wall, his throat closing, his eyes blurring, and the air around him impossible to grasp. Sobs erupted into a wail—"My Emma, my Emma. Oh, where is my Emma? My beautiful Emma. Noooooo!"

"Mr. Husting! Mr. Husting! It will be okay. Everything will be fine. We're here to help you. Let us take your baby to the nursery now. Here we go, let me take her from you." One nurse was trying to retrieve the bundle of pink from Robert's arms, now in a stronghold on the only thing left of Emma.

Another nurse sat next to Robert, trying to console him. "She'll be fine in the nursery; just let us take her now. You need to get some rest." Robert felt his arms drop into his lap as the baby was pulled away.

How he made it through the rest of the night, Robert did not know. His head was pounding when he awoke late in the morning in his own bed. He had no recollection of how he got there. Staggering to the bathroom, he ran through the events of that evening two days ago. A call from Emma. A rush home from his downtown office. The drive to the hospital. Emma. Her breathing becoming more and more labored with every contraction. He remembered her crying out to him to stop the pain.

Then the first two hours at the hospital. Prep for delivery. Robert in the waiting room, alone. Emma somewhere behind those doors. Doctors and nurses giving him updates. *Emma is doing fine. Emma is resting. Emma is having a little bit of difficulty, but everything will be fine. These things happen sometimes. No need to worry.* Then, things started to change.

Well, we'll keep you updated as we can. It seems the baby is distressed, but we can take care of that. It's likely that we will need to do a caesarean delivery. We're prepping Emma for surgery.

She has started to bleed. We want to be sure the baby is okay. No need to worry.

Emma has lost quite a bit of blood. We're doing all that we can for your wife and the baby. No need to worry.

As he thought through that evening and the aching pain he felt to be with his wife, Robert's heart felt as if it literally broke. He couldn't even think about what his beautiful Emma must have suffered. Hospital policy kept him from being by her side. She'd left him. No one cared that he had something to say to her. He needed to tell her that he loved her, that he was happy to be married to her and ready to be the father of their baby. He needed Emma to know that she really was important to him and that she was not just his trophy. But it was too late.

He didn't recognize the man in the bathroom mirror. He shook away the image, relieved himself, and returned to the bed. Pulling the covers over his pounding head, Robert sobbed.

At one o'clock in the afternoon, the telephone rang. The crass ring reverberated, pulling him from his dark hole. His head throbbed with every sound. Reaching for the nightstand, he grabbed the receiver. "Hullo."

"Mr. Husting?"

"Speaking."

"This is Nurse Farris at DuLoche Memorial Hospital."

"Yes?"

"Mr. Husting … we are very sorry for your loss. I know you are probably not feeling up to much today. But will you be coming to the hospital to see her today?"

"Um. Well, I'm not sure. See who?"

"Well, were you planning to come by to see your baby girl?"

"Uh, I hadn't really thought about it." Robert rubbed his scalp and dragged his fingers through his curly black hair.

"I realize this is a difficult time for you, but there are several things you need to take care of. And you really should do those things today." The nurse maintained a businesslike demeanor.

"Like what? What day is this?"

"Today is Saturday, of course."

What could be so important? Why do I need to be in the hospital now, on a Saturday?

"Mr. Husting? Maybe we should talk about a few of the things you need to take care of in person. Can you come by the nurses' station on the fourth floor before three o'clock? Ask for Nurse Farris. Okay?"

"Sure."

Robert hung up the phone and continued to rub his scalp, seeking relief from the pain and throbbing he felt in the top of his head.

─── ᘒᘓ ───

To Robert's surprise, there were very few parking spaces at the hospital. He swung into a space at the very rear of the lot and killed the engine. He pulled his coat collar up, pushed open the door, and dragged his aching body out into the balmy gray November day. Even with temperatures in the midfifties, Robert felt a chill. Tightening the belt of his black trench coat and pulling on the black leather gloves that lived in the pockets, he slumped across the lot. A blaring horn stopped him from stepping in front of a pickup truck. "Get outta the way. My wife's having a baby!"

Emma. My wife had a baby. When?

Less than forty-eight hours had passed, but it could have been a year. Emma was gone. Time was irrelevant. A baby was irrelevant. Life was now irrelevant.

Left, right, left, right, left, right. Robert focused on every movement. His world became surreal. No familiar or tangible things existed for him. Everything looked suspended before his eyes as if he were looking down from another place and time. Left, right, left, right, left, right.

A door. ENTRANCE. He pulled the heavy glass door and stepped inside. The sudden climate change made every breath a wheeze in unbearable heat. Gloves off and onto the floor. The coat belt pulled apart, the buttons quickly pulled apart, and the shoulders pushed down around his upper arms. Sweat beaded his forehead. Robert dropped to the floor.

"Mr. Husting, can you hear me?"

The air felt cold; the lights seemed too bright.

"Mr. Husting?"

Distant voices called to him. He opened his eyes to see blurry figures moving about the room. His eyes were tearing in the glaring white light. He closed them quickly.

"Mr. Husting, you're in the hospital. Can you hear me?"

He kept his eyes shut. "Yes." Then finally he said, "I hear you."

"Can you open your eyes and look at me?"

Slowly, Robert opened his eyelids. Bright light caused him to flinch. "Ahhhh." He closed his eyes immediately.

"What is it, Mr. Husting? Does something hurt?"

"My head. The lights. My eyes."

"It's okay. You're fine. Let me get something for you. You fell in the lobby and hit your head on the tile floor. Do you remember that, Mr. Husting?"

"Vaguely." Robert didn't recognize his own voice. It sounded faint, far away—deep and lacking his usual tight, tense tone.

"We've tested you and see nothing significant. Did you have a headache before you arrived?"

"Migraine, I think." His eyes remained tightly shut without conscious effort.

"So we can get you something for that. The doctor wants to keep you here for observation for a little while. We've tried calling your home phone to let someone know you've been here. No one answered. Is there someone we should call?"

"Emma. Call my wife; she'll get here soon. I'll just sleep till she does." His head fell to the side, and the tension around his eyes released.

"Good morning, Mr. Husting. How are you feeling today?"

"Basically horrible."

It had been three days since Robert returned to the hospital. Multiple attempts to get out of bed had resulted in blackouts. Intravenous fluids, medications for migraine, and rest were beginning to pay off. Things were becoming clearer to Robert. He knew he was in the hospital, that his wife had not survived childbirth, and that he was now the single father of a little girl who remained without a name in a hospital nursery.

The hospital staff had been unsuccessful in contacting any family members for Robert Husting. They accepted his loner status, treated him and his new baby with care and concern, and just left his past alone. The Husting name carried enough weight. They could worry about details later.

"You've had quite a time of it. I don't think I've seen migraines that severe in anyone before. You may not know it, but you've been in that bed since Saturday afternoon, and today is Tuesday."

"I think I know it. The day calendar there on the wall." Robert lay propped up in the bed. He nodded at a paper calendar hanging across from the foot of the bed.

"Well, you were sleeping off and on, so I wouldn't be surprised at all if you lost track of what day it is."

No point in arguing.

"How are you feeling?" The nurse fussed with bedcovers, showing no real interest in what Robert had to say. "Do you want to try a little bit of breakfast?"

"Coffee."

"We'll keep it simple—a little toast, maybe?"

"Sure. Coffee."

Regardless of what he wanted, the tray was already in the room. Tea and toast. *Emma would serve oatmeal with fresh fruit, dark coffee, and sweet rolls. Even on a Tuesday, especially for my first meal in three days.*

The nurse fluffed his pillows and slid the tray in front of Robert. "All set?"

"Sure." Robert stared at the tray as she left the room.

He managed to eat some of his toast with added jelly. The tea actually soothed his aching head a bit.

When he had eaten all that he wanted, he pushed the tray away, slipped the pillows away, and lay back to think. Instead, he dozed back to sleep.

"Mr. Husting, you have company."

Awaking with a shiver, Robert rolled over. The curtain around his bed was being dragged back, shrieking metal against metal, and the sound of squeaky shoes on hard floor came closer. He opened his eyes to find a woman holding a pink bundle. "Who are you? What is that?" He struggled to focus on the swaddling clothes in her arms.

"I'm Nurse Leeder. This, Mr. Husting, is your little girl. She is just beautiful."

Robert felt the sweat forming on his forehead. His hands were clammy, his breathing shallow. "Did you say 'Nurse *Leeder*'?"

"Yes, that's right. And this is your little girl. You know, she has been patiently waiting for you to wake up from your little nap. The one you started three days ago." Her upbeat voice felt too energetic for Robert.

He swallowed hard, missing most of what Nurse Leeder said. He leaned on his elbows as the bed was lowered, making it difficult for him to actually look at this "beautiful little girl." "I can't see her."

"Are you okay? Can you see me?"

"Of course! The bed is too low. Of course I can see you!" *Nurse Leeder*. Robert had no patience, having been awakened by scratching and squeaking and now being probed as if he were some kind of anomaly. *By Nurse Leeder, not someone I want to see.*

The nurse bristled at his reply. After gaining a bit of composure, she added, "I can prop the bed again, as long as your vision is back."

"Back? What are you talking about?" Robert, surprised by his own sharp reply, ran a hand through his hair.

"You had quite a migraine, Mr. Husting. I don't think you

were seeing very well at all for quite some time. It's good to know you can see today."

"Oh." He nodded agreement but remained distracted from the topic.

Fluffed pillows were strategically placed, allowing Robert to rest his elbows to help support his little girl. "There you go; spend some time just getting to know your daughter. I'll be back in a few minutes." She left the room, leaving Robert holding the pink bundle without an opportunity to say no.

My little girl. Emma's little girl. Staring straight into his face, Emma's daughter opened her eyes. Blue. Crystal blue, not at all like Emma's. Sucking on a pacifier, she looked content as her eyes closed softly. The little being felt so right in his arms. But Emma was gone. *This is all I have left of my Emma.*

His eyes filled, and tears streamed down his cheeks, landing on the swaddling clothes that caressed this precious little thing. "Oh, sweet Emma, my precious Emma." Letting his head drop back against the pillow, he used every ounce of strength he had to refrain from sobbing.

"So you have decided to name your baby Emma? What about a middle name; do you have one?" Nurse Leeder was standing by the bed again.

Robert pulled himself together enough to respond. "Well, I suppose Jean would work. Don't you think that sounds okay? Emma Jean?" *Nurse Leeder.*

"Very southern, I'd say. I thought you were a Yankee." She smiled wryly at Robert.

"Indeed. So what about Emma-Mae?"

"Do you have someone in your family by that name?"

"Well, not exactly."

"Mae, I mean."

"Yes, I know. No, no one in the family is named Emma-Mae or Mae, or Jean for that matter." Robert thought perhaps Nurse

Leeder reveled in this exchange a little too much. She didn't look like the Miss Leeder he expected to see, and he felt no interest of any kind in casual, comfortable conversation. It was clear that she was looking for him to handle the naming of this child, and he didn't want to just slap a label on Emma's daughter.

"Sometimes it's good to have a connection in the name, but sometimes it's nice to use something unique. You already have the name of her mother, so it might not be too important to use another family name."

"Yeah. I like Mae. It will be Emmamae, one word, as her middle name." Robert was fussing with the receiving blanket, straightening the folds and tucks so they exposed the round face in a perfect frame of pink.

"Wait. Are you changing your mind about her first name?"

"Yes. I can't call her Emma. There was only one Emma to me. I can use that as part of her name, but not alone. Do you understand? Do I make sense?"

"Certainly, Mr. Husting. Why don't you record the name right here on this line, just the way you want it?" She took the baby from his arms as she moved the bed tray in front of him with pen and documents.

Nurse Leeder pointed to an official-looking document. It appeared as the be-all and end-all of his deliberations. *Why didn't Emma leave me with the name of the baby? Why didn't she tell me what to name this child? We never talked about that. Or did we? Was I just not listening, again?*

Oh, Emma. I'm so sorry. I failed to pay attention to you.

Reaching for the pen, and thinking one last moment about the name, Robert wrote, "Veronica Emma-Mae Husting." Done. No changing it now.

Chapter ———

TWO

The estate bustled with hired hands. Balloons decorated the dining room. Packages filled the corner table. All were wrapped in the little girl's favorite colors. Soft pink and creamy yellow decorations strewn about the room set a calming yet festive atmosphere.

The smell of freshly baked cake wafted through the entry, and the sun streamed in through the sidelights of the front door that faced the southern landscape.

The day grew very warm, not unlike other fall days in the Delaware Valley. Often the forsythia at the back of the estate showed new blossoms of vibrant yellow at this time of year. Such was the case this year. Veronica Emma-Mae Husting's third birthday was an occasion to celebrate. Robert had been waiting for that magical age. Somehow three years old seemed to him a passage into childhood, away from all things baby related. He had anxiously awaited this time so he could move on with his life and forget about those difficult early days. He longed to regain some levity in his demeanor and begin, again, to field his masculinity. He wanted to find another woman to love. But in this place, around this estate that Emma filled with her love, it felt impossible to escape the past. He equated the feelings to being trapped. Everything overwhelmed him.

Upstairs, her nanny dressed little Veronica. After a warm bath and a light dusting of sweet-smelling Bouquet of Flowers talcum powder, Betty led Veronica to the dressing room that connected the washroom to the nursery. "Now, Veronica, which one of your fancy dresses do you want to wear today? You have lots of pretty ones to choose from."

Veronica wrinkled her nose. "Why?"

"Why what? Why wear one of your pretty dresses?"

"Let's just wear my nightie. It's soft."

"Oh, Veronica, your daddy will be here today. It's your birthday luncheon! You want to look really pretty."

"Oh. I'm three! Yeah!" Raising her arms into the air and smiling brightly, Veronica let her brown curls bounce as she bobbed her head playfully from side to side.

"Indeed, you are. You are a big girl, aren't you?" Betty smiled in return, warm and loving.

"Yes, Miss Betty. Daddy will be happy today?" She asked this very important question often.

"Oh, little one, of course he will be. Now let's get dressed."

"Okay, Miss Betty. If you say so." Veronica marched to the carpet, where she knew to stand while Betty dressed her.

Betty turned to the closet, wiped a tear from the corner of her eye, and selected a lovely pink dress. Sewn in soft cotton, the one-piece dress featured a scalloped yoke. The puffed sleeves were short and ended in silk piping. The dirndl skirt gave just enough fullness to add a charming little-girl look.

"How about this pink one?" Betty held the dress up for Veronica's approval.

The little girl giggled with glee, telling Betty she had made a good choice.

After slipping the dress over Veronica's head, Betty spun her around. "You are beautiful, my dear. Let me button you down the back."

Veronica turned dutifully around and stood with her head down as Betty buttoned her dress. "Ouch!" The loud response with a pouting face was part of Veronica's game of getting dressed.

"I'm sorry! Did I catch your hair?" Betty responded with her standard line and expression of remorse.

"Uh-huh." The child nodded and wiggled, all part of the game.

"Well, that's nothing a quick kiss can't cure!"

As Betty smacked the back of little Veronica's neck with a loud kiss, the child squealed with pleasure. "The kiss of cure!" Betty called out.

Veronica giggled with glee and waited for Betty to tie the simple bow that adorned the back waist of the dress with crisp white.

"You are such a silly little girl."

Veronica tipped her head back and giggled with joy.

"Okay, now. Let's get your tights and shoes on so we can get downstairs to see your daddy." Betty tried diligently to move things along just a little faster, knowing that Robert would not wait forever.

"Yeah! I'm three years old!" Again, Veronica threw her arms in the air and tilted her head to the side, a pose she had perfected to gain the attentions and melt the hearts of the Husting estate staff.

Betty laughed and hugged Veronica, who snuggled into Betty's arms as if her whole world were secure in that embrace.

———❧☙———

"What is the holdup here, Arthur? How long does it take to get a three-year-old dressed, for goodness' sake?" Robert paced the floor of the dining room, repeatedly dragging his fingers through his hair and fussing with the handkerchief in his breast pocket.

"Well, Mr. Husting, she's not just any three-year-old. She's *your* three-year-old and very special to all of us, indeed."

"I don't need your comments, Arthur. I need to leave for a meeting in Washington before five. So we need to get this party on the road."

"Yes, sir. Just trying to help, sir." Arthur's curt reply reflected his all-business approach as he realized Robert was losing patience.

"Well, that's enough. Go find Veronica for me." Robert pulled out a chair at the head of the lavishly set dining table and planted himself there. He fussed with the napkin and flatware, aligning the water goblet and coffee cup the way he liked them.

"Yes, sir." Arthur turned to hunt down Betty, but as if on cue, Betty turned the corner, holding Veronica's little hand.

"Daddy!" Veronica ran to Robert. He turned in his seat and welcomed the giggling and squirming little girl into his embrace. She smothered his cheeks with kisses. "I'm three. Are you happy?"

"Oh, little Veronica Emma-Mae, you are a very big girl today. You look very pretty."

"But are you happy, Daddy?"

Putting her down in front of him, Robert looked Veronica over. "Let me see you walk across the room for me," he demanded, ignoring her question.

"What for?"

"Just do it. I want to see how you are doing. Last time I watched you walk across the room, you were still wobbly."

"Oh, Daddy, I can run!"

And run she did. Veronica headed right back out of the dining room, around the corner, and up the stairs. She flew into her nursery and shoved the door closed. Betty and Arthur were right behind her.

"Little girl, open the door. Your daddy needs to have your party and get off to an important meeting." Arthur's disappointment in

Robert Husting interfered with his ability to be his typical gentle and kind self. He loved this little girl like his own child, and it crushed his heart to see her treated like a china doll—taken off the shelf, inspected, and returned for another day.

"Oh yes, your daddy is always working hard so that he can give you wonderful birthday gifts and all the pretty things you have." Betty always came to the rescue.

Arthur nodded in her direction, let his eyes drop to the floor, and worked his way back down the stairs and toward the dining room.

"Oh." A sad face appeared around the door as Veronica opened it cautiously. "Daddy is leaving soon."

Betty sensed the disappointment. "Come on, sweetie. This is a very special day, and you are going to love it! Your daddy will make sure of that! He loves you very much, even if he does have to travel a lot."

It was no secret that Robert Husting had not regained his zest for life since losing Emma. At least not when he stayed around the estate. But the amount of time he actually remained home and in the presence of Veronica had greatly diminished over the past year. He spent more and more time working and traveling, all in the name of accumulating a substantial amount of wealth for Veronica's future.

Lifting Veronica in her arms and balancing the child on her hip, Betty walked down the hall, down the grand staircase, and through the main hallway. Just outside the dining room entrance, she stopped and put Veronica on the floor. "You are getting just a bit too heavy for me to carry you around, young lady. A big girl indeed!"

Arthur stood ready to greet them. "Now, Miss Veronica, you will stand up straight and proud and show your daddy just how three-years-old you are! Are we ready?" His smile brought a twinkle to his eye, and little Veronica raised her shoulders, giggled, threw her hands in the air, and shouted out, "Yes! I'm three!" Her excitement showed as she bounced toward Arthur to take his hand.

Arthur, Betty, and Veronica entered the dining room as proud as could be.

Robert Husting smiled. "Well, little missy, you certainly can run! I'm proud of you."

Veronica ran across the room. Robert stood to greet her. He lifted the child into a hug, her little arms curling around his neck. She planted a wet smooch on each of his cheeks. "I'm three, Daddy! I'm three! You happy?"

"Oh, of course, honey. You are a big girl now." Robert lowered Veronica back to the floor. As he did so, he turned toward the windows that overlooked the backyard. *Emma, I never had a chance to tell you.*

"Did you say something, Mr. Husting?" Betty sensed that he had mumbled something.

"Oh, no. I'm just admiring the balmy November day we're having. Seems to me we had similar temperatures on the day Veronica was born. Funny weather we have around here. Wet and warm when we should be getting ready for Christmas lights." With a turn and a shake of his head, Robert continued, "Oh well. So let's get on with the festivities, shall we?"

Two more domestic servants arrived with perfect timing, carrying trays that served a perfect lunch.

On this occasion, the staff were invited to join in on the celebrations. Veronica's favorite soup accompanied by small tea sandwiches brought a smile to her face. Fresh fruit compote followed, and a lavish birthday cake, complete with a ballerina on top, was served with Veronica's favorite vanilla ice cream. Three tall candles marked the occasion.

At the end of the meal, Veronica turned to Robert, sighed, and rubbed her tummy. "I'm too full, Daddy."

With a deep chuckle, Robert reached across the table to take Veronica's hand in his own. "Well, you certainly ate your share of soup and tea sandwiches, not to mention cake! No wonder you're full."

"No more." Her distressed face would win compassion from anyone.

"Okay. Let's take a little break from the table and wander over to that corner of the room. Do you see what I see?"

Veronica slowly got down from her seat and moved toward the corner. Sucking in a great volume of air that could be heard across the room, Veronica exploded with delight. "Oh, Daddy, Daddy, Daddy. Presents! You're happy."

"Yes, sweetie. Now go ahead and open the packages, I've got to get going very soon."

"Oh, cuddle me, Daddy. My belly hurts."

Robert's vision blurred. He choked back the sobs that welled up in his chest. Feeling ready to crumble, he squatted down and welcomed Veronica onto his knee. "Of course."

Righting himself carefully with Veronica in his arms, Robert shifted his weight to balance the small body on his left forearm. He walked across the hallway into the sitting room and lowered himself into the settee as Veronica once again wrapped her little arms tightly around his neck. Once the two of them were resting against the corner of the settee, Veronica slid down onto Robert's lap, her arms slipping away from her father's neck, her head resting on his chest. With heavy eyes, she moved her left hand flat against her daddy's heart, and her right thumb found its way into her mouth. Robert smoothed his pants leg as best he could, swept the curls away from Veronica's forehead, and leaned back. He used the pillow that sat squarely in the middle of the settee to rest his elbow and support Veronica. Within minutes, father and daughter were dozing.

Mr. Husting! Mr. Husting! It will be okay. Everything will be fine. We're here to help you. Let us take your baby to the nursery now. Here we go, let me take her from you.

"What?!" Robert was startled and awakened abruptly.

"It's okay, Mr. Husting. I guess Veronica got worn out today. I'm sorry. Let me take her up to the nursery for a short nap." Betty stood in front of Robert. "You can then get a proper rest before your travels."

"Yes, yes, of course." With a quick kiss to Veronica's brow, he released the child to Betty, who gently lifted the limp body and carried her off.

Robert stood up, heavy sweat on his brow. He reached for the handkerchief that always stayed in his breast pocket. His shaking hands made the task difficult. The white linen cloth, hand-embroidered with the initials R. H., held a faint scent of Bouquet of Flowers talc, Emma's scent. Shoulders racking and arms stiffening, Robert felt the sobs coming on once again. He fell to his knees, leaning his upper body against the settee, his head falling into the pillow, his hands on the seat.

Just for a moment he was back in the hospital waiting room. Once again, his baby had been taken away to a nursery—his Emma taken away. The tears flowed without constraint, and Robert struggled to his feet. In staggering steps, he made his way up the stairs and down the hall to his own suite across the hall from the nursery. Closing the door in a teary fog, he fell on the bed and succumbed to his sadness.

A loud rapping on the door pulled Robert from his sleep.

"Mr. Husting? Are you okay? Mr. Husting?"

"Yes, yes, Betty. I'm fine. Go away."

"But, Mr. Husting, you must get on the road for your meeting."

"What time is it?"

"Nearly three o'clock, sir. You must have dozed off."

"Okay, okay. Let me be. I'll be out shortly."

"Little Veronica is awake, sir."

"Okay. Thank you."

Betty stepped away from the door, looking carefully around to be sure no one would see her. She spoke loudly enough for her voice to be heard through the door. "I've brought you a cool drink to help refresh you, Mr. Husting. Cook made fresh mint iced tea today." After tinkering with the ice cubes and adding a cube of sugar, she left the beverage on a tray outside his room. "It is here on the tray, sir."

Betty hurried to the dining room. There, near all of her presents in the corner of the room, Veronica sat wide-eyed and ready to tackle the packages.

"Miss Betty, are these all mine?"

Smoothing her uniform skirt and watching over her shoulder, Betty replied as naturally as possible: "Yes, Veronica. You are one very lucky three-year-old!"

"Where's Daddy?"

"He's in his bedroom, sweetie. He must have taken a nap at the same time as you! Did you wear him out today?"

"I'm not tired."

Forcing a little laugh, Betty replied, "I know you're not tired; you just had your nap! So let's get some iced tea. Cook made a delicious mint tea today. It will help settle your tummy if you're still feeling full. Then maybe your daddy will be ready for you to open your gifts. Is that a good idea?"

"Yes, Miss Betty. I'm thirsty."

The two of them made their way to the kitchen, just missing Robert as he came down the stairs.

"Arthur?! Arthur, where are you?!"

"Yes, sir. Good afternoon, sir. How may I help you? Would you like some tea or coffee? What about a cool drink instead, since it's a mild afternoon?"

"Stop, Arthur. I just had some iced tea. What I want is my daughter to open her presents so I can get on the road. Where is she?" Robert tugged his tie and adjusted the knot.

"I'll go look for her. I'm sure Betty is with her. How about if you go to the sitting room, and I'll bring Veronica in to you."

"Yes, fine."

The sitting room. Where the air smells of Emma and the furniture is filled with her personality. Robert could not deny the strange presence in that room—everything always tidy, clean. He walked slowly to the window that looked out onto the side garden. *Emma used to sit on the bench.* A garden bench aligned to the south side of the footpath. The roses were directly across the path, and their fragrance could be enjoyed from that spot. Emma spent many summer mornings in that spot, just enjoying the lofty scent of pink and yellow. *Bouquet of Flowers. Emma's scent.*

"Here we are, Daddy!" Veronica bounded into the room. "Let's get presents!"

"You go ahead and get started. I'm coming."

Veronica and Betty moved to the dining room. Robert closed the drapes before leaving the room. *Goodbye, sweet Emma.* He gained his composure, straightened his suit coat, ran his fingers through the curls on the top of his head, and left the sitting room.

Without much forethought, Robert called to James, his driver. "Bring the car around, James. My bags should be in the trunk. We'll be heading out shortly."

"Yes, sir." James came running from the study, where he'd left the mail for Arthur to sort later. "Do you plan on catching the 4:30 train, sir?"

"Yes, I will. Veronica will be finished in time."

"Yes, sir." James scurried off. Robert continued on to the dining room.

There stood Veronica, holding up a Shirley Temple doll and drawing in quick, deep breaths. "Daddy! Daddy! She's mine."

"Indeed, she is all yours. What else did you find?" Robert chuckled loudly, enjoying her mood.

"A duck!"

"A rubber duck to make those baths much more fun! What else?"

"Doll clothes. Dollhouse! Doll buggy. Yeah! I'm three. You happy, Daddy?"

"If *you* are happy, that's all that matters, Veronica."

"I'm happy!" Veronica twirled around and bobbed up and down, her hair bouncing and shining in the low light that streamed through the southern-facing windows.

"Well, that's settled then. I'll let you play with your new toys, and then I'll be on my way."

Stooping down to lift Veronica, Robert felt a strange aura. Quite suddenly, an insurmountable fatigue struck him. "Oh my, sweetie. I'm afraid I need to sit down. I'd better not lift you right now."

Slowly rising up, Robert balanced himself against the dining room table. When he had steadied himself, Betty came to his side. Walking in a wavering path, Robert found his way back to the sitting room and dropped into the settee. Veronica had scurried in behind him. She climbed on the seat next to him and watched as Robert dropped back into a deep sleep.

"Daddy? Daddy, you 'wake?"

"Leave him be, Miss Veronica. Daddy is very tired. He'll be fine. Come with me to the playroom. We can set up that dollhouse and dress your new dolls and ..."

Betty nodded at Arthur and James, who had appeared in the sitting room doorway. "That should detain him just long enough."

"What, Miss Betty?" Veronica showed confusion.

"I just said that we can move your toys up to the playroom and begin to set up the dollhouse. Let's go play."

Arthur and James slipped back to their respective tasks as Betty led Veronica up the stairs to the nursery and playroom.

Arthur returned to the office to package the mail that Robert needed to see. In usual fashion, Arthur prioritized the most important things, labeled them, and put them in a leather satchel that Robert carried on his trips.

In the garage located at the back of the property, James had to focus on the car. The fan belt had been cut and the tires slashed. He'd made a phone call about thirty minutes earlier, as soon as he discovered the vandalized car. Knowing that Robert would not have handled the news very well at all, James and Arthur worked with Cook and Betty to detain his trip. Now he just needed to be sure nothing looked unusual when Mr. Husting awoke from his unexpected nap. Working swiftly and quietly alongside the local auto service station attendee who had arrived with all the necessary parts and tools, James had the car ready to roll within an hour and a half. Robert would have to catch a later train.

James parked in the front circle driveway, waiting for Mr. Husting to awake. The local newspaper was tossed through the open car window by the carrier, who hollered out to James, "Headline looks like something Mr. Husting will want to see on his way out of town!" Before he could respond, the delivery boy was gone.

James scanned the headline and the following article: MISS CAROLYN LEEDER—MAKING A COMEBACK IN WILMINGTON. A celebration at the Wilmington Dinner Club marked her return. Any person of social standing in high circles would be expected to attend. And everyone would be waiting to hear the sordid details of her quick disappearance and her flamboyant return. All of the notables had been interviewed, and excerpts were spread across the page. Pictures of Miss Leeder from 1942, when she debuted on the Broadway stage, were a treat for any man's eyes.

Robert walked quickly down the front steps of the mansion, Arthur at his side.

"Arthur, we need to hurry. I'm not going to catch the 4:30 train, but I definitely need to be on the 5:20. Let's go."

"Yes, sir. Here is your mail."

"Thank you, Arthur."

Climbing in the back of the black sedan, Robert barked instructions: "James, we need to be at the station by five o'clock so I can be sure to get a ticket for the 5:20. Arthur, I looked in on Veronica. She's fine. But you need to get her a tricycle. She's ready. Needs to be outside on these balmy days getting some fresh air. Take care of that right away."

"Yes, Mr. Husting. I'll do that. Any particular color?"

"If they come in pink, do that." Robert paused to brush the lint off his shoulders.

"Yes, sir."

"And tell Betty to stop calling the child's bedroom a nursery! She's not a baby anymore."

Robert settled against the back seat and pulled his door closed. "Let's go James." He straightened the handkerchief in his pocket.

James held up the newspaper. "You might like to take this on the train with you, sir."

He had gingerly folded the front page inward so the headlines were not visible.

"Good idea, James. I've not seen the local paper when the news is still fresh in a long time! I'll do that. Thank you." He reached for the newspaper and tucked it inside the satchel that carried his mail.

James pulled the car away from the house. As the sedan headed down the long, tree-lined driveway, Arthur stood on the driveway watching them drive away.

The car remained silent all the way to the train station.

———— ❧ ————

James unloaded the bags from the trunk and handed them over to the porter at the train station.

"Anything else, Mr. Husting?"

"No, James. I'm fine. Be sure Arthur gets that tricycle. In pink."

"Of course, sir."

Gripping his leather satchel of mail, Robert gave a nod. Then he made his way on board the train without looking back.

Finding a relatively quiet car, Robert took a seat that would allow him room to thumb through the mail and make good use of his commuting time. The stack seemed a bit larger than usual, perhaps because it had been a fairly long time since he had been at the estate. Arthur generally did a good job of sorting through the nonessentials and passing along only those things that needed his attention.

At the top of the stack were two letters, one from his aunt in Milwaukee and one from a distant cousin in Minneapolis. Robert settled in for the usual, long-winded diatribe committed to paper that was customary for Clare. She had a habit of giving him every morbid detail of her social affairs, the latest recipe she thought he should give to Cook, and other such innocent and boring details of life back home. She'd never married—a spinster with too much time on her hands. He'd never had the heart to tell her that he just had no interest in petty things. Telephone calls were equally painful, so he read her letters. This particular letter mentioned a set of pearls she was sending to Betty for Ronnie's wedding day. *Wedding day—how many years till then?*

Reaching for the second letter, he noted that Dwight Bastien's handwriting was sloppy—nothing new there.

September 28, 1948
Dear Robert,

I hope all is well with you and little Veronica. She must be getting big.

I'm in Los Angeles on business, and I met an old friend of yours. The name is Carolyn Leeder, and she was part of the entertainment at a club in downtown LA. The dancers mingle with the crowd there. You know what I mean? She joined me for drinks, and one thing led to another. Anyway, I was shocked to hear that she knew you years ago! It's a small world.

Anyway, I just thought I'd drop the enclosed brochure to you. You can see the club where I met Carolyn. She's the one on the far left in the picture of the dancers who perform. Great place.

We really should try to get together. I think at this time in our careers, we could do some good things together. My business is growing in leaps and bounds!

Regards,
Dwight

Robert looked at the brochure stuffed in the envelope. Yes, that was definitely Carolyn Leeder. *Dwight Bastien. The bastard. Probably drunk again.*

Robert shoved the two letters back into the satchel. He would deal with those later. Right now, he needed to look at the more pressing pieces of mail. A letter from a nearby estate owner complaining about property boundaries took most of his attention. The latest election of officers at the Wilmington Dinner Club proved to be an entertaining read, but the headline of the *Daily News* sent Robert into a polarized state of mind: MISS CAROLYN LEEDER—MAKING A COMEBACK IN WILMINGTON.

Perspiration started to dampen his neck. There were pictures of Carolyn in various stage performances in Wilmington, New York City, and Philadelphia. A beauty, Carolyn had been a singer for some very sought-after big bands, playing the role perfectly. Offering sex appeal to the all-male ensembles, she kept swing music ever popular in the Northeast. Grabbing the handkerchief from his suit pocket, Robert started sweeping his brow and blotting the back of his neck. *What is she doing?* Memories of Carolyn. The scent of flowers colliding with his rapid pulse ended in guilt. Two very different women. The two lives of Robert Husting.

Chapter ———
THREE
— NOVEMBER 1948: RETURN TO THE PAST —

"This is Robert Husting calling. I'd like to speak with Miss Carolyn Leeder, please."

"One moment, sir."

Robert was in Washington, DC. The train ride seemed unending. The anticipation of getting Carolyn on the line weighed heavily on him, and the wait only exacerbated his anxiety.

The newspaper said she was back in Wilmington. After several calls to area hotels, he gave up and contacted the Wilmington Dinner Club. The manager told him the details of Carolyn's itinerary, and this call produced the gem.

"Robert, how wonderful to hear your voice. It's been ages." Carolyn's singsong voice reflected her buoyant personality.

"So it has. What are _you_ doing in _Wilmington?_" Robert needed to get right to business. He didn't welcome her presence in his town.

"Well, you must know already if you've tracked me down here. But I am performing at the club tomorrow evening. I hope you'll be there."

She acted innocent, and Robert had no patience for games.

"No, I won't. I gave you enough to keep you away from Wilmington for the next thirty years. You agreed. Now what are you doing?" _Be direct. Don't get sucked in._

"Oh, really, Robert. You didn't think that measly little bit of cash was really going to do it, did you? My fan base is here, and they have been after me to return for the past year and a half. It wasn't a good enough story for them that I had to leave to take care of a relative in California. Besides, who would really buy that story?"

"I know you've been getting around, but I didn't think you would have the nerve to show up on my doorstep." *Stick to business.*

"Oh, that's right. How could I forget? Your cousin. What was his name? Was it Darren? Dylon?"

"Dwight." *Damn him.*

"Yes, that's it! Dwight. What a charming man. He absolutely swept me off my feet that night. Not too far from your own skills, Robert. Or have you lost that touch of yours?"

What did they do? "Carolyn, we need to have a talk. How long will you be in Wilmington?"

"As long as you need me here, Robert. I'll be waiting for you." Carolyn still used that sexy vocal asset of hers.

"I'll call you in a week. Good night, Carolyn."

"I can't wait to see you again, Robert. Good night, love."

Robert slammed the phone receiver and bolted to the bar in the lobby. He ordered a double scotch on the rocks.

Back at the estate, Veronica enjoyed all her birthday gifts. Betty and Arthur selected the perfect tricycle for her and had it delivered the very day after her party. James helped her learn to drive the bike around the circular driveway. The November days were warmed with sunshine and offered nice afternoon hours for outdoor play. Veronica took to her new freedom of motion and enjoyed every moment she could on the wheels.

By the time Robert returned a week later, Veronica had mastered her tricycle.

James was pulling the car into the garage, and Veronica came down the front steps of the house, followed by Betty and Arthur.

"Daddy, watch me, watch me!"

Veronica climbed on the tricycle and began to pedal her way around the circular drive. She gained enough speed to cause alarm in everyone who was watching. In no time at all, she had circled back to the front steps and plowed into the post at the bottom step. She tumbled over into the grass and started to make mumbling noises.

"Veronica, are you all right? Did you hit your head? Let me look at your knees."

Robert dropped his satchel and rushed to her side. Kneeling in the grass, he checked her knees and elbows. Veronica's big brown eyes opened wide, and she giggled. She laughed so hard, Robert couldn't help but smile.

"Was I good?"

"Oh my, little one. You are a daredevil. Well, I guess you did fool me!" Robert glowed with love.

Little Veronica wrapped her arms around her father's neck, and he lifted her into a great big bear hug, the two of them laughing their way up the stairs and into the house.

Betty and Arthur followed.

"I don't know how much more of these little antics I can tolerate. When did you teach her that trick, Arthur?" Betty sighed and shook her head.

"Did you like it? Thought it might scare him a little bit. He ought to be paying a little more attention to the child," he responded, his voice trailing off as he moved ahead of her.

"And you think that kind of thing will work?" Betty almost yelled out at Arthur.

"Maybe! Look at them now!" Arthur called back over his shoulder and continued on inside.

The two went their separate ways. Betty tended to Robert's belongings and escorted Veronica into the washroom to clean her knees.

Arthur returned to the study to sort Mr. Husting's mail and prepare for the weekly review of household expenses.

Robert went up to his suite to prepare for dinner.

Cook always prepared a good meal for Mr. Husting's first day home. He had been traveling a good deal over the past several months, and his time on the estate was very limited. This time, rumors were that he might be home for a little while longer. Betty heard from her friends in town that his plans might have something to do with Miss Carolyn Leeder.

❧⸙

"Miss Leeder, please."

Robert stood in the lobby of the Wilmington Inn, an exquisite hotel frequented by those traveling on both business and pleasure. Heavy red velvet armchairs adorned with gold fringe were nestled together in a cozy corner of the lobby near a stately marble fireplace. The unusually warm fall weather didn't call for a fire for heat, but its glow added to the ambiance of the tall-ceilinged space. Crystal chandeliers hung above, and dark wood tables were strategically placed, welcoming the weary to rest with a drink and reading material.

Robert had a pleasant dinner with Veronica at the estate, but his edginess about this personal call caused him to cut their after-dinner interactions a bit short. He focused on the creases in his pant legs, lifting the fabric to help the creases fall in a straight line all the way to his shined dress shoes. Robert looked about the lobby, waiting for the concierge to call Carolyn. To his surprise, a porter escorted him to her room.

"Miss Leeder, Mr. Husting to see you."

"Thank you, Albert. Come in, won't you, Robert?" Carolyn had command of the situation.

The concierge left the doorway. Robert stepped inside, and Carolyn closed the door behind him. In one smooth movement she flipped the lock and wrapped herself around Robert.

Her touch sent him into uncontrollable desire. It had been three years too long. He responded to her kiss without inhibition, and the two lost themselves in one another.

A train rumbled by. Robert checked his watch. It was the last train to Washington for the evening: 8:45. He ran his fingers through his thick black curls, trying to tame them. The satin pillowcase served its purpose for Carolyn but maybe not for him.

"Where have you been all this time, Robert? I expected to hear from you from time to time." Carolyn was propped on her elbow, leaning over Robert's face.

"Let's not talk about that. We have a little bit more time right now, so let's not waste it." Robert rolled toward her in the bed.

"Not so fast, Robert. I want to hear why you haven't contacted me."

Pulling back now. She's after something.

When he didn't respond, Carolyn pressed on. "Well? Tell me, Robert. Why didn't I hear from you?"

"We had an agreement." He tried to sound cordial and not flustered or panicked, even as he felt an increasing pulse.

"Yes, so you thought. Your precious Emma fit into your high-society world better than I did. But what happened to good old love?" *The old Carolyn is returning.*

"I loved her too." He had a sense of melancholy mixed with guilt as this simple fact spilled out.

"And that's why you *kept* me? Because you loved her enough to have her be your wife and the mother of your children, but you needed me for *real* love?"

She's sexy when she's angry. "I loved you too. It was all so complicated then, Carolyn. But that's over. Let's just enjoy this reunion for a few more minutes." In an effort to gain the upper hand, he reached toward her, but Carolyn moved out of the bed. She slipped into a silk robe. "What makes you think you can just have a tumble in my bed and owe me nothing?"

"Owe you? What do you mean? You had plenty of cash from me when you left three years ago. You couldn't have possibly needed anything more from me." *So this is her point—money.*

"What about an explanation? Don't you think I deserve that much?" Her face flushed, and the lines around her eyes tightened.

"What is it that you don't know, Carolyn?" Robert's voice was louder than he intended with clear, crisp diction, his anger audible.

"What did you tell Emma about us?"

"I didn't get to tell Emma anything. She died in the delivery room before I could explain that you were gone for good." His words were still deliberate, his palms were sweating, and he had to look away.

"Gone for good?" Carolyn's voice grew louder. She began pacing, her body visibly shaking. "Is that what you planned to tell her?"

Robert didn't answer. He rolled over on his side and stared at the wall.

Now Carolyn was almost screaming, and her questions spilled out quickly. "You were going to tell her I was gone for good! What were you going to tell her about *our* daughter, Robert? Did you forget that I was pregnant? Did you forget that you promised to care for *our* little girl just as well as the baby she had? Or were you just going to leave that part out?" Even more flushed and with tears welling in her eyes, Carolyn flopped down on the edge of the bed.

Robert threw the covers back, jumped out of the bed, and stormed across the room to the chair that held his clothes.

"If you don't want to have a quiet, peaceful reunion, then forget about all of it." His words were definitive. He intended to leave no room for negotiation.

He pulled his pants on, tugged his shirt over his shoulders, and buckled his belt. He sat down to put on his shoes, and when he looked up, Carolyn was standing right in front of him. Her robe slipped down to her waist. Her lips were parted, and she reached down to run her fingers through the hair at the back of his neck. Tears streamed down her face. Clasping her hands behind his head, she pulled his face up to hers and met his lips with passion.

Damn. Robert succumbed. The kiss was passionate, sweet, and confusing all at the same time.

"Why do you do this?" Robert whispered. He looked Carolyn directly in the eyes, holding her face in his hands.

"What are you talking about, love?"

He had no restraint left. Robert had been through enough, and he welcomed the opportunity for distraction.

The sun peeked through the drawn drapes; Robert listened for the train. The first run to Washington would be leaving at 6:45. He glanced at his watch. It was 6:40.

Carolyn rolled over. Her eyes were glistening in the bit of sunlight that reached her face. They were a deep shade of green. Robert remembered the first time he'd seen those eyes. Carolyn was a singer in one of the luxury hotel lounges in Atlantic City. He made it a point to frequent that lounge as often as possible, and he and Carolyn enjoyed a relationship that spanned many years.

She was his lover; he was her dream come true. Each had different ideas of where things would lead.

"Are you hungry?" Carolyn broke his gaze with her practicality.

"Just some coffee would be good."

"I'll order."

"No. Please don't."

"Afraid to be seen with me still?"

Maybe. "Carolyn, we have to talk."

"We do, but last night you didn't want that."

"True, but you were right. We need to have a conversation, but this morning I need to get to work."

"Well, if we can't talk now, and since I'm working the club tonight, which means I'll be busy late this afternoon, when do you propose we have a conversation?" Impatience set the tone of her question.

Robert got out of bed, dressed, ran his hands through his hair, and came back to sit on the edge of the bed. He fussed with his shirt collar. "Let's have lunch. I'll pick you up at 12:30. Then you can have the afternoon to prepare for your show." She nodded her agreement.

With a kiss to her forehead, Robert made his way out of the room, through the hallways, and across the hotel lobby without suspicion. He hailed a cab.

When he arrived back at the estate, he could smell the coffee percolating, the wonderful aroma filling the house. Robert moved quietly up the stairs and into his suite to prepare for breakfast. No one would be the wiser about his escapade with Carolyn, especially not the estate staff.

From the edge of the stairs, Betty watched Robert slip through his suite door. She twirled a loose strand of hair into place and continued on to the kitchen.

"G' mornin', Cook. Looks like another mild day. This crazy weather brings on all kinds of crazy things."

"What?"

"Nothin' important. Let's get breakfast on the table. Mr. Husting will be in a hurry, I'm sure."

Betty started grabbing flatware and plates, putting the sugar and cream in their china holders, and moving in and out of the dining room. Cook was on her heels with a dish of scrambled eggs, bacon, and potatoes.

"Where's little Veronica this morning, Betty?" Arthur was right behind with the muffins, toast, and jellies.

"Sound asleep. I'm not going to wake her. Somethin' tells me to leave the child alone today. She'll wake up when she's good and ready." Betty exercised her intuition to do what she thought would be best for everyone.

"It is still a little early; you're probably right to let Miss Veronica stay in bed awhile. It's not often that Mr. Husting is here on a weekday for breakfast; I forget how early he gets up and out."

"Depends on what's goin' on, I suppose." Betty believed Robert had been otherwise engaged at the Wilmington Inn last night. She had heard rumors around town about Carolyn Leeder staying at the Wilmington until she could find a place of her own.

———— ❧ ————

With a quick breakfast and two cups of coffee, Robert called for his car to be brought to the front. "James, please bring the Princess around to the front. I'll drive myself downtown today."

"Sir? Are you sure you don't want me to shuttle you to the office, sir?"

"No. I'll be perfectly fine. I will be running about town today and won't want to be waiting for you to arrive between stops. Thanks for your concern."

"But, sir, the Princess is quite ..."

"I said thank you for your concern, James. Just bring the car now." Robert's voice was sharp and demanding. James knew better than to continue his line of reasoning.

"Yes, sir."

James pulled the black Austin Princess from the garage to the front of the house. The paint shined with James's meticulous care. Robert impatiently waited at the front. With his satchel tucked under his arm, he moved to the driver's-side door before James was even out of the car. With a quick nod and spin out of the way, James made way for Robert to get seated.

"Sir, you didn't get a chance to review the mail and household details last evening. Will you be interested in having that conversation with Arthur later today?"

"Why isn't Arthur asking me this question?" *What's going on with these two? Can't they do their own jobs anymore?*

"He tried to, sir, but he missed you as you were leaving the dining room this morning. He asked me to check with you, sir."

"I see. I must've been in a hurry. So yes. Now let me get on with my day. I'll talk with Arthur this afternoon."

Robert pulled the door closed, and before James could reply, the Princess was heading down the driveway. *I need to have a talk with James and Arthur. It's time they started making some decisions about household matters, the petty stuff.*

James stood on the driveway watching and wondering what had been distracting Robert these past few days.

Robert worked through the morning in his office. The hours flew by, filled with telephone calls to customers, a new project for the company that involved some legal attention, and the typical review of financials. Before he had finished a meeting with his assistant, it was time to drive by the Wilmington and pick up Carolyn. "I'm sorry, Jeannette, but we'll have to pick up with this when I return from lunch. Please excuse me."

"But, Mr. Husting, these reports are due to the accounting department before 2:00 today. I don't know if we'll have enough time to review all of the line items for your input if we don't finish up now."

"Let them do the financials without my review. I can look at the results later. Sorry, I've got to go. This meeting can't be postponed." *Petty.*

"Yes, sir." Jeannette left the office, shaking her head in disbelief.

Robert draped a scarf around his neck, reached into his breast pocket, and removed the embroidered handkerchief. He tucked it in his top desk drawer and shoved it closed. *No Emma today.* Looking in the mirror on the back of his coat closet door, he straightened the scarf, tugged at his coat collar, and ran his fingers through a few stray curls on the left side of his head. He strode out of his office and into the parking garage.

Feeling rather debonair, Robert slid into the Princess. He checked his appearance once more in the rearview mirror before pulling out of the garage. *This could be a long process. Or not. Depends on Carolyn's willingness to relinquish her claim on me. Do I really want that?*

—⟷—

Carolyn sat in the lobby of the Wilmington. Robert pulled in front, and the valet greeted him. "Mr. Husting, Miss Leeder is ready."

The concierge escorted Carolyn, and the valet opened the passenger door. Robert hadn't seen such a beautiful woman in years. Three years, to be exact. Carolyn was voluptuous and knew exactly how to move her body in ways that sent chills through any man. She sauntered her way through a room, and when she performed on stage, that voice was enough to excite even the resolute married man. Carolyn's performances with jazz bands helped to popularize and localize the scat singing style. She could translate the Creole sounds of Duke Ellington's music to please the blues and swing crowds. Her versatility in vocal style was unprecedented in Wilmington clubs, and without a doubt, Carolyn was on her way to stardom. She was not easily resisted. Relocating to Los Angeles was not the best move of her career, and Robert knew that. He had been selfish in getting her far away from the Northeast. Today, he hoped to settle all the old conflicts.

"Well, look at you, Miss Leeder. Dazzlingly beautiful as always." *Damn. Why does she have to be so gorgeous?*

"Thank you, love. But the flattery isn't necessary." Carolyn's deadpan response said it all. *She hears that from all the men.*

Robert pulled the car out of the drive and headed north out of the city without explanation.

When Carolyn realized where they were headed, she queried the choice. "Wait! Where are you taking me? Aren't we just going to a local joint, somewhere nearby?"

"I think it would be good to get a little way out of the city today. Don't you?"

"I need to be in town to prep for tonight."

"Don't worry about that, Carolyn; you'll be back in plenty of time." *Or not.*

They headed north out of the state of Delaware entirely. Just north of the state line, they entered Chester County, Pennsylvania, and Carolyn commented on the gentle rolling hills. "It's as if God made this part of the country just so people would know what beauty really is, don't you think, Robert?" She was enjoying the scenery—a plus for Robert.

Robert thought for a long moment before he replied warmly,

"Perhaps. But all anyone needs to do is look at you to know the definition of beauty."

Carolyn reached across the seat and stroked his cheek with the back of her gloved hand. "You are still as sweet as ever. But don't try to sucker me into something."

Robert smiled wryly. It was true: the rolling hills of Chester County were truly beautiful, even in November. The air was crisp, but the sunshine removed the chill. Carolyn's presence had an effect on Robert. He hadn't been this relaxed in a long time. She was relaxed as well. His own response to her comment shocked him. He'd never intended to let her know how he still felt about her. She was comfortable to be with, and her presence alone penetrated his body with the afterglow of their lovemaking.

They turned down a long dirt road toward the west. The winding way took them to an inn located deep in the heart of the hills.

"The Dilling Inn!" Carolyn clearly showed her excitement with no restraint.

"Yes; remember it?"

"All too well, my love!"

They parked the car. Robert offered Carolyn his arm, and they strolled to the front entrance. Robert turned and gave Carolyn a peck on the cheek and whispered in her ear: "Let's make the best of this time together."

"We will, for sure, Robert. But don't think for one minute there won't be many more opportunities to be together."

What am I doing? Robert didn't know in which direction he really wanted things to go. At that moment, he resolved to let things unfold as they may.

"So it's settled." Carolyn looked straight ahead.

Robert was content. They had enjoyed a wonderful lunch, had

discussed several awkward topics, and were making the return trip to Wilmington. In his mind, this was a successful mission. He would have his mistress back, and there would be no need to discuss anything more.

"Yes, I think so!" Robert felt quite pleased.

"I still have a few questions. What about *our* daughter? I don't think I can live as a *mistress* forever, Robert."

"Let's just take it a step at a time. Besides, you're not my mistress. I'm not married. My daughter is three years old, and I'm free to begin a relationship. Let's just see where it goes from here. Sound good to you?" Robert was confident that they could be an item without any disruption to his current lifestyle on the estate.

"You really need to get to know Margaret. She's a darling little girl. Also three years old, by the way. *And*, once you know her, you will feel that she belongs on that estate right along with Veronica."

"Not so fast. Let's just take it a step at a time, like I said." Robert felt a little bit of panic. *Is she after the Husting family estate?*

"Look, Robert, I can't stay in Wilmington forever. You need to provide for me and Margaret. The nanny thing in Los Angeles isn't working out that well. Margaret will be joining me in a week or so."

"That's not my problem. I gave you plenty of cash to support that child. You just have to deal with that." Robert was sensing a shift in Carolyn's objective for the day.

"I don't think I *can* deal with that, Robert. And she's not *that child*! She's *our child*. What I think we need to do is get married. That will take care of everything."

"Marry you? When did that become a part of this conversation?" *What if she tells the press everything about my infidelities? What will happen to Husting Manufacturing? What about Veronica? What about Emma's reputation?* Sweaty palms made it difficult to hold the steering wheel firm. Robert shifted hands, wiping them on his pant legs. In between, he ran fingers through his hair and kept glancing at the rearview mirror.

"I'm a celebrity, and you should see the chance of a lifetime right here before your eyes."

"Carolyn, let's be reasonable. I need more time, what with everything going on at the office right now and financials for the year-end transfers needing review. How can I possibly have time to think through everything you're asking for? Besides, do you really want to marry *me*? Think about that!"

"There should be nothing to *think about*, Robert." Carolyn was definitive.

Robert thought that a visit to one of their old tryst locations would soften her heart enough to give him time—time to find a way to convince Carolyn that they made a wonderful couple, just not publicly. *I should have known better. Her line of work doesn't demand a respectable lifestyle. She can get away with anything and still have a following. What would that lifestyle do to me, my business? What about Emma? Veronica?*

They drove in silence, Robert deep in thought about the repercussions of his actions, including meeting Carolyn at the Wilmington, falling prey to his own desires, inviting her to lunch at a place that held memories for both of them, wanting her more than he cared to admit. *Maybe it is time to own up to my other family members. But marry Miss Carolyn Leeder, club singer?*

Chapter

FOUR

DECEMBER 1948: MOVING FORWARD

The Christmas tree was the pinnacle of opulence. Plush velvet ribbons in gold and white ran from top to bottom. Globe ornaments of crystal and silver glimmered in the light, and a star crafted of crystal, pearl, and gold leaf sparkled at the top. Beads of white were draped from branch to branch, offering the jewelry that so beautifully accented the creation.

Robert had hired florists and groundkeepers from the nearby DuLoche properties to create the Christmas decor at the estate. It was breathtakingly beautiful. Mr. DuLoche had agreed to the arrangement and offered to send an interior decorator along to assist. Robert graciously accepted the offer with the understanding that together they would host a dinner for some joint business associates during the holiday season, perhaps just after Christmas. This affair would be at the Husting estate rather than at the customary Lochewood Gardens location, DuLoche's official estate. Husting Manufacturing was a benefactor of the newly formed Lochewood Foundation, and thus began the relationship between the two businessmen. The association was mutually beneficial, and the gentlemen got on well with one another.

Robert prepared for the season with a renewed sense of being. He walked the halls of the estate with greater ease lately. The tree adornments didn't align with Emma's tastes. She was a simple woman with elegance and poise. Today the mansion reflected southern charm and northern warmth, all wrapped together in that mid-Atlantic way. He felt nearly exuberant as he wandered the entryway and adjoining rooms, studying the grandeur of the style. Fresh greens and berries gathered from the grounds were trimmed in burgundy velvet ribbon with gold edging. The rooms were filled with the scent of evergreens and spice, replacing the light waft of roses that had become disagreeable to Robert. The flowery scent of Emma encumbered him with sadness and guilt.

Veronica was in her upstairs playroom with Betty. The plan included Arthur with the day off and James on a two-day visit with his family in the city. Cook was preparing dinner. Robert expected visitors at any moment, and he felt resolute in his ability to make this evening a complete joy for everyone involved. Plans were for Betty to entertain Veronica and the visiting little girl, Margaret. Cook had been asked to serve dinner to Carolyn and Robert in the dining room. After dinner, Cook had time off until lunch the following day, and Betty would put the two girls to bed. Margaret would be spending the night. Betty planned to spend the night with her own relatives in town, also returning to the estate at noon the next day. Robert had worked hard to choreograph all this time off for his staff. He wanted to be sure the evening ended with no one in the house except him and Carolyn and their two little girls sound asleep in Veronica's suite. Where the evening would lead from that point was entirely open to Carolyn's imagination.

Robert walked back to the front entry after inspecting the sitting room, dining room, study, back hallway, and living room. Every nook and cranny reflected the season. His heart was full, his life finally getting back to normal. He could stop worrying about Veronica's needs as a baby. She was growing up; he was moving on.

A tap on the front door was punctual, as he expected: 4:30.

The sun was low in the sky, silhouetting Carolyn and Margaret on the front porch. He opened the door with a grand sweep of his arm. "Good afternoon! How lovely to see you, Miss Leeder."

Carolyn played along. "And you, Mr. Husting. What a delightful afternoon. And, oh!" She paused as her eyes took in the grand entry. "What beautiful surroundings and decorations. You certainly have prepared for the Christmas season, haven't you?" A genuine smile met Robert directly.

Little Margaret looked stunned. Her eyes opened wide, revealing deep blue diamonds rimmed in lush dark lashes. She peered up at Robert and held tightly to her mother's hand, her red curls reaching down her back and poking out from under her white rabbit fur hat, framing her face. The blue wool coat included a skirt that ended in black braided cord, and the double-breasted front included frog closures in matching black. The collar and cuffs were trimmed in white rabbit, making this little girl an exemplar of current fashion. Rosy cheeks and pursed lips spoke of innocence. As Robert took this scene in, he could also see Carolyn standing on a stage, scat singing and swinging her hips. *This little darling will have to ward off the creeps when she's a little older.*

"Robert?" Carolyn was trying to bring Robert back to the present.

"Oh yes. I'm sorry. What were you saying? I was taken by this lovely little girl here." Some unusual sensation connected him to Margaret, and he felt off-kilter.

"I was saying that you certainly did prepare for the Christmas season. Why, the decorations are just beautiful!"

"Oh, yes. Well, thank you. You see, I'm preparing to entertain some business associates between Christmas and New Year's, so yes, I uh, I uh … We, we did a little more this year than usual. You understand, of course. This is not normal for us. We keep things simple. Usually." He reached up with both hands to straighten his hair.

"Robert, relax. It's okay. Margaret, I'd like you to meet Mr. Husting. Robert, this is Margaret."

Robert searched Carolyn's face for a clue. *"Mr. Husting." That's good. That's good; I can work with this.* "Hello, Miss Margaret. It's very nice to meet you." *She has my eyes.*

Shy eyes relaxed from their wide-open pose, and Margaret turned her face into her mother's coat.

"Can you say hello to Mr. Husting, honey? He's a very nice friend of Mommy's."

"Hullo." A whisper was followed by a twist that buried Margaret deeper into her mother's side.

"I'm sorry, Robert. She'll warm up in a few minutes."

"Oh, no, that's fine. I understand. Really." He was shifting his stance from side to side, uneasy in the moment.

Realizing that he was still holding the door open, Robert felt awkward and clumsy. *This is not working.* "Come in. Come in, won't you? Let me take your coats."

I don't know how to do this. Where is Arthur? Where does he put people's coats when they come in the house?

As if she had read his mind, Betty appeared on the stairs. "Mr. Husting, would you like some assistance?" Veronica stood behind Betty, just one step above her. Holding onto Betty's upper arm, she peeked around Betty's body to see the visitors.

"Oh yes, Betty. That would be fine, thank you. If you just take Miss Leeder's coat and little Margaret's coat and hat, I'll take these other things into the study until later." He felt his shoulders drop to a much more comfortable position. *Thank you, Betty.*

Betty moved into action, and Veronica followed right after, holding onto Betty's skirt from behind. Robert took the other child's pink train case from Carolyn and made his way to the study, trying to ignore the pounding in his chest. *Is this a mistake? The two girls don't even know each other. What was I thinking? They're here for the night!*

Betty managed to get Veronica to let go so she could take coats and hang them in the entrance closet. Veronica just watched Carolyn and Margaret. She followed Betty's movement with her eyes and never swung her head in any one direction. Robert returned to recognize a confused little Veronica.

"Veronica, sweetie. Come here and meet Daddy's friend, Miss Leeder." He reached for Veronica's hand, and she followed his lead. "Can you say hello to Miss Leeder?"

Veronica nodded. "Hi. I'm 'Ronica."

"Well, yes, hello. I've heard a lot about you. It's very nice to meet you."

"Me?"

"Oh yes. Your father has told me about you. And this is my daughter, Margaret."

Again, Margaret had her face buried in Carolyn's skirt. Carolyn struggled to pull Margaret away and turn her toward Veronica. Betty saved the awkward moment.

"Excuse me, Miss Leeder, but I was planning to take Miss Veronica back upstairs to put some toys away before dinner. Margaret is welcome to join us."

"Of course. Sure."

Margaret looked up at her mother, her pink lips dewy and her eyes wide in anticipation of her mother's direction. "Go ahead, Margaret. You can help Veronica upstairs. I'm sure this lovely lady will have things for you to do up there."

Turning to Betty, Carolyn queried, "What should she call you?"

"'Miss Betty' is fine."

"You heard the lady, Margaret. Her name is Miss Betty, and you can play with this lovely little girl here. I bet she has *lots* of dolls and other *toys* that she'll share with you."

Robert felt a sense of nausea. *Yes, Veronica has every toy imaginable. What will that look like to Carolyn? Why hadn't I thought about that?*

"Come! A dollhouse! You have one?" Veronica was excited to show her toys to someone her own age.

Margaret let go of her mother's skirt. She shook her head no and followed Veronica in silence. Betty led the two of them up the stairs.

"Well, then. How about if we go into the living room? Can I get you a glass of wine?" Robert wanted to get things under way and move beyond this very clumsy beginning to the evening. *This was not the best idea.*

"That would be very nice, Robert. Thank you."

Robert led the way. Carolyn followed, noting every piece of furniture, fine carpet, lovely piece of crystal, decorative vase, crystal chandelier, and exquisite piece of imported china that adorned the walls and surfaces. The grand piano that filled the front bay window of the living room was a focal point of the room, accompanied by appropriate lighting and music storage along the nearest wall. Its white finish spoke to a feminine touch that denounced a traditional style. Carolyn was drawn immediately to the instrument.

Robert caught Carolyn's expression as she eyed the piano. *I forgot about the piano. What was I thinking?*

"Oh, Robert! This is wonderful! May I play just for a few minutes?"

"How about we have a nice glass of wine first, hmm? We can think about some music a little later, if you don't mind." Robert's heart was beating hard in his chest, making him realize that his weakness for Carolyn's style of music would win out before the night was over.

"If you insist." Carolyn ran her palms down the front of her green dress and along her thighs as she wiggled her hips slightly. Her shoulders throbbed alternately as if she were controlling the rhythm that rose in her soul at the sight of a beautiful piano. "I'd actually like a mixed drink if you have that, Robert. You know my preferences."

"Of course. Let me make you a rickey then. Cointreau?"

"Yes, thank you."

Robert wondered why she was calling the shots. He'd invited her to dinner, he'd invited Margaret to spend the night, and he'd prepared for some private space. Yes, he had also prepared for Carolyn's favorite cocktail, but he had offered her a glass of wine. *This evening has to be on my terms, not hers. Right after this drink.*

Robert handed Carolyn her drink and set out the prepared olive tray and hard cheese. She helped herself to a bite of cheese and sipped her drink delicately. He sipped his burgundy and reached for something to open a topic of conversation he suddenly felt eager to approach.

"So tell me, Carolyn, how are your living arrangements working out? Are you and Margaret comfortable in the apartment?"

"No, we're really not, Robert. You know that."

Robert's eyebrows shot up, and his eyes opened wide. He felt his face flush. His first reaction was to lash out. *One, two, three, four, five … breathe.* Robert sat quietly.

"You know that the space is too small for two of us, and I need to have a live-in to help with Margaret because my performance schedule is very full. But we had that conversation already, Robert."

Yes, we did. "So how long has it been? Almost two months since you arrived there?"

"That's right. But Margaret joined me full time just a couple of weeks ago. She needs more space; I know you agree. After all, look at what you have here for Veronica. Little girls require lots of space. They have toys and clothes; they just need room to roam on cold days when they aren't outside. And besides, the chances of Margaret playing outside aren't great in the city. The parks are not too close, and getting there is just a hassle. So I know we need to be thinking about an alternative. I have the monthly arrangement set up through January, then I'll need to make a move."

Robert hadn't expected the situation to take this turn. The apartment, a lovely five-room unit of about twelve hundred square feet overlooking the Christina River and Brandywine Creek, seemed like a wonderful location. The apartment on the eighth floor in a building constructed in contemporary architecture within the past three years suited Carolyn's lifestyle very well. The nearby Brandywine Park offered a great outdoor space within easy walking distance. The rent was not inexpensive, and Robert was surprised that the amenities offered there were not sufficient for Carolyn and Margaret. The management booked services for residents, including nanny services and cleaning. Robert paid all of these extras for Carolyn just to be sure she did not expose the nature of their relationship, and their child, to the public.

Robert asked what kind of move Carolyn had in mind, but she was very vague. All he was able to get was her desire to have a private residence outside the city. He decided to let the conversation go and not appear overly eager about the situation.

Robert swallowed the last of his wine, stood, smoothed the front of his trousers, and ran his free hand through the top of his thick hair. Carolyn eyed him closely. She followed his lead. Drinking down the last of her cocktail, she sauntered in front of Robert to place her empty glass on the buffet. "Shall I play a song for us, Robert?"

There was no need to respond. As quickly as the question had been asked, Carolyn was sitting on the piano bench. Her fingers moved sensually across the keys. Relaxed and swaying to her own music, Carolyn allowed her eyes to gently close as she got lost in the melody. Slowly opening her lids long enough to check the keys, her voice started low and raspy. The lyrics of her song were unfamiliar to Robert. She impressed him with her impromptu serenade. Moving closer to her side of the piano, Robert placed a hand on her shoulder and stood mesmerized by her art. Carolyn whispered the words: "And you are my only man. Only you can … touch me."

With those final phrases, Carolyn dropped her head, closed her eyes, and nodded as the ending chords faded away. Robert didn't stir. He grew warm and flush. Carolyn looked up at him over her right shoulder and simply stated, "And that's the truth, Robert."

He bent over her and kissed her passionately, trying to push back the memory of Emma, who'd sat on that very piano bench innocently playing classical works of the great composers of the world. The two women were, in many regards, worlds apart. Carolyn drew from something deep inside him. She fulfilled his manly desires. Emma was a sweet woman and stable wife.

Carolyn always received Robert's advances willingly and openly. She bore no embarrassment and was comfortable with her own sexuality.

Making every possible excuse to postpone the inevitable, Robert managed to get Carolyn to refrain from a completely physical encounter. They found their way to the dining table, enjoyed a wonderful dinner, and extended all appearances of casual friendship until the appropriate time. By eight thirty all the house staff had left for the evening. Betty had assured Robert that the little girls enjoyed a nice meal of their own, had played until they were tired out, and were sound asleep. The quiet house was completely unfamiliar to Robert.

Carolyn attempted to pick up where they had left off at the piano bench. Robert, completely out of sync with the cadence of things, graciously found a way to end the evening. He phoned for a taxi to carry Carolyn back to her apartment.

"I'm quite disappointed that you are not feeling up to par this evening, Robert. I was so looking forward to a more complete reunion with you."

Robert sniffed shortly, clasped his hands together in front of him, and adopted a very businesslike demeanor. "Yes. I am disappointed as well, Carolyn. But you wouldn't want to catch whatever this is that has me. I don't think it wise for us to continue together tonight. You understand, I'm sure."

The taxi pulled around the circle drive. A horn beeped, and Robert opened the door with the same wide swing he had used to usher Miss Leeder into the house.

"Good evening, Carolyn. I'll ring you in the morning when the girls are about."

"Thank you, Robert. And do take care of yourself."

Robert couldn't close the door soon enough.

He leaned against the back of the door and breathed in deeply. A long, slow exhale pulled his shoulders down. He let his head sink until his chin touched his chest.

"Daddy!"

Robert opened his eyes to see little Veronica staring straight into his face. All thoughts of illness left him, and Robert squatted down to hug his little girl. Veronica hugged him back as he lifted her off the floor. Together they moved to the settee in the sitting room.

Robert awoke as sun shone through the east window early the next morning. Veronica's head was leaning against the small of his shoulder, and he was leaning into the corner of the settee. He reached up with his right hand to move the straggling curls out of his little girl's face. She turned a natural, warm, smiling face in his direction. "Morning, Daddy. Are you happy today?"

"Indeed I am."

But that may not have been the full truth. Something seemed awfully wrong.

He lulled Veronica back into napping.

Before the sun had fully appeared, Robert had carried Veronica up the stairs to her bed. There, sleeping soundly in the spare twin bed, lay Margaret Leeder. Her little body was curled into the fetal position, and the back of her head bubbled with red curls. Robert moved quietly, shushing Veronica so as not to wake Margaret. He succeeded in settling her into her own bed and then quietly slipped out the door.

Across the hall in his own suite, Robert removed his shoes, slipped out of his clothing, and made his way to the bathroom. There, staring at him in the mirror, was a man of much older stature than expected, a man he didn't recognize. The past three years clearly had taken their toll on him. Shaking off the immediate despair, he reached for his toothbrush and toothpaste and went to work with vigor. Moments later he was spitting blood into the sink and thinking of the need to have Carolyn at his side. It was tempting to make a phone call, but instead he succumbed to the comfort of his bed. As if it were a typical part of his routine, Robert pulled the covers up over his head and willed the world to leave him alone.

Close to eight o'clock, there was a tap on the door. Robert pulled himself together and called out, "Yes?"

"Mr. Husting, it's me, Betty. I am here to start breakfast. Will you be leaving early today?"

"Betty. Yes. I thought you were off until lunchtime. What's going on?"

"I thought better of it, sir. Are you leaving early?"

"No. No, in fact, we have Miss Margaret here for breakfast today, Betty."

"I'll get started."

"Thank you, Betty." *Thank God Carolyn is not here.*

Betty backed away from the door. She walked across the hall and peeked in on the two girls. Neither was stirring. Quietly closing the door, she retreated to the kitchen to begin her work. *I wonder who else is here?*

In the meantime, Robert lounged in his suite, trying to enjoy his favorite time of day. The dark furniture and plush linens were smothering, not comforting. The dark flocked wallpaper that spoke to the error of the estate only added to his suffocation. With sweat popping out all over his body, and with shaking hands, Robert shook his head to clear the feelings. That didn't help. He sprung into the bathroom, stripped out of his nightclothes, and walked into the shower. Turning on tepid water, he hung his head down and let the stream pound the back of his neck. He wasn't sure if the water on his face was salty, but he didn't care to know. If these were tears, then let them be. *My Emma. Why did I treat you so poorly? I wasn't fair, was I?*

A cup of Betty's strong coffee helped Robert find his senses. As he sipped from his cup and perused the morning paper, melancholy gave way to renewal. Headlines of city events in the coming 1949 led to thoughts of a new start. Life could be fresh and alive if Robert would just accept the past as the past and stop reliving his failures.

"Daddy! We got dressed. We're hungry."

Veronica was running through the entryway, seeking her father's attentions. Margaret trailed behind her, dragging a stuffed giraffe by the neck. The two looked a bit unkempt. They had clearly dressed themselves.

"Well, well. Look at the two of you! Did you dress by yourself today?"

Margaret nodded. Veronica pointed. "She showed me!"

Margaret swung from side to side. Her wide eyes took in the sparkle of shiny crystals hanging from the dining room chandelier. *She definitely has my eyes.*

"Now that's a great thing, to dress all by yourself! Wait until Betty sees you."

Veronica ran toward the kitchen looking for Betty. Margaret followed.

Robert smiled to no one. *Indeed, this is a good day. Veronica becoming independent. Emma would be proud.*

By eleven o'clock, Robert had Margaret and Veronica loaded into the Princess and was driving them to Brandywine Park. They were bundled in their winter coats, although only a dusting of snow lay on the ground. The cold air lost its effect in the delightfully warm sunshine. The children were sitting in the back seat, content with the whole situation. Robert had promised them a ride on the carousel, followed by lunch with Miss Carolyn Leeder.

As planned, Carolyn met them on the outskirts of the park. She greeted her daughter warmly and shifted her attention to Robert. "So you must be feeling better this morning."

What about Veronica? No greeting for her? Having forgotten all about his illness, Robert was caught off guard. He picked Veronica up as if protecting her. "Yes, I'm fine now."

Carolyn gave a shifty look out of the corner of her eye as if to warn Robert that she was fully aware of his tactics. "Just remember, I know how to make you feel better."

Robert simply smiled in return and redirected the attention to the girls. "You know, these two little ladies have had a wonderful visit together. They dressed themselves this morning, and then after breakfast they played in the nursery for a bit." He shook his head to clear his mind. "That's Veronica's room. It used to be called the nursery." Carolyn pinched her eyebrows together. He continued. "Well anyway, now they're both looking forward to a ride on the carousel before we go to lunch. So, shall we head that way?"

Robert put Veronica down and took her hand. He led the way. Carolyn followed his example; she and Margaret walked behind them. Each parent–child pair was absorbed in the moment. The carousel ride did not disappoint. Both adults and children found laughter and good nature in abundance, and the end of the ride came much too soon. Without carrying on, Robert highlighted the positives of the day and swept the children to the ground from their perches on highly ornate horses. Piling into the Princess, the four of them drove to the edge of the park and took pleasure in the wonderful smells of fried dough and popcorn. Robert continued out of the park and into the city, where he had made a reservation at a favorite family-style restaurant. The children giggled at fuzzy soda and ate hearty amounts of noodles and meatballs. Had no one thought twice, the four would have appeared to be a happy family. But the girls were not quite twins.

Chapter
FIVE

May 1964: A Decision Made —

Ronnie checked her watch. It was not like Quentin to be this late. They were meeting for dinner at the Wilmington Club, and he was the one who had stressed the importance of being on time.

It didn't make sense that he would be twenty minutes behind schedule, even with traffic.

"Terrance, has Mr. Simarillo called?" Ronnie knew how to win the attention of the club manager.

"No, Miss Husting. I've not heard anything. Would you like me to check with his office?"

"Please. I'll be at our table."

Ronnie walked away from the club entrance, hips striding forward, shoulders swaying slightly as if she were on a runway. A waiter greeted her, pulled a chair back, and placed the linen napkin in her lap once she was seated. "Good evening, Miss Husting. What can I bring you?"

"The usual, please, Raymond."

"Would you like some pâté while you wait? Chef's favorite, foie gras, today."

"No, I'll wait for Mr. Simarillo to join me. Thank you."

From across the room, Ronnie could hear a familiar voice. *What is she doing here?*

"Miss Husting, I contacted Mr. Simarillo's office. The concierge said he left about fifteen minutes ago and should be here shortly. I would say you have about a ten-minute wait. Can I bring you anything?"

"Thank you, Terrance. I think I'll retire to the women's lounge. Hold my drink."

"No problem. I'll alert the waitstaff to freshen your table."

Curious about the presence of Margaret Leeder, whose voice was very recognizable, Ronnie strolled through the dining room, down the hallway, and into the women's lounge. Sure enough, there sat Margaret at the vanity, checking her powder and lipstick.

"Well, hello, Miss *Leeder*. What brings *you* here?" Ronnie couldn't help but let her disdain ring out in her greeting.

"Ah, of course, Miss Husting. It's nice to see you also." Margaret remained herself, cavalier.

"Are you here seeking a proper mate, or are you still strutting about to attract anyone willing to bite?" Ronnie knew how to be snide and didn't care to cover her loathing of Margaret.

"And you believe that you are above such activities? What about your pending catch of Quentin Simarillo, Daddy's right-hand poacher?" Margaret held her own with Ronnie, this not being their first tango.

"How dare you. Quentin and I are very much in love, and you know it."

"Right. And so are our daddy and my mother."

"Don't you call him your daddy. Just because he fathered you doesn't make him your daddy. Your mother just happened to be a convenience when my father worked long hours to establish his manufacturing business. Don't even consider yourself a part of my family."

"It's a little late for that, don't you think? Daddy has acknowledged me, and he and Mother are getting along swimmingly these days. Or haven't you noticed?"

"I've got better things to be doing. I suggest you leave this club. Now."

Ronnie turned on her heels and left the lounge, jaw clenched and fists formed at her sides. She traipsed back down the hallway at a quick pace. Turning the corner to the dining room, she walked right into Quentin.

"Whoa there, Miss Husting!" Quentin said with obvious surprise. "I do believe you are in a hurry! May I distract you?" Ronnie noted an uncharacteristic playfulness in his approach.

Releasing her breath and shaking her head, Ronnie's jaw loosened, her fists uncurled, and she moved her shoulders from side to side. "Hello, Quentin. Yes, I guess I am in a hurry. I was missing you. Is everything okay at the office?" She coyly tilted her head the way she had learned very early in life.

"Are you sure that's it?" Quentin gave a puzzled look.

"It's nothing. I'm fine, really. So is everything okay with you?" Ronnie looked Quentin straight in the eye, playing sweet and innocent.

"Let's take our table, and I'll tell you all about it. Shall we?"

Quentin gave Ronnie a quick kiss, gently took her left elbow in his right palm, and directed her to their table. They moved as one, as only a year of practice could accomplish.

"We've made it all the way through dinner and you've not yet mentioned why you were so late, Quentin. What held you up?" Ronnie's patience had expired.

"I needed to have a talk with your father, and he was tied up until almost 5:30. Then when he *was* available, he had two phone calls to return. So I ended up waiting until almost six before I could get in to see him. Then, with the traffic today, it just took longer than I expected. I'm sorry."

Ronnie became self-absorbed as she listened to what seemed like a very lame excuse to her. She cast her eyes down at her empty coffee cup and began to broil inside. *He's late, he doesn't call, and I encounter her! All that because of my father? Really?*

Before she could restrain herself, Ronnie started blurting out her thoughts in rapid fire, looking downward, shifting her eyes back and forth, unwilling to meet Quentin's look from across the table. "Why did you have to see my father today? You were insistent that I be on time, and then you didn't seem to make any efforts. You didn't even call. That's just rude, Quentin. I don't understand you."

Quentin propped open a small ivory box that was lined with plush pink velvet and placed it in front of Ronnie on the table.

"Will you marry me, Miss Veronica Emma-Mae Husting?" He spoke with a calm, deep, and very romantic voice.

Ronnie shifted her eyes enough to catch the sparkle of the clearest, brightest, largest diamond she had ever seen. Set in a band of platinum and flanked by large baguettes, the center, square-cut stone caught her off guard.

"Why, Quentin, I don't know what to say!" Ronnie surprised herself with that reaction. She felt her face flush, the heat running into her cheeks.

"Really? You didn't see this coming?" Quentin's voice pitched higher now. He hadn't anticipated anything other than a resounding yes.

"Well, I guess maybe I did. But really, Quentin. I'm not very pleased with you right now! Why were you so late today?" The response was Ronnie's way of buying time to gain control of the situation.

"Ronnie, do we really need to talk about that right now?"

"I suppose not. Yes, Quentin."

"Yes what?"

"My answer to your question is yes."

"Yes, you'll marry me?"

"Of course." Her voice trailed off as if she were bored with the topic.

"That's good news. Your father will be happy."

My father? "And what about you? Are you happy that I want to be your wife?" Ronnie was matter-of-fact in her inquiry. Her father's happiness was always at the heart of everything she had done as a child, and now it seemed that her father's happiness was most important to Quentin too—but for different reasons.

"Oh, of course, dear. Right now, though, I need to get going. Your father and I have to be back in New York first thing in the morning, and I've got some work to do before then. So I'm going to head out. I'll call you tomorrow night."

"Quentin, is that it?" Disbelief at the situation and his lack of attention to her set Ronnie in a new frame of mind.

"What do you mean?"

"You just proposed to me, and now you're going to walk out on me?" Her temper started to show.

"Don't be silly. I'm not walking out on you. I'm heading off to get some work done that very much needs to be done. Your father and I have to be really prepared for this proposal to a potential customer in the morning. I don't have all of the details of the cost analysis together yet, and that's really important to the sales pitch. So I want—"

"Quentin! Stop!" Her face was red, her voice was tight, and her hands were shaking.

Quentin stopped talking abruptly. He looked Ronnie directly in the eyes. Then he pulled away to scan the dining room. Several members were looking their way. He smiled, nodded at two tables, and reached out to take Ronnie's hand. "Shh. Everyone's looking at us." He continued to smile at her.

Ronnie looked down at the ring. She smiled and batted her long, lush eyelashes. Looking around the room quickly, she refocused on

Quentin and lowered her voice. "Quentin, I have lived my entire life with a traveling father, so I know this life. But when we're married, you may need to spend just a little more time around me. Do you think that will be possible?" Her voice quivered, the tone high. She was losing control of her emotions and wasn't happy about it.

"Of course, Ronnie. I wouldn't have it any other way. I really do need to get back to the office now, though. Let me walk you out. Is James around to drive you home?" Quentin clearly tried to avoid the topic.

"I believe he's waiting in the billiards room. Please go get him for me. I need to powder my nose."

"Sure. And tomorrow, why don't you work on selecting a few dates and run them by my secretary. Then you can get started making the plans. I'd like to have our wedding as soon as possible."

Ronnie paused before responding. "Whatever you'd like, Quentin." She succumbed to the situation. The two parted with a brief kiss to seal the proposal—or to appease the onlookers. *Ware wouldn't treat an engagement this way. Do I even have a choice here?*

James brought the car to the portal of the club, got out, and opened the rear passenger-side door. Ronnie slid into the seat and laid her head back. James returned to the driver's seat and pulled away from the club.

"James, when did life get so difficult?" She sounded defeated and distressed.

"When you turned three, Miss Ronnie."

"Were you around that day, James? The day of my big three-year-old party?"

"Oh, indeed I was. You were the cutest little thing. Your daddy spoiled you rotten. Right after your party, I drove Mr.

Husting to the train station. That was the day the big news broke about Miss Leeder coming back to town."

James looked in the rearview mirror to see Ronnie with her head leaned back and tears floating down her cheeks.

"It's all going to be fine, Miss Ronnie. You are one beautiful lady." James sang out that last sentence. He knew how to win her back from her moments of despair.

"You've always been optimistic, James. Always."

"Guess so, Miss Ronnie. It's the only way to be. You'll see."

Miss Betty was waiting at the door when Ronnie walked in.

"How was your dinner, Miss Ronnie? Did Mr. Quentin look handsome in his fine work suit?"

"Oh yes. He always looks fine. Daddy is sure of that." Her resentment rang through her words.

"Is there anything I should know, Miss Ronnie?"

"Well, somehow I feel like you already do."

"Well, tell me, sweetie, what is it?"

"Tonight was the night."

"The night for what?" Betty feigned ignorance.

"Quentin chose tonight to propose to me." Ronnie's voice rang flat, no emotion attached.

"Well?" Betty leaned toward Ronnie with wide eyes.

"Yes, we're going to get married. I have to find a date tomorrow." It sounded like a chore.

"Aren't you happy, Miss Ronnie?" Betty loved Ronnie like her own daughter, and her happiness meant more than anything to her. Just as Ronnie always wanted Robert to be happy, Betty wanted only for Ronnie to feel love and happiness in her own life.

"Oh, of course I am, Miss Betty. I'm just very tired right now. Is there tea brewing?" Ronnie's voice revealed her exhaustion.

"Sure. Cook's in the kitchen."

Instead of walking toward the kitchen, Ronnie made her way upstairs.

Betty stood, shaking her head. "That child's never going to learn how to be happy with anything." *Neither am I, until I finish my work here at the Hustings'.*

"Ware, are you awake?"

Ronnie had tried to sleep, but too many thoughts raced through her mind. She got out of bed, read some of her favorite Agatha Christie novel, and took a warm bath but still could not stop thinking about all that was happening in her life. She finally gave up. With the house totally quiet and all of the staff tucked in for the night, it was safe to make her way out the back door and across the yard to the pool house. Ware Treallor, a twenty-two-year-old gardener, lived on the grounds. His responsibilities as pool attendant had expanded to include all exterior maintenance. Robert Husting offered him housing in the pool house and free meals in exchange for hard work year-round. With no family nearby, Ware had accepted that position graciously at the young age of eighteen.

Even though he was a bright young man, Ware just didn't enjoy school. He'd left as soon as he was old enough and traveled from Virginia to Wilmington with an older buddy who was moving to Delaware to be near a sister. Ware tagged along, looking for a job as a landscaper. He loved the outdoors and wanted to see if he could support himself doing that kind of work. For two years, he worked for a landscape company that Robert had hired to work on the estate. Ware struck Robert as the kind of kid who would do well with a little bit of independence and the freedom to work at his own pace. With a background of farming and working with his own dad on landscape projects in Virginia, Ware knew the ins and outs of grounds maintenance from hands-on experience. He turned out to be a good addition to the Husting estate staff, and now he was the go-to person for all things related to the property, including the grounds and the exterior maintenance of the house and outbuildings.

"Ware, are you there?"

Ronnie grew impatient. Usually Ware appeared immediately when she called his name.

"Ware, open the door! I know you can hear me."

"Go away, Ronnie." Ware's gravelly voice carried softly through the door.

"But, Ware, I need to talk to you."

"About what?"

"Well, something happened tonight. I need to talk to you."

"Yeah. You're going to marry him." The disappointment was obvious in Ware's response.

"How do you know?" Ronnie threw back an answer.

The door opened. There stood a strong, tight body clad in blue jeans only. Bare feet, tousled blond hair, unbuttoned waistband, dangling belt. "Why are you here?"

"Can I come in?"

A nod, a sweep of the arm, and a step backward indicated Ware's response.

"Drink?" Ware usually kicked off their encounters with an offer.

"Sure."

Ware opened two beers and handed one to Ronnie.

"So. Why did you say yes?" Ware didn't need the full story.

"Ware, please." She knew that Ware had struggled with her relationship with Quentin for a long time.

Leaving no room for a different conversation, Ware fired back, "No, Ronnie. Answer my question."

"You know why, Ware. We've been through this before." She shook her head and searched his eyes for understanding.

"All because I don't have a swanky job in a flashy office next to your father at Husting Manufacturing?"

"It's more than that."

"Really? Like what? Tell me so I can understand." Ware's curt tone reminded Ronnie that she was unfairly hurting him.

"I don't know. I thought we talked about this already." Her voice trailed off. *He's right.*

"And you also thought I would just stand by and watch you marry someone you don't love?"

"Maybe I shouldn't have come here. I'll just go back to the house and …"

Ware had moved toward Ronnie with a suave and unwavering action that was his signature style. He literally swept her off her feet.

Without warning, Ronnie was on the couch, wrapping herself around Ware's strong body and weeping. He smothered her sobs with long, hard kisses until the two of them gasped for air.

Each responded to the other in utter abandonment of their reality. Pleasure and heartache intertwined, and neither allowed the other to utter a word. The night moved slowly enough for them to fully embrace their love.

The morning sunlight poked through the window curtain. Ronnie rolled over and grabbed her clothes that were still strewn on the floor beside the bed. Ware stirred. "Are we busted?"

"Not exactly. I'll find a way to my room without being seen."

"One last kiss."

"Coffee, Miss Ronnie?"

"Huh!" A loud suck of air sounded as if Ronnie were gasping for her life. "You scared me, Miss Betty!"

"Someone needs to scare you! Just what do you think you're doing?" Betty was stern and motherly.

"I just took an early morning walk." *She's on to me.*

"Mm-hmm. Right out of Ware Treallor's quarters and into the kitchen?"

"Miss Betty, please. Understand this. I was just talking to Ware about …"

"Never mind. I know what goes on with the two of you. You need to think about that relationship. You're betrothed to another man now, and it's time to stop the partying!"

Betty whirled around and left Ronnie standing in a puddle of guilt.

Oh Lordy! What have I done now?

Grabbing that much-needed cup of coffee and making her way back to the second floor, Ronnie felt more determined than ever to make the marriage to Quentin the most lavish event the county had ever seen. And she did have the know-how and the resources to make that happen. No one would suspect anything about her real feelings for Quentin.

After a hot shower and a dab of makeup, she was prepared to do all the planning. She started with the list of tasks, the appropriate timeline for invitations and responses, a review of the social calendar, and consideration of the best time of year for a lovely wedding on the grounds. From there, she came up with three dates and proceeded to contact Quentin's secretary, as he had requested.

After several failed attempts to bump into Ware on the grounds later that morning, Ronnie succumbed to the idea that she needed to let that relationship cool off for a little while. If he wanted to continue seeing her, he would have to make it known. Their trysts were not common knowledge, and Ronnie could easily convince Miss

Betty that it was her own wild imagination that had created the relationship. Cool and casual would be her ploy. But she did need to know how much advance notice he needed to get everything on the estate ready for an event like the one she had in mind.

"Ware, are you in there?"

Ronnie tapped on the pool house window. "Come on, Ware!"

"Well, well. Are you looking for me, Miss Beautiful?"

She jumped. "Where did you come from?! You scared me." Ware stood not three feet behind her.

"Sorry." He smiled, sending goose bumps down her body.

An uncomfortable pause fell between them while Ronnie remembered the purpose of her visit. "Yeah, well, I've been looking for you all morning. I need to talk to you." She was very business-like as she worked to push other thoughts from her mind.

"About the fabulous night I showed you?"

Ware's gravelly voice sent her spinning. Instead of giving in, she reached deep inside to gain that cool, collected demeanor that seemed necessary right now. "Stop, Ware."

"I can't."

"Please. We need to have a serious conversation."

"Every conversation I have with you is serious."

"No, really. Please. I need you to work with me on something."

"On what, better moves? I think you have them down just fine." Ware moved closer. She could feel his heat.

"Oh, please!"

"Okay. I'm sorry. I just can't help myself. You're my soft spot."

Ware's hazel eyes were shining gray, and the sun picked up on the gold flecks that added to their depth. Ronnie noted the unique sparkle that always distracted her. She looked away to concentrate. "Well, let's get beyond that and talk about a party that I'm planning."

"And what kind of party would that be? You don't happen to

mean a wedding, do you?" His voice returned the business-as-usual tone that hers projected.

"Well, I actually do." Ronnie worked to stay focused as she looked him in the eye again. *Lower status or not, this man has me.*

Ware shifted his eyes downward and kicked a pebble off to the side. "I thought maybe you were having second thoughts."

"Ware. We've already been through this. We're not right for one another, and I am engaged now to Quentin Simarillo. He's Daddy's pick for me, and I think it will work out just fine."

"What about me and you?" A palpable sadness echoed in his voice.

"Well. I've actually been thinking about that. My feeling is that our relationship depends entirely on you." Ronnie became very matter-of-fact now.

Ware seemed puzzled. Stepping back to look at her from a little farther away, he tilted his head and asked, "What does that mean?"

"It means all of that is in your hands."

Ware's eyebrows raised, and his face brightened. "Plan on my hands being full then. With you."

"Ware ..." Ronnie was cut off.

"Mark my words."

The awkward silence lasted seemingly forever.

"So tell me about this party you're planning." Ware rescued the moment.

Thankful for the shift, Ronnie began to lay out the details of her plans.

"Well, I'm hoping that we can pull off a wedding on the grounds. Don't you think the estate is the perfect place for an outdoor wedding? Either late summer or early fall. We can set up a chapel in the west rose garden while the roses are still in bloom. The fragrance is just delicious. The reception can be under tents that can be set up on the north side of the house so that the afternoon sun is not too strong. What do you think?"

Ware only partially listened. His mind wandered as soon as she started talking about the estate being the perfect place. Indeed, it was the perfect place, perfect for love, for celebrations, for raising a family, for him to be with Ronnie. His only option was to play along and keep Ronnie in his grasp right here on the estate.

"I think the estate is the perfect place, Ronnie. Perfect in every way."

"So can we talk about timing?"

"Of course. But let's do that in the rose garden. It should be really pleasant there right about now."

Ronnie wore a pair of close-fitting yellow pedal pushers. It was warm, and her long, dark hair was pulled up in a French twist, loosely pinned at the back. A few free strands of wavy hair cascaded around her neck and touched her shoulders lightly. The black slip-on canvas shoes were adorned with red and yellow brocade flowers, and her white blouse was fitted at the bodice.

Ware purposefully fell behind Ronnie so he could watch her walk. The swing of her hips was luscious to his eyes, and he couldn't help but stare as she moved in front of him.

"Come on! Don't stare at me like that; you make me uncomfortable."

Ronnie had spun around to find Ware fixated on her lower body.

"Sorry. A man can only dream."

"Let's go. We've got lots of things to talk about."

"Yes, we do."

When they reached the garden, Ronnie moved to her favorite spot, a small bench positioned to provide the perfect view of the garden, the fields in the distance, and the open countryside beyond that. She always chose this bench. It was a place to think and be peaceful.

Ware sat down beside her on the bench. He turned toward Ronnie and looked longingly at her.

"You really are beautiful, Miss Veronica. And I do mean that most sincerely."

"Thank you, Ware."

A familiar silence lingered uncomfortably until Ware got down on one knee. He reached in his front jeans pocket and produced an exquisitely delicate diamond ring. "Miss Veronica Emma-Mae, will you spend your life with me?"

"But when? How did you …? Why …?"

"You do love me." It was a statement of fact.

Ronnie couldn't stop the whirling. Her chest was rising and falling visibly. Her hands shook, and tears welled up in her eyes.

"Tell me the truth, Ronnie: do you love me?"

Leaning forward and wrapping her arms around his neck, Ronnie rested her forehead against his. "You can feel that, can't you, Ware? Do I have to say it?"

"I take that as a yes."

Ronnie was softly crying, her tears rolling down his cheeks. "Yes."

Ware moved from his knees to the bench, and her hands floated back into her lap. His arm wrapped around her shoulders, and she laid her head against his chest. "Ware, what will we do?"

When he didn't answer, Ronnie filled the silence.

"You know, Ware, this is hard for me too. I can't deny the way I really feel about you. But at the same time, I feel like we aren't really meant for one another. My life has been filled with high-society events, parties, travel to faraway places. That's not you. You are a homebody, someone who needs to work the land and be in nature. We're just total opposites."

"Ronnie, answer one question: do you love Quentin?"

"Ware, don't do this."

"Just answer me."

Ronnie was trapped.

"I can spend my life with him."

"Do you *love* him?" Ware was getting impatient and pressing for Ronnie to be honest.

"In my own way."

Ware swallowed his pride, stood up, tucked the ring in his pocket, and faced Ronnie directly.

"I swear that one day you will be mine. When you're ready, I'll be here waiting. In the meantime, I hope our love doesn't ruin your daily life."

"Oh, Ware, thank you. Thank you for understanding." Ronnie was wiping the tears from her cheeks. *What have I done?*

"I can't say I understand, Ronnie. I can only say my love for you can weather the storm."

Ware has been my rock.

Ware stood still. Ronnie stood up, moved closer, and gave him a strong, loving embrace. "You are my rock, Ware Treallor."

"Remember that you said that."

The silence returned. Instinctively, they started to stroll the garden path, not a new walk for either of them. It was Ware who spoke this time.

"I think you could put a small freestanding lectern right about here. That way the minister can use it to put things down if he needs to. But then he would stand right about here to actually perform the ceremony. You could have chairs lined up along that back wall and coming forward ..."

"Ware," interrupted Ronnie. "I trust you to figure all of that out. I know it will be perfect." She sincerely didn't want to be bothered with the details.

With a forced smile, Ware tipped his head in acknowledgment. "Thank you. Only the best for my love."

Betty pulled the sitting room drapes closed with a snap. She had seen more than she wanted of Ronnie and Ware, but she felt the sadness herself when she thought about her husband, Alej, so far away with little opportunity to be with him.

The tent was in place, the tables were set, and the roses, pink and yellow, were being placed around the grounds. They were spectacular in Ronnie's eyes. The fragrance filled every corner of the grounds. She knew that her guests would swoon at the sea of color.

All the arrangements were coming together beautifully. Wedding guests were due to arrive in the next thirty minutes. With her hair perfectly coifed, nails beautifully manicured, and makeup complete, Ronnie felt like the princess she always knew she was.

Robert stopped in Ronnie's room to check on his little girl.

"So. This is it." His voice quavered a bit.

"Yes it is, Daddy. My wedding day is here." She was poised and proper.

"Are you feeling ready for this big step?"

He's just being fatherly.

"Of course! Why wouldn't I? I've been planning it for months now. Besides, you know how much Quentin and I love each other, and you've said yourself that we make such a ..."

"Ronnie." Robert stopped her midsentence.

"What?"

"What do you really feel for Quentin?"

Now you ask … Ronnie responded quickly: "I love him, of course. He's perfect in every way. We'll have a family, and I know he'll give our kids the best of everything. He works in the family business, and I know you'll be sure he continues to give me everything I need and want. And what with living here on the estate and having all that it offers, we'll be just fine." She was selling the idea to him and to herself at the same time.

"Sweetheart, I just want you to be happy." Robert sounded almost melancholy.

"Happy. Yes, of course you do. That's why you've always worked hard and were gone all the time, so you could provide everything I want. Quentin will continue that for you, right, Daddy?" There was a hint of mockery and cynicism in Veronica's voice, but Robert didn't want to hear that.

"Ronnie, are you happy?"

Ronnie turned to face her father squarely. With a slower, more empathetic tone, she replied, "Sure, Daddy. I'm happy."

Robert smiled. "Well then. It's settled. Let's get on with it."

Robert kissed his daughter lightly on the forehead. He turned and walked out of the room without another word. He ran his hands through his dark, curly hair.

Ronnie felt the tears well up in her eyes. She watched her father adjusting his tuxedo jacket as he left her alone. *When did everything get so difficult?*

She moved to the door and locked it so that no one else would walk in on her.

The string quartet had arrived, and the sweet sounds of Tchaikovsky floated through the open bedroom window. Down below, Ronnie could see guests beginning to gather in the west garden. It had all been beautifully arranged by Ware. White chairs were strung with bridal netting with roses woven in the soft bows that draped to the ground along the aisle that she would walk down. A sinking feeling hit Ronnie when she thought about the care and attention Ware had given to all the prenuptial planning. It was he who had seen to every detail that she just somehow didn't have the energy to tackle.

Ware strolled the garden, checking every last detail. It was immaculately trimmed, and light rose petals were scattered along the pathway from the front porch to the back of the seating area. Guests would face the front of the garden, where Ware built a small platform that would allow Ronnie and Quentin to step up so guests could watch them exchange vows. Ware even covered the steps with beautiful white fabric so that her train would not catch on any uneven wood or splinters. The walkway had been leveled and covered with the same white fabric, so there was no need for the bride to watch for uneven ground as she moved down the aisle on Robert's arm.

Ware had let no detail go unattended to. He'd made sure that Ronnie would be free of all distractions on her wedding day. It was important to him that she was completely aware and focused on what she was doing and the commitment she was making to Quentin Simarillo. Ware had not prepared this ceremony with a light heart. He noticed the sadness mounting in his core as the music filled the air and he seated guests.

Ronnie had insisted on keeping the guest list smaller than anyone expected. There were the usual business associates of Husting Manufacturing, Quentin's family who lived nearby, the staff, and a few more-than-acquaintances from the Wilmington Dinner Club. In total, there were probably under a hundred people present. The day was brilliant in every way.

Ronnie recognized some unwanted sensation stirring inside. *My wedding day. Where is the joy and expectation, the bursting excitement? This is Quentin. What about Ware?*

A light knock interrupted her thoughts. "Can I come in now, Ronnie?"

It was Betty, the maid of honor. Without Betty's support through her life, Ronnie wouldn't have made it during those difficult times. Betty always came around for the cookies-and-milk moments. Growing up without a mother in a huge house full of waitstaff did have its disadvantages. Betty was there amid all of them.

"Just a minute, Betty."

Taking a quick look in the mirror, Ronnie wiped a little smear away from her eye, touched it up quickly with a lining pencil, and hurried to the door.

"What are you doing in here, girl? We need to get that dress on you. People have already arrived!"

Betty always kept things on track. Yes, Ronnie needed to get the dress on. But she needed Betty to help her do that.

"Well, you look beautiful in that gorgeous yellow dress, Betty. Don't you love yellow?"

"I suppose I do, now that you ask. It sort of suits my coloring. But I'm not the one everyone will be looking at! So get to it, girl."

The two of them synchronized every movement to get Ronnie into her wedding dress. The empire line that had become so fashionable in recent years accentuated her slender shape. The long sleeves of lace accented the silk gazar dress and organza train that flowed from the shoulders. Short silk gloves with beaded trim matched the beading of the neckline and headpiece. A veil of organza fell just past her shoulders, and the tips of her shoes peaked out from the bottom of the gown, adding a touch of the same beaded pattern. Betty and Ronnie had designed the dress together, but Betty gave more attention to details. Ronnie went along with every decision.

Ronnie admired herself in the mirror. *What a waste of a beautiful event.* Betty reached over to add a couple of touches to Ronnie's hair. She twirled a loose strand of hair around her finger and added a spritz of spray to hold it in place. *Betty is so attentive; does she think this wedding is right?*

"So here's the something borrowed. Your great-aunt Clare insisted that you wear her pearls today. They're beautiful. And here's something blue—your mother's garter. Slip it on."

"Okay. What's all of this about anyway?" Ronnie wasn't sure what she felt. *My mother? No one has ever said much about her. Why all of a sudden on my wedding day am I learning about my mother's garter?* "I have a garter, but we're not doing all that hokey stuff, you know."

"I understand. It's just tradition."

"Okay. If you say so." Ronnie sounded skeptical.

"Well, I do say so. And besides, with those two things, you've covered it all—something old, something new, something borrowed, and something blue."

Shaking her head, Ronnie complied. "If that's some old wives' tale that brings good luck, we don't need it. Quentin and I will be just fine without all that nonsense." She muttered, "I don't even know an Aunt Clare!"

"Trust me. She existed. She passed on when you were about twelve. These pearls have been in an envelope in your father's jewelry box since you were three!"

Ronnie turned argumentative. "So, if these things have been here forever, how is either of them *borrowed?*" She shook her head and turned away.

"Just consider them borrowed. You didn't own them." Betty coaxed Ronnie out of the bedroom to end the rift. She lifted her train as they moved down the stairs, out the front door, and onto the porch. Robert was there to greet her.

"Oh, my Emma." Robert's eyes filled with tears.

"Daddy, what's wrong? Are you okay?"

Breathing deeply and shaking his head from side to side, Robert lost his composure.

"I don't think I've ever told you how much you look like Emma, your mother."

"No. You never did." Ronnie's heart pounded; her breathing became shallow.

"If you had dark eyes, you would be her double."

Taking the monogrammed handkerchief from his pocket and breathing deeply to gather the scent of Bouquet of Flowers that Betty perpetuated, Robert exhaled long and slow. "You are beautiful, Veronica Emma-Mae Husting." He ran his fingers through his black curls and tucked the handkerchief inside his coat. He straightened his boutonniere.

"Thank you." *On my wedding day? Why now?* She looked away, unable to contain her sorrow, the melancholy associated with that scent of flowers and with her memories of snuggling into his lap in the sitting room. Ronnie had never wondered about her mother until now.

Robert gained his composure, put his arm out for Ronnie to hold, and began the walk down the front steps of the house and into the west rose garden.

After lifting Ronnie's train as she walked down the front steps, Betty moved ahead of Robert and Ronnie. The string quartet began to play Pachelbel's Canon in D. They made the walk with heads held high and smiles of deceit, covering heavy hearts.

Quentin stood tall and austere, watching Ronnie and Robert approach the head of the aisle. He stepped forward on cue, took Ronnie's gloved hand from Robert, and nodded. Robert kissed Ronnie on the cheek through her veil, backed away, and moved to his designated seat.

The minister moved through the ceremonial nuptials without a hitch. He hardly knew Ronnie or Quentin, but he'd agreed to do the service for a fee and a good meal. Quentin played the part of a groom perfectly. He removed Ronnie's glove to place the wedding band on her finger, he gracefully lifted her veil to give her a ceremonially sweet kiss, and he proudly marched her back down the aisle on his right arm as a piece from Handel's Water Music filled the air.

No one shed a tear during the perfunctory demonstration of a wedding.

Ware moved guests from the ceremony in the rose garden to the northeast side of the house. The afternoon sun was growing strong, but the strategically placed tenting provided delightful shade. The clubhouse on the edge of the tennis courts served as a prep station, and its covered patio was staged for hors d'oeuvres and cocktails.

None of the typical wedding rituals were planned. Ronnie had no interest in what she called "weddings of the less sophisticated." Instead she opted for white-glove service, the string quartet, and champagne and caviar. It was her vision that added the ice sculptures on the side hors d'oeuvre tables and the finest crystal stemware. China and silver adorned the tables, and waitstaff attended to every guest's individual needs. Dinner was served with elegance. Ronnie didn't allow standard wedding fare.

The only traditional act she agreed to was the cutting of the cake. And for that ritual, she made Quentin promise not to play foolish games. They would not feed one another, and they would not act as if this were some childish play with hidden meaning. Instead, they would act as grown adults cutting a cake ceremonially, and then turn the plating and serving over to the staff.

Ronnie noticed Ware watching her as she and Quentin made the rounds to each table, talking with their guests and thanking them for joining them on their special day. She tried to see Ware's eyes. *Is he crying?* Each time she came close to making eye contact, he shifted his gaze in another direction. *Is he playing games with my psyche? Why won't he look at me?*

More tables, more small talk. Still no direct signal from Ware. As a waiter passed, Ronnie took two tall glasses of champagne off his tray, excused herself from Quentin, and made her way across the garden.

"I'd like to toast to a beautifully executed wedding plan." She stared into those hazel eyes.

Ware nodded, took the glass of champagne, and swallowed it down in one long drink.

"Thanks. Just what I ordered. Did I tell you how fabulous you look?"

"Ware, I'm sorry."

"Sorry? For what?" He was trying to be casual, but Ronnie knew better.

"You know."

"Hey, don't worry about me. Remember, you said everything is up to me. You might live to regret that, because there is no way you're getting away from me. When you come back from that honeymoon of yours, we'll just pick up right where we left off." There was a little edge in his tone.

"Now we never said …"

"Yes." He paused for effect. "You did say. And I know you never go back on your word to me. That's just *one* of the things I love about you." His tone reverberated flirtation.

Ronnie replied with a raised voice and a casual attitude: "Ware, you made this property absolutely beautiful for the wedding, and I just wanted to say that Quentin and I really appreciate your work and the way you put so much into every detail."

Quentin walked up behind Ware. "Indeed. Nice work, Ware. Thanks. Even the weather held out. You didn't have anything to do with that. Or did you?"

Ware smoothly replied, "Thanks, Quentin. No, I'm afraid I'm not that good. If I could control the weather, then we'd all have something to worry about. In the meantime, I'm just pleased that things turned out for you two today. You have one beautiful lady here, Mr. Simarillo. I hope you treat her kindly."

Ware left the scene before anyone could reply.

Quentin pulled Ronnie to him and kissed her lightly on the top of her head.

"You know, I've got some things to take care of back at my place. I'm going to have to exit here as soon as the last guest leaves and pick up some papers."

"What? It's our wedding day, Quentin." Ronnie was incredulous.

"I know, sweetheart, and I promise I won't be gone long. But I want to take a few customer folders with us to Paris. I can review the materials on the flight. I should have packed them, but somehow I must have been distracted. They're on the desk in my home office."

By ten o'clock the party was over. Rental equipment was ready for pickup the next day, but otherwise all the silver, china, crystal, and roses were long gone.

And so was Quentin. He'd left within minutes of the last guest. It had been two hours, and still he had not returned.

"Dad, where are you going?"

Ronnie was in her casual clothing. Robert was walking out to the front porch.

"I think I'll run by the office. There are a few things I need to attend to. Besides, you'll want to get a good night's sleep so you and Quentin can get up early for your flight. You have a big day ahead of you tomorrow. I won't be long."

"Good night, Dad."

"Good night, sweetheart. You were beautiful today."

"Thanks," she said as if she were talking to a checkout clerk.

Betty and other staff were busy with cleanup. Ronnie slipped out the back door.

"Oh my God! Ware, what have we done?" A sense of panic set in.

"Nothing, precious." Ware was calm and exuding victory.

"How am I going to get back in the house?" Ronnie was in high gear.

"The same way you always do—through the kitchen door."

"But everyone's in there cleaning up. What if Betty sees me?"

"Come on, you really think she'd be surprised?"

"Ware!"

"What? I'm just being honest with you."

"I've got to go."

"Wait!" Ware stopped her. "Tell me you love me."

"Really? Do you think that would be wise tonight of all nights?" Ronnie was shocked to hear him ask for this now.

"You just wrapped yourself around me like you were meant to be only with me. How can you deny the way you feel?" Ware pushed her yet again.

"You know how I feel. Save it for another time."

Ronnie pulled her clothes on and scrambled out the door of the pool house. Ware smiled, rolled over, and went to sleep.

Ronnie woke up at 5:00 a.m. Quentin was nowhere to be found. They had planned to spend their wedding night at the estate and leave by 6:00 a.m. to catch their flight to New York. There, they would change planes and land in Paris by midnight, local time. Her bags were packed, and all she needed was a quick shower and breakfast. Instead, she threw on a robe and ran downstairs to see if Quentin was there.

"Good morning, dear. You look harried. Is everything okay?"

Quentin stood in the entrance of the dining room with coffee in his hand.

"Where were you?"

"Here. Why?"

"You didn't come here last night."

"Oh, but I did. You weren't in the house, love. I decided to wait for you in the sitting room. But I guess I fell asleep there. Where were *you* last night?" Quentin showed no suspicion, only curiosity.

Ronnie panicked.

"Nowhere. I mean, here. I was here."

She brushed stray strands of hair away from her face. She felt her cheeks get hot.

"Right now, I've got to get a shower." She turned and ran up the stairs, flew into her bedroom, and closed the door behind her. Shaking all over, Ronnie drew her robe around her slender body and felt a nausea that was coated with guilt and fear. Making her way to the bathroom, she stripped off her sleepwear and stepped into a steamy shower. The tears, water, shampoo, and soap all mingled together, but none of them felt cleansing.

Quentin and Ronnie boarded their plane in NYC at 11:30 a.m., the start of a new life already on the wrong road. Just before pulling a mask over her eyes, Ronnie pulled the window shade down and relied on the airsickness pills to work their magic. In minutes she was asleep.

Chapter ──────

SEVEN

── December 1965: Secrets of Love ──

"Where are you going today, Ronnie?" Quentin was returning to work after two weeks away.

"Nowhere. Why?"

"I just thought you might want to do some Christmas shopping downtown. I thought perhaps we could meet for lunch or dinner. I'll be at the office until at least ten tonight, maybe later, trying to catch up. But maybe we could have a meal together."

"Oh, no worries, Quentin. I'll just hang around the estate. I want to write Christmas cards today and think about some of the decorations that will be hung on the weekend." A pause in the conversation made Ronnie self-conscious. She tried to cover her anxiety with more explanation. "There's always plenty to do here." She tried to avoid his eyes. It seemed to her that he peered at her lately in a way that instilled guilt every time they were alone, even if only for a few minutes.

"I guess it's best if I just go with whatever comes my way today. It might be pretty unpredictable. I'm wondering if your dad has some things for me to handle; this new product line is getting a lot of attention lately." The disappointment in Quentin's voice was obvious, but he tried to sound engaged in his work.

"Daddy certainly will need you. You know that!" Ronnie

feigned her support without actually being flippant, but she knew she had failed to sound sincere. Quentin didn't take notice.

"So I'll look forward to seeing you tonight, then?"

"I'll be here, Quentin." She looked down at the floor.

"Are you okay, Ronnie? You seem a little nervous or something."

"Oh, I'm really fine. You go ahead. I'll see you tonight." *Please just leave.*

After a brief kiss on the cheek, Quentin was down the stairs and out the front door. James waited with the car.

Quentin had been traveling a good deal. Husting Manufacturing launched a new product line, and potential customers were clamoring for Quentin's and Robert's attention. The two men had been traveling literally all over the world. Since their return from a two-week trip, Quentin had been completely engrossed in his work. He showed no interest in Ronnie's little projects. They had moved into the suite that was previously occupied by Robert, and he relocated to the first floor into a suite that had been his father's before him. These changes were a part of the plan to offer housing to Quentin and Ronnie as part of Quentin's employment package. Ronnie, wanting the suite to feel new, took on a redecorating project. Quentin didn't concern himself with that at all. Nor did he care if the latest social event required a new outfit. Comings and goings around the estate meant nothing to Quentin. Christmas was fast approaching, and he didn't seem interested at all in the parties or decorations.

Ronnie, on the other hand, appreciated a man who cared about her concerns. The doting attention that she always received from the staff became even more important to her now. Betty made sure all her needs were met, and Arthur was just as attentive where her interests outside the home were concerned. James, her ever-faithful driver, was there to hear her every complaint and dream. Ronnie often reflected on her nonblood family. *What would I have done without these people in my life? And Ware, my rock.*

Life on a daily basis was not as simple as life on the three-week honeymoon in Paris. Ronnie managed to put her connection to Ware aside and fully enjoy Paris. Her longing for his love was something she was just going to have to learn to handle. His words rang true: *I hope our love doesn't ruin your daily life.* From a distance, it was easy to put Quentin and Ware into separate compartments of her life. She even found it possible to consummate her marriage and enjoy Quentin. Once she returned to the estate, the guilt was overwhelming.

This morning's suggestion from Quentin to have lunch or dinner seemed a little bit out of the ordinary. He never gave her his attentions in their daily life, only in Paris, between business calls, and telegrams, and financial reports he was studying. *Maybe he's figuring out that I need a little more attention than a dog, but not today. Not from Quentin, at least.*

"Hello?" Ronnie tapped on the pool house door. She pulled her coat around her neck and lifted the collar up against the cold. "Are you there, Ware?"

The door opened quickly. "Well, well. Look at you this morning. Aren't you just the beauty of the estate today?"

Blushing, Ronnie looked at her shoes. She pushed her hair back from her eyes. Then, looking up at those gorgeous eyes, she posed her question: "Can I join you?"

"I'm not doing much. But you can always join me. Come on in."

Ware closed the door, pushing shoes away from the entrance. "What brings you here today, lovely lady? Something to drink?" As always, he was cheerful, upbeat, and genuinely happy to see her.

"Ware, I've really missed you. Since I came back from my honeymoon, we haven't had much time to talk. I've been thinking about you a lot." Ronnie was sincere. Her heart was on her sleeve.

"I never stop thinking about you, Ronnie. You know that."

Ronnie tried to relax. She started to unbutton her coat and stopped abruptly. "Do you think I made a mistake?"

"Whoa! Let's start that over again." The quick change in topics surprised him.

"What do you mean?" She looked at him with her tilted head, wreaking innocence.

Ware looked at Ronnie. She sincerely wanted to hear his answer, but she tried to be coy and play the part of the innocent child seeking an honest opinion.

"Ronnie. Don't play games with me."

"But, Ware, I don't know if I've made a mistake or not." Her lips turned downward, and her narrow chin protruded slightly.

"Of course you made a mistake, if you're talking about marrying Mr. Right!"

Ronnie shot a look at him that exposed her vulnerability. "Ware, please ..."

"*But* we already had that conversation. So you have to just walk through the steps, Ronnie." His deep voice softened as he said, "In the meantime, you know I'm always here for you."

The howling wind created a draft around the windows. Ronnie felt a chill, more from Ware's reaction to her than from the temperature. "So what's this all about?" Ware searched her eyes for answers.

"He's never around. He's always traveling. His work is more important than me. He doesn't care about spending time here at the estate, and he just wants to earn big dollars so he can flaunt that fact in everyone's face. He thinks of me as the prize."

Ware must be shocked at my honesty. It had only been a few months since the wedding. Christmas was right around the corner, and she had been busily preparing for the holiday season. *He's probably been thinking everything is just fine with my life.*

"What do you really want, Ronnie? Do you want the lifestyle of the wealthy? I thought you already made that choice." She knew that her roller-coaster ride could be hard to understand. But she wanted Ware to take the ride with her.

"I did make my choice; you're right." Ronnie started to melt. *Ware is my rock, my number one man.*

Ware moved toward her and offered his open arms. Ronnie moved toward him and fell into his embrace. With her head nestled in the hollow formed by his rounded arms and shoulders, Ronnie let the meltdown flow. "I feel so empty, Ware. I've been feeling out of sorts all week. I don't know what's wrong; I can't seem to focus on anything. I'm distracted all the time." She was crying without abandon. "I cry without warning; I don't even know why."

"Just let it go, sweetie." Ware rubbed her back and hugged her gently.

"I don't know where to turn." Her voice cracked. "Ware, I'm so sorry."

"But you *do* know where to go. You're there now, with me. There's nothing to be sorry about. We'll work through this. I'm here for you, always."

Ronnie turned her head upward. She looked into the eyes of a caring, loving man. Ware kissed the tip of her nose. He wrapped one arm fully around her and wiped the tears away from her cheeks with the thumb of his other hand. Taking her chin in his fingers, Ware guided her lips to his. The two accepted one another as if it were the most natural thing they'd ever done.

"Come with me. Quentin is gone. Robert is gone. No one will bother you."

He's right. Ronnie needed nothing more. She linked her fingers with his and followed him to his bed. He closed the door to the world, and they made their own reality for a few hours.

The sun hung low in the sky. Ware and Ronnie sat in the sitting area of the pool house, sipping hot chocolate. The day had been the best she had had in months. Ronnie felt whole again. She needed Ware to fill the void in her life.

"You are awesome, Ronnie. Quentin's one very lucky man." Ware was sincere, his voice soft, gravelly, and incredibly magnetic to Ronnie.

"That name. Why did you mention him?" Sadness and guilt filled her.

"Because it's true. He's your husband, and he's very lucky."

"Yeah. I think I'd better go now." But she couldn't move.

The two sat looking at one another. Words were not available to either of them.

Ronnie leaned over, kissed Ware sweetly on the lips, and stood to put her coat on. He accepted her need to leave and helped her with her coat, then led her to the door. "Remember that I'm always here for you. You can depend on me for anything, Ronnie. That's what love is really all about."

"Thank you. You're my rock." Ronnie reached deep to hold herself steady and then left the pool house.

The door closed gently behind her, and the earth crackled under her feet as she walked across the yard to the kitchen door.

Betty was waiting just inside. "Did you have a nice visit in the pool house today?" Her voice had just a hint of sarcasm and cynicism in it.

"Betty!" Ronnie was taken aback. She pulled at the hem of her coat sleeves, shook her head to move the hair out of her eyes, and stomped her feet on the doormat. "It's brisk out there today!"

"Mm-hmm. Can I get you some hot chocolate?" Stepping closer, Betty took in an audible sniff. "Or did you already have some?"

"What do you mean? Sure! I'd love a cup of hot chocolate. I'll come back for it in just a few minutes." *Caught, again.* Ronnie made her way to the front hallway to hang up her coat and change her shoes. The real shock hit when she bumped into Quentin in the front hall.

"Quentin! I thought you were at work until late tonight. What brings you home this afternoon?" *Oh no. How long was I gone?*

Quentin smiled wryly. "Maybe I thought I needed to check on you."

"Why would you think that? I'm just perfectly fine." The onus she felt was nearly paralyzing.

"You seem to be fine now. This morning I wasn't quite sure. You seemed a bit down. What have you done to boost your spirits?"

Does he suspect something? "Nothing."

"Really? Where have you been?"

Why is he suddenly so interested in me? "Nowhere."

"You're taking off your coat; I can't believe you needed to wear your coat in the house. Your face is flush too. Are you feeling okay?"

"I'm perfectly fine." Instinctively, Ronnie was wiping her face with the back of her hand as if that would change the rosy glow she was feeling. "I just … I took a little stroll in the yard. The air is crisp, and the cool felt good."

Shallow breathing accentuated the heartbeat in her ears. The palms of her hands were clammy, and a sense of panic settled in.

"Well, what did you do in the yard?"

"Nothing. Really. I was just breathing the air. It was very invigorating." Ronnie avoided Quentin's eyes. She hung her coat and carried on the conversation. "So what's going on for you today? Don't you have lots of work to do at Husting?" She focused on her breathing. She walked with exaggerated casualness.

"I do. But, as I said, I was worried about you and thought I

would stop in to see how you were." Filling a particularly awkward moment, Quentin made small talk about how busy the new
project was keeping him. "Anyway, if everything is okay here, I'll
get back to work."

"Yeah, sure. I'm fine. Really. You could have just called; you
didn't need to come home! I plan to go upstairs and write some
Christmas cards to relatives."

"Well, I'll just be on my way then." He avoided her eyes.

"Great. See you tonight."

Quentin leaned in to give her a kiss, but Ronnie turned away.
She feigned a cough to avoid his lips. Escape was so close.

"Are you sure you're okay?"

"Oh, yeah. Just a tickle in my throat. Maybe you'd better
just stay away, just in case I'm catching a cold or something." She
feigned another cough.

"Right. Okay then."

"See you tonight." She cleared her throat.

"Yeah."

Quentin walked out the front door.

Ronnie bolted up the stairs. Instead of going to the new suite
she shared with Quentin, she ran into her childhood bedroom
and closed and locked the door. She fell on the bed and cried until
she fell asleep.

Betty walked by the old nursery. Something didn't seem quite
right to her. Maybe it was the pink rug peaking under the door, or
maybe it was the sound of something rustling inside. She stopped,
listened, and decided perhaps it was her imagination. As she
turned to continue on her way to Ronnie's suite, the doorknob
clicked. She turned back around.

"Oh my!"

Ronnie's red swollen eyes and unkempt hair were a dead give-away for Betty. "Ah, sweetie. Come here." She put her arms out and offered Ronnie solace. Ronnie accepted. She let her head rest on Betty's shoulder and cried softly. The two swayed back and forth without worrying how long they stood there.

Ronnie finally lifted her head and stepped back. "I'm sorry, Betty. I think I'm just overtired."

"I'm not so sure, Ronnie. There's more going on here. I know you too well."

"I guess you do, don't you?" She smiled through her tear-streaked face.

"Uh-huh." Betty sounded very self-assured on this point. "Now, do you want to go to your suite and have a heart-to-heart talk?"

"No. Not my suite, Betty. How about if we just go to the back study and sit for a few minutes? Can we do that?" Ronnie was referring to the room that used to be her playroom. Years ago, the room had been converted to a second study. That space was where Ronnie read and reviewed mail in the afternoons. It connected to her childhood bedroom with a second door that led to the hallway, just opposite the two rooms that now comprised the suite she occupied with Quentin.

"Sure. Should I get some tea for us? I'm sure Cook has a pot on the sideboard. At least he did a little bit ago."

"That would be nice." Ronnie continued down the hallway, and Betty went back downstairs to the kitchen.

Ronnie sat by the window in her study. From this vantage point she could look down at the pool. The window faced the north. The pool house faced the west, and sun was shining on the side door that opened into Ware's living quarters. With a deep breath in and a sigh that cleansed her soul, Ronnie let her head fall back against the wingback chair. *What I wouldn't give to walk back through that door right now.*

"Here we go!" Betty entered with a tray with two cups of orange pekoe tea, already fixed to Ronnie's liking. Just a little bit of milk, no sugar.

"Hmm." Ronnie took a sip, careful not to burn her mouth. "Betty, you always know what I need."

"I should. I all but raised you myself."

"I know. But you were so young, quite a bit younger than my own mother would have been. How did you know what to do?" Ronnie invited the distraction and welcomed the opportunity to think about her childhood days for a little while.

Betty laughed lightly. "Oh, I don't know. I always loved children, and you were a precious little girl who needed that love. All I wanted to do was make you happy. That's all."

Ronnie reflected on that for a few minutes. *She wanted to make me happy.*

"Was I a happy child, Betty?"

"Well, I certainly hope so. You had everything any child could ever want. Everyone around here doted on you." Betty chuckled at the thought.

"Did I smile a lot as a little girl?"

"Most of the time. Yes, I believe you did smile a lot."

The two sat in silence, sipping their tea.

Ronnie set the saucer and cup down on her lap, holding them in place with one hand and tracing the rim of the cup gently with the index finger of her other hand. She was staring into the tea as if there was some answer floating in the creamy mixture.

Betty finally broke the ice. "What's going on in that mind of yours, Ronnie?"

"Oh, Betty, I don't know. I don't remember what it's like to just be happy." She lifted her gaze back to the door of the pool house. Ware was just pushing it open. He stepped out wearing a brown leather coat trimmed with a sheep's wool collar. His hair was messy, and he had on the same blue jeans she had wrestled with earlier in the day. She stood up abruptly. The cup of tea crashed to the floor, splashing tea everywhere and sending shards of china across the wood floor.

"Oh! I'm so sorry, Betty." Ronnie was shaking and didn't know where to look. Without facing Betty directly, she offered assistance. "Oh, please. Let me get that, Betty. I'm … I'm really sorry. I didn't mean to drop the cup and make such a …"

"There's no need to be so distraught. I'll take care of this. Go change your slacks, and I'll get this." Before she started to take care of the mess, she added, "But then we'll continue our talk."

Ronnie choked back the tears and ran out of the room. A loud slam of the door across the hall signaled that Ronnie would be cloistered for quite a while.

Two hours passed. Ronnie didn't leave her room. Darkness settled in for the night, and so did a sense of dread. Not knowing where to turn or what to do, Ronnie lay on her bed staring into the blankness all around her. *What am I doing? Where is that happy little girl Betty said I used to be? What is wrong with me?* A chill ran through her body. The light tapping on the door grew louder.

"Ronnie. Ronnie, sweetie, open the door for me."

It was Betty. *I have to face this sooner or later.* "I'm fine, Betty. I just need to rest."

"Just open the door. Let's finish our little chat."

Ronnie blew out a sound of exasperation. "Why can't you just leave me alone?" Her voice was louder and angrier-sounding that even she had expected. "I mean, I'm really fine, Betty. We can talk tomorrow."

"Open the door *now*."

Something in the directive tone that Betty used made Ronnie move quickly. She scrambled from the bed, flipped on the bedside lamp, and moved to the door, unlocking it quickly to invite Betty in. When she opened the door, there stood Ware.

"Hi, Ronnie. Can I come in?"

"Where's Betty?"

"She had to go help Cook in the kitchen. Something about leftovers that needed to be stored."

Ronnie looked up and down the hallway. "What are you doing here? What time is it? Is anyone else around?"

"Take it easy." Ware was smooth and casual. He stepped over the threshold and closed the door behind him. With fluid movements, he locked the door. "Relax. No one's home but Betty and Cook. They know more than you realize."

She let go. "Oh, Ware. What are we going to do?"

"We're going to figure out what's going on with you, together. And then together we'll do whatever we need to do. Do you understand?"

"No. I don't. I can't—"

Ware walked closer to Ronnie. He wrapped his arms around her and held her close. The tears came again, and Ronnie relaxed in his arms.

"Ah, yes. Just hold me." Her voice felt too weak. Ronnie didn't know what had come over her. She didn't want to let go of Ware, and at the same time she was afraid of Quentin returning home like he'd done earlier in the day.

"I'm here. Shh."

Ronnie bolted upright. "I just heard something. Quick, you need to leave."

"Take it easy. It's just Cook bringing dinner up for you." Ware spoke confidently as if he was in on a plan.

"How do you know?"

He always has everything under control.

"Why did you lock the door? What are you doing here any-way?" Ronnie talked fast and felt as if things were spinning out of her control.

Ware stepped away from Ronnie and moved to the door. He unlocked the door and opened it with a wide swing. Then he walked into the hallway. "She's ready for dinner, Cook. It smells fantastic! Any left downstairs for me?" Typical, affable Ware.

"Sure. Just go tell Betty you're hungry. There's plenty of this stew in the pot. Good for a cold December night."

"Thanks." Ware turned to Ronnie. "Be sure to eat well. You'll feel better with a good meal. We can talk later if you want to." He shot a smile in her direction, eyeing her from the side and adding a wink before turning away.

Cook moved into the room with a tray. He pulled the small serving table to the edge of Ronnie's bed. "Here you go, Ronnie. This should give you a little lift. It's your all-time favorite comfort food, beef stew with soft, warm bread. The salad is nice and fresh. Enjoy." Just as quickly as he had entered the room, Cook was walking away.

"Cook!" Ronnie called out abruptly.

"Yes, Miss Veronica?"

"Thank you. You're the best." Her words were genuine.

"No problem, Ronnie. If you need anything else, you just let me know."

"I will, Cook."

Ronnie took small bites of the hot stew. The soft bread topped with just the right amount of butter made her feel loved and content in her own skin, even if only for a few minutes.

When she had had her fill, Ronnie felt human enough to leave her room. She carried her own tray to the kitchen, where she found Betty. "I'm ready for that heart-to-heart, Betty."

Betty took Ronnie's hand in her own and patted it, offering her love and understanding. "Let's go find a good spot in the sitting room, shall we?"

Without a response, Ronnie led the way through the hallway and into the quiet room.

Chapter

EIGHT

FEBRUARY 1966: WONDERMENT

The Christmas holidays at the Husting estate had been hectic. With business in growth mode and a newly married couple living on the estate, Robert Husting put together some very extravagant parties, from cocktail parties, to dinner parties, to an open house children's charity event. Veronica played the role of the perfect hostess at each one. The festivities ended in mid-January. When the events were finally past, Ronnie ended up very unmotivated, suffering physical exhaustion and feeling generally weary. Her home was a comfort, and knowing that she had the luxury of staying in her suite all day if she so desired made the prospect of getting through the winter months a little easier to bear.

Quentin continued to travel the world, promoting Husting Manufacturing. Robert was gone most of the time as well, but he was not doing as much international traveling. Instead, he was occupying himself with local functions. His company was important to him, but other things also claimed his time. Ronnie believed Carolyn Leeder was to blame for his absence from the estate. Although he never admitted as much, Carolyn was his love. Ronnie knew better than to think that Carolyn and Robert were not involved, but she also couldn't hold that against her father. She did love him, even if she had never developed a particularly strong bond with him.

All Ronnie ever wanted was to please Robert. She wanted him to be happy. It seemed, however, that she couldn't give him happiness no matter how hard she tried. Eventually, she had come to understand that her father had other interests and that she was not the love of his life. Robert Husting provided stability for her with a staff he had selected to raise her. His money and his property were all she really needed to survive, technically. But she longed for a strong bond with someone who truly cared about her more than anything else, like only a parent or a husband could care. Neither her father nor her husband provided that security and unconditional love, and her heart ached for more. *Or is there something else going on?* She couldn't quite name the way she felt; it was foreign to her.

Two weeks passed, and Ronnie was still spending much of her time in her suite. She rarely came to the kitchen or left the second floor. She slept most of the time. Food was not appetizing, and she had no interest in much of anything.

"Ronnie, why don't you go to see Dr. Clark? A good checkup might be in order. You might be anemic or something. He can give you something for that, and then you'll feel like yourself again."

"Maybe you're right, Betty. I can't say I'm enjoying this feeling at all. I don't seem to have any energy, and I'm not interested in doing much. I'm not even reading the new mysteries I was given for Christmas."

Betty made the appointment, and three days later Ronnie was driven to the medical center located near DuLoche Memorial. Much to her surprise, Ronnie found it nearly impossible to walk into the doctor's office on her own. Because she hadn't ventured out in so long, this short trip was overwhelmingly tiring. James helped her into the waiting room and stayed until a nurse took Ronnie to the exam room. He decided to remain in the waiting room, expecting her to be finished shortly.

About forty minutes had passed when the nurse returned.

"Are you Mrs. Simarillo's husband?"

"Uh, no, ma'am. Is there something wrong?" James was clearly shaken.

"Well, nothing to be overly concerned about, but the doctor wants to put Mrs. Simarillo in the hospital for some tests and observation. We'll try to reach her husband and take care of the transfer from here. If you'd like to leave, that would be fine."

"Leave?" James was a little bit surprised. "I can't just leave her here. Who will help her?"

"There's no need to worry. We'll get an ambulance transfer; it's just across the street. The doctor doesn't want to send her on her own. So a gurney will wheel her into a transport, and the medics will take good care of her."

James rubbed his head. "Can I go see Ronnie?" His eyes were searching the nurse's face for a response.

"I suppose that would be fine. Just follow me."

James followed the nurse into the office.

"Judy, please go ahead and call the contact number on Mrs. Simarillo's card, and then call the medics to transport her." The nurse took charge of getting things started.

"I can call her father." James offered his assistance without thinking. "Where's the nearest phone?"

The medical assistant led James to a telephone he could use. She picked up another phone and called the medics to pick up Ronnie.

It was late in the evening before Quentin could be reached. He was in St. Louis, not planning to return to Delaware for several days. He spoke with James and Betty but was never connected directly with Ronnie at the hospital.

Robert had stopped by to visit Ronnie in the early afternoon, but he had found her sleeping, and the nurse told him she was not to be disturbed.

When Ronnie started to stir, well into the evening hours, it was Ware she found next to her bed.

"Hi there, beautiful. How are you doing?"

That voice. "Ware?"

"That's right. I'm here." Ware stood up and leaned over her bed. She met his eyes and felt safe.

"What's going on? Why are you here?"

"Do you know where we are?" Ware poked to see if she knew what had happened.

"Yeah. The hospital, right?"

"That's right. You apparently have reached a level of exhaustion that has people a little worried. What are you feeling?"

"Tired, not pain anywhere."

"Do you want a sip of water? Or something else?"

"I guess water would be good." Ronnie tried to sit up, but she was connected to IVs and an oxygen tube. "What's all this?"

"Nothing to worry about. I guess they have you on a little bit of oxygen and some fluids. You should be feeling better soon. Did you eat anything today?"

"I don't think so. I don't think I've had much of an appetite for a few days."

"That's what I've heard."

"From who?"

"Betty. She's definitely worried about you."

"Well, that figures. She's sweet."

There was a long silence. Neither Ronnie nor Ware seemed to care. They just looked at one another. Ware pulled the chair closer and sat back down. He held Ronnie's left hand in both of his. He kissed the back of her hand gently and smiled warmly. Ronnie just smiled in return, but still neither of them spoke.

"Well, well. Are you coming back to life?" A nurse had entered the room.

Ware nonchalantly released Ronnie and slipped his hands onto his own thighs. Ronnie turned her head the other way and, with her eyes, followed the nurse as she came closer to the bed.

"I guess so, but I didn't know I had left."

"Oh, you didn't really. But you were definitely sleeping deeply. Do you feel a little more rested?"

"Foggy is more like it, I think."

"That's pretty normal. When is the baby due?"

Ronnie couldn't answer. She glanced at Ware. Ware shot her a look and then looked at the nurse.

"Would you repeat that?" Ronnie wanted to be sure she had heard the nurse correctly.

The nurse responded as if nothing was unusual: "I asked you when the baby is due. You know it isn't at all unusual to get overly exhausted early in a pregnancy. It is a little unusual, though, to let it go so far that you need to be in the hospital. You should be taking those vitamins the doctor orders for you. There's a reason they give us those prenatal vitamins."

"Oh. Um. I-I-I don't know." Ronnie was baffled.

"About the vitamins?" The nurse was clearly confused.

"No. I mean, yes. I mean, I don't know." Ronnie looked at Ware for help.

"Oh, we didn't … I mean Ronnie, or Mrs. Simarillo, didn't know she was pregnant, I don't think. Well, if she did, she hadn't told me." Looking at Ronnie, he added, "Did you?"

"Uh. No. No, I didn't. Tell you, that is—I mean, know."

The nurse just shook her head and walked out of the room, only to return again with a glass of apple juice and a packet of crackers taken from a tray that was in the hallway. "Here you go. Let's get a little something in you so you can begin to get some energy back."

Ronnie followed orders. She didn't know what else to do. *Baby? What will Quentin say?*

Ware let his head drop back against the chair. He stared at the ceiling. The nurse walked around to his side. "You need anything?"

Ware sat up. "No thank you. I'm fine."

"Okay. I'm going to be out at the nurses' station. You have about ten more minutes before we have to ask you to leave the hospital for the night. Mrs. Simarillo, I'll be back in a little while. We'll see if we can get some soup or something into you." She left Ware and Ronnie alone.

"Congratulations. You'll make a wonderful mother," Ware spoke with genuine sincerity.

"Please don't say that. I can barely take care of myself. How will I take care of a baby?"

"You'll know what to do. Quentin is really a lucky man."

Tears ran down her cheeks, but Ronnie remained silent. She looked at Ware and said, "Good night, my rock. Please visit me tomorrow."

Ware took the hint. He stood, kissed Ronnie on the forehead, and left the room.

Ronnie lay back and cried without restraint.

Three days later, James drove Ronnie home from the hospital. Ware had visited her every day and stayed for as long as possible each time. On the second night, the nurse on duty thought he was Mr. Simarillo. Feeling no need to explain, Ware just let that misunderstanding remain. Ronnie never made an effort to set the record straight. After all, the real Mr. Simarillo never graced them with his presence.

By the time Ronnie returned to the estate, both her father and

Quentin were scheduled to return from their travels. Robert had been called to Boston for the past couple of days, and Quentin was finally returning from St. Louis. The evening would be busy with their respective transportation needs, and Ronnie planned to stay out of the way. She made her way to the upstairs suite but retreated to the back office. There she sat in the wingback chair with a view of Ware's front door. *A baby. A love child or a baby. Which is this?*

Though she didn't find it to be a particularly welcome situation, Ronnie started coming to terms with the fact that she was pregnant. She didn't know how or when to break the news to Quentin. Ware was the only person who knew the truth. He promised he wouldn't say anything, not even to Betty or James. She trusted his word. The story was that she had allowed herself to become dehydrated and was a little bit anemic, as Betty had predicted. Other than that, no one needed to know anything until she was ready to talk. And definitely not tonight.

Chapter — NINE

Years later, those same gray hospital doors separated Robert Husting from his daughter, Mrs. Veronica Husting Simarillo. These should have been happy moments, but Robert struggled to keep the memories at bay. Emma had been in this same place just twenty-one years ago, and now their daughter was experiencing some of the same things.

The nurses came and went. Robert asked questions, but no one said much.

"She's resting, Mr. Husting. The baby will come soon."

Quentin was in Europe. Robert had rushed from the office to the estate, picked up Veronica, and drove her to the hospital. It all felt so familiar.

Betty had stayed at Ronnie's side all day. Off and on, Ronnie had strong contractions, but nothing seemed to be consistent with no pattern forming. Eventually, strong pain had triggered the call to Husting Manufacturing. Robert was very attentive and had stepped in for the absent father, but now he wished he could leave.

When the next nurse walked through the waiting room, Robert stood up.

"Excuse me, but it's my daughter in there. I know you are busy, but I need to know what you think the timing of this delivery will be. I'm thinking I could step out for a few minutes and get a bite to eat."

It was about 6:30. Robert just needed to escape.

"Of course, Mr. Husting, that would be fine. Is there a phone number where we can reach you?"

Robert rattled off the number at the estate, expressed his appreciation, and exited.

There were two other men in the room, who just looked at him. Clearly they too were feeling a bit weary. "Good night," he said with a nod of his head.

They nodded in return.

———— ⌦⌧ ————

The telephone rang, causing Betty to jump. She wiped her hands on her apron and picked up the telephone in the hallway.

"Hello, Husting residence."

"Good evening. This is DuLoche Memorial calling. Mr. Husting just left the hospital. We thought that Mrs. Simarillo would be awhile longer before giving birth, but it looks as if she will deliver that baby sooner than we thought. Mr. Husting asked us to call this number."

"Oh! Oh, thank you. Yes, I'll be sure to let him know. Thank you. Thank you very much!"

Betty put the phone down and sprang into action.

"Cook! Arthur! Miss Ronnie is about to have the baby! What will we do? Cook? Arthur?"

Ware was coming in the back door to inquire about a quick grocery run.

"Ware! Ronnie is having the baby! What will we do?"

"What do you mean, 'what will we do'? I thought Robert was with her." He acted shocked to think that Ronnie was at the hospital alone.

"He was. He's not. Oh, I'm confused. The nurse said he left, but he's not here. Is he?" Betty started to search the house, calling for Robert.

"Betty. It's okay. I'll get on to the hospital. Don't worry about a thing."

Ware was out the door before anyone could stop him.

He hopped in his truck and made it into the hospital maternity ward within twenty minutes. Stopping at the nurses' station, he explained his presence and his need to be with Mrs. Veronica Simarillo, who was about to have a baby. He never gave a name.

"Oh, Mr. Simarillo, we're so glad you made it. They just delivered the baby. Let me take you in."

Ware didn't have a chance to correct his name. He just followed the nurse through the gray double doors and down the hallway.

"Mrs. Simarillo is right in there." She pointed to the right, and Ware followed her directions.

"I'll be back with your daughter in just a few minutes."

"My daughter?"

"Why yes, Mr. Simarillo. You have a beautiful little girl."

"Thank you," Ware said to the nurse's back as she walked away. He found Ronnie looking absolutely beautiful, glowing in a pretty pink robe trimmed with yellow piping. She was sitting up in her bed, hair a bit unkempt but otherwise looking radiant.

Ware walked closer. "You are beautiful." The words were only a whisper.

"Ware! What are you doing here?"

"I'm here for you."

"I thought my father was waiting out there somewhere."

"He was, but I guess he left. The hospital called the estate. I was heading in to see if Cook needed me to pick up anything for tomorrow since I had to make a grocery run. I walked into a flustered Betty, who was trying to find Robert." He smiled broadly.

"Figures." Ronnie was disappointed again.

"It's okay. I'm sure he was here for quite some time. He probably needed dinner or something. You know what time it is, right?"

My rock. Always optimistic. "Yes. I understand all of that." Looking away so that Ware wouldn't see her disappointment, Ronnie asked, "Did anyone reach Quentin?"

"I have no idea, Ronnie. I can go back and find out where he is and try to send a telegram if you'd like me to."

"Later, Ware." Ronnie paused. "Did you hear? I had a little girl."

Ware nodded and offered a smile. "Yes, and I bet she's as beautiful as her mother."

The nurse walked in at that moment, carrying a little bundle of pink. "Here is your little baby girl. Meet your mommy and daddy." She handed the baby to Ronnie.

Ronnie's mouth dropped open, and her eyes grew wide. "No, this is not …"

"Oh, sweetie, this is your daughter. Just enjoy these first precious moments as a family. I'll be back in a few minutes."

Before Ronnie could say anything more, she was looking at a beautiful little face and Ware was sitting on the bed beside them. The baby had Ware's chin, Ronnie's almond-shaped eyes, and a full head of dark hair. "Oh, she's so precious. Ware, she's the spitting image of you."

"No, Ronnie, she looks just like her mom."

"Wait, this child is Quentin's, of course." Ronnie was trying hard to sort things out. Her mind was spinning. *When did I last have sex with Quentin?* It had been awhile, of course, with the last month of the pregnancy making her so uncomfortable. Before that, Quentin had been traveling a good deal, but neither of them was surprised that she was pregnant early in the year. Certainly this was his child. *Why does she look like Ware?*

"Ronnie, let's not rush to any conclusions here. It is possible that I'm the father. Right?"

"Oh, no. No. That *is not so*. This child is a *Simarillo*."

Ware decided to let things be for now. They could tackle this mystery at a later date. "You're probably right." He smiled lovingly at the little girl.

"What do you mean, 'probably'? This baby is Quentin's and mine."

"Yes, Ronnie. Only you and Quentin could have made this beautiful child. Did you decide on a name ahead of time?" *Obviously, this is my baby girl.*

"No. We, um, we never talked about it."

Ronnie turned her head away as tears streamed down her cheeks.

The nurse came to take the baby back to the nursery, rescuing them from the awkward moment. Ronnie was encouraged to get some rest, and Ware found a comfortable spot in the chair next to her bed. Before long, the nurse returned and asked him to leave for the night.

Reluctantly, Ware stood up, tugged at his collar, and straightened his rumpled pants legs. He stalled until the nurse left the room.

"Ronnie, sweetie, I have to leave now. The nurse is clearing me out. I promise I'll be back in the morning." He bent down to kiss her forehead.

"Good night, Ware. I love you," Ronnie whispered innocently. *She really does love me.*

Not wanting to spoil the moment, he placed the back of his hand against her cheek for a brief moment, then turned and walked away.

With a body soaked in sweat and shivering, Ronnie reached for the call button. *What is wrong with me?* She slipped her legs over the edge of the bed and tried to sit up. Instead, her feet hit a cold floor and she couldn't find her balance. Leaning back on the bed, she collapsed to her left side.

Again reaching for the buzzer, she discovered her arm was wrapped in the side rail, so she tried to roll over to free herself. The pillow felt heavy and wet as it fell off the propped head of the bed and rested in the nook between her right shoulder and neck. Thrashing her head to and fro, Ronnie began to cry out: "Help me. Help me, please. I'm suffocating."

A nurse appeared with an oxygen tank and mask.

"Relax, Mrs. Simarillo. We have something to help you."

Another nurse came in with towels and needles. The two nurses stood on opposite sides of the bed.

"What are you doing? Leave me alone. What is the mask? Why are you …"

"Relax, Mrs. Simarillo. Take a deep breath. It's just oxygen."

Ronnie succumbed to four heavy hands holding her shoulders against the bed. She breathed as instructed and found her composure.

"That's it. That's good. Just begin to breathe normally now." Nurse Kathy was very sweet. Her brown eyes were compassionate as she coached Ronnie.

Ronnie felt her arms relax. She let her head relax and closed her eyes. She began to breathe at a more normal rate, and the tears began to trickle down her cheeks.

"Are you feeling pain, Mrs. Simarillo?" This time it was Nurse Laurie speaking. Her tone was more businesslike, though still kind and caring. "We can't help you until we know what's hurting, if anything."

"No."

Kathy removed the oxygen mask and replaced it with a small tube that fed oxygen into Ronnie's nostrils. "There you go. This will just give you a little more oxygen so that you aren't lightheaded. You were hyperventilating. Are you doing okay now?"

"Yes. I'm cold."

"We'll get you some dry sheets. After delivery, as hormones fluctuate, you can experience shivering and sweating. That's very normal. Was there anything else going on though—I mean, when you first woke up? Hmm?" Laurie was stating the factual side of things. Kathy turned to her and nodded, indicating that she could leave the room.

Ronnie turned toward Kathy before she responded, "I had trouble breathing. My bed was shaking. I got scared." Tears were still streaming down her face.

"We saw a change on the pulmonary monitor at the nurses' station; that's why we came in with oxygen. It doesn't look like anything to worry about, though. I do think you are dealing with hormonal fluctuation, but I'm a little more concerned about your emotional state. What is making you sad right now?"

Ronnie's stomach was quivering with her short, rapid breathing. She felt the corners of her lips uncontrollably dragged downward. With eyelids firmly closed, she let the sobs begin.

Kathy held her hand and waited.

Ronnie couldn't stop crying, and Kathy simply stood there, offering an occasional, "It's okay, just let it out."

"What do I do now? How do I live with this?"

"It's okay. Being a new mother is overwhelming at first, but you'll be a great mother."

"That's not it," Ronnie whined. She didn't recognize her own voice. It was raspy, soft, and lower than normal. *I have lost all control.*

"Do you want to talk to someone?"

"Who?"

"I can call for a staff counselor to come talk with you, or I can call your husband to come back."

"*No!*" Ronnie surprised herself with the rapid response that felt so emphatic.

Kathy patted Ronnie's hand. "Should I just leave you alone for a little while?"

"Yes" tumbled out in much more composed manner. "I'm fine. Thank you. I'd like to be alone now."

"I'll send an aide in to change your sheets. Please leave the oxygen under your nose for a little while. We'll be able to remove that in about thirty minutes or so." She released Ronnie's hand.

"Okay."

"If you need anything else, here's the buzzer." Kathy wrapped the buzzer back around the side rail, positioning it in such a way that would make it easy for Ronnie to reach.

"Thank you."

Kathy left the room and pulled the door closed behind her.

Ronnie sighed, tears streaming down her face again. *Oh my dear Ware, what will we name our love child? She is your creation. We can't deny it.*

Three days later, Ronnie experienced another episode of fear and panic. Her doctor ordered a full examination that resulted in nothing of concern. He determined that she was handling the hormonal fluctuations fine but that her sleep had not been sound since the first twenty-four hours in the hospital. The doctor felt that getting her back to familiar surroundings might allow her to rest more easily. Ware arrived early on the morning of the fourth day to escort the new mother and baby to their home. In a stream of paperwork that was generated, Ware signed papers that were put before him, including release forms, doctor's orders for follow-up visits, and any other thing that was needed. He never realized how much paperwork was involved in having a baby, but he just wanted to get Ronnie home and did whatever was necessary. He knew that Betty would be able to work magic in getting Ronnie over whatever was bothering her.

They exited the hospital with lots of well-wishes for "the new family." Ware just went along with the comments. It didn't seem to bother Ronnie that he continued to be mistaken as the father of her baby. After all, he might well be.

Betty greeted Ronnie and Ware at the front steps. She bubbled with excitement. Her face lit up when she looked into the beautiful face of little Sandra Elizabeth. Ronnie reacted with relief at the familial love. Her Betty, her only mother, was as happy as any grandmother would be, and she was honored to know that Ronnie had chosen Elizabeth as the child's middle name. Ronnie cried at the sight.

The first week at home with Sandra was a challenge for Ronnie. She had never been around babies, and she certainly didn't feel like a mother. Quentin continued traveling, and she worked on accepting that fact. His work with Husting Manufacturing took him away from her more than she had ever expected or wanted. Her own father had lived that life, and now her husband followed in those footsteps. The whole environment created discontent. She didn't believe that Sandra would be affected as long as she could be a doting mother. At the same time, it was challenging to be that doting mother when she was tired, sad, and feeling unloved. Betty was the only one who knew how to handle that. And she did a wonderful job of it.

Ronnie's sleep became a priority, and she slept until any hour she desired. She received breakfast in bed and enjoyed being driven to have her hair coiffed and her nails manicured every week. Betty took the night shift and the day shift in answering the calls of baby Sandra. For the sake of Ronnie's happiness, Betty would do anything. She understood the sadness and the loneliness of the beautiful Miss Veronica Husting Simarillo. Having a baby only compounded those feelings.

Quentin arrived back at the estate three weeks after Sandra's birth. Because he had missed the birth and couldn't make it in a timely fashion to be with Veronica, he had chosen to continue his business travels and not worry about rushing back to the States. In fact, he'd extended his stay in Europe to pursue unexpected expansion opportunities.

Quentin finally arrived home in early October. The air was crisp, and Ronnie was beginning to find her way back to normal daily routines. Quentin came in the front entrance and took the stairs up to their suite two at a time. Ronnie was standing in the hall, waiting for him. He made his way directly to her with open arms. "My dear wife, how are you?"

Ronnie felt her guard rise. "Fine, thank you, Quentin." She allowed him to hug her, but she stepped back readily. "I hope you had successful travels and are ready to see your little girl."

Quentin stepped toward her again. "Things were fine, yes. But how are you? I'm so sorry that I was not ..."

Ronnie shot her hand into the air. "No, Quentin. Let's not go into that right now. Come see Sandra Elizabeth, your baby girl." Ronnie turned abruptly and marched ahead of Quentin down the hall and into the nursery. The nursery that had once been Veronica Emma-Mae's nursery, and then her childhood bedroom, decorated to correspond with every stage of her development, was once again a pink and yellow nursery, albeit updated to meet the needs of the modern mother. The rocking chair was a glider-style rocker, and the drapes were tapered, not ruffled. The walls were pastel, but the rugs and other decor spoke to the times with elephants, giraffes, and other animals offering a more generic motif than a typical all-girl pattern.

Ronnie watched Quentin as he stepped into the room. With lips tightened into a straight line, she simply observed. Her insides knotted up, and her throat felt tight. Her instinct was to offer criticism of his absence, but the words didn't present themselves. Quentin walked slowly to the small bassinette that held a sleeping, suckling infant. Working to stay still, Ronnie's heartbeat quickened. With hot cheeks and blurred eyesight, she looked away to avoid seeing Quentin in a tender moment.

With her lower lip quivering, Ronnie found her voice. "She's a beautiful image of us, isn't she?" Swallowing the lie, Ronnie looked at the floor.

Quentin reached into the bassinette and touched the back of his hand to a warm pink cheek. Ronnie wondered what he was thinking. *Does he see Ware in that face?* Forcing herself to remain focused on the moment, she raised her head and looked at Quentin. He was staring back at her.

"This can't be my child. These are not my family's features; in fact, how can this not be the *pool boy's* baby, Veronica? Look at that chin—just like Ware. I'll find my way out of your life, Ronnie. I see what's going on here." He turned and walked out of the nursery, down the stairs, and out the front door.

There was no denying it. Quentin was right. Ronnie sank into the glider rocker and let her head fall back against the hard wood with a thud. She felt nothing.

TEN

Ronnie was wallowing in a deep place. Never before had she visited the depths of her being in such negative ways. Through all those years of feeling unloved by her father, Ronnie never felt this level of despair and dread. Under all of the loneliness, she could always depend on the house staff to entertain and love her. They did love her, and she knew that. Robert, on the other hand, was never particularly affectionate toward her.

The mother she never had added a barrier of some kind to her relationship with her father. Perhaps to Robert she was a painful reminder of Emma. Her mother was no more than a ghost roaming the halls of the estate, but some presence there influenced her father's behavior at all times. Lately that influence had grown stronger. It was palpable at times, especially in the sitting room. Though she'd never asked, Ronnie sensed that her mother, Emma, spent a lot of time in that space. The particular scent of Bouquet of Flowers talcum powder lived in that room. Betty would sprinkle Ronnie with that powder after her bath when she was a little girl. The powder felt especially cool on the sticky hot creases behind her elbows and knees in the heat of the summer, and the unforgettable fragrance of roses filled her senses. She now remembered snuggling into her father's lap on the settee as a child and being comforted by the same smell. He would hold her near, but it was the smell of the talcum powder, not his embrace, that comforted her.

The air chilled and a breeze rushed through the slightly opened window, bringing Ronnie back to the present. A faint cry from the adjoining nursery caught her attention, and the steps in the hallway alerted her. Betty was rescuing Sandra. Ronnie sat at the desk in the back study, reviewing her schedule for the week. She stood up to lower the window. She could see Ware coming out of his quarters in the pool house. Ronnie froze. *I need him.*

Quentin had left the estate over three weeks earlier, and she hadn't seen him or heard from him since. Her father remained vague about Quentin's travels and business affairs, and Ronnie didn't care to know more. Ware had tried to approach her in the kitchen a few days earlier, but she feigned a need to make a phone call and retreated to her suite.

Seeing him now stung her soul. He brushed against the door as it swung closed behind him, and Ronnie glimpsed his opened Barbour. She remembered the day he bought that coat. Being completely practical about his choices, Ware was careful to spend his money wisely. The cost of such a garment was a true extravagance for him, but he had every reason to own a work coat of royal choice. Proud with his purchase, Ware had shown it to Robert. Robert, of course, insisted that he reimburse the expense as the coat was a part of required working attire. Ronnie smiled as she remembered the exchange between the two men. Ware was sincerely surprised at the generosity of his employer, but his pride caused him to refuse the offer.

Shaking her head and chuckling silently, Ronnie relived the moment when Robert placed several hundred-dollar bills in Ware's hand and told him to add a lining and hood to the outerwear. He went on to explain that Ware would be expected to wear that coat whenever he represented the estate in inclement weather. He was told to submit the receipts for additional purchases of the protective wax used on the outerwear if necessary. Robert walked away abruptly as he did after any other command given to his staff. What Ronnie noted then was something she was feeling right now. Her father had found something special in Ware, and he had walked away with a broad smile, pleased by Ware's choices.

Indeed, Robert Husting had the upper hand over everyone he interacted with, especially the men in Ronnie's life. Quentin and Ware were both under the direct influence of Robert Husting, the international manufacturing mogul.

"Miss Veronica! It's Robert! Quick! Hurry!" Betty startled Ronnie.

"What is it, Betty? Where is he? Where's Sandra?"

"Come! Quick!" Betty was already heading back out of the room.

"What's wrong?! Answer me, Betty!" Ronnie moved in panic. Without thought, she followed Betty.

"Don't know. He might be dying. He's not responding."

The two ran down the stairs and into the sitting room. *Emma Husting; Bouquet of Flowers.* Robert lay draped across the settee, his tie loosened, his left arm splayed across the back of the furniture and the other over the armrest. His head hung back.

Tears were streaming down her cheeks as Ronnie swept into the room and knelt on the floor in front of her father, her body tight and shaking. "Daddy! Daddy, can you hear me? Can you hear me, Daddy? Answer me!"

"We've called the ambulance. They should be here any minute." Arthur scurried into the room with Ware at his side.

Ware moved immediately to Ronnie. "I'm here for you, Mr. Husting." His arm went around Ronnie's shoulders, and the two attended to Robert as if he were father to them both. Ware was the strong one. "Let me know if you can hear me, Mr. Husting. Just move your fingers." Both Ware and Ronnie looked at Robert's hands, waiting. "Can you hear me, Mr. Husting? It's Ware. Ronnie is with me. Just give us a signal so we know you can hear us."

Robert's eyelids fluttered but never opened. The fingers on his left hand moved slightly.

"He hears you." Ronnie moved closer to her father's face. "I'm here, Daddy." Ronnie was gaining composure as she followed Ware's lead.

"We'll go with you when the ambulance arrives. We'll make sure everything is fine. You're going to be fine, Mr. Husting." Ware continued to assure Robert that everything was under control.

The medical crew rolled a gurney through the double doors of the sitting room. Everyone cleared out of the way.

Ronnie made her way to the window that overlooked the rose garden, looking for distraction from the scene. Through blurry vision she tried to focus on the last roses of summer. Yellow and pink. Bouquet of Flowers filled her senses, and tears once again rolled slowly down her cheeks. *What will I do without Daddy?*

Ware surprised Ronnie when he touched her elbow. "Shall we go now?"

"Of course." She pulled herself together.

Ronnie let Ware lead her out the door and down the front steps. There were already three medics climbing in the ambulance. "I'll pull my truck around, and we'll follow them." Before Ronnie could respond, Ware was gone.

The ambulance doors closed, the red flashing lights were turned on, and the vehicle pulled away. Ronnie stood there, stone still.

"Keep us updated, Miss Veronica. Don't you worry about

Sandra. You know she's in good hands. I'll be right here with her."
Ronnie turned to see Betty and Arthur standing on the porch.

"You just make sure you call us as soon as you know anything.
Here's your purse and a jacket." Arthur wrapped her in a jacket
and handed her purse over.

Looking up, she saw Betty snuggling the baby. *Sandra. My
love child. In Betty's love, of course.* "Of course." She was feeling
vulnerable, scared, and inadequate.

Ware was in front of her now with his truck. He reached
across the front seat and pushed the passenger door open for her
to climb inside. Pulling her jacket tight and throwing her handbag
over her shoulder, she grabbed the doorframe and stepped up on
the running board. The smooth leather seat was cool through her
lightweight slacks, causing a chill to run through her body. *Fear,
or just cold leather?*

Ware drove carefully but fast. He kept the ambulance in sight.
Its sharp siren pierced the air as they sped through the winding roads. Closing her eyes tightly, Ronnie could see red circles
growing with the expanding sound of the siren, receding as the
shrillness died to lesser decibels, growing again with the cyclic
crescendo. Expanding, receding, expanding, and receding. Red,
pink, yellow. The visual patterns and ringing sounds created a
rhythmic nodding of her head. Ronnie felt the anxiety grow. Her
fingernails dug into the palms of her sweaty hands.

A spasm of her left thigh and a quick breath in through the
nose brought her back. Ware was squeezing her leg with one hand
and driving with the other. "Hey, it's going to be okay." His voice
was calm.

Thankful for the interruption of the siren's pattern, Ronnie
let the air gush out of her mouth, not at all conscious of the immediate relief Ware's attention brought. Ware's hand left her thigh
as he reached up to turn. He swung the truck to the curbside just

outside the emergency room entrance where the ambulance had stopped. The medics were unloading Robert, transferring him to a hospital gurney. Ronnie stared through the windshield at IV drip bags and tubes. *What will I do without my daddy?*

Ware hopped out of the cab and reached the passenger door unceremoniously. He opened the door and reached in to assist Ronnie. Her hands were again balled up into tight fists, her face pale. The strain of tight lips and clenched jaw gave her a look of shock. As Ware reached in to take her arm and guide her out of the cab, she couldn't control the shaking. Her right elbow rattled against her side. "Ware, what will I do?"

"I'm here for you, Ronnie. Everything will be okay. Just breathe a couple of deep breaths."

"How can that help me get through this?"

Ware just looked at her, his tender eyes reflecting deep under-standing. She could feel his real knowledge of her feelings. He was not pretending to be there; he *was* there. He was there for her now as he had been when she married Quentin, when her baby was born, when she was most vulnerable, and always. *Ware is here for me. Not for what my father can do for him. For me.*

Pulling from the deepest pool of energy she could muster, Ronnie swung her feet out of the truck and toward Ware. He put his hands on her waist as she slid her way to the ground. "Thank you for being here with me, Ware."

"I'm always here for you, Ronnie. Don't forget that."

She looked down at the ground, avoiding eye contact.

Ware broke the awkward silence. "Are you okay now? I need to park the truck, but if you want me to go in with you, I will."

"No. No, I'm fine. I'll go ahead in and figure out what's going on. You can just meet me in there."

Ware kissed Ronnie's forehead. "He'll be fine, Ronnie, and so will you."

Ronnie closed her eyes briefly and then looked up at those gray and gold eyes. "I believe you."

It took a few seconds to refocus, but Ronnie's resolve gained momentum. She turned in the direction of the emergency room, stood straight, and walked in with the determination she had gained from Ware's encouragement. Ware returned to the truck.

Inside the hospital, Ronnie was just one person among many seeking information or registering for services. When she finally made her way to the information desk, what repose she had garnered just a few minutes earlier diminished. Her patience had run out by the time a middle-aged woman of kindly demeanor greeted her: "Good afternoon, ma'am. How may I assist you?"

Ronnie lost control. She wanted to scream. "What is going on with Robert Husting? He was brought in on a gurney, but I don't know where he is. I'm his daughter, and I need to see him. Now." Her voice was firm, even though her body was visibly shaking.

"I'm sorry. Please bear with me while I look for his paperwork."

"I said I'm Robert Husting's daughter. I need to know what's going on." She was brusque, demanding.

"And your name is?" The nurse was trying to be efficient.

"I'm his daughter; just let me know what's happening. Where is he?"

"I'm sorry, but I need your name, and I'll need to pull his file." The nurse smiled at Ronnie, maintaining her pleasant attitude.

"Fine." Ronnie dug into her wallet and handed over her driver's license. "Here. What else do you need?" At this point, she was ready to pull her social rank and explain her father's deep pockets.

Without her noticing, Ware was standing behind her. He bent down to whisper in her ear: "How are you doing?"

"I'm fine." Her words were brusque, but Ronnie's body relaxed as her shoulders lowered with the warmth of Ware's presence.

The woman addressed her again. "Well, Mrs. Simarillo, let

me check in with the nurses who are with Mr. Husting. Please have a seat. I'll be right back."

Ronnie blew out a moan as she leaned her head back on Ware's shoulder. He put an arm around her, and the two of them retreated to a corner of the waiting room. They settled into hard green chairs. People were sitting on all sides of them, but they had a clear view of the hospital-gray double doors that shielded them from the reality of Robert's experience. Neither of them spoke.

Ronnie's thoughts were traveling in all directions, taking her down paths of happy days remembered and through tunnels of darkness adorned with unspoken sentiments for her father. She mostly stared into nothingness and tried to grasp the meaning of all that filled her mind. *Ware is here with me. What would he think if I told him all that I'm feeling right now, right this minute? Would he wonder about my emotional state? Would he run away as fast he possibly could? I wouldn't blame him.*

"Mr. Treallor?" a nurse called out across the room.

Ronnie had to nudge Ware. "I think she just called for you. Who could need you here?"

"Mr. Warren Treallor, please." The name rung out again, and this time Ware responded.

"Right here. I'm here." Ware stood up.

The nurse came closer, carrying a clipboard. She was a pleasant enough person with a slight smile on her face. Her wavy red hair and healthy-looking freckled face radiated a nurturing yet robust personality. Ronnie had an immediate repulsion toward her. *Looks like Margaret Leeder.* The white uniform fell comfortably close to her body, and her green eyes danced when she saw Ware. Ronnie missed none of the electricity that sparkled from her.

"Well, it's a pleasure to meet you, Mr. Treallor. My name is Robin, and I'll be caring for your father during his stay here."

"There must be some mistake." Ronnie was on her feet. "I'm Veronica Husting, Robert Husting's daughter, and I'm the one waiting to hear about his status. This is one of our estate workers. He accompanied me here."

Ware just looked at Ronnie. *One of our estate workers.*

"Oh, I see." Robin was addressing both of them as she looked back and forth from Ware's face to Ronnie's face twice. Then she directed her attention specifically to Ronnie. "It seems as though Mr. Husting has designated a Mr. Warren Treallor as his contact family member. There is no information about a Veronica Husting on this list of allowed visitors right now. So I'm afraid I'll have to ask you to wait a little longer."

"That can't be right. I'm his daughter. My name is Veronica Simarillo."

"I'm very sorry, but we can only allow people who ..."

"I don't care what you can allow," Ronnie interrupted. "This is *my* father and I need to see him and know what is going on! Don't you understand that *I* am his next of kin, his *only* next of kin? My attorney will be happy ..."

"Miss Husting! Or Simarillo, whichever it is. We don't need to have a scene here."

"Maybe we do if that's what it will take." Veronica's head swung slightly from side to side with each word, and her lower jaw protruded forward.

Ware stepped in. "Robin, would you excuse us for just a second? Ronnie, let's just go over there for minute and figure this out." He pointed to a corner of the room that was unoccupied. Taking her by the elbow, Ware escorted Ronnie away from the anxious moment and into a state of reasoning.

"Ware, how can she do that? What does she mean that you are my father's son?! You're not his son! What's going on here?"

Ware tilted his head to the left, and his lower lip curled as the edges of his mouth dipped. "Sweetie, I don't know. No, I'm not your father's son, not even close. But I hope I'm more than just an estate worker to you."

Ronnie's eyes filled. She batted her lashes to avoid the spillage. *Hold tight. Get a grip. Don't cry now.*

"I didn't mean anything by that." *Ware. My rock.*

"Right now, I'm going to follow the nurse. We can talk about that little slip another time." Ware turned and left Ronnie standing alone.

Ronnie moved back to the sticky green chair. Ware joined Miss Electric with her perfectly shaped hips, vibrant smile, and sparkling eyes. *I wish you would trip over your pretty little white clogs. And Ware better not even look at you the wrong way when you do.*

The wait was unending. Ronnie tried to occupy herself with out-of-date magazines. She flipped through the pages, never really seeing their contents. She paced the floor more than once and even interrupted the nurse at the desk with more inquiries of her father's status. None of her approaches were successful. There was no breaking through the barrier. Only Ware was listed as a visitor, at least for the time being.

When Ware finally did return to Ronnie, he was solemn. Ronnie couldn't read his face or his body language. She asked lots of questions and only received one answer: "I'll take you in when they say we can go back." Clearly he was preoccupied with something very serious. Ronnie was afraid to know what that was.

Chapter
ELEVEN
February 1967: Transition

The holiday season proved difficult for everyone. Ronnie never saw Quentin again. Robert came home from the hospital and was on bed rest for three weeks. When he regained his strength, he returned to work half-time until the beginning of the New Year. Then he returned to the office three full days each week and worked from his home office the other two days. His business was beginning to take a turn. Quentin was not keeping up his end of the negotiations that had started the business into its growth mode over the past two years. He was often unavailable for Robert's needs, and their relationship faltered. Ronnie sensed that all of this downturn was her fault. Quentin didn't see Sandra as his child, and she'd never tried to convince him otherwise. He hadn't given her a chance.

To everyone else, Sandra Elizabeth was the daughter of Quentin Simarillo. Ronnie thought that even her father, Robert, believed her. At all costs, Ronnie would not be suspected to have had a baby from an extramarital affair. Even if Ware did think Sandra looked like him.

The postholiday blues were sinking in. Ronnie needed a breath of fresh air and wasn't sure where to find it. Her father was engaged more fully in his work, but his mood was terrible. She felt too much guilt to be in Ware's company. Betty and the staff were constants, but they certainly didn't help get her out of her blue mood. She was desperate for a fling without a baby in tow.

As always, Ronnie was determined to get what she wanted. In this case, she would tell her father she needed a change for her mental health. *Of course he'll send me off to Paris for a couple of weeks. That's what I need—a vacation.* Ronnie set her plan in motion, but the result was not what she expected.

The developmental years of Veronica Husting Simarillo's life were complicated. She was influenced by money and her own desires to be satisfied. Stepping down to the needs or desires of another person was not in any way her modus operandi. She would never give up something of hers for another being—not for her father, a husband, or a daughter. Few people were important enough to win her service in any form.

Betty was very special to Ronnie, but only because she cared more about Ronnie's satisfaction than her own. Ware was a strong attraction. He did things to her that she could not and chose not to understand. He was there whenever and wherever she needed him. Her most vulnerable moments were in his presence. His steadfast devotion was something that she knew would always be there, and she expected it. Her affections for him were genuine, but she was not able to accept the responsibilities that love demanded.

Robert made his way to the dining table. The sun was very low in the sky, and rays streaming through the windows bounced off the mahogany tabletop. The crystal chandelier shone in multicolor, sending rainbows onto the walls. Ronnie joined Robert at the table. She pulled out a chair, sat next to him, and took his hand in hers. "How are you feeling today, Daddy?"

"Just good enough to get through the day. After dinner, I'll retire to my suite for some rest."

"Are things going well at Husting?"

"Why do you ask?"

"Well, I'm just worried about you."

"Since when do you worry about me, Ronnie? Hmm?"

"Daddy, you know I've always wanted you to be happy."

"Happy, yes. What is that to you, Ronnie? What does it mean to be happy?"

"I don't know. I guess I've never thought about it much."

"Really?" Robert was incredulous. All Ronnie ever pursued was her own happiness. She used her influence to make the world around her match her every desire, and she thought Robert was blind to her ways.

"Well. I guess I know when I'm happy. I know when things around me make me feel good. I just think we all need to be happy all the time! Don't you?"

"That might be a very lofty goal for some of us. Very lofty."

Ronnie just stared at her father. His words bit her. She dropped his hand, stood up, and moved closer to him.

"I hope you're always happy, Daddy."

Ronnie turned around and walked straight upstairs to soak in a tub. Robert grabbed at his chest. He tried to call out to her for assistance, but she didn't hear him. She didn't see him struggling. Grabbing the edges of the table, Robert gasped for air. It did not come. Gasping sounds continued. Minutes passed. No one came to Robert's rescue.

His head began to bob forward, and his grip loosened.

Twenty minutes later Betty entered the dining room to find Robert slumped over, his face down in his dinner plate. She removed an empty glass that held a strong scent of mint tea. Holding it up high to allow light to shine through, she nodded, smiled wryly, and took the glass to the kitchen. No one was around. She washed the glass and returned it to the back of the top cabinet, careful not to touch it with her bare hands. She poured regular tea into a new glass and returned it to the table. With a sense of accomplishment, Betty sought out Arthur and Cook, acting with urgency.

"Oh my! Oh my! Cook! Arthur! Come quick!" She scurried through the hallways, calling into the office where Arthur sat doing his evening record keeping. "It's Mr. Husting! I think he's not breathing. Hurry!"

Cook joined them from the basement storeroom.

Betty called up the staircase to alert Ronnie. "Hurry, Miss Ronnie. Where is Sandra? Come here, but be sure little Sandra is in her playpen."

Betty was running up the stairs. In the hallway she bumped into Ronnie, who had stumbled out of her bathroom, throwing a robe around her shoulders.

"Your daddy is in trouble. Go downstairs! I'll check on Sandra. Make sure someone gets Ware and James and calls an ambulance!"

What followed was a blur to Ronnie.

Robert's final words haunted her: *Happiness. A very lofty goal for some of us. Very lofty.*

Ronnie returned to a deep and dark state of mind after her father's death. What she learned about the events surrounding Robert's initial heart attack became a mark of venom. Ware had made a pact with Robert that day when he was summoned to Robert's hospital bedside and she was not allowed in the room. Ronnie sensed that true-blue Ware had traded his loyalties.

Chapter

TWELVE

May 1968: Facing Reality

A delicious spring day on the estate gave everyone a new outlook. Azaleas in full bloom along the property line added crisp color—pink, purple, and white. The sun was bright and the sky azure. Ware was tending the gardens on the west side of the house when Ronnie found him, his shirt wet with sweat, his neck dewy, and his arms covered with earth. Ronnie could feel his masculinity from a distance.

Ware turned to see Ronnie approaching. He kept his head low and focused on the soil he was tilling. He often replenished the soil of the rose gardens in the spring. Tools lay on the ground beside him, and a wheelbarrow of peat moss was at his side. Ronnie stopped next to him. She waited and didn't speak. It had been too long since she had felt him close to her. Her dark mood could use his embrace, but she would never admit that under the circumstances.

"Hello, Ware."

Acting as if he hadn't seen her walking up, Ware gave a casual reply: "Oh, hi there, Ronnie. I didn't even hear you. Lost in my own thoughts, I guess."

Ware stood up. He cocked his head and looked her square in the eyes.

"Yeah, I know what you mean," Ronnie answered awkwardly.

"What are you up to?" Ware put on his casual charm.

"Nothing much."

Neither wanted to break the quiet that ensued. After a bit, Ronnie spoke first. "I guess you're getting everything in order for the realtors, huh?"

"Ronnie, I know this is …"

"No, Ware. Don't talk about it. It's done. What my father wanted, my father gets. I don't have any say in that. He left the estate for you to handle, and I have to accept that."

"Okay, then, yes. I am getting things ready for the realtor."

Ronnie started to walk away. Something strong drew her back, but she fought the pull. Instead, she flew the words over her shoulder and kept moving: "Don't sell it, Ware." Her walk broke into a run, and she didn't look back.

Ware chased after her. He caught up to her under the flowering crab apple tree on the north side of the house. He pulled her by the upper arm, and she spun around to face him. Both were out of breath. "What? What did you just shout to me?"

Ronnie started to cry.

Ware probed: "I thought you didn't care about this place."

"You're right. I don't."

Ronnie pulled herself away and ran into the house. Betty stood in the kitchen. Ronnie pushed past her without noticing that Sandra was with Betty. The tears were streaming down Ronnie's face, and Sandra caught on to her mother's sadness. She also started to cry.

"Now look what you've done! What is going on here?!" Ronnie stopped and faced Betty and Sandra but did nothing to explain. Betty scooped Sandra into her arms. The child was not yet steady on her feet, but she had a very keen sense of emotions. If anyone was distraught, Sandra cried sympathy tears. Ronnie left the scene and ran up to her suite on the second floor.

Why did Daddy do this to me? Ronnie was desperate to understand how Robert could have left the estate to Ware and left Husting Manufacturing to her. She had no business sense and had never worked a day in her life, and he expected her to carry on in his footsteps.

Husting Manufacturing was not continuing to grow. In fact, not long after Quentin left the estate, he'd also left Husting. Ronnie suspected there was more to his exit than she knew. And she suspected her father knew what was coming well before she did. Quentin had been absent from the estate for weeks at a time before she gave birth to Sandra. He was never too concerned about being around Ronnie, even spending time on business affairs on their wedding night.

Ronnie never fully understood what Robert saw in Quentin but was quite sure that the marriage was Robert's idea. After all, her engagement ring was given to Quentin by Robert. Ronnie learned that it was the ring Robert had chosen for her mother, Emma. In some respects, Ronnie thought of that as a sentimental and touching act. In others, she wasn't sure if Robert just wanted to pass her off to someone. And her father had tested Quentin as the person to continue running Husting Manufacturing after his retirement. Whether the ring was a sentimental gesture or a way of forcing the timing of the engagement, the point held no relevance to Ronnie now. She just wanted to be out from under all these warped situations. She felt totally distanced and left to her own devices—no father, no husband, no Ware. She would have to pull herself out of this hole and figure out exactly what action made the most sense. Tomorrow.

She fell onto her bed and let her feelings win. She sobbed openly and loudly until there were no tears left.

About an hour had passed when Betty knocked on the door. Without waiting, she stepped inside. "Cook made some fresh mint tea. Have some; you'll feel better." Ronnie blotted her face with a tissue and accepted the cool glass that Betty held out. She drank thankfully and returned an empty glass to Betty.

Betty stepped out of the room. Ronnie never said a word. Within minutes, she was asleep.

For several days following, Ronnie chose to sequester herself. She only appeared for meals that were enough to sustain her. She lolled in the upstairs suite. Occasionally she sat at her desk in the back office making notes. Sometimes she lounged on the bed. Throughout the day and night Ronnie was contemplating her next move.

It was a Tuesday morning, not exactly the start of a new workweek, but close enough. Ronnie awakened to Betty's strong coffee. She opened her eyes to the golden sun that shone through the yellow curtains, magnifying the cheeriness of the day outside. Rolling over to reach the edge of the bed, she let her long, dark hair fall across her face and tickle her nose. Rather than adding playfulness, the sensation created frustration and impatience, propelling her exit from under the covers as she blew out through a forced underbite, sending a stream of air that removed the irritating tickle. Grabbing the lightweight pink robe that was draped over the bedpost, Ronnie quickly wrapped herself and headed to the bathroom. The vanity clock showed 7:10, perfect timing for what Ronnie had planned for the morning. She took a quick shower, put on her makeup, tugged on a trim suit, and slipped out of the suite. Sandra's nursery door was still closed tightly, a sign that Betty hadn't gotten Sandra out of bed yet. Ronnie took the opportunity to get out of the house before becoming involved in Betty and Sandra's morning.

After a quick "good morning" to Cook in the kitchen, a mug of coffee, and a call to James to drive her to the Husting Manufacturing offices downtown, Ronnie took a minute to double-check her appearance in the full-length mirror mounted on the back of the door of her father's suite on the first floor. Staring straight into the mirror, Ronnie met her own eyes. *Husting Manufacturing is not Ronnie Manufacturing. Be strong.*

James pulled into the front circle as Ronnie exited the front door. Her blue business suit and crisp white blouse were an unexpected outfit in James's perception as he had never seen Ronnie dressed for a business meeting.

"Well, well, Miss Veronica, you look quite sharp! What is on your agenda today?"

"I have some important business to tend to today, James, and I mean to be successful."

"And you will. You will indeed. I've never known you not to accomplish your goals. Ever."

"Thank you for the encouragement, James. We'll see."

The ride was silent. Ronnie was planning her approach to Husting Manufacturing's legal and financial teams. She was determined that today she would begin the process of selling the business. The estate would be on the market in the next week, and with Husting out of her life, she would be completely rid of her father's legacy, Quentin Simarillo, and anything that reminded her of either of them. Then she would be free to have her own life her own way, even if that way was still in conceptual development.

As the car pulled up to the lobby doors, Ronnie's stomach churned. She felt sweat gathering insider her suit. *Don't take the jacket off.* James came around to the rear passenger side and opened the door. She blotted her upper lip with the back of her hand, stepped out of the car, thanked James, and told him she would have him paged when she was ready to return to the estate. Standing straight and taking in a deep breath through her nostrils,

Ronnie slowly exhaled through her mouth and stepped forward. An attitude of power and strength struck Ronnie without anticipation. Almost immediately, she became self-assured. *Thank you, whoever you are watching over me. I can do this.*

Unsure where this newfound confidence was coming from, Ronnie decided to take the change as a sign that she was doing the right thing. She was supposed to get rid of this huge business that she could never manage. At least she knew her limitations and was determined to make money, not to seek power as a female executive in a male world. Too many hours of work and too much stress had taken their toll on her father, and Ronnie knew that would never be the life for her. The fringe benefits, though, were important: luxuries, vacations, and lots of personal assistants to handle the mundane parts of life.

The revolving glass doors spun Ronnie into the lobby. She stepped onto the white marble floor, noting their highly polished surface and the abutting black granite walls. *Contradictions, black and white. Husting Manufacturing and Husting Estate.* Hers was the less desirable of the two, the dark, upward-expanding face of a slippery slope. There was no easy climb to the top. There would be no assistance in reaching the summit of Husting Manufacturing. She knew her plans made sense.

Ronnie had visited Robert's office enough times over the course of her life to be allowed through to the elevators without question. She stepped inside the mirrored car and confidently pushed 12, the top floor, which housed only the executive suite.

The ride up felt slow and laborious. She had never before been alone on this elevator ride. *Alone. At Husting Manufacturing, my company.* Confidence waned. Her stomach started to churn again, her legs felt heavy, and her breathing became shallow. She could feel her heart beating in her ears, and her head throbbed to the rhythm. By the time the car stopped and the doors slid opened, Ronnie's body shook with fear. It took all her willpower to move her legs. The only thoughts were to find a restroom—and fast. It was a distance down the first long hallway.

Her shoes tapped out a near-running pace on the marble floor. Her handbag slipped off her shoulder, and the toes of her shoes felt too long. The weight of the bag pulled her to the side. The toes of her shoes prevented her from cross-stepping to save a fall. She tumbled to the right, banging her shoulder into the hard granite wall, and slid to a stop on her side, her back against the wall and her right shoulder on cold marble. Throbbing pain shot down to her elbow. Her head was light, and her ears were ringing. Dark rings flashed before her eyes. A voice called her name.

"Mrs. Simarillo? Are you okay? Can you hear me?"

Ronnie couldn't see anyone in the blackness. The strong scent of ammonia wafted through her nostrils, snapping her out of the dark hole. The voices came closer. The light at the end of a long black funnel widened. Slowly, she came back.

"Get some water. Don't move her too quickly."

Ronnie rolled her head back against the wall. She became immediately self-conscious, worrying about her posture, her skirt, and her awkwardly splayed legs. A blanket appeared and was spread over her. Three faces came into clearer focus. All women. *My father's women. The women who tended to his every need during his working hours.* "I'm fine. Please step away, and let me stand up."

A bit uneasy and definitely lacking a sense of balance, Ronnie was resolute in forcing herself back into command of the situation.

"Mrs. Simarillo, you took quite a slip. Maybe we should have you checked by ..."

"I am fine. Just step away." Her tone was crisp and definitive.

The three women backed up, rising to standing positions. Each took a couple of steps backward. "Go!" Ronnie was forceful. They knew she meant what she said. In seconds, Ronnie was alone in the hallway, still on the floor.

What a fabulous entry. She propped herself into a sitting

position. The blanket slid off her upper body. The contents of the outer pocket of her purse had spilled, and she reached for the lipstick and compact that seemed nearby. The pain in her shoulder suggested something different. *Breathe. Ware would tell me to take a deep breath.* Ronnie composed herself, moving her arm and shoulder up and down until the pain was less intense. She retrieved her personal effects and concentrated on getting off the floor.

Thankful for the presence of the blanket, she used the drape to shield herself as she slowly rose to her feet. She carefully folded the blanket over her arm, repositioned her handbag on the opposite shoulder, and used the wall to steady herself before proceeding down the hall. The urge to run to the women's room had long passed, and all she wanted now was a sip of hot coffee. Her nose led her directly to her father's old office.

A pot of coffee was brewing. The assistant, one of those women who had been in the hallway, must have anticipated Ronnie's need. She was nearby with a china mug, sugar, cream, a spoon, and a napkin. "Would you like a nice fresh cup of coffee, Mrs. Simarillo?"

"Please tell me your name, since you know mine so well." Ronnie tried to be cordially businesslike but really had no idea what that meant. Still unsure of her balance, Ronnie nonchalantly held the corner of the big mahogany desk and eased herself around to the oversized brown leather chair. Carefully she lowered herself into the seat, inconspicuously losing the blanket under the desktop.

"I'm sorry. We've met several times, but I know that you were introduced to many people the last time you were here. I'm Nancy. Your father and I worked together for many years, so I know you've heard my name before. He was a wonderful man, your father. He and I made a great team here at Husting, and I just hope that ..."

Ronnie heard nothing that Nancy was saying. She was mesmerized by the soft voice, the blue eyes, and the blonde hair. While Nancy was not young, she was very attractive in that mature way that Ronnie couldn't define. *Is this one of my father's kept women? Could she have been more than an assistant?* "So don't worry. Dwight and I will do whatever we can to help you out."

"Dwight? Who is Dwight?"

"I guess I was blabbering, wasn't I? Dwight is my husband. He and your father were cousins, and they joined together in the business quite a few years ago. I think it was in the late 1940s. When that happened, I came on as an assistant to the two of them. Oh, it has been a wonderful time. Dwight is getting on in age, so he doesn't come to the office every day anymore. But I'm several years younger than him, and I have a lot of sprite left in me! You and I will be able to ..."

Dwight? A cousin? Part of Husting? "Grand. Nancy, I think coffee would be perfect, and then just leave me to myself. Thank you."

Nancy Bastien took the hint as if she had practiced many times. Ronnie was alone with her coffee. Her shoulder was aching, her senses in need of revival. The mysteries of Husting Manufacturing were beginning to unveil themselves. And it was already Tuesday.

The morning moved quickly. Ronnie leafed through the mail that had accumulated for her review. Most of it made no sense to her, but she tried to put pieces of information together to form some overall idea of what Husting Manufacturing was about. There were invoices that required payment, letters of credit that extended buyers' agreements for product delivery, and financial statements from banks. With her limited understanding of business operations, and not really knowing what to do with the mound of paper, Ronnie succumbed. She called Nancy back into the office and asked for assistance.

Nancy went to work as if handling those documents was her daily responsibility. She explained why a few invoices were in the mail and assured Ronnie that they generally were quickly directed for review and payment. Nancy knew exactly who should receive each and every item, and the status of each was in her memory. Ronnie was awed. *Women do this kind of thing? Could I do this? Is that what my father was thinking?*

With the 9:30 meeting just minutes away, Ronnie started to question her intent. If women were already a part of Husting, and if they could know as much as they did about the workings of the business, could she, just perhaps, become a successful business owner? That feeling of fear, confusion, and near-panic set in again. Ronnie didn't understand what was happening around her, yet she wanted to ask the legal and financial teams to sell this whole mess. *Dwight? What about him?*

As if they had been summoned, a team of six people arrived in the adjoining conference room. Nancy was knocking on the office door.

"Mrs. Simarillo, it's time for the 9:30 meeting. Would you like another cup of coffee to take in with you, or would ice water be better?"

"Water, please. And, Nancy, would you kindly join me in the meeting?"

"Of course. I was planning to."

"Good."

Planning to? So my father didn't do anything without her? Who really runs this place, me or her? Or someone else?

What transpired in the following thirty minutes was completely unexpected in Ronnie's world. Never would she have assumed that this group of businesspeople expected to meet with her to feed her information about Husting Manufacturing's current financial status, including any current or pending legal issues and their impact on the business, and to make suggestions for immediate actions that were needed to correct potential downturns in profitability. Nancy responded to every suggestion as if nothing were out of order. Ronnie just listened with a furrowed brow.

"Do you have any questions for us, Mrs. Simarillo?"

It was the chief financial officer, Donald Bastien, asking the question.

"No. At least not about any of these things."

"Will you be coming into the office on a regular basis, Mrs. Simarillo?"

"Call me Ronnie. And no. I won't."

Ronnie stood up, walked to the credenza to pour herself a fresh glass of water, and with great poise requested that Nancy excuse herself from the room. Without hesitation, Nancy followed orders, closing the door as she exited. Ronnie moved back to the head of the table but chose to remain on her feet.

"I do have a question or two, unrelated to the conversation we, or you, just had." Her head was swimming with thoughts. *They know I don't know anything! What are they expecting?*

"Of course! Go ahead and ask." It was Donald Bastien speaking for the group.

With a lift of her chin and a quiet breath in, Ronnie proceeded to make her desires known. She had practiced in front of the mirror many times. She knew when she needed to tip her head, when to pause, when to look someone directly in the eye, and when to sit back down. The execution was flawless, the sense of success in her delivery of a difficult message obvious. She was smiling broadly when she sat down. With ease and grace, she simply rolled the leather chair under the table, picked up her pen, and began to write on the legal pad in front of her:

Suggested retail price:

Buyers:

Expected sale date:

When she lifted her eyes, Ronnie was met with six pairs of wide-open eyes staring back at her. She moved from face to face, her own smile fading and the glow of success diminishing into uncertainty. As her gaze moved around the table, her shoulders slumped and her chin dropped. Moving her eyes back to the legal pad, she continued, sheepishly this time. "So what are the first steps in selling Husting Manufacturing?"

Nancy tapped on the door and announced the urgent need for the financial team to move on to a meeting that was about to start. Four men excused themselves from the table, profusely apologizing for the need to cut the conversation short and promising to get a follow-up meeting scheduled quickly. Before Ronnie could respond, they were gone, led by Mr. Bastien. The two attorneys who remained in the room found this the perfect opportunity to exit. One insisted that the conversation should not continue without Donald, and the other followed his lead with the need to attend a deposition in ten minutes. The two left the room, gathering up documents and briefcases absentmindedly. Ronnie was left contemplating her legal pad, a sweating glass of ice water leaving a puddle on the table.

James arrived within minutes of her page. Ronnie maintained her composure through the walk down the marble and granite hall, into the elevator, and across the same cold, hard black and white floors and walls of the building lobby. She pushed through the rotating doors and stepped into the fresh air. James opened the rear passenger door, and she escaped into the plush interior. The door closed on Ronnie's first experience as owner of Husting.

Ronnie retired to her suite after a very light dinner. Betty made sure that Sandra had some time on her mother's lap, but that was clearly an obligatory act on Ronnie's part. She had other things on her mind. With a quick kiss on the cheek and a hurried "you be good for Betty" as a typical send-off for the night, Ronnie returned to her desk. Her thoughts focused on the web that had been woven since Quentin's departure.

Ware was the full owner of the Husting estate. Ronnie was full owner of Husting Manufacturing. People whom Ronnie didn't know existed were beginning to appear. Dwight, a distant cousin, was involved in Husting Manufacturing. She didn't know exactly what his role was at the company, but it was clear that Dwight and his wife, Nancy, were part of the inner circle. They had more information than Ronnie had been able to gain in her days of reading and her time spent today with staff.

Ronnie detected things that she needed to investigate. Nancy and Dwight clearly had a very intimate knowledge of Robert Husting's life. They knew her mother, Emma; they knew Carolyn Leeder and, of course, the newly married Margaret Leeder Bastien. Something smelled rotten to Ronnie. *What is happening? Why me? How did I get this business? What do Nancy and Dwight do here at Husting, and why are they running the show? Why is Margaret married to the head of finance? Daddy's match? Like my own to Quentin? Are these the "undisclosed persons" in the will? How can it be? A will with undisclosed persons? Really?!*

Her own penchant for mysteries led Ronnie's imagination in many different directions. *Was Daddy killed off by one of them?*

Chapter

THIRTEEN

SEPTEMBER 1968: LETTING GO

The moving vans were packed. All the oriental carpets were rolled and ready for pickup. They had been auctioned off by International Estate Sales Consortium, along with many artifacts from the estate. All had been removed except for six rugs. One buyer took everything. It was all removed in one day. The auction house refused to disclose the name of that person.

The estate was empty and damp. Ronnie walked from room to room, her boot heels clicking loudly on the wood floors, echoing off the tall ceilings. She shivered, more from anxiety than from cold. The power had been turned off, and the lateness of the day created strange shadows across the foyer. She paused and looked through the sitting room windows to the rose garden. Walking slowly into the sitting room, her senses were heightened by the last rose of summer, visible through the side windows. It was yellow and drooping slightly, but still beautiful. A deep inward breath produced the near scent of Bouquet of Flowers, at least in her imagination. Ronnie's eyelids gently closed as she exhaled and her shoulders lowered. A second deep breath in, and her chest rose as her chin lifted high. She could feel the corners of her mouth curl upward. A tremendous sense of love and compassion for Betty filled her heart. A small hand reached into her palm. "Mommy, go now?"

Ronnie squeezed the tiny hand and opened her eyes. "Yes, Sandra. We are."

Mother and daughter walked out of the mansion into the low sun, closing the door on a chapter of Ronnie's life.

Ware was waiting in his truck. Ronnie and Sandra climbed in, and before Ronnie even closed her door, the truck was rolling down the driveway.

"If we don't get going, you two will miss your flight." Ware was all business.

"Thanks for driving us. You didn't have to take us. I could have called a cab."

Ware had insisted that he drive Ronnie and Sandra to the airport. They were on their way to Los Angeles. Ronnie's efforts to sell Husting Manufacturing were continuing, and she wanted to follow a lead on the West Coast. The financial team in Wilmington was not particularly excited about her activities, but she didn't care. In the final analysis, Ronnie knew her strengths, and they did not include playing CEO of a large company. Perhaps Nancy was a great assistant and she could probably cover all of Ronnie's mistakes. But there was something about that woman that created high levels of suspicion in Ronnie's mind. After careful investigation of Nancy's comings and goings, and after spending time with *Cousin* Dwight, Ronnie decided it was not her love of mystery novels creating some kind of warped scene. Instead, she had uncovered some unusual travel patterns, interesting connections between Dwight and Carolyn Leeder, and large amounts of money in some accounts that even the best of the financial department could not, or would not, fully explain. Ronnie needed some help.

Her greatest suspicions were of the Bastiens. Margaret Leeder never came into Ronnie's life in the way the death of their blood father might have resulted. Instead, Margaret quickly married Don Bastien, a name Ronnie had never heard until that wedding, which she refused to attend.

The purpose of a trip to Los Angeles was to seek a buyer for Husting. At least that's what everyone thought. In reality, Ronnie had met an intriguing and mysterious man named Fredrick Whatton, a movie producer. He was visiting Wilmington that summer and had attended a fund-raiser at the Wilmington Club. Ronnie had been swept off her feet when she met Fredrick that night. This trip would be an opportunity for her to explore some opportunities with him. He had enough money to buy Husting Manufacturing or to connect her with someone who could. Ronnie pulled enough weight to get the right people on board with her ideas, and her interests would be well represented.

Ware pulled onto the highway. Sandra was singing in the jump seat and sat right behind Ronnie. Ronnie was staring out the passenger window. Ware slipped a pair of sunglasses off his head and over his eyes. Ronnie looked at him. *Where will he go after he drops us off?*

"So when will you return?" Ware asked that huge open question, the one Ronnie preferred to avoid.

"I haven't really decided yet. We'll see how negotiations go."

"This buyer, is it someone who can close the deal pretty quickly? These things generally take a long time."

"I'll leave all those details to the legal and financial teams. I don't really know anything about it. They've just asked me to be there."

"There must be a return flight booked then. I can't imagine this is an open-ended trip."

"Ware, don't expect to hear from me. I'll find my way around just fine."

The atmosphere chilled. Ronnie's message had come through

loud and clear. Ware coughed, or hiccoughed, or did something that Ronnie couldn't figure out. It was a strange noise accompanied by a deep breath. She didn't want to ask. *Is he crying? He doesn't really need those dark glasses.* The sun had slipped lower in the sky, and quickly. It was that time of day when darkness suddenly appears and streetlights replace daylight. Cars merged into the right lane and formed a long line on the exit ramp. It was a busy night at the airport. Ronnie recognized her own reaction—nervousness. Sandra was still happily humming in the back seat. No one paid attention.

—— ❧ ☙ ——

Ware acted the perfect gentleman, as expected. He opened the passenger door and helped Ronnie and Sandra out of the truck. He hugged Sandra firmly and wouldn't let her go. He held her with one arm as he retrieved their suitcases from the closed compartment in the back. She hugged his neck and giggled when she almost slipped out of his grasp. He laughed with her as he gracefully caught her. She tugged at his sunglasses. "Mr. Ware. Can't see you!"

Ware let Sandra pull the glasses away. The gray and gold eyes twinkled at her, and he gave her a kiss on the cheek. She squirmed and giggled. "Thank you, Mr. Ware."

Clearly distraught over the situation, Ware smiled through curled lips and moist eyes. "Oh, my little Sandy—you be a good girl for your mommy, okay?"

Sandra nodded as Ware lowered her to the ground.

"See you?" Sandra's innocence was killing Ronnie.

"We'll have to figure that out later, Sandra. Let's get going right now, okay?" Ronnie knew she had to take control of the situation or else she would have second thoughts. Ware was not the man for her, and she needed to end all of this quickly. She signaled for a porter to take her bags for check-in. As suitcases were being loaded onto a rolling cart, Ronnie made the break.

"Goodbye, Ware. And thank you for the lift. I hope that things work out for you."

"Sure. They will. You too."

Ronnie was tugging Sandra by the hand, and they were walking away. Sandra looked back over her shoulder. Ronnie focused her eyes forward.

Ware stood watching until they were out of sight.

Takeoff was uneventful. Sandra was excited to be making a trip in an airplane, her first flight. Ronnie hoped that Sandra would fall asleep so that she could do the same. The last thing she wanted to do was entertain a two-year-old. *How was Betty always so happy taking care of me and then Sandra? What a saint.*

Sandra squirmed about, looking out the window, pulling down the seat tray, standing on the seat, and peeking over the top at the other passengers. In short, she acted like a typical two-year-old little girl. Not Ronnie's favorite thought. As fortune runs, a very kind grandmotherly woman was seated next to Ronnie. She took an interest in Sandra and offered to read a story from a book that the stewardess had handed to Sandra as she boarded the plane. Ronnie asked no questions; she simply said that that would be lovely. As the story began, Ronnie faded into a deep nap.

More than five hours later a stewardess was tapping Ronnie on the shoulder. A blanket draped over her body, Sandra was snuggled in her seat with her head resting on Ronnie's lap with the lovely woman resting comfortably next to them. The stewardess collected blankets in preparation for landing. Ronnie never asked what happened; she just accepted her good luck.

Ronnie and Sandra spent the night in a local motel in the greater Los Angeles area. They arrived in the late evening, both feeling quite rested and not able to sleep when the clock indicated differently. It was a difficult night of jet lag, and an even more difficult day followed. With a tired and cranky child in tow, Ronnie struggled to get her thoughts in order. She didn't know where to begin. The moving van was on its way here. Everyone in Wilmington believed that she was in Los Angeles for a short stay, meeting with the Husting Manufacturing team and a potential buyer. In reality, she planned to make this a permanent move. Her goods were scheduled to go into storage. All arrangements had been made well in advance. *How did I manage all of this without help?* She had picked up a few tips from watching Nancy, and now she was taking control of things for herself. Her eyes were set on Frederick Whatton, the perfect sugar daddy. He was the man who could give her anything she wanted, and she knew she would win him over in short order.

Chapter

FOURTEEN

SEPTEMBER 1968: LEAVE-TAKING

Ware managed the final phases of the Husting property sale with mixed emotions. His dream of spending the rest of his days on the estate with Ronnie and Sandra at the center of his life had been shattered. Ware respected the wishes of Robert Husting. He had clearly stated in his will that Ware should sell the estate because Veronica didn't show interest in the property, and he left specific instructions for the disbursement and investment of the proceeds. Ware was well rewarded for his loyalty to Robert.

Cook quickly found employment at the Wilmington Club, where over the years he had served as the chef for many events when Robert Husting served as the club's fund-raising committee chair. James started driving for members of the DuLoche family, but only on occasion. Their chauffeur staff included many drivers, and James took the work he could get gratefully. He had no concerns about his own welfare. Arthur had the opportunity to butler for one of the DuLoche family members who had moved closer to Philadelphia. He adjusted to being a part of that estate staff as if he belonged there and nowhere else. Ware knew they were happy with their new employment, and all the staff vowed to stay in contact. Except Betty, which was no surprise to Ware. Both Betty and Ronnie had been vague about when they would be in touch. Each went their own way.

Ware opened the door to his apartment. He shed his coat, dropped his keys into the tray on the hallway table, and kicked off his loafers. The coat tree in place next to a hall table received his outerwear, and without thought or effort he made his way toward the couch. Most of the boxes were unpacked, and what remained in crates or boxes was not critical to his current needs. Ware waded through the obstacle course of empty packing cartons, wrapping, and miscellaneous items that had no specified resting place yet. Finally, within flopping distance, he threw himself down on the soft bench seat of the sofa. Grabbing a throw pillow, he curled into a near–fetal position, hugging the soft pillow. He managed to remain stoic throughout the sale of the Husting estate and his goodbyes to staff who were like family to him. Sending Ronnie and Sandy off was more than he could bear. For the first time since childhood, Ware sobbed without care. He made no attempt to stop the flow of raw emotions. When there was nothing left to release, he fell into a deep sleep.

The bright sun shining directly in his eyes through the uncov-ered living room window was an unwelcome start to a new day. Though it was not particularly glamorous, Ware had been drawn to this small apartment complex. It was near the docks along the Christina River and offered an interesting view. The warmth of late summer days still lingered, and the fourth-floor space was hot and stuffy. Clammy skin and cotton mouth added to the dis-comfort of the streaming sunlight piercing his swollen eyes. He still clutched the pillow close, and he could feel the wet fabric. When he realized where he was and what had taken him over the night before, Ware threw the pillow to the floor. He rolled off the couch, landing on his knees: the perfect position. Leaning over the couch seat, he clasped his hands together, rested his forehead in the palms of his hands, and prayed. Prayers turned into moans, which turned into yet another round of tears. An hour passed. The sun was no longer glaring through the window, and the room turned gloomy.

With boxes all around him, indications of the work ahead, Ware was overwhelmed. He saw little worth in putting effort into this place. This place was not him, not his home, not where his heart was calling him to be. That call had left with Ronnie and Sandra.

Exhausted and weak, Ware pulled himself to his feet. A shower and a shave would deliver some energy, but he was dehydrated and suffering a headache. Two days earlier, when he moved into this flat, he bought some orange juice, coffee, milk, and cereal—just enough to cover breakfasts. The rest of his days were spent elsewhere, so stocking other foods made no sense. This was a place to crash, not a place for life to happen. Life, too, had left with Ronnie and Sandra.

A tall glass of orange juice helped. Some energy returned to his legs. He plugged in his old percolator and started a pot of coffee. Waiting for it to brew, he showered and shaved.

Ware returned to the living room with a clearer head. Boxes, cartons, possessions, all just staring back at him. *What does all of this stuff mean? Why do I have it? What will I do with it?*

These were just the beginning of many questions that began to haunt Ware. He couldn't focus on finishing the move-in. He found no purpose. He had no job, no reason to stay in Wilmington without the Hustings. It had been wonderful to connect with Betty. She was his older half-sister and had always been a bundle of energy and ambition. Betty was born to Harold Treallor and Mary Elizabeth Zane. Her mother died of pneumonia during a rough winter when Betty was only seven years old. After Mary Elizabeth's death, Harold married Lucille Zane, cousin of Mary Elizabeth.

Harold Treallor was a faithful and pious man. He believed it was in his child's best interests to give Betty a mother who was already committed to the little girl's well-being. Harold and Lucille Treallor lived a wholesome life. They welcomed Warren into their family when Betty was nine years old. Warren, lovingly nicknamed Ware by his big sister, grew up in a hardworking churchgoing family. He adored his older sister.

When Betty was old enough to realize that her father was married to her cousin, she rebelled. It didn't take long for Betty to determine her own path. By age sixteen, she left their home. Ware received only occasional communications from his sister.

How the two of them had landed on the staff of the Husting estate was such a foreign thought to Ware. He never dreamed Betty would be a domestic employee. Her aspirations as a young girl were to become wealthy and live on a plantation in the hills of Virginia, where she wanted to breed horses. That would take an incredible bank account, and certainly their minimal upbringing would never afford that.

When Ware first reconnected with Betty, he was shocked to see her. Betty had assumed the name of her birth mother. He expected to meet someone by the name of Betty Zane, not Betty Treallor. It took Betty less than thirty seconds to give Ware that eye, the one she always used when they were kids and needed to tell him to shut up and not give their parents any information about her activities like slipping out her bedroom window at night to meet up with her high school boyfriend. Or when Ware found her with friends, drunk in one of the empty stalls. As young as he was, Ware knew that what Betty was doing was wrong.

Betty had a bit of a wild side, but deep down she was a good person. She was compassionate and loving, and clearly cut out to be a nanny like she was for both Ronnie and little Sandra. Ware appreciated that very much. Ronnie was not quite as attentive to that beautiful little girl. *Oh, that beautiful little girl, my baby.*

Tears were again flowing down his cheeks. Ware reached up and wiped away the streams. Then he licked the corners of his lips where the salty moisture stung his newly shaven face and closed his eyes. *Will Sandra be like Betty? Does she have that sense of adventure and independence? Or is she like me? Or Ronnie? Will Ronnie take care of my daughter?*

These thoughts took the soul right out of Ware, leaving him limp and listless. His mind could not address the tasks ahead of him. He grabbed his keys from the table, stuffed his feet into the loafers that still lay on the floor by the door, threw the Barbour sloppily on his body, collar half tucked in, and walked out of the apartment. His hair was tousled but clean. Jeans and a light jersey were sufficient for the fall day, which was becoming overcast and windy.

<hr />

The plane landed late in the afternoon. Her escort stood outside the terminal, and Betty was greeted with a brief hug.

"Was your journey safe? Were you followed?"

"It was fine." Betty looked the tall man in the eyes, planted a soft kiss on his lips, and stepped back. There was no response.

"Let's get going." Her partner was distracted and uninterested in any kind of warm welcome. The couple climbed into the back of a limousine, and the driver put Betty's bags in the trunk. They pulled away from the curb and headed into the hills of Los Angeles. She thought what awaited her there was a reunion too long in coming. Her work in Wilmington had lasted much longer than anyone expected, more than twenty years too long. Robert Husting proved to be a much healthier man than anyone would have guessed. His demise was long and slow and included many more attempts than she had wanted—some of them botched and some of them close calls. Betty had become a member of the

Husting family on many different levels, successfully covering her true intentions and motive. In the end, those connections made it very difficult to finish her work.

Disguising her work under the role of personal assistant to the lady of the house seemed like an easy thing. The original plan included an eight- or nine-month assignment during which Betty would take down the estate. And ABS, the company owned by Alejandro Stanis, would be a major beneficiary. What no one anticipated was the death of Emma Husting and Betty's resulting role of nanny to her infant. Once Betty became entrenched in the Husting family, it seemed that the goal of her work for ABS was never going to be realized. Multiple attempts, years of plotting and planning, and running into unexpected hurdles made things very complex and nearly impossible. Betty became very attached to Veronica Husting, and in many ways her work for ABS left her living in a world of guilt and fear. Until today.

Today was a reason for celebration. She was back in Los Angeles, reunited with Alejandro. Together they could begin to breathe easily. Only one piece of business remained unfinished, but that was just around the corner. Alejandro would be meeting with Ronnie Husting and her advisors from Husting Manufacturing in just a few days. Soon enough, Betty and Alejandro Stanis would be one of the richest couples in the United States, and they could retire to Mexico as they had always planned.

Living in Wilmington, separated from Alejandro for as much as a year at a time, had been more than difficult. Betty couldn't wait to be with him again. At the same time, she grieved the loss of her adoptive family and particularly Ware, her biological half-brother. It had been very challenging to live in the same household as he for so long and to watch the interactions he had with Ronnie Husting. Betty loved Ware. Their early years were wonderful. They grew up on the farm in Virginia. Parents who loved them dearly spent time nurturing them into lovely young adults. Both left their home to pursue their dreams, and neither of them regretted their choices.

It was pure happenstance that Ware and Betty ended up together on the Husting estate. But it was a wonderful gift of quite a few years. Neither of them had ever let on that they were siblings. They had no resemblance to one another, one being dark and tall, the other fair and of average height. Not a single person ever questioned the story they concocted about different backgrounds. Their first introduction to one another by Robert Husting was a bit awkward, but they found time to corroborate a waterproof story.

Ware was totally unaware of Betty's marriage to Alejandro many years earlier. She told no one. Alej was involved in some interesting businesses, and Betty feared her family would reject him. Ware and Betty left their childhood home as they developed the need for independence. After they had both moved away, a tragic farm accident led to a barn fire, and both their parents were killed in the incident. The farm was sold. After paying back taxes and settling all the outstanding debt, there was virtually no cash. The two siblings had the same opportunities—each had had the same early formation—but their ways of life were diametrically opposed.

Ware led a wholesome and moral life. He believed in doing the right thing always and was steadfast in his commitment to people. Betty's attraction to Alej was so strong that she abandoned all she had learned from her parents about honesty, integrity, and ethical living. She could draw on those traits to create a visage when she needed to, but the allure of Alej and all his promises led her in a different direction. Her first assignments with him fed a side of her personality that she had never explored in her years on the farm.

Betty's first assignment for ABS was in Chicago in 1944, just six months before she was hired by Robert Husting. An elderly gentleman needed a home caregiver because he experienced levels of anxiety that caused him to panic, resulting in a need to remain in his home most of the time. The adrenaline she experienced when she served the deadly potion to him was addicting. Betty found a dark side that she never expected would become a way of life. But Alej promised her many things, including a world of pampering and jewels that she would otherwise never see as the daughter of a farmer. ABS, a financial consulting firm based in Los Angeles, was expanding and offered many opportunities for quick accumulations of cash in the form of bequests assigned to its nonprofit division, all managed by Alejandro Basil Stanis. All Betty had to do was convince the family to give to the nonprofit and then deliver death.

Betty was worried about Ware. He was head over heels in love with Veronica Husting Simarillo. From Betty's perspective, Ronnie never understood how to be happy, but Ware filled a huge void in her life. Underneath, Betty knew that Ronnie had real love for Ware. She also knew that Ronnie couldn't admit to loving the pool boy. Ware was the loser in this scenario. The strong, steady, and committed man was being thrown away. And that beautiful little girl, undoubtedly Ware's daughter, was never going to know the wonderful father he could be. Sandra accepted her life without thinking about a father. She was too little to understand.

Quentin Simarillo disappeared when things got tough at Husting Manufacturing and Dwight Bastien started taking a more active role in the company. It was Betty's job to keep Alej well-informed of everything she knew about Husting Manufacturing. She took that responsibility very seriously. Her own life might depend on it. Certainly her vision of riches and the good life rested on the success of the business.

Betty had to sit back and watch all these things unfold so that she could protect her own motives. But tonight, she felt another pressing issue. Alej was not himself. He presented differently to her; his affections were not palpable as they usually were when they reunited after a long absence.

The drive to the mountain retreat was quiet, cold, and calculated. *Maybe I'm just weary. Tomorrow will be better; the sparks will be rekindled, and all will be well.*

Chapter ——

FIFTEEN

—— November 1968: Readjustment ——

The California weather agreed with Ronnie. Sandra enjoyed the swimming pool at the hotel, and Ronnie found boutiques and restaurants that suited her tastes. Motherhood, however, was not agreeing with Ronnie. She had no calling for nurturing a child. She loved Sandra, but that love didn't translate into hugging and cuddling, reading stories, and playing patty-cake. It took every ounce of her energy to play in a swimming pool or to read a story. Instead, she looked forward to nap time and bedtime. Sandra longed for the cuddles and care that Betty always gave her. She became sullen and cried easily. Betty was the mother that Ronnie had never had, and in turn, Betty mothered Sandra like a grand-mother would. Ronnie couldn't be that kind of person. Her patience was running low.

It was less than two weeks into their stay, and Ronnie had learned how to leverage the services of the hotel staff completely. They started delivering breakfast to the room each day as a routine part of their work. The concierge arranged childcare for Sandra so that Ronnie could do the things she felt she had to do—shopping, going to the beauty parlor, and dining in places where she would be seen. Her way of honoring her role as a mother was to make sure that she was in her hotel room every night with her daughter, though there were times when that was a challenge for Ronnie. On more than one occasion, she met interesting people with whom she would have loved to spend long nights of conversation and partying. Instead, she forced herself to focus on her goal: Frederick Whatton and his riches.

At the age of twenty-three, Ronnie felt grown up and independent. She was enjoying the freedom of moving about as she pleased without Betty, Arthur, James, or Ware checking on her whereabouts. She had to balance reasonable responsibility of her toddler daughter, even though this newfound liberation tempted her into less-mature behaviors. This struggle was no more prevalent than on one particular morning when she woke Sandra earlier than usual.

Sandra complained about being awakened early. Ronnie shrugged off the guilt and pushed on. "We have important people to meet today. Let's just move quickly. Please."

She pulled the covers off the bed, lifted Sandra up, and carried her to the bathroom. Sandra started to cry. "You will not stop us today, little girl." Ronnie used a firm and deep voice, causing Sandra to cry all the harder.

Ronnie reasoned that perhaps she would be better off trying to console Sandra with a hug. But Sandra had different thoughts, and she would not to be convinced that easily. The sobs continued. Ronnie ignored the temptation to take the easy way out and call for a babysitter. She needed to have Sandra with her today.

She moved through the motions of getting Sandra dressed into a lovely pink outfit. Combing the dark, wavy hair caused more tears. Ronnie clipped a yellow and pink bow on one side of Sandra's head to restrain the wild nature of her hair. She poured on every bit of nurturing motherhood she could muster. Offering Sandra a sip of water, she stroked her daughter's back, calming her down.

"You look pretty, little one."

The tiny lower lip was curled, corners sucked downward. Bright blue eyes were moist and sad.

"I know you're unhappy about getting out of bed, but there's a surprise waiting for you."

Ronnie scooped Sandra up, grabbed a sweater for each of them, and threw them into a canvas tote bag. Slinging her purse over her right shoulder and balancing Sandra on her left hip, tote bag dangling from her left forearm, she exited the room. The two made their way out through the front lobby, where James was waiting for them.

"Well, looky here!" James beamed at the sight of Sandra.

Sandra recognized James and squirmed to get down from Ronnie's grip. James gave her a big hug. Sandra giggled and buried her face in his shoulder. "Mr. Ware?"

"Sandra, this is James, remember?"

"Mr. Ware too?"

Ronnie could feel her throat closing, her eyes welling with tears, and her heart beating hard. "He won't be here."

James led the way to his parked car, carrying Sandra. Ronnie followed, swiping the wetness away from her eyes and focusing on the task ahead of her.

"James, thank you for being here today. I know you had to make special arrangements, but you will really be a big help."

"It was not difficult at all, Miss Veronica. When I left my position at the DuLoches', I was hoping I would find you. They were nice enough, and I was doing fine there, but they just weren't a family to me. They never had full-time work anyway. I'm free for a while, and I would love to be your assistant. Besides I have some kin in this part of the country. It will be good to see them too."

Ronnie smiled. *I know how to call the shots. James will be my ace.*

The conversation lagged at times as James drove through the hills of Los Angeles. Idle chatter filled some of the airtime, but generally Ronnie was more focused on the meeting she had planned with Frederick Whatton. Her goal for the day was to convince Frederick that they needed to become quick partners. The plan was to entice him with her riches and then lure him into her life. She had no intention of giving any part of her fortune to another person, but she also knew that money attracted money in all the circles she had run during the past several years.

Ronnie also knew that Sandra was an irresistible appendage to her life. Cute as a button with her wavy dark hair and violet-flecked blue eyes, she had a way of batting her eyelashes and winning any heart in her path. By playing the role of unfortunate single mother whose child is accustomed to extravagant surroundings, Ronnie anticipated a rapid catch.

The morning sun was bright, and shadows of tall trees stretched across the pavement. It was challenging to follow the winding pavement on an eastward route, but James managed as if this excursion were a familiar one. Ronnie was beginning to get nervous about the pending conversation with Frederick. She queried James about his confidence in the direction they traveled, but he assured her that he had studied two different maps after she contacted him.

Two days earlier, Ronnie had called James with a special assignment. He caught a flight, arranged for a car, and appeared at her hotel, ready to work. Always ready to serve, James had been a staple of Ronnie's past life. She would love to have him around as long as he was willing to stay in Los Angeles.

After thirty minutes in the car, Sandra was more than ready for breakfast. James stopped at the first restaurant they encountered, and they enjoyed a hearty breakfast.

Within minutes of getting back into the car, Sandra dozed into a restful sleep. Ronnie put her head back, closing her eyes to take a nap, but her mind raced with thoughts of her upcoming meeting with the very rich Mr. Frederick Whatton. She spent the time planning her approach.

Less than three hours after leaving the hotel, the car moved through the gates of a magnificent abode nestled in the hills. The manicured property overlooked a large area of undeveloped land, giving a magnificent view. Taking in the vastness of the terrain, Ronnie understood the insignificance of her physical being. She breathed in three times, just as Ware would have told her. *Let go of insignificance. This is my chance.*

Sandra slipped out of the car, taking the large hand extended to her. Looking up into the eyes of a towering male, her eyes grew wide, and she turned to find Ronnie. Ronnie sat staring at the endless landscape with its multiple shades of green. "Mommy?" The small voice gave Ronnie a start, jolting her back to the present. She gasped aloud and noticed her hands shaking slightly.

James stood at the open rear passenger door. Sandra stared back into the car, holding onto Frederick Whatton's hand.

"Good morning, Veronica. It's a delight to see you again." The deep raspy voice had a calming effect on her. Ronnie brought herself out of the momentary freeze. She felt her chest sink, her shoulders drop. This man had a powerful influence on her physical being.

Swinging her legs out of the car, Ronnie stood to greet Frederick with a full smile and sly eyes. "The pleasure is mine, Mr. Whatton." *Steady. Keep it together.*

"Frederick, please."

"Frederick." Ronnie nodded slightly and reached for Sandra. "My daughter seems quite at home with you. Sandra, please come to me."

Sandra dropped Frederick's hand and moved to Ronnie's side. She held her mother's wrist with both hands, her head back and her hair trailing in curls down her back. Her face told the whole story. Like Ronnie, Sandra was confused by this man's aura. He radiated a welcome that led to immediate trust that captured both Ronnie and Sandra. *What is this feeling? Ware? Don't drop my guard. Protect Sandra. Be careful. Snatch him for his riches. Don't give away my heart.*

James saved the moment. He graciously offered to park the car and wait for Miss Veronica. Frederick directed him to pull the car around to the back of the house, where he would find a guest garage and a comfortable cabana stocked with beverages and snacks. Before departing, James shot a questioning look at Ronnie. A quick nod assured him that she was comfortable with this suggestion.

Sandra had relaxed enough to wave goodbye to James. "Mommy, the bathroom."

"Right this way, Sandra. My housemaid can show you to the facilities." Frederick led the way up the long stone steps to the front entrance of the house. The tall columns created a stately appearance. The white facade contrasted with the rich green hills surrounding the house, imbuing Ronnie with a sense of insignificance once again. Her resolve to be strong and confident was challenged in this vast arena. Walking behind Frederick with Sandra just in front of her, Ronnie paused long enough to take in the scene. A quick calculation of a potential escape route provided a bit of comfort. She moved forward with caution.

James rounded the corner of the house, following the drive behind a grove of large evergreen trees. About a quarter of a mile ahead stood an outbuilding with three bays for vehicles, each with its own set of double doors. The building was in keeping with the architecture of the house and equally regal. As the car neared the structure, one set of doors opened. A woman stood inside, waving an arm and directing him to drive into the garage.

As the black Lincoln pulled ahead, the double doors closed, and the woman opened the driver's door to assist James out of the car.

"It's good to see you again, James."

James pulled Betty into a bear hug and held her for a long time. "I'm so glad you're here and safe," he said. Holding her by the shoulders and pushing her an arm's length away, James inspected Betty from head to toe. "It is really good to see you too."

They hugged again, and Betty wiped a tear from her cheek. "I wasn't sure this was going to work out at all."

"Well, it did. Now let's get on with our plans."

Chapter

SIXTEEN

FEBRUARY 1969: STARTING OVER

The holiday season proved very busy for Ronnie and Sandra. Their time in the Los Angeles area turned quickly to a flurry of social activities throughout the entire season. With few connections in the area, Ronnie expected a quiet and uneventful month. As it turned out, James was full of connections. He had family from the East who had settled in the Los Angeles area. Ronnie's plan to quickly attach to Frederick Whatton was maturing into a very typical love relationship.

Frederick's resources were boundless. Even the Husting estate and reserves appeared limited in comparison. Frederick answered to Sandra's every whim. He provided ponies and carousels, playmates and caregivers. His outpouring of affection was uncharacteristic of an older gentleman with extensive business concerns. He had no family of his own, and the care he showed seemed genuine enough to Ronnie. She welcomed every bit of his attention and sent caution to the winds, at least temporarily.

She and Sandra spent weekends at his estate in the hills, and they continued their hotel lifestyle during the week. Ronnie's days were filled with shopping, connecting with more and more of Frederick's acquaintances, and doing the research she thought was important to unloading Husting Manufacturing at a top price.

Her understanding of such transactions was clearly lacking in every way.

James stayed in town. He was at Ronnie's disposal whenever she called upon him. Otherwise, he maintained a low profile, never letting Ronnie know what he was doing. She trusted him completely. Her assumption was that James was enjoying the reconnection with his family. She never pried into his personal business.

Sandra started attending a preschool program for toddlers. She was thriving in the company of other children, learning how to share and socialize, and becoming more and more verbal. Ronnie enjoyed the freedom this arrangement gave her. With the assistance of the hotel concierge, she secured a regular nanny who stayed in an attached room, tending to Sandra the same way that Betty had cared for Ronnie.

Even with these conveniences, Ronnie was very eager to seal the deal. She wanted the home in the hills with Frederick Whatton caring for her every whim. It was her ideal life with every material desire she verbalized at her disposal and with time to indulge herself in any way at any time. *Daddy left Husting Manufacturing to me so that I could live comfortably forever. Frederick can do that for me instead.*

During the holidays, Ronnie noticed how very much at home she felt at Frederick's estate. She even imagined the scent of Bouquet of Flowers. She could feel the presence of a feminine touch, much like that at the Husting estate. Every room had an eerily familiar tidiness. The pillows were arranged in the same manner on every couch—always squared off and placed in the middle of the seat back. There were no signs of tolerated clutter, and items on sideboards and side tables were aligned with the corners of the furniture. While she had never thought much of these things in the past, these small style indicators were in keeping with the Husting estate. She continued to reflect on the similarities and continued to notice their consistency. Even after all the holiday celebrations, these little curiosities remained.

Eventually, Ronnie concluded that style and habits in home living were not worth questioning. She believed these were a sign that this was her home. *But only after Frederick closes a major deal with me.*

James lunched with Betty in a Los Angeles bistro known for its private tables and discreet staff. Betty took the opportunity to unload her greatest fears on James. Theirs was a close-knit relationship, forged from years of working together on the Husting estate and covering for one another's faults and errors. His mishaps were never difficult to explain away. Hers, on the other hand, required a good deal of finesse. James knew of her many occurrences of drugging Robert as a way of giving the young Veronica more time with her father, or covering for a mishap that could be corrected while he slept off the effects of a special iced tea. Most of the estate staff were aware of her antics. Ware was never included in these secrets. All of them who knew about Betty's actions believed she was well-intentioned and assumed she used drugs as a way to give Robert a little extra sleep and a little extra time at home, and even as a way for all of them to survive in stressful situations.

Betty was trusted to know how to handle every melodrama with grace, poise, and ease. James, for one, was grateful for her help when he needed to cover his lack of vigilance around the Hustings' automobiles. More than once, the cars were vandalized, always during times of turbulent politics or social indiscretion. James could always depend on Betty to buy time enough for the cars to be repaired and ready to transport Robert to his next destination. Today, though, Betty unloaded far more than a little confession about slipping drugs to Robert. Today, he was learning all about her marriage, something that she never had shared with him.

"So I was married to Alej long ago. Before I even came to the Husting estate. He uses the name of Frederick Whatton for all his US business dealings. I still call him Alej."

"Why? Why didn't you tell us you were married? Robert could have found someone else. I don't understand."

Betty became very uncomfortable with the questions. She had miscalculated James. Betty thought that he would buy her story at face value. Her concern was about her husband falling in love with Ronnie and his recent mention of divorce. She had felt the change the minute she returned from Wilmington. Nothing was the same. Alej was cold and hadn't welcomed her in his normal manner. The passion was gone, no love left in his eyes. She saw only a man with a mission, but the mission didn't include her as a partner.

Alej had commanded her to get lost whenever Ronnie and Sandra were around. She and Ronnie had not yet laid eyes on one another. As far as she knew, Ronnie was totally unaware that Alej was even married. Ronnie knew him as Frederick Whatton, his US business name. Ronnie saw money, not the Alej who would take the Husting fortune, not the Alej whom Betty loved and with whom she had committed to live a life of crime.

"It's not that simple."

"Help me understand, Betty. You were our number one person at the estate. And you never told us you were married. How can that be?"

Now she felt the squeeze. *How much can I tell him? Will he betray me?*

"Just listen for a minute, James. I had an assignment. Alej was originally my boss. I worked for him in Chicago first. Then I learned what he really does, and I wanted more. I married him to work with him in his business."

James got suspicious. He furrowed his brow and looked Betty directly in the eyes. "And what exactly is his business, Betty?"

She looked away. She licked her lips then drew them into a tight line. Her gaze searched the ceiling, then the far away wall. The waiter drew near.

"More wine, please." Betty needed a distraction.

The waiter left, and James pressed on. "Tell me, Betty."

"It's really complicated."

"I'm listening. Real careful like."

"He manages wealth for some very prominent people, and he uses nonprofit organizations as a means of growing the wealth."

"How can that be? I know I'm no accountant, but I thought that nonprofits can't have profit! I mean, that's what it's all about, right?"

"Yes. You're right."

"I'm completely confused."

"I've already said enough. Just leave it at that. ABS is a non-profit organization that people often bequest money to in their wills. Alej uses those funds to help people." Betty stopped short of giving the most telling details of ABS.

James was exasperated. He wanted to call Betty out on her vague description of her own husband's business activities. He wanted to accuse her of being careless with the lives of people he loved by withholding the truth about her personal life. He wanted to threaten to pull Ronnie aside and tell her about Betty's long-term marriage that she'd failed to reveal. He wanted to crush all the trust everyone had in Betty.

James wallowed in the betrayal. He was tired and couldn't even begin to confront Betty with all these thoughts. Instead, as she started to cry, he reached across the table and took her hand. At that moment, her vulnerability was unveiled. James knew he had been sucked into something that would own him from that night on.

Ronnie moved freely about the grounds, enjoying the warmth of the sun, taking in the expansive views, and wondering how she could be so lucky. Frederick treated her like royalty. She enjoyed the way he doted on her and offered her every indulgence she could imagine. And she let him spoil her to no end. Underneath all her intents, something else was brewing. In fact, she found Frederick to be very attractive—maybe too attractive. She hadn't intended to fall in love. She had only wanted to marry him for his money and have him take over Husting Manufacturing with all the proceeds of the sale being put in her own coffers through special accounts that he could not access. Things in that arena were a little less clear. In fact, Ronnie wasn't sure what was going on with the Husting attorneys.

Several attempts at getting a layperson's explanation of the sale of the company failed. Ronnie trusted her counsel and had to depend on their business sense to finalize the transfer. Frederick remained cool and calm throughout all the dealings. Eventually deciding that he was looking out for her best interests, she trusted everyone around her to act on her behalf.

By the end of February, the sale was finalized. She would receive a healthy monthly payout, and the major value would be transferred to Frederick Whatton and become part of his company, ABS. Ronnie didn't quite understand the details, but her team of negotiators was confident that things were in good order. She signed and sealed the deal. Frederick and Ronnie celebrated in high fashion with an evening in Beverly Hills: dinner, dancing, strolling the lighted streets, and collapsing together in the poshest hotel on Rodeo Drive. Frederick received the treatment of the stars, and Ronnie learned just how well-known he was in this part of town—all the more reason she wanted to adorn his arm.

The extravagant evening culminated with the offer of her

lifetime. Frederick proposed marriage with a four-carat diamond ring. With little regard for reason, Ronnie accepted. She never questioned his motives, his background, or his plans for the future. She fell for the sparkle and glamour of the night. *This marriage will be very different from the last. I'll be calling all the plays in this game.*

Chapter

SEVENTEEN

MAY 1969: ESCAPE

The early spring was busy with wedding plans. A simple ceremony and a lavish party were held at Frederick's country club. He insisted on keeping the event very low-key and stylish. No expense was spared, but no major splash occurred to raise the lenses of the press. Frederick preferred a quiet celebration with his elite circle of friends, and Ronnie didn't object. She had all she wanted.

Sandra enjoyed a wonderful life as the daughter of a wealthy stepfather who doted on her with every material possession she wanted. Frederick enjoyed watching her play in the yard and even took her on walks in the fields. Sandra's energy and spontaneity resulted in Frederick calling her "Lizzie," insisting that the name Sandra was much too formal and proper for the likes of her boundless enthusiasm for all things new. Sandra took to her nickname handily, refusing at times to respond if someone called her Sandra.

Frederick spoiled Lizzie with attention, something Ronnie could not muster. It still was not in her makeup to dote on anyone—not even her gift horse Frederick. The distance she felt with him was unwarranted. He seemed to have fallen deeply for Ronnie and accepted her with all her baggage. She, too, thought she had fallen in love in a way that would only enhance her decadent living.

Ronnie was impressed with the amount of understanding that Frederick had for her past life. Yes, he had been to Wilmington several times, and yes, she had met him there. He had toured Husting Manufacturing while she was still going in and out of the office. The two of them connected at a cocktail party or two in Wilmington prior to the negotiations. Of course, that's how she selected him in the first place. But there was more to his knowledge. He had an in-depth understanding of her personal story that included details she didn't remember ever sharing with him. Something about that level of knowledge was unsettling. Ronnie pushed it out of her mind. She was living the high life of a society woman, and that was what she'd wanted more than anything else since she could remember.

——— ⚚ ———

A very quick divorce left Betty virtually homeless. Her instincts about Alej had been spot-on. He was after Ronnie. There was nothing Betty could or would do to stop it. Truth be told, Betty loved Ronnie like her own daughter but could not degrade herself by revealing the truth. Somehow she'd managed to get away without ever bumping into Ronnie or Sandra. She thanked the heavens every day for that small miracle. There was no way she could have admitted to being the wife of one known as Frederick Whatton. She could never tell Ronnie of the work that she had done or what Alejandro was planning.

Then again, maybe she had been fooled all along. Maybe she was Alejandro's doormat. Maybe she had been played for a fool, and now she was a murderer with nothing to show for her indis-cretions. *What would James say if he knew the whole truth? What would Ware say?*

Ronnie relieved James of his duties as soon as she married Frederick. It made sense. Frederick's estate was well staffed, and James longed to get back east. He never betrayed Betty's con-fidence, and the best answer was for him to leave. He couldn't trust himself to remain quiet over time, so getting out of the city completely made the most sense to him. He took Betty with him. Her hope was to find Ware, her beloved brother, another secret that she hadn't shared with James. *What would James think of that?*

The drive back to Wilmington took a full three weeks. Neither James nor Betty was in any great hurry; they needed time to adjust to the new realities of their lives. She was depressed and suffering the throes of Alejandro's treatment. James was feeling a major letdown and betrayal from the people he thought he knew well. Nothing called them, and they responded accordingly. Instead, James and Betty relied on one another in every way, loving when the moment was right and retreating into solitude whenever appropriate. It all felt right.

Ware couldn't understand his world. His sister was gone, the love of his life had left him behind, and his beautiful little daughter was out of reach. The long winter gave way to a vibrant spring, and that made matters worse. In a better time, he would have relished this time of year when he spent long hours pruning the lush plantings around the Husting estate. He always found great pleasure in caring for the grounds, opening the swimming pool, interacting with all the other estate staff, and mostly breathing in the love of Ronnie. *My mainstay. Gone.*

Before May gave way to hot summer days, Ware embarked on a new adventure. He found a group that was backpacking the Appalachian Trail, including some wilderness sections. This was a trek intended to help the soul reconnect with what was important and meaningful. It was arranged through a local outdoor equipment shop with a couple of spiritual mentors from a nondenominational parachurch organization. The hikers varied in age and circumstance. Many were searching for the necessary support needed to shed negative habits.

With little training, Ware outfitted himself and joined the hikers. The four-week trek opened his mind to new possibilities. The rugged terrain, unpredictable weather, and camaraderie of people he'd never met taught him to step outside his comfort zone. He digested his past and began to feed on a new way of gaining sustenance.

The trek as a spiritual experience brought out the true person of Warren Treallor. He emerged from the wilderness clear and complete. A new purpose and a new drive carried Warren into the future. He was feeling confident, secure, and ready to reach his potential. With short notice and very little fanfare, Warren packed up his apartment, moved to Connecticut, and pursued a totally new way of living. His new work required training in information technology. He found purpose and joy working and giving back to the community. He worked in downtown Stamford and served at local soup kitchens and homeless shelters in the evenings and on weekends. Warren was finished serving the significantly rich. It was now his time to serve people who needed and deserved his time and companionship.

Betty's so-called "family members" who resided in the Wilmington area were welcoming. They had played the role of surrogate relatives for all the years she needed that cover. Mostly, this was a group of women who worked as hotel maids, household staff for the wealthy, and other domestic staff. Robert Husting never questioned the people Betty visited on her days off. She simply described them as some distant cousins who had lived in the Wilmington area for a long time. No need to explain any more than that.

Today, these "distant cousins" were definitely needed to help her find her way back to gainful employment. The divorce paid her enough to live on, but she needed a place to stay and time to find Ware. Together, brother and sister would figure out what to do next.

The unexpected piece of recent history was Ware's clean departure.

Chapter

EIGHTEEN

APRIL 1995: HAUNTINGS

The cool evening was wonderfully vibrant. Frederick and Ronnie hosted a patio party for business associates. The elegant food and classical music complemented one another. A local and highly demanded quartet of musicians entertained not only with music but also with short interludes of humorous skits. Ronnie moved about the estate comfortably and confidently. All her efforts to win a place in the upper echelon of Hollywood were paying off. She often lunched with movie producers' wives, entertained screenplay writers, and even found her way to an occasional film opening seated next to the stars.

Some of these events lost their allure over time. The Husting fortune and all the mundane acquaintances it produced may not have been so bad. Even though none of those connections had been important over the past twenty-five years, Ronnie wondered what it would be like to rub elbows again with rich financiers and business moguls instead of ostentatious stars.

The sun was setting, and the sky left a dusting of pink on the landscape. Light yellow touched the horizon in the final moments of the day, the sun slipping below the mountainous seam between sky and earth. Ronnie turned away from the view and felt an unusual melancholy. She wandered up the stone steps and through the patio doors, noting the number of women wearing pastels. Her favorite childhood colors seemed to dominate the palette. Yellow and pink were particularly noticeable from sky to dress. Regardless of the actual number of pink or yellow outfits, Ronnie's senses were heightened to notice even the slight hint of coral-turned-pink in an otherwise blue ensemble, or the hint of yellow in a predominantly green skirt. These colors became infectious to her steadfast demeanor, creating a distracting homesickness.

Ignoring the signals, Ronnie stepped a little more quickly into the front parlor of the mansion. Turning brusquely to the corner of the room, out of view of guests, she found that the settee blocked her path. The curved back and rolled arm spoke of a room from her past—the sitting room of her childhood. The shape, color, and placement of pillows struck her as eerily comforting. A few steps more and she collapsed into the welcome cushions. The scent of Bouquet of Flowers wafted through her senses. Across the room a vase held yellow and pink roses. The whole of the scenario pressed in on Ronnie's chest. Her breathing was cut short. Gasping for air, she doubled over onto the settee, temporarily unconscious.

Three days passed. On the evening of her collapse, Ronnie had been taken via ambulance to a local hospital. She was treated for asthmatic reaction to pollens and was released a day later. The reaction was severe enough to have her homebound for several weeks, moving about with a mask to filter pollens. All florals were removed, and all surfaces had been dusted with damp cloths. While this was all fine and understandable to everyone around her, Ronnie knew something was very wrong. She had been around floral pollen since she could remember; Betty always kept her home decorated in roses.

Approaching age fifty, Ronnie experienced relentless anxiety.

She was desperately longing for her roots, whatever those were. Currently she had no parents, a daughter who had moved to Connecticut after college, and no relatives of any significant connection. The dread of each day, the prospect of aging alone, and the lack of meaning in her daily routine overwhelmed her. She became dependent on the medical system—doctors, psychologists, therapy, and medication. It was a virtual roller-coaster ride of emotions, and Frederick's patience ran very thin. He was not the same gregarious man she had married. Instead, he seemed determined to have everything his own way. The trophy wife role was a demand that Ronnie could not maintain in her current state of mental anguish. He was aging and very set in his ways.

During one of the many ABS-associated trips that required Ronnie's presence, she feigned that she was too exhausted to join Frederick. This declaration broke the final strand of patience that the man had left in him, and he stormed off for Europe without her and without a goodbye. In Ronnie's mind, this was the perfect storm that she had unconsciously been waiting to create. Her dreams of living among the high rollers of the movie industry had taken on a new meaning. Those were empty existences. She felt a voice pulling her back to her childhood, back to the Wilmington area. Frederick's response to her decision not to travel with him gave her a reason to leave Los Angeles.

Within two weeks of Frederick's departure, she was back in Delaware, drinking in all the melancholy she could collect. Remarkably, she needed no mask and had no asthmatic reactions to her surroundings. Ronnie trusted her gut and knew that something other than pollen had caused her collapse. She indulged herself in the past, traveled about her old hometown, and tried to locate the Husting estate staff, particularly hopeful of seeing Ware Treallor. She visited local restaurants and shops, asking about Ware and other members of the Husting staff. Only bits and pieces of information were available.

Betty's whereabouts were not known; James seemed to have returned to Wilmington for only a short time; and Arthur had died of cancer four years earlier without her knowing. Wilmington, her home and her draw, held nothing. Ronnie's fears were a reality; she was completely alone in the world, yet she could not muster the courage to contact her daughter, Sandra. She had Sandra's address and phone number from years earlier when Sandra and her husband first moved into a house in Greenwich, Connecticut. To Ronnie's knowledge, Sandra still lived there, but she certainly did not have Sandra's attention—ever.

Years earlier, Ronnie had met Dr. Michael Channing, Sandra's fiancé at the time. The couple were traveling in the Los Angeles area, and Sandra wanted to see Frederick. The Channings married in a private ceremony and sent Ronnie and Frederick an announcement after the fact. Since the first meeting, Ronnie could count on one hand the number of encounters she had had with Sandra and her family.

Contacting Sandra would mean facing her own shortcomings, something Ronnie was not ready to do. Even with all this disarray, Ronnie was comfortable in her hometown. But she worked hard to muster that same sense of determination she possessed most of her life, a determination she needed to reclaim her home, the former Husting estate.

Wilmington had many lovely condominium complexes. Ronnie set out to find one that would suit her needs, a greater task than she realized when she had to identify needs and wants. In the past that would have been easy. Now her heart was guiding her in new directions. Simple and quaint called out to her. No concierge, no posh club feeling, no signs of the beautiful people. She ended in a small cottage that gave her a sense of security, something that was never really present in her opulent homes. It was good not to be rattling around in large spaces. Ronnie's understanding of who she really was as a person started to surface. Simple things were important: her past, her relationships, her lost love, and even her daughter. These were the things she longed for in her life, not diamonds and champagne.

Chapter

NINETEEN

Sandra Elizabeth (Lizzie) Simarillo Channing was a typical Greenwich mom. She had taken on the nickname Lizzie while living in California as a child but had reclaimed her given name of Sandra after college. Right after college graduation in 1988, she married Michael Channing, a doctor who was several years older than she. The relationship was good. He found long hours at the office to be a natural part of who he was.

Sandra enjoyed growing her own career in real estate management. Neither Michael nor Sandra cared if they didn't have dinner together every night. They enjoyed having new and exciting things to tell one another when they did find themselves at the same table at the same time.

Within five years, they had a lovely home and two daughters, Kathryn and Rachel. Sandra didn't give up any time in her career for the sake of the girls. She depended on good childcare arrangements and continued to pursue challenges in her professional work.

Both girls grew to be quite independent, as Sandra wanted, each with her own set of friends. As most teens in the neighborhood, they were spoiled, but not by the presence of parents. Sandra commuted to Manhattan four days a week. She reaped the many benefits and rewards of her dedication at work. Michael was equally involved in his medical practice; they were busy living the lives of a dual-income family. Anything their daughters needed could be bought, and it was.

On a particularly warm April Saturday night, Sandra drew the short straw and was relegated to driving Kathryn home from a high school dance. It was highly unusual for her to play this role, but something drew her to the assignment as a welcome reprieve from an otherwise boring evening at home. As a high school junior, Kathryn usually drove herself or rode with friends to social events. With her car in the shop for maintenance, Michael and Sandra committed to helping out. Michael had to work late again, and Rachel was with one of her friends. A typical weekend. Why Kathryn didn't find a ride with another schoolmate was curious to Sandra, but she chose not to ask questions.

The warm air was heavy, and rain soaked the roads. Starlike reflections from oncoming headlights made the windy road difficult to navigate, so Sandra drove much slower than usual. A large vehicle crept up behind her, causing her to press the gas pedal just a bit harder. A long curve gave way to a slide, then a spin. Hands gripping the wheel, heart banging, lights glaring in her eyes, Sandra's breaths shortened. Lights were traveling in multiple directions. Slamming the brakes, she landed the car just at the edge of the road, two tires in soft terrain. One final release of breath emptied her lungs, and her shoulders dropped.

Putting the car into park, Sandra let her head fall forward, her chin resting on her chest. The wipers gave credence to the conditions, screeching on the upswing of each sweep across the glass. A tap on the side window startled her. A light was shining, and a man was looking in at her. Fear gripped her body, and she simply stared out the window at an intriguing pair of eyes.

"Put the window down. I'm here to help."

Sandra didn't know how to respond. She shifted her eyes to

her handbag that had found its way to the floor in the spin. *What's in there?*

"Do you need help?"

My cell. "No."

"Are you sure? I'm heading to the high school just up the road."

Oh! A parent. "Me too," Sandra yelled through the closed window. *How foolish.* Slowly reaching for the window control, she allowed the window to lower slightly.

"Tell you what, I'll pull my truck in front of you. If you want to follow me to the high school, I'll drive slow enough for you to stay behind me. Your passenger tires are off the road, but you'll be able to pull out."

"Yeah. Okay. Thanks. That would be good. I'm going to the school too."

"I'm Warren."

"Hi. Lizzie. Well, Sandra. Thanks for the help."

"No problem. I'll pull in front of you."

Sandra put the window up. *Lizzie? Really?* Her heart was pounding and her mind was whirling, but she was confident that this would be okay. *Parents stick together.*

Warren Treallor pulled his truck in front of Sandra's car. He drove slowly enough for her to follow him. Within five minutes, they were pulling into the circular drive at the front of the high school. Watching the students exit the building, Sandra noted that Kathryn was holding hands with a nice-looking young man. The two of them parted on the steps. The young man jogged to Warren's truck and hopped in the front seat, and they drove away. Kathryn climbed in the front seat before Sandra realized it; she was preoccupied.

"Who was that guy you were with?"

"Nobody."

Of course.

The two of them drove home in silence. Kathryn had a headset on. Her music was loud enough for Sandra to hear the sounds of Rihanna. She just wanted the road to straighten out so the night could end. The ten-minute ride was sheer torture for her as she drew from every resource she had to avoid a display of fear in navigating the dark, windy roads.

"Good time tonight?" Warren was keeping an eye on his rearview mirror as he drove a bit slower than usual out of the school drive.

"Yeah! It was great. The band was really fun. It was great."

"Glad to hear that."

Warren noted that the car behind him was not holding a steady speed. *Lizzie? Or Sandy.* He slowed down even more to provide a taillight guide.

"Why are you driving so slow, Dad?"

"Roads are actually a little slick tonight. Can't hurt to be cautious."

A few minutes of quiet passed. Rob had become intent on the road ahead, and Warren kept one eye on the rearview mirror. Soon enough they reached the main route. A turn right and they were on the home stretch. The car behind traveled in the opposite direction.

"So who was the young lady you escorted out the door tonight, Rob?"

"She's pretty special. Her name's Kathryn Channing. We started sitting together at lunch and stuff about two months ago. I really like her a lot."

"Hmm. Does she play in the band with you?"

"No."

"In some classes?"

"Yeah. But that's it."

Warren pulled the truck into the garage. The two got out of the truck, went inside, and confirmed their Saturday morning plans before retreating to separate parts of the house.

Warren quietly prepared for bed, crawled in, and snuggled up to Leslie. She was facing the wall and dozing lightly. A long day had caught up with her, and she was thankful for a little bit of quiet time in the evening. Her work as a nurse at a local homeless shelter was taxing, both emotionally and physically. Warren had met Leslie in his volunteer work at the same shelter, where he was servicing the two computers that served as a lifeline in soliciting donations, scheduling volunteers, and spreading the mission of the organization. Both of them were dedicated to this work, she as a paid staff member and he as a volunteer.

Leslie was a wholesome woman. Her unassuming presence was enhanced by her natural beauty. The thirteen-year difference in their ages was not a concern for her. She saw in Warren a real man who was willing to give of himself in ways that she had not seen in men her own age. Warren had a genuine interest in helping others. Leslie had fallen in love with him quickly, whereas he had taken a little longer to respond to her signals. By the time Warren emerged from the Appalachian experience, he had found contentment in being alone. Leslie had come into his life within six months, and he was not looking for any kind of relationship. Eventually he was convinced that a much greater power guided their connection. He relinquished his own reasoning to that power.

Leslie Irons and Warren Treallor were married in May 1973 in a small outdoor chapel at the rear of the homeless shelter. The pigeons cooed as a justice of the peace, a dear friend of Leslie's, offered the vows. No one fussed. Leslie's coworkers served as witnesses, and the director provided a cake and a small celebration. That night, the shelter guests congratulated the two. A day later they took a long weekend to consummate their union. They spent four days in a small cottage along the Connecticut shoreline in Branford. The time was passed reassuring one another that nothing would come between them, ever.

Tonight, Leslie was receptive to Warren's affection. She rolled over and received his kisses with warm love. They embraced and fell into a peaceful sleep.

Sandra calmed herself with a long pull of Jack Daniel's. Her nerves were unraveling. *Never again will I drive myself to that godforsaken place in the dark! Never! What the hell was Michael thinking?*

Sandra was not used to running the late-night errands. The train, the bus, the subway, all fine. Driving? Not her favorite activity. *And in the rain and the dark no less. Who was thinking about that? No one.*

There was a strange feeling lingering that Sandra could not quite identify. That man, Warren, had sent a weird vibe. *Why was he banging on my window? Why Lizzie? Why did that name come out? Why did he let me follow him? Both ways. And who is he anyway?*

She answered her questions with a little more Jack Daniel's and a sleeping pill. Before long, Sandra was in a deep sleep, snuggled in her king-size bed under the down comforter. The world faded away, just the way she willed it. When Michael crawled into bed, she never stirred. He kissed her shoulder and rolled over to his own side of the field. Neither of them needed more.

Saturdays in the Channing household were filled with busyness. Sandra used the morning hours to check her work voice mails, review the personal mail, and enjoy a second cup of coffee. Michael generally reviewed medical reports, did some dictation, and sometimes held office hours for post-op patients. Today was exactly one of those days. Michael planned to meet three patients at the hospital clinic, and Sandra buried herself with work. The home office was a good retreat for days like this. She closed the door so she could get down to business.

The girls were still sleeping. Kathryn was known to stay in bed until early afternoon, and her sister, Rachel, generally took an early morning run before getting into her studies. Rachel was looking forward to moving away for college next year. She anticipated and prepared for a rigorous course of study at Amherst College in Massachusetts. She hoped to become a college professor someday and wanted to focus her studies on history. The prospect of her leaving the nest had no effect on Sandra or Michael. They considered this move a natural part of life and were prepared for Rachel's departure—no melodrama ordered.

Sitting at her desk and looking out across the back lawn, Sandra sipped her coffee, waiting for the caffeine to propel her into the latest project. Somehow she lacked energy, caffeine notwithstanding. She found herself reflecting on the past—little Kathryn and Rachel running through the backyard, taunting one another. A lovable shaggy sheepdog bouncing around with them. They laughed and carried on as if they were alone in a fantasy. The nanny of the day would try to keep up with them, and without fail, the girls would wear out the strongest, most haughty of caregivers. Sandra never stepped in. She always made sure her payments were healthy enough to keep even the weariest nanny interested and committed to working solely for the Channing family. It would never have worked out to share a nanny's attentions with anyone else. Sandra was sure of that and worked hard to ensure that any nanny dedicated herself to serving Sandra's needs.

Thinking of her own younger days, Sandra recalled running

through a sea of green touched by an azure backdrop. There she played with Frederick, whom she remembered fondly as Papa Fred. Even though he seemed a bit elderly as her father, he was indeed the father she remembered fondly. He always made time for her. He enjoyed teasing, calling out, "Lizzie, where are you now?" when playing hide-and-seek, and simply showing her the beauty of nature that grew on his land. She remembered very dry areas near their home, almost desert. But whenever she thought of Southern California as her hometown, she remembered Papa Fred playing with her high in the hills of his estate. There was plenty of grass and foliage. Wildflowers in yellow and pink, sometimes blue, would spring up along the edges of the grassy slopes at certain times of the year. *Beautiful.*

Did I share those things with my girls? Do they understand the cycle of nature? I can't remember even talking about those kinds of things when they were small. A nanny must have, of course.

A sharp knock pulled her from her memories. "Mom!" It was Rachel. "I'm leaving now. Bye."

"Wait!" Sandra jumped from her chair and sprang for the door.

"What's a-matter?" Rachel's brows were knit together.

After the slightest hesitation, Sandra responded, "Nothing. Never mind."

"You sure?"

"Yes. I'm sure."

"Okay." Rachel just looked back at her mother and smiled sweetly. "See ya later, Mom."

"Goodbye." She was gone. *A run? A study session? Doesn't matter. She's gone.*

Sandra moved to the window, still holding her coffee cup that had never left her hand. Now she wrapped two hands around the large ceramic vessel and slowly brought it to her lips. The creamy bitter drink was a comfort in moments like these. *Why? What was different about those days in California?*

The early morning fog gave way to sunshine. She couldn't focus on the work she intended to accomplish during the quiet morning hours. Her mind wandered too much between thoughts of California and thoughts of her early days in the mid-Atlantic, remembering some lovely gardens. *Was it Wilmington? Philadelphia? Baltimore?* Trying again to focus on her work, Sandra returned to the desk, put down the coffee cup, and leaned back in the tall-backed leather chair. She breathed out a sigh of regret. *Mother, what didn't you tell me?* She picked up the phone and dialed the number that used to be her mother's cell.

"Good morning!" The woman on the other end of the line sounded chipper.

Sandra hung up. She snapped herself from the mental lapse and moved into the pile of documents she intended to review this morning. After a few minutes' study of the latest real estate listings, she realized that the picturesque setting of one particular property drew her in like an open door to a familiar home. The property was located in Wilmington, Delaware. The listing was being managed by a Wall Street financier.

The home boasted eight bedrooms and five full bathrooms, totaling over six thousand square feet of living space situated on close to eighty acres of immaculately maintained land. Photos in the latest publications would appeal to the imagination of young prosperous couples. The sitting room, as it was labeled, look like a storybook page from Sandra's past. The ceiling-to-floor windows were adorned with heavy drapes fringed in gold. The deep burgundy and gold accents played off one another in the professional photos. The arts and crafts rug sharpened the lounge chairs with contrasting navy and yellow. Pillows in lighter colors accented the furniture, and bouquets of roses graced the center table.

Yellow and pink. The smell of flowers. Sandra experienced a brief sensory immersion in the room. A clear splatter fell onto the page. Without thought, Sandra brushed the wetness away from the magazine and from her cheek. Then she turned the page and lifted her coffee cup.

She moved on to the next project. The house remained quiet, Kathryn asleep and Michael long gone.

The clearing of Friday night's dark rain led to a Saturday morning flooded with sunlight, a welcome morning for the Treallor family. They enjoyed pancakes and bacon before rolling out the door together. The day would be filled with community service work. Rob and his sister, Adrienne, were scheduled to prepare lunch at a new inner-city shelter that served unwed mothers and their babies. Warren and Leslie were heading to the Salvation Army store to begin preparations for the annual Memorial Day sale, when the seasonal items were basically given away to local families and monetary donations were received from major benefactors. It was a joyous event every year. Volunteers started working a couple of months ahead of time to make the event a huge success. Spirits were high, and the family was thankful for the good weather.

Final goodbyes were shared with quick hugs and kisses. They piled into two vehicles, Warren and Leslie into her sedan, and Adrienne and Rob into Warren's pickup truck. Everyone knew the plans to meet back at the house in time for dinner.

This scenario was a very typical pattern in the fabric of the Treallor family. Warren and Leslie were proud of their teenaged kids, who were more than happy to give back to the community whenever the occasion arose. Both were strong students, found joy in family events, and even offered to help with household maintenance. Rob would head off to college next year. Although he would miss his son, Warren knew it was the best thing for Rob. There was no way his children would skip out on a college education the way that he and his sister, Betty, had.

Warren navigated the windy roads carefully as the surface still held moisture from the previous night. Rob followed him out onto Route 1, the main road. They parted ways as the sedan turned toward downtown Stamford, and Rob and Adrienne headed in the opposite direction toward the homeless shelter. With his eyes, Warren followed the pickup truck in his rearview mirror until it was out of sight.

"Do you think the two of them will always be friends? Brother and sister?" Warren smiled at the thought as he anticipated Leslie's response.

"Time will tell. But we have to admit that they definitely do seem to enjoy one another's company. We did something right."

He thought carefully about the standard response of "time will tell." Leslie never wanted to predict the future. There were times when Warren just wanted an answer, and other times when he was happy with "time will tell." Today was a good opportunity to just let things go without more conversation. His mind turned to other things, specifically, the face of the woman he had helped through the treacherous roads the night before. Her eyes said something to him, but he didn't know what. *Lizzie, who are you?*

Leslie pulled Warren from his thoughts. "How many people do you think will show up today"

"Not sure. I know the Halprins want to help out this year."

"Oh, good. I really like them, and we never seem to get a chance to work with them on any of these projects. Nice."

"Yeah."

Warren didn't feel up to talking. Leslie took the hint and observed the morning sun on the shoreline. It was always a treat, no matter how many years she had seen it. As they traveled, she whispered her morning prayer of thanks.

"What was that?" Warren knew full well what it was. When she didn't respond, he simply said, "Amen."

Their vehicle pulled into a lot filled with other cars. Warren found a parking spot, turned off the engine, and sat for a moment. He turned to Leslie, tightened his lips, and simply said, "Thank you."

"No, thank *you*, Mr. Warren Treallor." These were their typical words of gratitude for one another and for all the blessings in their lives. Both believed deeply that they were living in God's grace.

After a gentle kiss, the two moved on to the storage building where the work of the day would take place.

The smell of coffee greeted everyone who entered, and job locations were posted. Warren and Leslie signed in, choosing their separate tasks, and got down to work. He would be helping clean out one section of the storage building in preparation for the big event in May. She had been working on publicity and moved to a nearby table to meet with three other women who were already busy reviewing press releases.

The day was off to a great start. Almost. Warren felt a nagging in the pit of his stomach that just wouldn't let up. *Those eyes.* He shrugged off the feeling and forced himself to focus on the mission work he had set out to accomplish this day.

Day's end brought together a happy, tired Treallor family. Gathered around the harvest table in the country kitchen of their home, and in keeping with their family custom, they each offered thanks for the blessings they enjoy before digging into the pizza that sat in the middle of the table. Adrienne told a story of a young mother who was struggling to feed two children and was expecting a third. The mother had shown up at the soup kitchen hoping to find more than a bowl of nourishment. Adrienne explained how the counselors offered the family a place to stay for the night and said that it reminded her of how lucky she was to have a safe, warm home with her own bedroom. Rob was happy that they as a family could sit down to just about any meal they wanted any night of the week—he was hungry, and pizza was the perfect quick fix. Everyone laughed at Rob's comment and helped themselves to the hot deep-dish meat-lovers' dinner.

Warren smiled across the table at Adrienne and was stopped midmotion by her eyes. *Her eyes. No.* The conversation faded into the background, and Warren ate in silence.

"You okay, Dad?" Rob looked concerned.

"Oh. Yeah. Just thinking how lucky we are."

"I'll say. Boy, after watching those kids with no food just dive into a bowl of soup, I think this pizza is heaven-sent!"

"Indeed. And so were you. Never forget that." Warren looked at both his children with a seriousness that seemed a bit out of keeping with the moment.

"No worries there, Dad. You and Mom taught us to remember what's important," Adrienne said, lightening the mood.

The meal continued with good spirits. Leslie laughed with the kids, and Warren participated occasionally. With the table cleared and dishes in the dishwasher, Warren excused himself for an early retirement to his room, where he said he would be catching up on some reading. The reality was that he wanted time to think about a few things. Leslie gave him a nod and explained that she and Adrienne had a girls' night planned in the family room with a movie they'd been waiting to watch. Rob retreated to his room with his music and video games. Warren appreciated having some space.

Sandra Channing never did figure out what the girls were doing for the day. The two girls were very different indeed. Kathryn lived in the moment, finished her schoolwork at the last possible minute, and basically enjoyed her social circles. Her parents knew little of what those social circles were like. Last night was a quick glimpse into Kathryn's selection of boys. Sandra didn't know enough about the "nobody" to make a comment, but she did know there was something about his father that was unnerving to her.

Sandra and Michael didn't bother Kathryn about her activities. She was the daughter who chose to play things low, not creating waves. They knew she enjoyed a few drinks, a little pot, and an occasional overnight drunk with a friend or two when parents were out of town—things that Sandra chose to ignore. Rachel was the perfect child; Kathryn, the rebel.

In another year, it would be Kathryn's turn to leave the nest, but she didn't want to go to college. She could think of plenty of ways to make a living without more school. That conversation was just beginning to hit the tables, and it was not a happy one at all. She and two girlfriends planned to leave town after graduation, and find an apartment and jobs in Trenton, New Jersey, where they had their sights on a two-year school that would give them just enough skills and knowledge to land decent employment. Sandra and Michael had given up trying to change the direction of the conversation.

By the time Sandra emerged from her office, the sun had set. Michael had gone to bed early or at least had retreated to the bedroom. She grabbed a yogurt, a banana, and a glass of orange juice for dinner. Dessert consisted of red wine, a chocolate bar, and a novel. When sleep became a possibility, Sandra made her way to bed. Walking past the girls' bedrooms, she noted a dim light coming from under Rachel's door, and an open door to an empty room where Kathryn might land eventually. As she lay back on the pillows, a sensation of *knowing* the estate that was for sale in Wilmington, Delaware, struck her acutely. *Oh my God!*

She rolled over and shook Michael.

"Wake up! I need to tell you something."

———— *Chapter* ————

TWENTY

‾ AUGUST 2008: ANOTHER CHANCE MEETING ‾

The long, winding drive into the estate looked different. Warren remembered a well-manicured road lined with layers of indigenous plants. Tall poplar trees that graced the acreage leading up to the main house were still standing, but the undergirding had become a bevy of creeping ground cover, unplanned and scruffy. The sunshine streaked through the majestic trees all the same, and the sense of stateliness still reigned. Slowing the truck for a careful drive into the front circle, Warren was keenly aware of his racing pulse. It had been a long time since he had been this close to the heartache that he thought had passed. *Why am I doing this? I love Leslie and my kids.*

Bringing the truck to a halt, he reached for the ignition key. *I can't do this.* Once he switched the key, the engine cut off, leaving nothing but the still hot air floating in through the open windows. And a pounding chest. *Ronnie, where are you? Sandy, my little girl, all grown, in her forties now.*

Taking a few moments to breathe in the thick air, Warren reached for the door handle. He pulled the handle up but couldn't push the door open. Extra weight held him back, beckoning him to rethink this move. He dropped his head, closed his eyes, and whispered a prayer for strength. Physical and psychological. He needed to overcome some deep-rooted pain, things buried and forgotten until now. *Oh Lord, forgive me. I have a promise to keep.*

Finally, the truck door swung open, and Warren found his feet touching that ground, the almost sacred land of his past. He pushed the door closed as quietly as possible, rubbed his hand across his hair, stroked his chin, and stepped forward. His eyes moved to the front steps. He saw flashes of Sandy standing there and beaming in her pink dress, looking up at Betty, seeking approval. A smile broke across his lips, and his eyes misted over. *My sweetheart.*

Warren walked up the long steps, across the vast porch, and to the front door. Turning back and looking down the long driveway, he could see the limo pulling away. *The day Quentin left my beautiful young Ronnie and our baby.* Shaking his head to clear the pain, he continued across the front of the house. The long front windows made easy work of poking around and casing things out. The front sitting room looked sad, empty, and unloved.

A walk around the side yard brought Warren to the garden where Ronnie had committed her love to someone else, the place where he had felt temporarily betrayed. He followed the path to the rear of the house. The same tree stood there. He touched the bark and could hear their conversation. Ware was holding a diamond ring. It was May 1964, a day he would never forget.

"*Miss Veronica Emma-Mae, will you spend your life with me?*"

"*But when? How did you ...? Why ...?*"

"*You do love me.*"

Warren could remember seeing her chest rising and falling, her hands shaking, and tears welling up in her eyes.

"*Tell me the truth, Ronnie. Do you love me?*"

Leaning forward and wrapping her arms around his neck, Ronnie had rested her forehead against his. "*You can feel that, can't you, Ware? Do I have to say it?*"

"*I take that as a yes.*"

Warren could almost hear her soft crying and see her face with tears rolling down her cheeks. *"Yes. … We're just total opposites."*

"Ronnie, answer one question: do you love Quentin?"

"Ware, don't do this."

"Just answer me."

"I can spend my life with him."

"Do you love him?"

"In my own way."

Ware had put the ring in his pocket.

He remembered saying something that reeked of sarcasm, wisdom, jealousy, and hope—all wrapped in one fat, ugly package. But he did manage to get Ronnie to admit that she was in love with him and not in love with the man she was marrying. That knowledge had kept Ware in a mode of determination for years. Guilt struck with these memories.

Leslie is my wife. I love her. We have two beautiful kids.

He turned away, reached in his jeans pocket, and touched the small black box. He instinctively flipped the top open, slipped his pinky finger through the ring, and lifted his hand out. *How many years will I carry this thing around?* The mist in his eyes became full tears.

Looking at the sparkling stone in the bright noonday sun, he found that blurry colors flooded his mind. Blue, red, yellow. Blue. Deep, sad blue, not the loving sparkling blue that filled him with hope that day in May 1964. He fell to his knees. *Ronnie, Sandy, I love you.* Sobs were flowing freely. Ware succumbed to the moment.

Warren was still on the ground, his hands on his knees, his head bowed. There were no tears left.

"Excuse me, sir? Can I help you?"

He lifted his head to see a familiar face staring at him with a quizzical look.

"Who are you?"

"Hello. I think we've met. I recognized your truck out front."

"I'm sorry. Yes." *It's her. Lizzie.* "You have a daughter at Greenwich High."

"Yes. Yes, I had two, actually. Daughters. At Greenwich High. One graduated."

Realizing he was on his knees, Warren stood up now and reached out his hand. A broad smile graced his face.

Sandra persisted. "Excuse me for asking, but why are you here on the grounds?"

"That's a long story, but I used to work here. Long ago."

"Oh! Now that's interesting. What did you do here?"

Careful. "Well, I guess you could say I managed the property. It was owned by Mr. Robert Husting. But that was over thirty-five years ago now, I guess. I was in the area and thought I'd just check up on the old place, just to see what it looks like now. Looks different."

"Right. So ... you were ... checking ... the grounds?"

"Uh. Yeah. Right. Well, I was reminiscing a little bit. Nothing big. Just took a little breather." *Why are you here?*

The look on his face must have given away the confusion that muddled his thinking. Sandra looked at him and spilled the reasons for her own presence: realtor in the city; has a client interested in a weekend getaway; local realtor gave her the lockbox code to get in; needed to look over the property for general state of repair; etc.

"So I'm basically thinking about showing the property over the next couple of months to at least two potential buyers." *Or buying it myself. I'm ready to come home and show my mother who I really am.*

There was no For Sale sign on the property, of course. Warren knew these tactics—no visible signs of a property being on the market. Instead, property traders had their own secret networks that served them better than a sign or ads. *Open Estates* was a well-known glossy magazine that circulated among the elite across the globe, and this property was surely on its list of available opportunities. Warren felt his heart beating in his throat. *Where are you, Ronnie? We need this property back.*

"Well, thanks for the update on the old property. Very nice." He put his hand out again. "Good to see you again." *And to learn a little more.*

"Likewise."

"All right then, I'll get going and leave you to your work."

"Safe driving back to Greenwich. Friday nights heading north can be brutal."

Warren moved away with a nod. He just wanted out of the trap he felt coming over his existence. *Lizzie or Sandra, who are you really?* His steps quickened, and he was on his way. He looked at his left hand—the ring was still sparkling. *I hope she didn't see that.*

Sandra watched him turn the corner at the front of the house. She heard his truck start and listened as the tires crackled the pebbles strewn on the old asphalt drive. *What in the world? Is that really the Warren who helped me?*

Warren made his way through the Wilmington roads, thinking about Betty and Ronnie. His ideal world would include both of them, his sister and his love. And of course Sandy. But all of those relationships felt like a century away. The years had taken him through a dark hallway. At the far end, though, he had found a comfortable and satisfying life of service to others. Not service to those who could care for themselves and wanted to be waited on, but service to people who mattered but didn't think they did.

The broken, the homeless, the forgotten, the downtrodden: those were the people Warren lived to serve. *But what about my heart and my love?*

Warren knew Leslie as a wonderful wife. She lived his ideals and worked side by side with him to serve the neediest of all: young families with no homes and single mothers with no place to go. Her work was where God sent Warren. He needed to be useful. And in Leslie's world, he could offer many things.

Together, they had two of the greatest kids he could ever imagine. Not a single day of distress from either of them. Rob would start his freshman year at the University of Massachusetts, so they would still have opportunities to see him regularly. Adrienne would be a senior at Greenwich High. They were great young adults. Warren thanked God every day for their love. *So what is this nagging?*

The drive back to Greenwich was not without its delays. The heat was enough for Warren to turn on the air conditioning, something he usually avoided on the highway. His day trip was planned around a midmorning call to a medical center located in Wilmington. He'd been called in to assess their needs for added bandwidth. The two-hour visit was worth the trip. The center had other infrastructure needs that Warren's company didn't know about, so a personal visit was definitely the right choice. *But why did I give in to the urge to stop at the Husting estate?*

He had skipped lunch to visit the estate. Somewhat frazzled emotionally, he found the slow traffic crawling north toward the mountains and the northeast shore on a Friday afternoon not to be a welcome situation. On the other hand, the time alone was probably a blessing. *Get my head screwed back on. For Leslie. And the kids. And me.*

He felt the buzz in his pocket. *Who's calling me now?* It was 3:00 p.m. At the first exit from the highway, Warren pulled into a gas station. He filled the tank and checked his phone. It was

Leslie. *Not now.* He turned the phone off, stuffed it in his pocket, and reached in the other side to check on the black box.

It was after eight o'clock by the time Warren rolled into the driveway. Leslie met him on the front step of the house.

"Hi!" Warren gave a big smile and moved toward Leslie with purpose. He reached out for their typical hug. She stepped back.

"Where have you been?"

Not the typical response.

Chapter —— TWENTY-ONE

August 2008: Dangerously Close to Home

It was time for Ronnie to change paths. Her will to conquer all was wavering, and that was not the path she would succumb to. The small cottage she found in the rolling hills surrounding Wilmington was stoking the need to reclaim what should have been hers twenty years earlier.

Ware was the lucky winner of the estate. She was the unfortunate heiress of a business she couldn't handle. Frederick was no help. Yes, she had her money, but she didn't have her home. Those physical displays of wealth and power were gone. *What had Ware done with all those things that I didn't take to California?*

Lost in her thoughts of her early years and how wonderful her life could have been, Ronnie missed the ring of her cell phone. Her coffee cup sat untouched on the table in front of her, the taste less appetizing than usual. She stared into the cup and tried one more sip. The skim that had formed around the edge repulsed her. Standing abruptly, she snatched the cup and stepped heavily to the sink, throwing the cold coffee toward the drain and slamming the faucet on to splash water around the cup.

The buzz of the phone on the counter wouldn't stop. It was a voice mail. Again. There were more than ten voice mails left lately, none with a message.

With shaking hands, Ronnie flipped open the phone and

pressed the speed dial to her voice mail. It took great control to enter her pass code, and the effort only led to hearing a hang-up. No message. *Who the hell keeps calling and hanging up?* An unfamiliar phone number was displayed on the Missed Calls list again.

Enough. She held the send key until the line was ringing on the other end.

An answer with no voice. "Who is this?" No answer. "Stop calling me if you can't leave a message."

Click.

"Hello?"

Beep, beep, beep … "If you'd like to make a call, please hang up and dial …" Ronnie slammed the phone shut and slid it across the counter into the pile of yesterday's newspapers. She could feel her face tense, her head throb, and her teeth clench.

She grabbed a jacket, her purse, and her car keys and headed out the back door. She hopped into her leased Volvo and spun away with no idea where she was heading.

Winding roads took Ronnie to places that looked vaguely familiar. So much had changed. The foliage was thicker, the roads were narrower, and the hills were smaller. Trees lined the way, making every turn a mystery. The Volvo hugged the curves, and the afternoon sun cast shadows across the open road. Pressing on as if by instinct, Ronnie moved with an unknown purpose. Something pulled her, and she knew not to where, until the entrance to the Husting estate was looming ahead of her.

Visions danced in front of her. *Sandra? Ware? Daddy?*

She slammed on the brakes; the car spun out of control.

Blackness.

Sandra was just finishing her inspection as the day came to a close. Still air made the Husting mansion feel sticky and hot. This time of year in Wilmington was the epitome of the dog days of summer, and the house emphasized that discomfort with its own set of sounds and smells.

The drapes in the sitting room drooped and smelled musty. Their fringe looked like snarled hair, and the doors were too swollen to open onto the side patio.

Wandering from room to room, making sure everything was locked up and in the same state as when she'd entered, Sandra was distracted by an eerie presence. She stood perfectly still in the entry and listened hard. Several seconds passed; no sounds were audible. She took a couple of steps toward the front door and stopped again.

A shadow passed across the sitting room floor. She listened again.

A creak. A whoosh. Nothing more.

In a panic, Sandra grabbed the front doorknob and ran out onto the porch. She managed to lock the door on the way.

Sandra got off the Husting estate property in half the time she'd taken to drive in. A quickened pulse helped. Speeding down the winding road to get to the highway as quickly as possible, she wasn't paying much attention to her surroundings. The scary feeling in the mansion and all of the strange happenings of the day were pushing her homeward. She wanted a drink and her bed.

Rounding the bend, she set her sights on the sign that read, "To I-95 N." In the rearview mirror, she caught a glimpse of emergency vehicles. "Damn. Not now." But they pulled to the side of the road and stopped. *Good. I gotta get home.*

Awakening to the sound of sirens and red flashing lights only added to her state of shock.

An acute awareness of the pain in her left arm added to the

urgency she felt to do something—fast. A quick review of the circumstance left her in shock. Blood everywhere. Blood on the dashboard, all over her hands, and flowing into her eyes. A salty flow of rich liquid in her mouth was repulsive, and she felt herself heaving. Her head throbbed with every convulsion of her stomach.

The door was being pried open, and men in heavy gear were pulling her from the driver's side of the car. Stretched on the warm tar of the road, Ronnie tried to focus on the scene. Within seconds the car went up in flames. Fire trucks came closer to the scene, their sirens wailing. Then, again, blackness.

Sandra opened the door of her home after battling a nasty ride home in the traffic on I-95. The day had been much longer than she had hoped. It was already 10:30, and tomorrow was another full day.

Her first stop was the bar in the great room. Her second stop was the closet to remove her coat.

A trip to the bathroom, followed by a second walk to the bar for another shot of whiskey, set the pace for the evening.

She grabbed a slice of cold pizza from the refrigerator and moved to the comfort of the sectional to watch TV. The headline news story scrolled across the bottom: "Car accident: heiress of the Husting fortune narrowly escapes death."

She turned up the volume: "Ms. Veronica Husting Simarillo Whatton was pulled from a car just before it went up in flames. Someone traveling along the narrow winding road that leads into the former Husting estate spotted the car against a tree and called 9-1-1. That caller, however, did not stay on the scene. Officials are tracking the call for more information. In the meantime, Ms. Veronica Whatton is being treated at …"

Shit. She hit the remote to end the story.

Sandra took the bottle from the bar and moved to the master suite. She closed herself in and found comfort in Jack Daniel's and a sleeping pill.

—⚬⚬—

Leslie was pressing him: "It's not like you to miss my calls."

Warren was feeling cornered. "You called me?"

"Yes, and I know your phone was on. It rang several times."

"Let me look ..." Warren reached into his pocket and pulled out the phone, careful not to disrupt the small black box. "It's not on! When did you call? How did that happen?" Warren felt the pressure building in his chest. His breaths shortened. *Calm. Deep breaths.*

Leslie gave him a quick kiss on the cheek. "It doesn't matter. You're home. I was just checking on your timing. Maybe the power button was bumped or something."

"Well, that would be odd. Maybe I need to check the power."

Warren turned his head, closed his eyes, and moved away. "I think I'll take a quick shower." *Thank you, Lord.*

"Sounds good." Leslie went to the kitchen and continued preparing dinner.

In the solace of the master suite, Warren moved into the walk-in closet, reached behind the sport coats hanging at the end of the bar, and opened an electrical panel. The bottom of the panel housed a small compartment that he had carefully crafted shortly after moving into the house. He returned the little black box, closed the compartment, and covered it with the thin piece of sheet metal that was cut to look like part of the electrical housing. He slid the clothes back into place and proceeded to let the water get steamy. *Someday.*

Ware stepped out of the shower feeling relaxed. The hot water pounding on his tense muscles had the effect he had hoped for.

Throwing a towel around himself and grabbing another to dry his hair, he turned just the right way to catch a glimpse of himself in the vanity mirror. He stopped short and stared at the stranger looking at him.

"Robert?"

"Hi, Ware."

"Warren."

"No. Ware. You *were* that wonderful young man named Ware who loved my daughter, Veronica, right?"

Warren could only stare and vaguely nod in agreement.

"Never forget that love."

Warren shook his head and blinked many times, but the face still stared back at him through the fogged glass. It wouldn't go away. He looked over his shoulder to see who was behind him.

"No. I'm not in the room. Physically, that is."

"Who are you?"

"You know who I am. You already called out my name."

"Robert?"

Leslie walked in. "Are you calling Rob? He's in his room. What's wrong?"

"Nothing. No, I wasn't looking for Rob." Warren was shifting his gaze from Leslie, back to the foggy mirror, and back to Leslie.

"Warren, what's going on? You don't look well."

"Yeah. I'm a little dizzy. I guess the shower was too hot and too long."

She touched his shoulder. "Throw something on and lie down for a couple of minutes."

"Yeah. I'll be okay. It was just the steamy heat. I already feel steadier."

"Getting some dinner might help too. What did you have for lunch?"

"My usual, a sandwich." *Why am I lying to Leslie?*

"Well, let me get dinner on the table, and then ..."

Warren heard nothing else. She was walking away from him. He grasped the vanity with both hands and stared back at the mirror. The fog had cleared. His own reflection looked back. Gray-flecked eyes. His own. He just stared until the sound of the evening news on a distant television captured his attention:

> We have an updated report on Ms. Veronica Husting Simarillo Whatton, claimed brain dead at the age of sixty-two after a single car crash on Route 52 near the Pennsylvania border. She was taken to DuLoche Memorial Hospital in Wilmington but has slipped into a coma. Earlier reports were hopeful that she would survive, but now things are not as hopeful. Ms. Whatton is the heir to manufacturing mogul Robert Evan Husting Jr., who owned and operated Husting Manufacturing, a family firm, until his death in 1967. Ms. Whatton spent many years in Southern California following the death of her father and the liquidation of the family estate. Ms. Whatton has been estranged from her family and friends on the East Coast for many years. The fact that she was near her family homestead has raised questions about her visit to the area.
>
> In other news today ...

Warren was frozen, still staring at himself in the mirror. His heart pounded; sweat beaded on his forehead. With shaking hands, he flipped on the water, cupped his palms, and splashed away tears. *I was there. Ronnie was there.*

Leslie called out very loudly, "Warren! Dinner is on!"

He smothered his face with a hand towel for a quick dry. "Coming!"

Warren had to muster up some strength. Throwing on a pair of jeans and a T-shirt, he stabilized himself and wandered toward the dinner table. Rob and Adrienne were in the kitchen, and Leslie was pouring iced tea into the glasses on the table. As he watched everyone move to their places at the table amid chatter that Warren didn't hear, he knew everything had to appear normal. He joined his adoring family for a typical midweek meal. They held hands around the table and said grace together.

Amen.

The telephone was ringing, but it was a very distant sound. Sandra pulled the pillow over her head. The Jack Daniel's and sleep aid had her numb, the way she liked to be at night. The house was completely quiet except for the ringing phone.

Willing the clatter of bells to stop, Sandra burrowed deeper in her bed, farther under the covers. Silence. She dozed back to sleep.

Thirty minutes passed. There were flashing lights sneaking through the cracks of the window blinds, decorating the walls of her otherwise darkened room. The doorbell was chiming repeatedly.

"Who is it?" Sandra yelled.

The chiming continued, and the phone started to ring again.

Struggling to get her arms out from under the plush bed linens, she snatched the receiver.

"Who is this?"

"Mrs. Channing?"

"What is it?"

"Is this Mrs. Channing?"

"Yes, it is! What do you want?!" Sandra's impatience screamed through every syllable.

"This is Lieutenant Randall Oberchaud with the Greenwich

Police Department. I'm at your front door. Would you please open the door? I have Officer Jessie Manash with me."

The news headline flashed through her mind. The Jack Daniel's bubbled up in her stomach.

"I'm coming."

She made a stop in the master bathroom and vomited before going to the front door.

———— ℮☙ ————

Michael Channing had become a highly respected trauma specialist. That particular week, he had been flown by a medevac unit to the DuLoche trauma unit from his home base, Yale University, to work with a team who had received two victims of a scaffolding accident in Newark, Delaware. He spent three days there working long hours to stabilize these patients.

It was on the third day, as the team was finalizing the extended-care plans with family members of the two construction workers, that Veronica was brought in. Michael postponed his return to Yale so he could assist with this new patient. He would never have recognized Veronica Whatton because of the facial injuries she suffered, even if she had been a regular part of his life.

Veronica's personal effects were given to him, but not before he had a moment to be with her—alone.

"Can you hear me, Veronica?"

No response.

Her face was lacerated, her eyes and lips gashed and swollen. She was struggling to focus on Michael's voice, searching the room to see his face. There was no eye contact made, and Michael knew she could not see well enough for that. He continued to talk to her in the hope that he would get some information about someone by the name of Treallor.

"Do you know who I am? Sandra's husband, Michael."

"My Sandy—I do love her. And I never forgot Ware."

"Where what?"

"Ware."

He knew she wanted to tell him something, so he pushed on, hoping she might tell him about the Husting estate. Maybe then he could start to put some pieces together, resurrect the puzzle, and get the answers he wanted.

"The estate?"

"Yes."

"Yes, you were near the Husting estate when you had a bad crash."

"Ware. The estate and Ware. I never forgot."

"What were you doing at the estate?"

"No. It was beautiful. Pink roses ..."

Her breathing was labored. Her chest rose and fell. The monitors beeped.

"Go ahead, Veronica. I'm listening."

Silence.

"Yes. Lovely. My love chi—"

Veronica was unconscious.

Michael felt his shoulders drop, his breath release. There was no sense in trying to revive her. He knew the signs well enough. Coma.

He left the room and called for nurses to do their work.

After completing all the necessary paperwork, convincing the staff that Michael could serve as family who vouched for the identity, and making arrangements for steps to take after Veronica died, Michael was left holding the bag. Actually several bags, some filled with bloody clothing, and another with Veronica's purse.

It wasn't too difficult to decide to dump the clothing in the hazardous waste receptacle. It was more difficult to decide how to handle the purse. Of course, the wallet had already been retrieved, and Veronica's license had been used for the first identification.

It was the letter staring at him that was most worrisome, a plain business-sized envelope with "W. Treallor" scrawled across the front.

He boarded the helicopter and was on his way back to New Haven's Yale University Hospital. The news was about to hit, and Michael wanted to get back to Sandra as quickly as possible. He knew the police had been trying to reach her, and he also knew that she was probably in a drunken sleep. He took the travel time to think about the letter. In the end, he decided not to do anything right away. He stuffed the envelope in the inside pocket of his blazer for later, if Veronica regained consciousness.

When the pilot landed on the hospital helipad, Michael's cell was lighting up in his pocket. It was the Greenwich police; they were with Sandra. He told them he would be there in less than an hour, and he was.

❧ ☙

The police delivered the harsh news to Sandra. They offered to contact Michael, which she was grateful for. Michael arrived home in record time. He put his arms around her, and she allowed herself to melt. It had been nearly a week since she had seen him.

After Lieutenant Oberchaud and Officer Manash left, Sandra and Michael settled down in the family room. He pulled her close. Sandra leaned into his shoulder, her head against the back of the curved, sprawling sectional. Michael felt something for his wife, but he didn't really know what it was. Pity perhaps. This was a lost woman with no roots, no family left, and no love in her world. Even he couldn't honestly say he loved her anymore. And if the girls did, they had never really let that be known.

When Sandra dozed off, Michael threw a quilt over her and left her on the sofa for the night. He capped the bottle of Tennessee whiskey that was still open on the bar and grabbed a sparkling water from the bar fridge. It was obvious that Sandra had been self-medicating again. All he could do was let her sleep it off.

As he was getting ready for bed, Michael wondered how he should tell Rachel and Kathryn about their grandmother. Kathryn was rebellious about most things. Rachel was preparing to head off for college and seemed to have her head on straight. *At least they didn't know Veronica; this shouldn't be too difficult. Maybe Kathryn is just another Veronica.*

Betty walked across the grounds of the Husting estate, her estate. James was parked near the pool. The years had taken a toll on the property. Three leases, each of multiple years, proved to be the death of the beauty Robert Husting had cultivated.

She was saddened by the condition of the rose garden. The landscaping around the pool had been neglected, and most of the flowering plants were looking fatigued. All the years that she and Ware had spent here doing their best to please Robert seemed to have been in vain. He was not one to show his appreciation except through material goods. And she was part of a plot to take his millions. Somewhere in that mix of working against him and working for him, she had become very confused. Betty didn't know really where her allegiance was.

Alej was a greedy man. The thrill of working for him was irresistible when she was young and impressionable. Now she realized that her energy had been very misdirected. Betty realized all that she had lost: a brother, Ware; a sweet girl whom she'd raised like her own, Ronnie; and Ronnie's little girl, Sandy, whom she treated like a granddaughter. In the end, she didn't get Alej. She did get this estate that he had bought when it was first sold by the Husting estate. But what good was that to her now? None of those people were here to share it with her, so the property was back on the market. Betty needed to wipe away the memories and move on. She was glad to be with James; he was a part of her past that had lasted. Her only regret was that now James was part of her evil side. And if she were being honest with herself, Betty would admit that she still had an inexplicable infatuation of some kind with Alejandro Basil Stanis.

She walked up to James, who sat in the SUV with the motor idling.

He tipped his head and asked if she was ready.

"I guess so, James. Let's get on with it."

She strolled around the front of the car to the passenger side. James pushed the passenger door open from where he sat, and she slipped in, her sandals dusty from the walk across the dry lawn. With little thought, Betty whispered, "... when ye depart out of that house or city, shake off the dust of your feet."[1]

"What's that you're saying, Betty?! I never knew you as a Bible-thumper!"

"There's so much about me you don't know, James."

She pulled the door closed and tightened the seat belt. She turned and looked him straight in the eye. "Let's go back to the cottage now. I need to take care of a few things."

Squeezing her lips into a straight line, she looked ahead. Without questioning, James drove out of the estate. The car circled around to the front of the mansion and past the front entrance. Betty squinted in the sunlight. The late day sun was low in the sky, and the air was heavy. She felt smothered.

As they rolled down the drive, she kept her focus on the passenger-side mirror. The dust from the car clouded her view, and she struggled to see the mansion for as long as possible.

"Are you with me, or are you back in that mansion?"

---

[1] Matthew 10:14 (KJV). Scripture quotations marked "KJV" are taken from the King James Version of the Bible.

James knew Betty had something on her mind. This was his way of letting her know that he was keeping an eye on her.

"I'm with you, James." There was a long pause before she added, "For a very long time, if you'll have me."

His bright smile and twinkling dark eyes drew her in. They continued down the long driveway in silence.

When they reached the road, James looked to the left. "Oh! Looks like a pretty big accident. There's all kinds of emergency vehicles."

"Oh yeah! I wonder what could have happened?" Betty looked interested, momentarily. *Got her.*

She coaxed James back to their destination. "You know what? Let's just go on our way. We can't help anyway."

"Well, that's probably true enough."

James turned right. He never mentioned the lights he was watching in his mirror. Betty silently did the same in her side mirror. Eventually a turn in the road obliterated the scene of Veronica's rental car and the Jaws of Life.

The winding roads were so familiar that Betty knew exactly where she was without paying attention. The curves of the road and the hills, and the feel of light and darkness through the tree-lined roads, was enough for her to know when James was nearing the cottage. She opened her eyes as he pulled into the gravel drive-way. The light shining through the trees cast moving shadows. Betty squinted, opened her eyes wider, and tried to refocus. James cut the engine and watched her blink a few times.

"James?"

"Yes, Betty?"

"Do you see Ronnie?"

"No. She's not here."

"Over there. Behind the tree."

James climbed out of the car. He paused in front of the car and looked in the direction of the tree Betty identified. He crossed the remainder of the driveway and motioned to Betty to join him. She cautiously got out of the car and went over to him.

James stood directly in front of her and placed his hands on her shoulders. "I think you were seeing things in the shadows. There's no one there."

Betty dropped her head and let out a sigh. *It* was *her on the road.*

Instinctively, James took her hand. They walked to the screened door of the cottage. With a few picks of the lock, Betty was able to open the screen and the main door. They cautiously entered the small kitchen.

Betty poked around the kitchen shelves. She located what she was looking for under a newspaper.

Betty was able to delete her phone number and all traces of her multiple calls to Veronica's cell phone.

The next item of business was to clean the coffee cup and replace it on the shelf. Betty cleared away all signs of ABS spice that may have lingered on the dishes that she'd tainted earlier that morning. She used a paper towel to wipe down any fingerprints she or James may have left in the cottage.

James turned the car around while Betty finished her work.

Before they reached the end of the short road that led into the cottage, the heavens opened and the rain poured down.

"God is watching over us, my love."

Betty nodded and smiled at James. The downpour was washing away their footprints and tire tread marks. "Hallelujah and amen."

Chapter
TWENTY-TWO
APRIL 2010: SHIFTING PLANS

Rob Treallor was finishing his second year at Boston College. He found many opportunities to continue community service in Boston's homeless shelters, doing the same kinds of things he'd done all throughout high school in Greenwich. His most rewarding hours were spent with young families or with single mothers whose children appreciated a positive male role model. Rob took the time to read stories to the children and listen to them tell the stories of their day.

Many of those tales were heart-wrenching. Rob was often reminded to be grateful for his family and the values they held. Evening family time was important to all of them. Now he really understood why. The children he saw a couple of nights a week didn't have the daily promise of a good meal or the love of two parents.

This work helped Rob define his life's work. He wanted to be a social worker. As a nurse working in the homeless shelter, his mother had instilled in him a desire to understand and help other people when they were at their lowest points in life. To continue helping the neediest children seemed like the best thing a person could do. He knew that some higher order had plans for his life, and this work was calling him. Somewhere deep inside, there was a nagging that had him wondering what that would really feel like.

Sitting in his single dorm room in the middle of the afternoon, away from his suite mates, Rob called his father's cell phone.

When the caller ID flashed on the screen, Warren answered immediately.

"Hey, Rob! What a pleasant surprise!"

Warren was always happy to get an unexpected call from Rob. He felt the smile spread wide across his face. The problems of the computer tech world could wait; he would always take time for his son.

"Hi, Dad."

"What's up with you?" Warren's delight was clear in his voice.

"Not much. Do you have a minute or two?"

This approach wasn't Rob's typical greeting. "Always, Son."

"We need to talk about a few things."

Warren's heart sank. He heard a troubled person, not Rob, on the other end of the line.

Warren listened to Rob anxiously spill his thinking for over an hour. His college career was becoming a very nerve-racking experience. It was clear to Warren that his son needed some real support.

"Rob, do you want me to come up to Boston? I can probably catch a shuttle and ..."

"No, Dad." At this point, Rob was emphatic.

"Well, it sounds like we should sit down together to hash this all out. I think maybe you just need ..."

"Dad! Stop!"

Warren was taken off guard by Rob's tone and immediate response.

"I've made my decision, and I'm asking for your blessing. That's not an approval or advice this time, Dad. It's just a blessing."

This kind of approach was a first for Rob. Warren had to stop and think about his own life's path. *Unkept promises to people I loved—still love.*

Without doubt, he'd made some real mistakes along the way, and he wanted to protect Rob from the pain he had suffered. At the same time, he recognized that Rob had a much better perception of reality than he himself had ever had. Warren knew that dreams left to grow unbridled by a dose of reality could be emotionally damaging.

After an uncomfortably long pause, Warren could hear Rob's sigh of anxiety and frustration, his lips rattling through the strong gust of exhaled breath.

"Rob, I do understand. If you think you have to test the potential of your dreams, then you are probably right."

Then there was another sigh in the phone, this time one of relief. With a cracking voice of near-tears, Rob replied, "Thanks for understanding, Dad."

"Of course."

There was another long pause. Rob was sniffling. Warren had many questions. He decided to take it slow.

"So do you want to share this decision with anyone, or do you want to get things all sorted out first?"

"How 'bout if we just keep it our secret for now? I should talk to the counselors here first."

"Okay. I think that's a good idea. We can touch base as you go through the process."

"Yeah. That's good."

Neither spoke. Warren didn't know if he should warn Rob that the counselors may try to convince him otherwise or mention that his mother would be devastated.

"Thanks for understanding, Dad. I knew you would."

"Goodbye, Rob. We'll talk on the weekend, huh?"

"Oh yeah, sure. I'll still call after church on Sunday."

"Hang tough. You'll be fine. Love ya, Rob."

"Love you too, Dad."

Warren hung up and stayed still at his desk. So many thoughts were running around in his head that he didn't know where to begin. *What if I'd been more careful to test my own dreams?*

The interoffice line buzzed on his desk phone, snapping Warren back to his day.

"Yes, Robin?"

"There's a Dr. Michael Channing here to see you."

Warren picked up the phone to cancel the speaker. "Who is that?"

"Dr. Channing?"

"He or she?"

"*He* doesn't have an appointment but said that you've done some work at the hospital he works at."

"Hmm. I need a few minutes. Ask him to wait."

"Okay."

"And, Robin, after we hang up, find out exactly which hospital, and then walk to the headend room. I'll meet you there."

"Certainly."

Who the hell is this guy?

Warren opened his customer database. The last visits he'd made to hospitals were two or three weeks ago. He stopped in at Sinai and New York University. Both were routine checks. Neither place was complaining about any security breach. There was no business reason for a doctor to stop by the company offices in Stamford.

Scanning the contact list, he found no Dr. Channing. His dealings were mainly with IT staff. On occasion, he might talk to a doctor or nurse in passing or ask a question about a specific tech-related problem. Other than that, nothing notable.

Robin made it to the technology headend room of the office just as Warren was rounding the corner near the digital display panels. There were boxes and wires everywhere in this tiny space. It could have been called "command central," but it was known simply as the headend room. The security screen for the reception areas was showing a clean view of Dr. Michael Channing. He was standing near the receptionist's station and seemed to be eyeing the work area.

"So who is this guy, Robin? Did you get any more information?"

"Well, he's on staff at Yale University Hospital. I think he said something about needing to get to his office, though."

"He probably is on staff there but might have a private practice at the medical center too. That doesn't explain anything. I don't work with doctors. Just IT guys."

Warren thanked his assistant and told her to go back. "Tell him I'll be about twenty minutes. And take your time getting back there. I'll see what he's up to at your work area."

Warren continued to follow Michael on the monitor, who was now eyeing the security camera but still scouting out the front desk. He reached into the breast pocket of his navy-blue blazer and retrieved a cell phone. He took several pictures of the work area and slipped the phone away as Robin was moving toward the room.

"Dr. Channing, Mr. Treallor will be with you in about fifteen or twenty minutes. He's got a couple of things he has to handle. Kind of important that he takes care of them right away."

"I'll come back another time."

Michael turned to leave.

"I'm happy to help you if I can."

"No. Nothing important. Thanks all the same."

"Can I tell Mr. Treallor why you were here?"

Michael was already out the door.

Warren appeared in the reception area before Robin sat down.

"What's on your desk? Don't touch a thing!"

"Why?"

"He took lots of pictures."

There spread across the work surface lay open the master calendar for all the firm's major projects for the next two months.

There was also a copy of Ware's scheduled appointments for the remainder of the month.

"Did he say anything before he left?"

"Just that he'd come back another time."

"Well, he's got our schedules. It won't be so easy to fool him next time."

Warren felt uneasy as he returned to his office. Things were just piling up on him. *What is this guy looking for? Channing. One of the kids' friends?*

Since the listing of Husting Estate nearly two years ago, life had been out of sync for Warren. Not only had Veronica been virtually killed in a car crash, but also he had felt haunted, literally, ever since the vision he'd had of Robert Husting on the day of Ronnie's accident. There were times when it felt as though Robert was with him, pushing him to do something. But Warren didn't know what it was. He couldn't deny the guilt that hung over him. How could he reconcile what he still felt for Ronnie and be living a lie with Leslie?

Now Rob wanted to bail on his college education.

There was also that woman, Lizzie or Sandra somebody, whom he'd met a couple of times over the years. There was just something about her that ate at him.

Warren returned to his desk and finished up a couple of emails. His goal was to get out of the office as early as possible. He asked Robin if she could move his schedule around for the next few business days. He wasn't up for any surprise visits from the mysterious Dr. Channing.

Driving into downtown Stamford, he replayed his visit to Wilmington about two weeks earlier. He again was pulled to Husting Estate. Whenever he made a call at accounts in the Philadelphia or Wilmington territory, he found himself back at the estate. It was getting more and more difficult not to walk around the grounds. When he last visited, there still was no For Sale sign and no signs of life.

The nagging question for him was related to Lizzie. Why, two years ago when the estate was first put on the market, was she there? If she lived in Connecticut and was a real estate executive there, or maybe in New York City, why would she be involved in a transaction in Delaware? *She must deal with some very high rollers.*

The story playing out in Warren's imagination was beginning to consume him. Too many questions needed to be answered. Maybe he needed to take on his past. The call from Rob had him questioning the wisdom of walking away from a child who may have been his daughter. All these thoughts brought on guilt. Leslie had been faithful and loyal, and he loved her, but she wasn't the love of his life.

After visiting a few installation sites locally and verifying that the work was on track for on-time completion in two of three buildings, Warren called his office. Robin successfully rescheduled his calls and appointments for the next week. She reported that the changes left the next day fully open.

"That's actually okay. Tell you what; I'll work from home tomorrow. I might make a couple of site visits unannounced. It's good to do that a little more often. I'll check in with you."

"Sounds good! Is there anything I can say to Dr. Channing if he returns?"

"No. I'm just in the field. If any of the partners are in, see if he wants to talk with one of them."

Robin didn't need to reply. She got the point.

"And, Robin ... maybe keep the schedules and any other sensitive information a little less visible?"

Adrienne had a soccer game late that afternoon. Warren and Leslie were supportive parents. They cheered her on and had dinner with her teammates. The next day was a Friday—a perfect day to drive back to Wilmington. Warren prepared Leslie for his long day by explaining he had two sites to visit. He planned to be on the road by 5:00 a.m. She understood, as she always did.

The need to get to bed early allowed Warren to leave the post-game dinner early without lots of questions. Adrienne and Leslie rode home with a neighbor.

Warren was in the shower and preparing for bed when they arrived. He joined them shortly, had a quick conversation about the great game, the school day, and work, and then headed off for bed. *Maybe I need to talk with Leslie about what I'm feeling. Maybe.* He was thankful again for such a trusting wife.

Kathryn Channing was at the end of her rope. Three days had passed, and the bruises were visible on her face, arms, and back. Marcus, her husband, was unpredictable. There were times when he was doting and kind, and there were times when he was drunk and mean.

After high school, Kathryn continued her rebellious attitude toward her parents and refused to go on to a four-year school. Her mother, Sandra, was a mess. She used pills and alcohol about as often as she brushed her teeth. Kathryn's father, Michael, had stopped trying to save the family. He spent more hours at the hospital or in his office than he did at home.

By the time Kathryn and her sister, Rachel, were finishing high school, they were expected to navigate their own way to college. Rachel did that very successfully one year ahead of Kathryn. Rachel was on track to graduate from Amherst in another year. She was focused on a strong liberal arts education but expected to be hired into a training program with a bulge-bracket financial firm, work for about three years, and then go on to business school. She was planning a very typical career path that would produce substantial income and not chancing the struggling lifestyle that might result from liberal arts academia.

In stark contrast, Kathryn and a classmate, Marlena, had left their privileged lifestyles in Greenwich immediately after graduation. They landed in Baltimore instead of Trenton. They both enrolled in a two-year postsecondary school and worked part-time jobs. Neither of their parents supported them because the young women had chosen to step out of the typical Greenwich pattern. Kathryn and Marlena were considered rebellious. Kathryn managed to get by. She indulged her wild side. There was no lack of a social life for her. Parties, booze, and occasional heroin use were the highlights of her weekends. Monday through Friday, she attended classes, studied, and worked at a local family restaurant. The restaurant owners were particularly kind to her, and if she needed anything, she knew they would give her an advance on her pay. She had had to resort to that a few times to pay the rent on time.

With one semester left in her program of study to become a certified medical technician, Kathryn learned she was pregnant. She made the mistake of expecting Marcus, the man whom she'd been having sex with for the past year, to be on her side, to understand that they shouldn't have this baby because of the drugs and drinking. She was met with a backhand slap across the face, followed by an incredibly remorseful, tender, caring Marcus who proposed marriage. He claimed that his reaction was totally unlike him and that he was just frustrated at the news.

She bought his story. Kathryn Channing and Marcus Bolten were married by a judge at the county courthouse. It was a dreary and bitterly cold February day that ended with Marcus in a drunken stupor. Kathryn cried herself to sleep that night on a

smelly brown couch in Marcus's two-room flat on the west side
of the city.

Within weeks of their marriage, Marcus had convinced
Kathryn to work more hours and drop out of school. He was worried about finances. She was able to get nearly full-time work at
the restaurant, but the pregnancy and the work schedule resulted
in relentless exhaustion.

By the time two months had passed, Kathryn was looking
for a reprieve. She tried to seek refuge with Marlena by stopping
by their old apartment, but she didn't find her there. A neighbor
told her that Marlena had taken an internship in Boston with the
hope of landing a good job. The apartment had been sublet for the
remaining two months that were on the lease.

Marcus sensed that something was bothering Kathryn, and
that irritated him. He accused her of not being grateful for everything he had done for her. An explosive argument ended with
Marcus slamming the door and Kathryn eating a frozen dinner.

Later that night, Marcus returned home drunk. He slapped
Kathryn around, screaming about how she should think about what
her attitude did to him. He shoved her into their bed and did what
he thought would make her understand that she answered to him.

When Marcus passed out, Kathryn packed as many things as
she could stuff into a backpack and a travel case. She slipped away
without taking a key.

Kathryn made her way to the local shelter for battered women.
The pregnancy had her exhausted most of the time, and getting
across town was nearly the hardest journey she remembered making in a long time, maybe since she was little and trying to follow
her father one time on the busy New York City streets. She had
that same fear. Those streets were filled with people walking too

fast, and she had to run to keep from losing sight of her father. She remembered the fear of being swept along in a sea of legs, none belonging to him. The same panic was with her now, only this time she feared Marcus would find her.

It was dark, and the familiar street corners took on an eerie silence. The church that sponsored a shelter was on the southeast side of the city, near the waterfront. She had been there once, the time that Marcus had threatened her with a meat cleaver. He was drunk. She went there before work the day after just to check it out. The restaurant had a few pamphlets, business cards, and flyers posted on a bulletin board at the checkout. That's where she'd read about the Saint Mary of the Immaculate Conception Center for Women. After her visit, she decided that Marcus didn't really mean to threaten her. So she went to work and home again on her normal schedule. He never suspected anything.

This time, things were different. She had taken too many beatings, and the emotional abuse was almost worse.

Kathryn knew it was too late for an abortion; she was too far along in the pregnancy. She hoped that maybe some kind person at Saint Mary's would help her find a good home for this baby.

The walk took over an hour with all the rest stops she had to take. Her fear was that she would arrive at the church and find no one there. At one in the morning, Kathryn knew there was no reason for anyone to be waiting for her.

The travel bag and backpack were getting harder to manage. Her breath was heavy, and her limbs felt like wet sponges. Fear became a source of strength that kept her moving forward.

The night air was cool, but she was sweaty all the same. Knowing she was now within two or three blocks of the center, she willed herself to continue on. The familiar sign with a cross lit on the top of it was within her vision. She'd memorized the landmark from the brochure, a night shot that begged women to seek refuge in the night. Her beacon of hope.

A light drizzle dusted Kathryn's face. She was thankful for the coolness that gave her renewed determination; she pushed on.

One block left to go.

The light on the church sign flickered. She tried to run but lasted only a short way. Cramps came on fast and hard. Retching, she squatted down on her travel case and panted. Then she took two deep cleansing breaths and panted again.

The cramps subsided.

She brushed the hair from her wet face, struggled to her feet, and started moving slowly.

Tears mixed with the rain on her cheeks.

Kathryn was surprised to hear her own voice. "Oh God, if you exist, please be home."

The wind started to blow hard. The rain came harder, the wind whipped her hair in her face, and Kathryn couldn't see. The church sign flickered multiple times. "Please be open."

She picked up the pace, willing herself to put one foot in front of the other. "Please …"

The sneakers on her feet were saturated. They rubbed her heels, causing pain that didn't matter. The wet backpack tugged hard on her shoulders, and she gave in to its weight, dropping it to the sidewalk. Her soaked sweatshirt clung to her big belly.

She sat on the travel bag and tried to gather herself together for the remaining stretch. The church sign went out. Several minutes passed. She hunkered down, protecting her face with her arms. Tears and fear mingled together. When she was sure there was no hope left, things changed.

The wind subsided and the rain tapered off. *God, thank you.*

The squall line was passing, and the weather was calming. But the horrible cramps started again.

With natural rhythm, she panted; she took deep cleansing breaths and panted again. The cycle repeated several times before the cramps let up.

This baby can't wait.

The realization of what was happening served as the force Kathryn needed to make the final trek.

When she reached the church, the sign was still in darkness. But the rain had totally stopped, and lights on the side of the building were working. The wet pavement was glistening. Along the side alley of the church, a very plain door with a cement stoop and two handrails was well illuminated by an ordinary capped light fixture. Nearing the door, Kathryn could read the plaque stating what she had felt at her visit to this shelter: All Are Welcome Here.

Just below the plague was a very plain black well-used door buzzer.

She leaned into the buzzer with her upper arm just as the cramps came on again. She slid down on the stoop and called out, "Please be home, God ..."

Michael Channing needed to find someone by the name of W. Treallor. It was no coincidence to him that when Veronica Husting Simarillo Whatton fell into a coma, she was carrying an envelope with that name on it. Now he'd been holding on to it for nearly two years—two years too many.

Sandra hadn't maintained a relationship with her mother. It had been so long that Michael wasn't sure he would have recognized his mother-in-law if he had just passed her on the street. Certainly age had changed her appearance, just as it had changed his own. He could recall seeing her only a few times, but the last time was a distant memory.

When the former Husting estate was put on the market a couple of years ago, Sandra withdrew from Michael. She spent a good deal of time investigating her childhood home, which she had neither seen nor visited since she was a toddler. After telling him that the property was on the market, she kept her inquisitiveness and exploration quiet, sharing nothing with Michael.

At that time Michael still wanted to save their marriage, and he had hoped to find Veronica and learn something that might help him understand what was going on with Sandra. He was not successful. Veronica was elusive. He could only determine that she had left California permanently. No one seemed to know anything about her whereabouts. The former Husting estate staff could not be found either. It seemed to Michael that Veronica didn't want to be contacted under any circumstances. He wondered if she would have wanted to know about her granddaughters or even her daughter. It puzzled him that a woman would totally remove herself from family. Michael's own mother and father remained actively involved with family until each of their deaths, which occurred within one year of one another. The first was when Kathryn and Rachel were just two and three years old, respectively.

The results of Michael's efforts were that he never located Veronica and never figured out why Sandra had become so focused on the estate. He had decided to give up all efforts to put the puzzle together. Then Veronica was wheeled into DuLoche Memorial Hospital on a gurney. He remembered the situation all too well.

Nearly two years had passed. Michael had made a decision not to deal with the letter written by Veronica Husting. His interactions with Sandra were minimal, and at the time it didn't seem to be too important. All indicators pointed to the demise of his marriage, so he kept the letter tucked away in his office at the medical center. He'd actually managed to forget about, or at least not to dwell on, his curiosity.

Michael knew that in the early stages of his relationship with

Sandra, she had some rather interesting stories to tell about her mother. They were related to the days they'd spent together in California. Sandra was very young then. She recalled times when they lived in a hotel and then in a condominium or an apartment. She talked about being cared for by different people, and she seemed quite fond of her stepfather. Frederick Whatton was an intriguing man based on what she relayed to Michael.

But those days were long gone. Michael saw Sandra as a self-sufficient, self-damaging person at this stage of their lives. Her goal was some kind of material gain that was unidentified. Michael provided very well for the family, and their two girls lacked nothing. Sandra, on the other hand, never had enough. Michael stopped trying to identify exactly what she did not have enough of. While Michael wasn't particularly domestic or fatherly, he didn't want his family to suffer at all. He did wonder a bit about Kathryn, though. She marched to the beat of a different drummer, and she was now off on her own little rebellious jaunt. He trusted that someday she would return. The fact that she was pursuing a medical certification of any kind gave him hope that eventually she might follow in his footsteps.

In a recent clean-out of his desk, the mysterious envelope surfaced, and now it was difficult to ignore. He started to open the envelope but saw visions of his mother-in-law lying on that hospital bed. He closed his eyes, tucked the envelope back in the drawer, and chose to do a little investigation.

It was quite easy to locate one family with the last name of Treallor. Warren and Leslie Treallor lived in his own town of Greenwich. Michael didn't know them, and he didn't want to raise suspicions by asking Sandra. Besides, he didn't know if he would even see Sandra anytime soon.

Warren Treallor, according to Michael's research, was a partner of an IT company that did most of their work in the Northeast and mid-Atlantic regions. He held many impressive certifications in technology systems management. A little internet research revealed that they may have done some work at DuLoche Memorial and at Yale University Hospital. Michael had an in. He could use his affiliations at both those hospitals to get a foot in the door.

And he tried.

He wasn't at all pleased with his first attempt to find Warren.

A case of insecurity trashed his plans. He'd actually visited Warren's office. Partway through his confident request to speak with Warren, he realized he didn't really know what to say or how to approach things. He had no intention of just delivering the envelope. At the first opportunity, he got out of there, but not without first figuring out where he might find Warren over the next few weeks.

He knew he should have been much more forthright when he showed up at Warren's door. But at the same time, he was conscious of the fact that Warren might have been his mother-in-law's friend or acquaintance, and Veronica wasn't exactly an easy person to know much about. He wasn't entirely sure he wanted to hand over the letter without a better idea of what might have been going on between this man named Warren and Michael's mother-in-law.

TWENTY-THREE

— MAY 2010: A WALK IN THE PAST —

The sun was strong. Sandra had actually enjoyed the three-hour drive from Greenwich. The arrangement had given her an opportunity to leave home early to avoid traffic. Highways presented straight roads with no blind curves or rolling hills. Her confidence behind the wheel had grown over the past several years, and making the trek was actually liberating to her. She stopped and enjoyed a cup of coffee in Bordentown and found herself thinking about Kathryn. Sandra hadn't spoken with her younger daughter in months. Kathryn had chosen her own fate, and Sandra didn't care to know where that would lead.

After a few moments of reflection about her two daughters, Sandra decided it was time to get back to the business at hand. She drained her coffee cup, paid the waitress, and made a visit to the restroom. Small diners along heavily traveled routes were not Sandra's favorite places. She used care with everything she touched, scrubbed her hands with warm, soapy water, and used an air dryer before opening the door with the sleeve of her sweater to avoid touching the door handle.

Sandra met her client at 11:00 a.m. on the front steps of the former Husting estate as planned.

"Good morning, Mr. Treallor." Sandra greeted Warren warmly as he was opening the door of his truck.

Warren removed his hat and looked up the steps toward Sandra. When their eyes met, both shifted uneasily. The silence was awkwardly long. It was Warren who broke the tension. Moving up the three long steps to the portico, he smiled with genuine happiness to be back at the estate. "A beautiful day in Wilmington, isn't it ... Lizzie?"

Sandra cast her eyes downward, feeling caught in her own mud. She straightened the purse that hung from her shoulder, although it didn't need it. Looking back at Warren, she responded, "Oh, I'm sorry. Did you say 'Lizzie'?"

"Yes. You do use the name Lizzie, don't you?"

"Why do you ask that?"

"It seems to me we've met a few times."

"No. No. We've talked on the phone enough times, and you've always called me Sandra. That's my name: Sandra Channing. I think you have me confused with someone else." Her voice projected at a somewhat higher pitch with a rushed pace.

"Okay. Have it your way." After a short pause, he added, "It's good to meet you in person, Sandra."

"Yes it is, Mr. Treallor."

"Warren."

"Warren." Sandra thought she'd recovered well from that little bump. She didn't want to think about the night several years ago when this man rescued her from that harsh rainy drive to Greenwich High, nor of the time she saw this man here in the side garden on his knees. "So shall we begin the tour of the property?"

Sandra began the tour with full explanation of the acreage, the age and square footage of the mansion, and a history of the surrounding area. Warren pretended he was learning about the Husting estate for the first time, but his heart was heavy with memories. He thought of Ronnie, Sandy, Robert, Betty, and James. He even could feel the presence of Cook and Arthur when they walked through the halls of the mansion. There seemed to be no significant changes in the property. To his surprise, the kitchen still looked as if Betty was in charge with the placement of utensils, pots, and pans. All the serving pieces were the same. With a closer look, he realized these were, in fact, the exact same utensils Betty used. *Whoever bought the furnishings from the estate sales company must now own this place.* Many questions rushed to his mind, and his heart rate quickened. Memories sparked emotions. *How did that happen? Separate sales. Estate. Furnishings. Who?*

Warren forced himself to ask a question: "So what did you say the taxes were last year? And did you say something about a recent change in assessment?"

Sandra answered as best she could, but she often had to promise to get back to Warren with updated information. She explained again that she was not the listing agent and that she actually worked in Connecticut and New York.

"Yes. I recall that from the first time I met you here."

Now Sandra could no longer play dumb.

"Oh. Yes! Now I recall! I'm so sorry." Stepping back a bit and smiling cordially, she acted as if she were recalling something casually. "You were here the first time I came to see this property in preparation for a showing, right?"

"Yes."

"And I don't remember exactly, but didn't you say you worked here?"

"Correct. But that was a long time ago. More than thirty years now."

"Well, if you worked the grounds at one time, you must know the site well."

"Indeed. Let's walk some of the property anyway."

Sandra let Warren lead the way. He moved out the back door, leaving Betty's kitchen the same way he had so many times. He could feel her presence and wondered where she might be after all these years. *My dear older sister.*

The May air was pure Delaware Valley, hotter and heavier than Connecticut's. The varieties of spring bushes were blooming in pastels, but they lacked the joy and radiance once projected through the careful maintenance of the Husting staff. Pink and yellow were predominant, and the fragrance of nearby hyacinths captured Warren's nostalgic side. He could smell Ronnie in the fresh floral scent of her signature perfume.

Warren naturally strolled down the paved walkway that led away from the kitchen porch. Then he turned left as if returning to his pool house quarters. Expecting to see the pool ahead of him, Warren moved with anticipation of a glorious return to his youth. Instead, he was greeted with a broken fence surrounding an empty concrete hole in the ground. The sidewalls were collapsed inward, and the once spectacular pool was nothing more than a pile of debris. Weeds stood tall between the slate slabs of the pool patio, and the tree roots pushed the far side pool apron apart. Warren felt the deflation of his lungs as his shoulders dropped, his face fell, and his heart sank. A lump was rising in his throat.

"As you see, there is a little bit of maintenance needed back here."

Warren tripped out of his stroll down memory lane enough to push the lump from his chest, fill his lungs, and resurrect his shoulders. "I can see the potential." His response was flat. He showed no excitement and no discouragement. "The seller will need to take this disaster into consideration before a final price can be negotiated."

"Mr. Treallor ..."

"Warren."

"Yes. This place is priced to sell. The market is not where it once was, and I highly doubt if the owner will go any lower."

"We'll see."

When Warren had spent an hour on the Husting estate, he had seen enough to know what his next steps would be.

Sandra approached the topic of an offer about to be made on the property, and Warren played things very nonchalantly. *Typical line. Seal the deal with a threat of loss.* He committed to get back in touch within a week. He also asked Sandra to alert him if there was any action on the property. Being a savvy business-woman, Sandra explained that she was under no obligation to do so. "If you tell me you expect to make an offer, then I will be sure to let you know if your timing needs to be adjusted."

"Fine. I'll let you know."

Warren returned to his truck. It took a few minutes for him to settle in. He checked his cell phone. Rob had left a text message asking for a telephone conversation that evening. Nothing from the office. Nothing from Leslie. He stepped back out of the truck to remove the light jacket he had on, and Sandra came through the front door of the mansion.

"I'm glad you haven't left yet." Sandra was walking toward Warren with purpose.

"Nope. Just settling in for the drive."

"I should have told you that the current owner of this estate does hope to have a very smooth transaction. Even though the price might not be too negotiable, there could be other incentives."

"Such as?"

"Property repairs, or live-in staff, or ..."

"Wait. Doesn't Frederick Whatton have his own properties in California to deal with? Why would he pump money and staff into this place?"

Sandra paused. She tilted her head and dropped her chin slightly. With a coy look, she responded to Warren's inquiry: "So, Mr. Treallor, you know the history of ownership here too?"

"Well ... yeah. And it's Warren." He didn't want to reveal that he was the beneficiary of the sale of the estate to Whatton after Husting's death. "Sort of. I was still on staff here when Mr. Husting died."

"I see. So you probably also know that Mr. Whatton bought this property for his first wife."

"That would have been Veronica Husting Simarillo."

"No. It wasn't."

Warren had no response. He gave a short nod.

"Anyway, think about some things that could be added to the purchase, as opposed to a reduction in sales price. With resources at his disposal, the owner wouldn't mind a cash outlay for maintenance, but a lower sales price would not be very attractive. He is open to selling the property as is with the furnishings."

Warren nodded. "Thanks. I'll think about that." He reached into the cab of his truck, grabbed his hat, and tipped it to Sandra before securing it in place. "Good day, Mrs. Channing." He climbed into the cab and started the engine.

Sandra watched as Warren drove away. The thought of her mother living here gave her reason to pause. She thought about Papa Fred and wondered if her mother ever knew she was not his first wife. So many puzzle pieces were left detached, yet Sandra was beginning to see a bigger picture, one that might put her in this mansion where her life had started.

Warren's truck turned the circular drive. He saw Sandra standing with her arms crossed and her head tilted. She appeared to be consumed with thoughts that made Warren wonder just how much she knew about the Husting family. Her posture indicated a determination that he had admired in Ronnie. *My Ronnie. Not Frederick's first wife?*

When the last tenant moved out of the estate, Frederick ordered all the original furnishings moved out of storage and placed back in their rightful places. Betty worked hard to restore the home to its original state. James was by her side, and they worked tirelessly with the hope that together they would realize a strong profit from the sale. James was only interested in enough cash to pay off a couple of debts and make a lifetime arrangement to stay with Betty wherever she landed. It was their unspoken pact.

Betty was walking across the back porch of the estate when she heard a vehicle in the front circle. She darted back down the steps and picked up her pace as she returned to the parking garage. She ran in, pulling the door behind her quietly.

James was there sorting through some tools and personal belongings left by multiple residents over the years. "Did you ever see so much junk that folks keep?" He was chuckling as he lifted an old coffee can filled with rubber bands and tacks. "Shh." Betty pointed toward the house.

"What's the problem?" James was whispering now, moving toward the door.

"Don't!" Betty stopped him from stepping out into the yard.

She pulled him down. They both squatted beneath the window of the door as she whispered, "I heard a truck in the circle drive. Didn't know anyone was looking at the house today."

They huddled there and remained out of sight for more than an hour. When all the sounds and voices stopped, James assured Betty that no one would be walking through the parking garage and that the coast was clear.

Chapter _____

TWENTY-FOUR

AUGUST 2010: A REUNION

Kathryn dragged herself and little Angela into the shelter. It was a hot day, expected for this time of year in Wilmington. Just a year earlier, Kathryn would have been out of sorts with the heat and humidity. But now she was at peace. Marcus was out of her life. She left him behind in Baltimore. To her knowledge, he had no idea where she was or how to find her. Saint Mary's of the Immaculate Conception had invited her in with open arms at the worst time of her life. When her baby was born and she held her close, there was no way she would forfeit that feeling to another mother. Not ever. Nor would she ever let Angela experience the likes of Marcus.

Kathryn and Angela stayed in the Wilmington hospital for several weeks after being transported there from Baltimore. When Angela was strong enough to leave, they were discharged to a shelter that worked with the hospital to assist new mothers with transition. Kathryn sought out employment with counseling from the staff at the shelter. She prayed every day that she would find a way to support herself and her baby. Her hopes included returning to school, finishing her certification, and landing a good job that would give Angela a better life.

When she opened the door that evening after spending nine

hours serving in the small diner just around the corner, a young man greeted her with a big smile and a look of warmth and care.

"Kathryn. Kathryn Channing."

"Rob?"

Kathryn turned away to hide her shame. She immediately moved to the back room of the shelter to find her baby. With a swift grab, she snagged Angela with the crib blanket and then scurried through the crowded room of cots and straight chairs. Nearly stumbling on the small children and their blankets, Kathryn found the side door and exited.

She ran two blocks to the nearest park, where she knew there were public restrooms. As she started to slow down, she heard the pounding footsteps behind her. "Kathryn, wait!"

"Go away; I don't want to talk to you."

She pulled on the women's room door, but it was locked. Panicked, she ran around the side of the building. But Rob anticipated her move and blocked her at the corner.

Kathryn broke down and cried.

Rob held her close while she continued to cuddle a crying Angela.

He rubbed her back, stroked her hair, and waited patiently.

Kathryn found her voice with "Why are you here?"

Rob lifted her face to him with a touch under her chin. "I guess I was meant to see you again."

Kathryn stared at his eyes, feeling the beautiful warmth of the blue pools of understanding. "But why here?"

"It's kind of a long story."

She only shook her head in question.

Rob filled the void. "It looks as if you have a story too. And it begins with this beautiful little baby. A complete replica of a beautiful mother."

Kathryn began to cry again, this time with relief.

Rob turned her around and walked Kathryn and Angela back to the shelter. The sky was getting dark, and Angela was fussing.

"I know they feed the babies on demand, but what time do you usually feed at night? It's already 9:30."

"It's time. I'm breastfeeding."

"Wow! Kathryn, that's awesome."

"It's also what I can afford."

"Sorry."

They walked back to the shelter in silence. There would be time for them to tell their stories. Rob knew he wasn't going anywhere until Kathryn was back on her feet. That would take some time.

When Rob finished school in late April, he had finalized his decision not to return in the fall. Instead, he found work in a not-for-profit organization that managed three shelters in different cities. He was placed in the Wilmington shelter because the needs there matched his desire to work with children. Rob's favorite assignments were the evening shifts in shelters for young families or homeless mothers. There was something about the innocence of the children that lured him in. He felt for those living in unfair situations that had nothing to do with their own choices. The sad eyes helped him remember just how lucky he had been to be born into a stable family. His own dad showed him how to work in centers for homeless people, and he and his sister spent many weekend hours together serving meals in Stamford. The tug on his heart for this work was very strong. Adding Kathryn and this beautiful baby to the mix only confirmed his choice as the right one.

Kathryn was still in shock over meeting up with her high

school love. Rob was one person she'd always looked up to, but she couldn't follow him into the traditional school track after graduation. They took alternate paths, and somehow now those paths were crossing. She couldn't understand it.

It was important to focus on feeding Angela. All Kathryn wanted was a cup of soup and a few crackers. Rob insisted that she add a tuna sandwich to get more protein in her diet. He also encouraged dairy products and fruit. While Kathryn didn't like his pushing her to eat his diet, she knew he was right. She was relieved to think someone was taking special care of her and her baby.

Rob had to tend to many other chores in the shelter. That night there were three new families taking the openings of the three families who had moved on over the past few days. There were rules in the shelter: As soon as a mother was no longer seeking employment or if she became unemployed because of drug or alcohol use, she had to move out. If a mother continued to work, she and her babies could remain in the shelter, with childcare, for up to ninety days. That was the time when a person was expected to have enough money for a deposit on an apartment and sufficient money to afford one week's worth of food. The number of children and ages of children in a family determined budgets, and counselors worked with the clients to help them reach the goal.

Kathryn was close to having enough money for a deposit on an efficiency apartment one block from the diner where she worked. It was a one-room, all-function space with a bathroom and one wall that served as a kitchen. The challenge would be childcare. It was possible to keep Angela at the shelter for a minimal fee if there was space. There were so many contingencies that Kathryn wanted to find a better alternative to the shelter. She hoped to free herself of the handouts given to her. It was not unusual to find her on her knees beside her cot. Rob witnessed that humble posture enough times to know Kathryn was in tune with his own soul.

Soul mates, no doubt. From their early days at Greenwich

High, Rob felt a closeness to Kathryn. Maybe their paths really were crossing for a purpose. *God sent me here for a reason.*

———— ❧❧ ————

Warren was working the mid-Atlantic area with more opportunities to travel into Delaware and Maryland on a regular basis. There were times when it made sense for him to spend the night away from home as multiple projects were under way in two medical centers at one time. One was the Baltimore Cancer Center. The other was a new wing at Children's Hospital at DuLoche. The network systems were in need of upgrading in the Wilmington DuLoche campus overall, so that particular project was extensive. When possible, he met up with Rob for dinner, but Rob's schedule of working evenings made that a challenge.

On a hot August night in Wilmington, Warren was sitting in his hotel room answering emails, reviewing blueprints, and checking specifications for all the work lined up for the next day. His cell rang. "Rob?"

"Hi, Dad!"

"It's good to hear your voice. What's going on?"

"Well, I'm wondering if you have a few minutes to talk."

"Of course. I'm actually in Wilmington at the Hilton preparing for a big installation."

———— ❧❧ ————

Rob walked into the lobby of the Hilton with Kathryn and Angela. When Kathryn saw Rob's father, she stepped back. His distinguished gray hair, glasses, and kempt facial hair surprised her. But when she saw his eyes, his calm and reassuring nature pulled her closer. He looked at her and her baby with kindness, not judgment. With ease, Kathryn reached up and hugged Warren without hesitation. Warren hugged her in return. Slightly embarrassed, she felt a need to say something. "I'm sorry. But thank you for letting me hug you."

Warren laughed warmly. "No need to apologize. Who is this little one?"

"Her name is Angela. She's my baby."

Warren and Rob exchanged glances.

"Dad, how about if we grab a bite to eat? Do you have the time?"

Warren looked back at Kathryn when he responded, "Of course."

Kathryn was clearly uncomfortable. She fussed over Angela and tried to avoid making eye contact with Warren again. Rob made sure that she ordered a substantial meal, and he assisted with Angela whenever possible.

"So how did you two connect here in Wilmington?"

Kathryn looked at her plate while she snuggled a sleeping Angela close to her breast. Rob responded, "Well, it's kind of odd, Dad. Kathryn is having some challenging times right now, and she walked into the shelter where I'm working. Strange, huh? We just kind of picked up where we left off, but maybe on better footing, ya know?"

Warren looked from Rob to Kathryn, raised his chin, and nodded slightly. "So, Kathryn, do you get back to Greenwich to see your family at all?"

"Not really, Dad." It was Rob who took the lead. "See, she didn't go to college like her parents wanted, so she kinda stepped out on her own."

Warren asked again, "But, Kathryn, do you get to see your family very often?"

"No. They don't know where I am. They don't know about Angela."

The silence spoke loudly. It was time to move on.

Warren ordered coffee and asked for the bill. He feigned a need to get back to his planning for a big day. Kathryn sensed the change in the warmth he'd first expressed, but she tried to ignore it.

Rob walked Kathryn back to the shelter and returned to his assigned tasks there. The kitchen needed cleaning up, and two new families were expected after nine o'clock. One had been referred from a local church, and another had stopped in during the day for intake. His role in that process was important if the families were going to have trust in the good work that the shelter was doing for them. Rob loved that part of his job. It was his opportunity to connect with children who needed his help.

Even with all these things to occupy his mind, Rob realized that the evening with his father hadn't really been successful. More than anything, he wanted a chance to talk about Kathryn, about how his feelings for her were rekindled, and about his desire to be with her. Instead, he may have shocked his father by having Kathryn and Angela with him.

Before leaving the shelter for the night, Rob found Kathryn on her knees. He walked behind her, rubbed her back, and knelt down beside her. She leaned into his shoulder and began to cry quietly. Rob wrapped an arm around her shoulders.

"Shh. It will be fine. God is on our side."

"He is good."

"Yes. Now get some sleep. I'm heading home now."

"Good night, Rob. And thank you."

He kissed her on the top of her head.

Angela was sleeping in a small bassinette on the floor beside Kathryn's cot. Rob rubbed the sleeping babe's back and quietly slipped away.

Out on the street, Rob dialed his father's cell.

"Rob, hi."

"Dad. I'm sorry. I should have prepared you."

"Look, Rob, it was a surprise to see Kathryn and her baby. I can't lie about that. At the same time, I'm not surprised that you two have found one another."

"Really? You mean, you knew how fond I was of her?"

"Let's just say I could tell that there was something important about her. You always seemed different when you talked about her, even years ago. And I can see that she's in need of some tender loving care. I would never expect you to shun her right now."

"So are you okay with the fact that I brought her tonight?"

"Yes. I was fine. But did you want to talk about something that we maybe didn't talk about tonight?"

"Actually, yeah. But it's late. Are you still in town tomorrow?"

"Probably for two more days."

"I'll call."

"Good. Sleep well."

"You too, Dad. And thanks."

"Good night."

Warren hung up the phone. He slid back into his hotel bed, but sleep escaped him.

Rob walked to his apartment. He opened the door and entered a lonely place. The efficiency flat was all he could afford. Working in philanthropy was not lucrative in the monetary sense. It was lucrative in satisfaction, and the ministry of his role gave Rob more riches than he could manage. Regardless of how many hours he worked or how late he arrived home, his small flat was warm and welcoming to him.

The apartment came furnished, and he'd used his college dorm setup to fill in the gaps. Inspiring posters in inexpensive frames provided focal points. The image of a stream of light coming through tall sequoia trees invited a walk through nature and hung over his bed. High tide crashed on white sand with streams of heaven shining through white puffy clouds. This one was mounted above a small couch next to the bed. The kitchenette along the opposite wall included two small plaques of psalms that Rob always recited when he needed to ground himself.

He pulled a cold juice from the small fridge under the kitchenette counter and collapsed on the couch. A small TV gave him a glimpse of the daily news, and a few minutes with a magazine gave Rob a chance to unwind before hitting the bed.

Kathryn awakened to Angela's cries. It was only 1:00 a.m., but she knew it was time for Angela to be fed. She rolled over, pulled Angela from the bassinette, and nestled the infant against her breast. The baby responded with ease, and mother and child molded against one another. By the time Angela was satisfied with her diaper changed and was back in the bassinette, Kathryn felt exhausted. She was physically tired but couldn't sleep for fear she might not awaken in time for work. She lay in bed thinking about Rob and Mr. Treallor.

Her mind wandered to the open suburbs of Connecticut where she grew up. She reminisced on lying in the grass outside her mother's study. Kathryn recalled trying to get her mother's attention by rolling around on the ground, jumping up and down, and antagonizing her older sister, Rachel. Kathryn's memory was that her mother didn't care much about being with her or Rachel. It was always a nanny who attended to them. *Why? Was I always a bad person? How can that be?* She sat up to see Angela—*my little angel*—sleeping. An innocent babe. *What is there not to love?*

A quiet resolve came over her when she touched the small Bible under her pillow. It was a gift from the Saint Mary's shelter. A few pages in the book of Psalms were well used and provided enough instances of distraction and solitude that Kathryn could now recite them by heart. She closed her eyes.

The Lord is my shepherd; I shall not want. He maketh me to lie down in green pastures …[2]

She stopped and thought about green pastures— the peace of an open pasture.

She lay back down and let the tears roll down her face until sleep came. It was 2:15 a.m.

Rob showered, made a sandwich, and turned on the TV.

He usually worked from three to eleven o'clock. Tonight, he finished the family intakes by 10:00 and managed to get home by 10:45. It was a good night. The evening shift always led to an inability to sleep. Rob knew that this was typical. People don't turn off the day at the end of a day shift, so why should he consider sleeping immediately after his workday? Late night news, late night talk shows, a chapter in a good book, and eventually Rob was ready to sleep.

He lay back and whispered thanks to God before switching off the lights. Tomorrow would be another chance to know what he was supposed to do about Kathryn and Angela. He closed his eyes and felt at peace. One of his favorite psalms ran in a visual like a movie on the screen behind his eyelids.

He leadeth me beside the still waters. He restoreth my soul: he leadeth me in the paths of righteousness for his name's sake.[3]

Sleep was upon him. It was 2:17 a.m.

---

[2] Psalms 23:1–2 (KJV).
[3] Psalms 23:2–3 (KJV).

Warren called Leslie later than usual. It took him time to process the surprise of seeing Rob and Kathryn together with Rob attending to a newborn baby. The scene had rocked him a little bit. Warren realized that he was old enough to be a grandfather, but he still supported two kids of college age. Adrienne was a freshman at the University of Wisconsin–Madison, where she was studying early childhood education. Rob unexpectedly shifted gears and left school at the end of his second year at Boston College. His original plans were to go to medical school. Once entrenched in studies, he had learned enough about himself to understand that a prestigious medical career was not in his heart. He was drawn to continue serving indigent people just as his parents had taught him. Now he was learning experientially.

Leslie and Warren struggled with Rob's decision at first, but they supported him. The agreement was that they would assist financially for one year while Rob worked through a decision-making process. He had to carry the weight of some living expenses so that there was a true understanding of all consequences. This agreement held only if he worked with an academic counselor at Boston during his one year away from studies. The school was willing to work with students who needed a one-year leave of absence, allowing them to pick up where they left off upon return in the fall semester of the following year.

Now Warren needed to share with Leslie this twist of events. "Hello?"

"Hi, sweetheart. Did I wake you?"

"Yes. What time is it?"

"About midnight. Sorry."

"It's okay. How was your day?"

"Good. Busy. Anything you have to share from today? Work go okay?"

"All fine. How 'bout you?"

"All fine. I'll let you go back to sleep."

"Okay. Love you."

"Love you too. I'll call earlier tomorrow."

"Okay. Bye."

They hung up. Warren let out a deep breath. He was spared the challenging conversation until tomorrow. By then, he might know what he should tell her and how he really felt about things.

Warren took a quick shower to unwind. He stepped out into the steamy room and looked into the mirror. Someone was behind him. He turned quickly, only to see the shower curtain.

"There's no one there. I'm here, in the mirror."

"Who?"

"You know who I am, Ware."

"Warren. My name's Warren."

"Of course. You and Ronnie were very much in love."

"Robert?"

"Yes, it's me."

"Where are you?"

"Here. I'm in a beautiful place. No need to worry."

"But how come ...?"

"Ware, I'm just here to tell you not to give up on Ronnie."

"She's gone. She must be with you."

"Oh no, Ware. She's there. She's ready. Dig deeper."

"Ready for what? There was a terrible car accident. You visited me then. Didn't you?"

"Just don't give up on her."

"How?"

"Look into those eyes of that little angel."

"Angel?"

The steam was clearing, and the image in the mirror faded away. Warren turned around, looked back in the mirror, and turned around again. Nothing. No one.

His legs felt weak, and his hands were shaking.

He reached for a cup and drank some water. Several large gulps of water didn't seem to help.

He grabbed a towel and moved to the bed. Sitting on the edge, he felt himself hyperventilating.

Calm. Be calm. Breathe evenly.

His racing heart started to slow down, and his breathing returned to normal. With his head between his hands, Warren bent over to restore his sense of balance. In a few minutes, he felt strong enough to get ready for bed.

Why? Where does this voice come from? What are you telling me? Is it God or my conscience?

He lay back on the pillow.

Yea, though I walk through the valley of the shadow of death, I will fear no evil: for thou art with me; thy rod and thy staff they comfort me.[4]

It was 2:19 a.m. when Warren fell asleep.

Kathryn's morning was typical. She managed to get on her feet, feed Angela, and make it to the diner for the seven o'clock shift. Breakfast was well under way, and she walked in to find a crowded breakfast counter.

In short order, she donned an apron and got two pots of coffee brewing to replace the empties. In the mirror behind the coffee makers, she saw a familiar face enter the door. She had two orders to take and three empty coffee cups to refill. She was on counter duty until 11:00. Then she would move to the tables in the back. Luckily the customers were regulars, so the orders were quick and easy. She anticipated filling the empty coffee cups and moving to the far end of the counter to grab a glass of juice for herself.

---

[4] Psalms 23:4 (KJV).

Instead, she stepped right in line with the stool that had just become available. Warren Treallor was shifting into place.

"Good morning, Kathryn."

"Good morning, Mr. Treallor." A lump formed in her throat. She didn't know where to look. His eyes held hers momentarily.

"Coffee, please."

"Of course."

Kathryn went about her work, hoping nothing unusual would happen.

Twenty minutes passed. Another waitress had taken care of Warren's order. He wasn't sure if that was on purpose, if Kathryn had stepped out of the way, or if it was just by chance that his stool was not part of her section. Warren stood up to leave. He leaned in when Kathryn was within hearing distance.

"Do you have a break soon?"

"Not usually until 10:15. But I can ..."

"Don't. I don't want you to jeopardize anything. I can stop back later. Lunch?"

"Okay. Yes, I usually eat at 1:30. Is that okay?"

"I'll make it work."

The rest of the morning was filled with anxiety as Kathryn tried to focus on her work. She spilled drinks, dropped a clean dish that broke on the tile floor, and nearly gave a customer the wrong change, having caught herself before closing the register drawer. That little mishap with a saving moment pushed her into the realization that just maybe she needn't worry. *Dear God, please help me to be present in my service to these customers today. I need you to be ever with me. Amen.*

Warren drove by the Husting estate. He couldn't avoid driving down the tree-lined driveway and around the circle drive.

Something drew him there again. He could feel Robert's presence as soon as he reached the front of the mansion. *Just a short walk.*

He got out of the truck and moved slowly onto the front porch. Warren always believed this place should have been Ronnie's.

His cell phone buzzed in his pocket. It was Rob.

"Dad?"

"Hi, Rob! How are you this morning?"

"Well, pretty tired. I got up early, hoping to catch you before you're on a project site. Was I successful?"

"You were. What's up?"

"Well, I really needed to talk with you. And I kind of blew it by bringing Kathryn and Angela with me last night."

"No problem. We can still find a time to talk."

"Can we meet now?"

Warren rescheduled his first stop to the end of the day. Within thirty minutes he and Rob were sitting in a coffee shop. Rob was clearly uncomfortable. Warren didn't know what to expect.

"Dad, I don't know what to say here, but I really want to be with Kathryn and Angela. She's been in a tough spot, and I don't want her to think I'm taking advantage of her at all. She's really vulnerable right now."

Warren just listened, nodded, and asked a couple of questions designed to keep Rob talking. By the end of their visit, Rob seemed to have worked through his problems on his own. He just needed Warren to be there for him. Warren had played this role many times. The father–son relationship was healthy and allowed Warren to know his son well enough to make the right suggestions at the right time.

Today, Warren was pleased to know that Rob planned to be a good friend to Kathryn for as long as she needed. Warren only needed to remind Rob of his and Leslie's agreement to support his choice to leave school for one year to give Rob time to solidify his decision. There was no threat. Rob had already worked through the possibility of paying his own way if his father disagreed with him. Instead, something told him it was time to stay the course.

"Rob, I have to tell you that I went by the diner this morning where Kathryn works."

"And?"

"I'm going to have lunch with her."

"Why?"

"There's something about her that I just need to figure out. Please trust me."

"Dad! Why are you digging into my business?"

"I'm not. I'm digging into my own business."

Rob just stared at his father in disgust.

"Look, Son. This isn't anything I can talk about right now. But when the time is right, I will definitely share everything with you."

Rob just shook his head.

"I know this seems unusual and out of keeping with our typical relationship. But, Son, I need you to trust me on this one."

"Okay, Dad."

"And please, this is only between the two of us."

"Meaning?"

"I don't want you to say anything to Kathryn to tip her off that I need to learn something from her."

"Okay. I guess I can do that."

"And please don't tell your mother or Adrienne anything."

"Our secret?"

"Our secret."

The two stood up to leave, and Rob slapped his father on the shoulder. Warren took that as a good sign.

Rob was confused, but he was glad to know that his father trusted him this way. They both had things to figure out.

———　❧　———

Betty was peeking out of the sidelight when Warren's truck pulled into the circle. She had heard the vehicle approaching. Since no one was expected at the mansion, she was careful to stay hidden. When Warren got out of the truck, she had a clear view of him. She felt herself gasp a breath. It took all her restraint to stop from throwing open the door and calling out to him.

When Warren answered his phone and climbed back in his truck, Betty felt relief and sadness wrapped together. Her eyes filled as a small smile came upon her. James put his hand on her shoulder. A series of short breaths in through her nose helped to suppress a full burst of tears.

"Come on, Betty. Let's drive into the country."

Betty followed him. Locking the doors and gathering up her personal effects, she walked in solemn resolve to make this mansion go away once and for all. It was filled with too many memories to be of any good to her psyche. It was time to move on.

Warren pulled his truck into the diner lot at 1:30 p.m. Kathryn walked out and climbed in the passenger side.

"What would you like to eat?"

"I don't eat much. Just a piece of fruit would be fine."

"Seems to me you need more than that if you want to be healthy for that beautiful angel of yours."

Kathryn felt frozen.

"Let's go to the market on the corner. We'll pick some things up and head to the riverfront or park."

"Oh, we can stop at one of the little bistros on the riverfront. I mean, if that's better for you. I have forty-five minutes. That should be enough time."

Warren took the cue to give this young woman a little bit of a treat this lunchtime. Clearly she was not used to having nice lunches anywhere in the area. *My treat. Probably used to grabbing whatever the diner manager will give her.*

When they were settled in with food and cool drinks, Warren broached the reason for his visit.

"Kathryn, you and Rob knew one another in high school."

"We did."

"Tell me what happened after high school. Did you two keep in touch?"

"Oh no. I pretty much ran off."

Kathryn told her story to Warren, even the stories of Marcus. She cried. She recovered. She cried again.

"Kathryn, I'm really sorry to hear all of this."

"I know. And you don't want Rob's life to be ruined. Don't worry. I wouldn't do that."

"No. That's not it."

"You should be worried about Rob. He's a really nice guy, too good for someone like me. I know better."

"Kathryn, stop. Don't belittle yourself. You've had some unfortunate turns. We're not that different."

Kathryn looked at him in awe. *Is this man telling me something? Is Rob not his real son? Does Rob know?*

"Don't let your mind run wild, okay? I have some things in my past, long before I married Rob's mother and we had our family. There was someone in my past whom I admired greatly. She never thought I was good enough for her. We were from very different economic backgrounds. In fact, I worked on the property her father owned. I had to let her go."

Kathryn looked at him quizzically.

"I just want you to know that you are a lovely young lady. You have a beautiful little girl, an angel from what I can see. Don't ever feel that you are less than great in God's eyes. He loves you."

"Oh, Mr. Treallor! Thank you! I do know that." She talked faster with excitement. "See, I started out at the Saint Mary's of the Immaculate Conception shelter in Baltimore. They helped me through the birth of Angela. And yes, she is my angel—that's why I named her Angela. Those people were so kind to me. And Rob is an extension of that. He is a godsend to me. I just know it." She spoke with passion, moving her head from side to side, never breaking eye contact.

Warren knew this young woman was special. "You stay strong. You'll make it through this time."

Warren got Kathryn back to work in time and headed on to his appointments for the day. But the challenge he'd received from Robert plagued him. *What is Robert telling me? Or what is God telling me?*

Chapter
TWENTY-FIVE
November 2010: Thanks Be Given?

Summer extended a bit longer than usual in the mid-Atlantic region. Warren worked long hours at the two installations in Wilmington. He was anxious for the projects to finish so he could spend more time in Greenwich and working around Stamford. Leslie was patient with his traveling. She trusted that soon they would return to a normal routine.

As the work wrapped up, Warren decided it was time to share his ideas about the future. He still didn't understand what he was feeling, but the guilt of not being open with Leslie about his past and the deep love he once held for another woman was beginning to bear down heavily. On a bright day early in November, Warren convinced Leslie to drive to Delaware with him. He wanted to show her his old stomping grounds. Together, he wanted to tour the former Husting mansion and open the conversation of purchasing the property. It would be a very challenging conversation.

Warren had never shared with Leslie that he had received all the profits from the sale of the estate in 1967. She never knew he held all that money in the hope of someday returning to that property. And she would never know that he had originally planned to return there with Ronnie. No one needed to know his dreams; he could share his revised dream. *But is Ronnie still in the picture, Robert?*

Not only did Warren make the drive a casual outing, but also he managed to arrange a showing with Sandra Channing. Warren made it clear to Sandra that under no circumstance was his wife to know he had already looked at the mansion a few months earlier. Sandra agreed. He explained that it would be a completely new look at the mansion with his wife. All Sandra needed to know was that Warren wanted to surprise his wife. She asked no questions; he gave her no information.

They drove up the long tree-lined drive. Leslie looked in awe at the tall poplars that canopied the naturally wooded land. Streams of sunlight made their way through the branches, creating alternating shadows and bright beams on Leslie's face.

"This is beautiful, Warren." Leslie was inspired by the serenity of the place.

"Yeah. It really is." He didn't want to reveal more than necessary.

They drove the rest of the way in silence. Perhaps for the first time in a very long time, Warren sensed a fondness for his wife that had been missing during his many trips. *She deserves more.*

As they rounded the last bend, the circular drive came into sight.

"Uhhhh." Leslie breathed out audibly.

"She's beautiful, isn't she?"

"The house or the real estate agent?"

"Come on, Les. You know me better than that."

"Sorry. She is quite attractive though. And so is the house."

"In real estate terms, this is a mansion."

Leslie and Warren walked up the steps to meet Sandra. *Lizzie. Who are you, really?* Warren shook hands as if he had never met Sandra before; he let his eyes lock with hers for a moment. Leslie introduced herself, and Sandra acted as the professional she was. With that exchange, the tour began.

Two hours later, Leslie's head was full of ideas about the

property and how it could be opened as a home for people who needed respite, or for indigents, or for the elderly, or, or, or ... Warren was depleted. *What about us? Why not open this home for us and our family? We could live here and enjoy the life I wanted. Of course our community service would continue.* He didn't say a word. He listened. His lower lip curled under as he nodded at Leslie's ideas. Sandra gave the first response.

"Well, I think the two of you have some things to talk about. In the meantime, here is my card. Can I answer any questions now?"

"I don't think so, Sandra. Leslie and I do need to think about quite a few things. This is a huge step for us."

"I understand. Well, it was nice meeting both of you. I'm going back in to be sure everything is locked up."

"Of course." Leslie extended her hand for a final shake.

Warren nodded and said his goodbyes.

The ride out of the estate property was very quiet. Sandra asked two questions, one related to how the couple could possibly afford such a huge piece of property and all that goes with the maintenance, and the other about why Warren would move out of his IT work and retire to such a huge undertaking as starting some kind of shelter.

Maybe Leslie and I have grown apart; maybe it wasn't just my travel.

"Tell you what. Before we leave town, let's try to connect with Rob!"

"Oh yes! That would be the frosting on the day! I'll text him." Leslie shifted gears.

As they drove to town, Warren was hit with a horrible understanding: *Sandra Channing. Dr. Michael Channing. Kathryn. Rob's Kathryn. Kathryn's Angela is Sandra's granddaughter.*

His palms were sweaty. The beautiful scenery became scary and suffocating with heavy trees bowing overhead. Leslie was talking about all the rooms, the outbuildings, the pond, and all kinds of possible day retreats for families that they could host on the property. She was thinking about staff who could live on the property to work as medical support, counselors, dieticians, and other service people. All Warren could hear was a voice—no words, just noise.

Twenty minutes outside the estate, Warren found a reason to stop at a convenience store. He left the truck without saying a word. Leslie didn't know what to make of his quick exit, so she slid out the passenger door and went in with him. They each selected a cold drink with no conversation. Warren chugged his and headed back to the truck.

"Are you upset with me?" Leslie almost had to run to keep up with him.

God help me. "I'm fine. Let's just get to Rob."

Sandra called the listing agent to let her know about the recent showing at the Husting estate. The agent was shocked to learn that anyone would think of turning those beautiful grounds into anything other than a grand family homestead. She alerted Sandra that it would be necessary to check into all of the zoning laws. It had never occurred to her that the property might be transformed into something so ordinary. With no shame whatsoever, the agent told Sandra that this purchase would be blasphemous, but she would do her due diligence. The seller would need to sign off on such a crazy idea.

Warren received this information almost immediately from Sandra.

"No need to investigate on my behalf, Sandra. We won't be

purchasing the property under these circumstances. If anything, it will be my home."

"Well, that's a relief."

"Why would you care? I don't mean to be crude, but it's just a business transaction to you."

Sandra hesitated. Warren could feel the tension over the phone.

"Well, yes and no."

"You don't live near there. You weren't a part of the Delaware real estate circles until this place was on your client's list. At least that's the story I remember from the first time I saw you there." *But you're not coming clean with me. You know something.*

"Yeah. Well, maybe there's more. And maybe I should tell you now."

"Do tell! I can't believe you've been so quiet." *God, guide my words.*

"Let's just say that at one time ..." She paused. "Well, I may have been to that place a couple of times. When someone was living there."

"Who did you visit? A friend? A relative?"

"Well." Sandra paused and then spoke with a fresh idea: "You do know it has been leased out for many years, right?"

"Uh-huh."

"Yeah, so there were lots of opportunities. I'll leave it there."

Warren decided to let it go. Eventually the truth would be known. This couldn't be it. *She visited friends there? No. Who is this woman?*

Sandra's shoulders relaxed as the conversation concluded with plans for Warren to get in touch in a couple of weeks. Sandra agreed to contact him if anyone else showed real interest in the property. This was a new arrangement, and Warren was thankful that she finally wanted to work *for* him. He concluded the phone call with a wry smile on his face. *We'll get to the bottom of this, Mrs. Channing.*

Thanksgiving arrived with much fanfare in the Treallor household. Rob had returned to school in the fall after less than three
months of summer experiential learning. What he'd learned serving homeless people for a philanthropic organization was enough
to confirm his thinking about what kind of work he wanted to do.
Meeting up with Kathryn had helped him sort things out. He
believed now that he needed to follow in his mother's footsteps.
She served needy people with joy and commitment. His decision
was to pursue a career in counseling, possibly child psychology.
The dean at Boston College welcomed him back with great satisfaction, and course work for a major in psychology with a minor
in early childhood learning filled his fall schedule. By all accounts,
he felt firm in his choice. He was keeping up with Kathryn and
hoping to see her sometime during the holiday season.

Adrienne was in an education preparation program at the
University of Wisconsin. She spoke passionately of the need for
people to understand brain development and how people learn.
Her latest project included research on current trends of technology used directly for student learning in classrooms. A pilot
school at Madison was being established, and in the spring semester, even as a freshman, she was going to have an opportunity
to observe teachers guiding student learning with technology in a
class of students with special needs. She was so enthusiastic about
her learning that no one wanted to change the topic.

Warren and Leslie were the ever-present parents for their
two kids who were in the peak years of figuring out just who they
wanted to be and what they wanted to contribute to the world.
They were very proud parents.

Warren was aware that just around the corner from the Treallor
household, perhaps a few miles away, was the Channing household. With recent connections in Wilmington over the Husting

estate, Warren confirmed where Sandra lived and practiced her profession. He thought it odd that they hadn't bumped into one another around the small Greenwich community. He pretty much confirmed that Sandra and Michael were Kathryn's parents.

Knowing about Rob and Kathryn made Warren a little uneasy. There was no expectation about the holidays and family or friends. But somehow Warren felt skeptical that just maybe those two would connect again. The biggest question in the whole picture was whether or not Rob had convinced Kathryn to rely more on her family. At one point, Rob told his father that he encouraged Kathryn to explore the support available through them. Kathryn didn't believe that was possible, but Rob was her coach in that regard since his own family had always acted as his support system.

Turkey was roasting in the oven and filling the house with that "home is the place to be" feeling. Warren and Leslie had worked together on the vegetables and other side dishes and fixings. He claimed fame to cooking the turkey, and she set a perfect table. While the kids were still in bed, they grabbed a cup of coffee in the family room. A sense of love and warmth always radiated there. Warren looked at the hearth. Something was missing.

"What's up, love?"

Leslie rubbed Warren's shoulders as she sat down next to him on the sofa, tucking her feet up under her.

"Just thinking about a lot of things."

"Like what?"

Warren raised his eyebrows, curled his lower lip, and tipped his head to the side and back before he answered. "Well, for one thing, it's great to have the kids home, to know Rob is settled in his studies instead of looking to 'find himself' for a full year. That worried me for a while."

Leslie nodded in agreement. She realized they were both staring at a blank fireplace. "It seems like a good day for a fire. Whaddaya say?"

"Works for me. After this great cup of coffee."

Leslie snuggled closer and landed a quick kiss on Warren's cheek. He responded with a wink and a smile. Then he continued to sip.

The Channing residence was just that on this Thanksgiving Day: a residence—with no heart or soul. Sandra thumbed through real estate brochures, planning her next big property showing. In the past two years she had been more interested in selling multimillion-dollar homes than in working with the upper-middle-class folks who wanted to make their way into the Connecticut shoreline scene. The remnants of the night before were all around: a dirty glass that still smelled of Jack, an empty Snyder's pretzel bag, and a few Dove chocolate wrappers. The morning coffee was intended to help her work through the fog, and brochures were meant to be a distraction. Instead, she had a persistent headache and a nagging thought that wouldn't quit.

Warren Treallor had sent her into a tailspin. Everything about him felt oddly familiar: the way his eyes talked to her, the body language he used when he ran his hand through his hair. She had done all kinds of research but turned up nothing more than what he was willing to share with her personally. He was a great IT consultant with lots of very big accounts in the mid-Atlantic states. He lived in Greenwich and traveled the Wilmington area regularly for his work. Nothing more. No digital footprint of significance. *Smart man.*

Dr. Michael Channing was on duty in the trauma center. An accident in New York City the night before had sent a very badly injured motorist to his unit. Michael would stay until the patient's vital signs were stable. He alerted Sandra that it might be a full forty-eight hours before he could leave the hospital. That news was of no consequence. Even if the patient was stable, the train would be running on a holiday schedule with fewer runs out to Greenwich. There were no plans for Thanksgiving. Rachel was arriving later in the afternoon from Amherst. No one knew where Kathryn was these days. Sandra knew Rachel wouldn't be expecting any kind of Thanksgiving celebration. They hadn't done that in years, maybe since the girls were in elementary school.

It was time for a little more Jack Daniel's. After all, it was close to noon. Sandra made her way to the bar and started to pour.

The sound of the front door opening sent her into panic mode. "Who's here?"

No answer.

"Michael, is that you?"

She put the bottle of whiskey back in a hurry, spilling two ice cubes from the minifridge as she moved too quickly to cover up her actions. Still no answer.

Sandra decided to be quiet and just listen.

Footsteps went up the stairs, the wood floorboards creaking all the way.

Rachel was trying to surprise her parents by arriving early, but she wanted to do it by coming down the stairs, not by walking in the front door.

Sandra walked in her socked feet to the entryway. No one was there. She continued quietly through the living room to the left of the entrance, through the back hallway that led to the family room, and out the back of the family room to the rear mudroom. No one. No signs of Michael. No keys on the foyer table or on the hook next to the back door. No dried leaves from the yard having traveled in on shoes. Nothing. She rounded the corner of the hallway that led back to the front entryway. She let out a scream. "Get out!" A body was coming down the stairs.

Rachel turned around with a huge smile on her face. "Happy Thanksgiving, Ma!"

"Good Lord, Rachel. What is this all about?" She punctuated each word with staccato.

Rachel continued to be upbeat and happy. "I wanted to surprise you and Dad."

"You know better. He's at the hospital, and I'm working in my study."

Rachel felt immediate deflation. Her eyes misted. She didn't know how to respond.

"There's some stuff in the fridge, probably, if you want to eat."

Sandra turned around and headed back to the study. She poured her whiskey, no ice. She stepped in a little puddle on the floor and cursed the fact that now her sock was wet.

Rachel was sitting on the stairs contemplating whether or not this was a good idea. Her cell phone buzzed in her pocket.

She saw the caller ID and jogged up the stairs to her room.

"Kathryn?" Her voice was a whisper.

"Rachel?"

"Is this really you?"

"It's me."

"Oh my God, where are you? You haven't been in touch forever. I tried to call you. Your phone didn't work. Is this really you? It's so …"

"Stop, Rachel!"

"What? What is it? Are you okay?"

"Do you really care?"

"Kathryn, yes. Of course I do." There was a long pause. "Kathryn?"

"I'm sorry. I didn't mean that. It's just that a lot has happened since we last talked. I'm trying really hard to turn my life around. I just thought it would help to talk to you. You know, the older-sister thing."

"Well, tell me where you are."

"I'm in Greenwich."

"Oh, me too! Tell me where. I'll be right there!"

The sisters found one another at the train station. Kathryn had Angela in a knapsack on her back. She was sound asleep. When Rachel ran up to hug Kathryn, she didn't see the baby at all. When she reached around Kathryn, she felt the small body and pulled away.

"What are you doing?" There was panic in her voice.

"Whaddaya mean?"

"There's something on your back. It feels like, I don't know, like a body or something."

"It is. My baby."

Rachel's eyes filled with tears that actually flowed down her cheeks this time. Her lower lip curled, and her forehead wrinkled.

"Rache, it's okay. I'm very happy with her in my life. Her name is Angela."

Rachel had buried her face in her hands and was visibly crying now. Her shoulders shuddered with every sob.

"Rachel. Look at me." Kathryn took Rachel by the shoulders and tipped her head up so she could see her sister's face. Rachel finally looked up, this time with an upward curl to her lips.

"Ah, Rache. It's all good. We've just got some things to talk about."

Angela started to stir.

Kathryn walked to a nearby bench and began to position herself to breastfeed.

Rachel looked at the beautiful baby in her sister's arms. "What a beautiful little angel."

Angela was dressed in a yellow bunting that showed only her face and two wisps of baby hair on her forehead. Her eyes were almond shaped, and her rosy cheeks were separated by a delicate nose. Pink lips were pursed in a circle, opening and closing softly with little murmurs. Rachel was mesmerized. When Angela opened her eyes, long lashes lifted her upper lids wide. Rachel felt her own eyes filling with tears. She reached out to touch the light brown curls on Angela's face. "You are the most beautiful angel." She turned and hugged Kathryn. The two sisters embraced one another with Angela in the center of it all.

The ride back to the Channing house was quiet. But Kathryn did take the opportunity to tell Rachel why she was in town.

"I've learned a lot about myself in a very short period, Rache. And I just needed to see my family. Now. On Thanksgiving."

"Yeah. I needed that too. To see Mom and Dad and maybe have a nice day together."

Rachel's tone of voice said it all. Kathryn got the point: no family dinner, no family day.

They pulled into the garage. Rachel was careful to park her mother's car exactly where she had found it. The two walked through the back mudroom, Angela in Kathryn's arms, sleeping once again. Rachel carefully returned the car keys to their rightful place, and the two made their way up the stairs to the bedrooms.

"Mom is probably still nursing Jack in the study."

Both of them laughed. Sister language was back. Kathryn felt a warm, admiring appreciation of her sister for the first time in a very long time.

Rachel suggested that Kathryn get settled into her old bedroom with Angela while she made her way downstairs to figure out what was going on.

Angela was small enough to fit in a dresser drawer, so Kathryn emptied her old T-shirts and gym shorts from the bottom of her dresser. She lined the drawer with towels from the connected bathroom and covered those with a pillowcase. Angela fit perfectly. Kathryn made sure the child was warm—but not too warm—and cozy, but not with fluffy pillow-like cushioning that could cause problems for breathing.

When the bedding was just right, she kneeled on the floor and admired her handiwork, both the little angel and the bedding. *Thank you, dear Lord, for blessing me in this way.*

A light knock pulled her from the floor.

Rachel was motioning Kathryn to join her. "Just leave the door open so we can hear the baby, and follow me."

They proceeded downstairs to the kitchen. Rachel had found the "some food in the fridge" that her mother had referred to. It was a box filled with catered food for Thanksgiving: turkey, mashed potatoes, carrots, green beans, a salad, and rolls. The two of them got to work heating the meal and setting the table.

Kathryn set the table for four just in case. *Maybe Mom does expect a Thanksgiving dinner after all.*

A blip on the monitor caught the nurses by surprise. Two nurses ran to room 2A. One stayed behind to contact the doctor on call. Another continued monitoring all the screens in DuLoche's trauma unit. It had been twenty-seven months; no one wanted to pull the plug. No one seemed to remember that this woman was in a coma. She had no family and no friends—no one. She was considered dead.

There was a rapid beat on the heart monitor and a flutter on the respiratory monitor.

Daddy. Sorry.

Nothing.

All monitors lulled back to their original readings.

Thirty minutes later, the doctor reported no change of significance.

Back to duty as usual.

Betty and James snuggled by the fireplace in the guesthouse, an often-forgotten outbuilding near the pond at the very back of the Husting property.

"What will you do when this place finally sells?"

"What will *we* do?"

James smiled in reply.

Betty picked up without missing a beat. "Well, I think that we'll get Ware back here." James didn't respond, so she kept on with her thoughts. "I don't know if I can stand up to everything and stay around—come clean, so to speak. Or if I'll have to book out of town. Not sure."

James didn't reply. He let Betty think on her own words for a few minutes. They were sipping on an after-dinner sweet wine. Betty had prepared a wonderful Thanksgiving dinner, though not particularly traditional. The appetizers were roasted chestnuts right from the property. She had cooked a flank steak laden with butter and garlic and used it to create finger sandwiches on soft potato bread. Neither of them felt deprived of turkey and all the fixings. Instead, they were pleased with their own version of Thanksgiving.

Neither was sure they were thankful for their current state of affairs. Neither could admit that they had failed to make a financial success of the property. Both were disappointed in the condition of the estate and were more than happy to take advantage of Alejandro, now known by Betty to actually be Frederick Whatton, and his deep pockets to get things in good repair for sale.

"Maybe we should try to leave before the estate sells. Go to the hills of California and enjoy more sunshine year-round."

Again, James was careful. "That would be nice, wouldn't it? But what about this place that you worked so hard to keep going all this time? You've invested more than time and money here. Do you really want to give it up?"

"Not sure. What if Veronica *had* owned this place? What would have happened then?"

James just shook his head. "She was a sweetheart. Too bad what happened."

"Mm-hmm." *I did a good job.*

They both laughed and sipped more wine. Betty and James couldn't have been thinking more differently.

———— ᥫᥬ ————

Another blip on the monitors. It had been three days.

This time, signs were reaching normal activity levels. This person was waking up!

Nurses, doctors, everyone, ran to 2A. The patient sat up in the bed.

"Daddy? Ware? Are you near?"

The nurses encouraged her not to worry about where she was, saying that they would take care of her and get what she needed.

Ronnie lay back down and closed her eyes. A smile came across her face.

It was a Sunday. A television station was audible, and Ronnie heard the words of a preacher praying: "Father in heaven, you have shown us love. You have tried to teach us about love. You sent your only Son in love. Bring to us your Holy Spirit this day. Let us feel love for Christ, and shine in our hearts abundant love, for without that, we have nothing. Amen."

"Amen."

A nurse swung back around at that last amen. "Mrs. Whatton? Are you awake now?"

"Amen! Wonderful love." Ronnie's voice was clear and powerful.

Staff were surrounding the bed, checking vitals, watching, and waiting. The church service continued in the background:

"But someone may ask, 'How are the dead raised? With what kind of body will they come back to us?' How foolish! What you sow does not come to life unless it dies."

"Dead; raised. Amen." Ronnie moved her head from side to side. "Ware."

"God bless you, my dear Veronica Emma-Mae."

Daddy? You're here! I'm sorry.

A doctor had come into the room. "Mrs. Whatton, please try to open your eyes."

Ronnie responded. The examination continued, and miracles were being witnessed.

"Call Dr. Channing." The lead doctor was ready to talk to the family.

Kathryn and Rachel felt lucky to reconnect. Kathryn shared her newfound love in God; Rachel detected the spark for life that her little sister had shown when they were small. She was a happy child who didn't have a care. Kathryn had a way of embracing life in ways that Rachel never felt free enough to experience. On the other hand, Kathryn took that free spirit a little too far and caused some heartbreak for everyone in the family. Rachel was pleasantly surprised with her little sister and more than in love with her beautiful niece, Angela.

Sandra was not quite so forgiving or understanding. In fact, she was infuriated by Kathryn's nerve at coming back to the house she had grown up in with extra baggage. The two had more than one encounter that ended in Sandra's slamming doors and drinking more whiskey. Her daughter simply snuggled with her little angel and prayed that God would see her through the next steps of reconciling with her family. She credited Rob Treallor with having given her the strength to take the first steps and the means to take action when she was ready. More than anything, Rachel admired Kathryn's approach.

Michael was more understanding of Kathryn's circumstance. He was happy to have her home, safe on his watch. He was also proud to have a beautiful granddaughter to nurture with love. It was clear to him that it was time to clean up the family a little bit more. There was just the nagging feeling about a few little secrets he was keeping about Veronica's real condition.

The letter he'd retrieved from Veronica's purse on the night of her accident was beginning to burn a hole in his desk drawer. The news out of DuLoche was scary: Veronica Husting was returning to life. Not what he'd expected at all. If anything, Michael was sure that Veronica would die. He so much as told Sandra that she was already dead. For all practical purposes, she was.

There was not a clue on this earth that Veronica would turn back the events of that accident. She had lost way too much blood. The coma seemed like a graceful way of dying with less pain and family suffering. But what did he know? He wasn't calling the shots on life and death; he left that to someone else. He turned the case over to other very capable doctors.

"Dad, what do you think about this idea for a Christmas present for Mom? I'd like to do a family tree."

"Oh, that might be a good idea. What makes you think of that now?"

"Well, now that I have a baby, and with Mom so upset with me about it, I just wonder if maybe showing her the family line might help smooth things a little bit."

Michael thought for a few minutes. He nodded thoughtfully. "So you're thinking about her side of the family? The Hustings?"

"Yeah. No? Not a good idea?"

"No. I actually think it is a good idea. She's been looking into the family estate lately, the one that was her grandfather's in Wilmington. I think it's on the market, and she showed it to one of her clients. I'm not sure how far all of that went, but it seems like it must have brought some kind of nostalgia to her. Maybe this would be a good thing."

"Can you help me a little bit?"

"How?"

The two of them started planning. Rachel was soon involved. They worked by the family room fire, little Angela snuggled in Michael's arms while the girls drew out a tree and made a plan for artistic display of their findings with Michael giving them ideas and what little information he knew. The Sunday afternoon soon became evening. Sandra never came out of the study; she had no idea what was brewing.

Michael managed to stay focused with his daughters and granddaughter. But he felt distracted. The baby showed signs of physical deformity that were becoming more apparent as time passed. He wondered if there was something about Kathryn that he didn't know. Kathryn seemed fine, but the baby definitely wasn't fine. Only his medical perspective would notice the characteristics that would take time to fully present.

Michael never mentioned the letter he was holding. He never spoke of Veronica at all. His own plans were not yet settled. He didn't know if he would try to find Warren Treallor before Veronica was fully ready for release from the hospital. He'd received several contacts from the DuLoche unit, and he was able to postpone going there or talking to Sandra. The big question was whether to contact Treallor or let it go. The letter remained sealed.

Kathryn eventually retreated to her room with Angela. Michael used the time probe a little bit.

"So, Rachel, how are things going for you?"

"Good, Dad. Why do you ask?"

"Oh, I don't know. Seems like you and Kathryn have a lot of lost time to recover."

"Eh, not really. She's the same Kathryn she always was."

Michael didn't answer right away. That's not what he was seeing at all. Kathryn seemed very different to him. He was worried about the baby's health and well-being, and he had never seen a nurturing moment from Kathryn in her whole life. Until now.

"Can you explain that to me a little bit?"

Rachel described Kathryn from the inside out. She didn't start with the decisions Kathryn had made to abandon a good college opportunity in return for living a life she wanted. She didn't show any sibling rivalry. She simply described Kathryn as a person who always sought out the right life for herself and mentioned that now she had found it. "I think she's really religious now, Dad."

"How so?"

"Well, do you remember her talking about a guy from high school named Rob Treallor?"

Michael took a deep breath. He forced himself to act casually. "Not sure. Who is that?"

As the words streamed from Rachel's face, all Michael saw was a blur of moving lips. *Rob Treallor. It can't be so. Treallor. Warren Treallor. A friend of my own family?*

"So, anyway, they reconnected when Kathryn was really down. She was in a homeless shelter and working for a diner in Wilmington. Rob helped her out. He even made sure she had her cell phone back so she could call us when she was ready."

"I can't bear to hear all of this. Your sister? Why didn't I know?"

"What would you have done differently, Dad?"

Michael was aghast. "What?! What would I have done?!"

Rachel was shocked that her father actually had strong emotions about things like this. She had assumed all along that she and Kathryn were expected to lead their own lives, fight their own battles, find their own way. Maybe she was wrong.

The baby let out a cry.

Kathryn's followed. "Rachel! Help me!"

Rachel and Michael found Kathryn cradling Angela on the floor. The little body was trembling. Blood slowly streamed from her nose, and her eyes rolled into her head.

_____ *Chapter* _____

TWENTY-SIX
— DECEMBER 2010: MYSTERIES UNFOLD —

Friday, December 3, 2010

A red bar scrolled across the top of the television screen. It read as follows:

> Breaking news. … Small plane owned by movie producer Frederick Whatton crashes in hills of Santa Monica, killing four people from the Delaware Valley. Details at 7:00 p.m.

Warren caught the banner while he was preparing a fire in the fireplace. Leslie was due home soon to enjoy the quiet Friday night they had planned. Pizza, beer, reading. *Whatton. Veronica's husband!* He fell back onto the couch. *Did Ronnie live? Where is she?*

"Hi, honey! I'm home."

Warren was in shock. He hit the TV remote as an instant reaction to Leslie's voice. He ran his hand through his hair and stood up. Sweat beaded on his forehead; he felt clammy. Leslie strolled into the family room. "Hi! How are you?" She walked around the back of the brown leather couch to kiss Warren quickly, balancing a pizza in one hand with a purse dangling from her other wrist and keys hanging from her fingers. "Did you pick up some of my favorite beer?"

Pull it together.

"Oh, yeah. Of course! I wouldn't forget our favorite date night beverage!"

Be calm. Warren moved toward the hearth, picked up the fire poker, and opened the screen. "I just need to get this fire perfect."

"Looks perfect to me." Leslie put the pizza on the coffee table. "I'll get everything else and change into some jeans. Be right back."

"Yeah, okay." Warren hung his head and breathed out heavily. *Ronnie.*

Leslie returned in what seemed a matter of seconds. She was carrying paper plates and napkins.

"I'll take care of the drinks." Warren left the room. He needed just a few minutes without Leslie. He needed to collect himself. *Don't seem too anxious. The 7:00 p.m. news—one hour to wait.*

Saturday, December 4, 2010
From the *New York City Daily*

> Yesterday, in unexpected circumstances, the private jet of Frederick Whatton went down in the hills of Santa Monica, California. Four of the five people on board were killed in what has been called "the perfect storm." A flight plan was filed at the Santa Monica private airport. The log indicated the six-passenger Eclipse 500 jet was in flight to Mexico City. The vessel was the last to take off from the airport on Friday afternoon, when winds picked up unexpectedly. All small jets were grounded beginning at 4:00 p.m. local time. The crash is considered accidental, though investigations are under way.

From *Los Angeles News Today*:

> Late yesterday afternoon, the private jet of
> Frederick Whatton, movie producer, was
> downed in what may have been a windstorm.
> Four people on board were killed, none from the
> area. Whatton was not on board. Investigators
> are looking into the crash. The six-passenger jet
> was the last to leave the Santa Monica private
> airport. Others were grounded because of high
> winds. The pilot survived the crash.

From the *Washington Writer*:

> Friday afternoon, the private jet of Frederick
> Whatton, movie producer, crashed in the hills
> outside Santa Monica, California. Whatton was
> not on board. Four people from the Wilmington,
> Delaware, area were killed in the crash. The pi-
> lot survived. Flight plans indicate the jet was
> expected to land in Mexico City. Investigators
> are looking at other reasons for the Eclipse 500
> to have crashed as this same aircraft has been
> known to fly in heavy winds without consequence
> in the past.

From the *Inquirer News*:

> Frederick Whatton, movie producer who stays
> out of the limelight, gave a trusted employee
> access to a six-passenger jet. The pilot, Randy

Bastien, worked for Whatton for many years, serving as personal pilot and occasional chauffeur. Randy is the grandson of Dwight and Nancy Bastien, both killed in the crash. Dwight Bastien, age eighty-six, was a cousin of the late Robert Husting, manufacturing executive. Nancy Bastien, age eighty-three, worked for Husting Manufacturing and was transferred to Los Angeles after the death of Robert Husting. Dwight and Nancy Bastien were the parents of Donald Bastien, CFO of Husting Manufacturing.

The jet was carrying cargo and four passengers to Mexico City, according to the flight plan filed at the Santa Monica private airport on Friday afternoon, December 3. Two others killed in the crash include Carolyn Leeder and Margaret Leeder Bastien, mother and daughter. Caroline Leeder, age eighty-seven, was a well-known jazz and scat singer in the 1940s, performing in many East Coast venues, including prestigious private clubs in the greater metropolitan New York area. Her daughter, Margaret, age sixty-five, was the daughter of deceased manufacturing mogul Robert Husting, wife of Donald Bastien, and mother of Randy Bastien. The relationship between Frederick Whatton and the Leeders is unknown.

People close to pilot Bastien report that the flight was intended to help the passengers get out of the country on Whatton's request. Reasons for leaving the country were somewhat vague, but Bastien indicated the need to prevent them from talking to the press about Whatton's dealings in another business that is undisclosed. Bastien is recovering from minor injuries and is expected to be released from a nearby hospital within days. Sources say that Randy Bastien has worked for Whatton for the past fifteen years as a private pilot, making frequent trips to Mexico City. The purposes of these flights is being investigated further.

The *Inquirer News* has identified Alejandro Basil Stanis as the owner of the plane that was used as Whatton's private jet. There is speculation that Stanis may have connections to Whatton's business dealings in Mexico. Sources continue to seek information on Stanis, who at this time remains unknown among our film industry connections.

Betty poured a second cup of coffee and flipped off the coffee maker. James was reading the *Inquirer News*. Flipping pages, unaware of specific headlines, sipping the final drops of coffee in his own cup, he did a double take when he reached page 4.

Betty, having heard the pages stop, turned to read over his shoulder. The cup dropped from her hand and shattered on the tile floor. "It can't be."

James didn't say a word.

Betty held the edge of the small breakfast table and sat down in the chair facing the window overlooking the backyard. "It can't."

James blinked a few times and read the article again, carefully. *Cousin to the late Robert Husting ... Nancy Bastien ... Carolyn Leeder ... Margaret Leeder Bastien ... Alej?* The past flashed before his eyes. He remembered the beautiful Carolyn and her little daughter, Margaret, many years ago staying at the Husting estate. And then there was Dwight and Nancy. *All connected with Frederick Whatton? Alej Stanis Basil—Betty's ex-husband. Carolyn Leeder, Miss Ronnie's hated half-sister. Always trying to get Husting's money.*

"Betty."

She turned to look at him, tears welling up in her eyes.

"What don't I know?" James was very serious.

Her head hung down. Tears ran down her cheeks.

Silence.

James got up from the table. He stared at his cup for a moment then walked out the back door. No coat. No hat. He just walked straight out to the open land along the pond and looked up at the cold December sky. He began to shiver.

What sin have I committed, O Lord? Forgive me. What is Betty doing? Did she try to kill Miss Ronnie? With me?

Betty appeared at his side just as James fell to his knees on the cold ground. She wrapped his coat over his shoulders and rubbed his back between his bony shoulder blades. "Shh."

James could not be consoled. He shook, and his tears streamed, as he repeated over and over, "What have I done? Why didn't I know? Forgive me. O Lord in heaven, forgive me."

Betty had regained her composure. She needed to be the strong one as always. Her own tears were present, but she controlled her emotions.

"Look, James. There's no way you could have known the Leeders were connected with Frederick! How could you?"

"You tell me, Betty!" Anger boomed from James's body; he was shaking and sweating, and veins stood out on his neck. "How could *you*?!"

Betty turned and walked back to the guesthouse.

James continued to sob.

She opened the door to the guesthouse just as the snow started to fall. Her path changed. Closing the door, she turned and made her way to the mansion. Pulling the key from a nail behind a shutter where it had lived for nearly seventy years, she opened the kitchen door. She made her way to the pantry that contained those clean—very clean—glasses, the glasses that she used to serve ABS iced tea. Reaching high onto the back shelf, Betty found the one glass that had done the first deed in a long list of conniving acts. Alejandro, her love, led her to all kinds of things. *How could I? What now?*

She pictured herself in orange. Maybe black and white.

Ware. Daddy. I need you now.

The glass fell from her grip and smashed on the hard floor. She took the remaining three glasses and threw them down as well. A tear fell as she turned away. Glass shards crunched beneath her feet.

She wandered through the empty building, letting the reality of her life sink in. She ran her hand over the sideboard that once held trays of pastries every morning in the dining room; felt the fabric of the heavy drapes; looked at the carpets that had seen so many guests come and go; breathed in the scent of bouquets of roses on the tables in the sitting room; and touched the velvet furniture—just soaking it all in.

Why have I committed these crimes? She cried out, "Alej, I love you! Where are you now?!"

Warren and Leslie pulled in the drive. The snow was falling hard for this time of year. Their Saturday morning started with breakfast out and a few Christmas errands. As they walked into the house, arms full of grocery sacks and pharmacy bags, Ware formulated a reason to be on his own for a little while.

"I need to run into town, stop at the hardware store. We should replace some of those outside lights."

Leslie bought his excuse without a second thought.

The evening news and morning headlines brought full-blown anxiety to Warren. Standing outside the hometown hardware store, he let the news of yesterday's plane crash in California bounce around in his head. The snow landed on his shoulders and covered his hair with white flakes that melted. The white beauty weighed heavily on him. His mind was racing. Thoughts of Ronnie's half-sister and almost stepmother left him in shock. *And Dwight? Randy? Did I ever meet Randy? Nancy. Where is Ronnie? My Ronnie.*

"Hey—you're in a bad spot, man! I'm trying drive through here!" someone yelled out of a car window.

"Sorry." *Thanks for bringing me back, dude.*

Warren shuffled out of the main thoroughfare of the parking lot. Shaking off the beauty, he walked into the store to buy something, anything, just to show Leslie he really had come to the hardware store. But he walked out empty-handed.

The radio reminded him of all the details of the crash as he drove back to his home, tucked away along the winding roads of Greenwich. Pine boughs were heavy with wet snow, and the roof was white with it, but by the time he parked the truck, the snow turned to rain.

Betty finished her tour, exited through the kitchen door, and returned to the guesthouse. No James. She gathered up two quilts, his coat, and a hat—and the handgun from the trunk in the corner. The snow still fell, but it tapered. The forecast called for rain to begin in the early afternoon. She made her way back to James. She found him just as she had left him, on the ground near the pond. The sobbing had stopped. He stared blankly into the frigid water. The snow that landed on his shoulders left wetness. Betty reached out in front of him, offering a quilt and the hat. He took both and wrapped himself. He put the hat on his head and looked up into Betty's eyes.

"Why?"

Betty only wrapped a quilt around herself and sat down on the cold ground next to him. There were no words to answer James. After a long silence, James had to ask.

"What have I been involved in, Betty? Can you tell me that much?"

"Two, James."

He only shook his head slowly, knowing completely what she meant.

"So, Ronnie too, huh?"

No response.

Betty let her head drop to her knees and began to sob.

James picked himself up off the ground, wrapped the quilt and extra coat around himself, and walked to the mansion, leaving Betty alone.

He retrieved the same key from the same spot and made his way through the kitchen. Betty kept the kitchen immaculate. He could smell morning coffee and baking breakfast pastries, the cinnamon that had wafted throughout. A few steps revealed glass shards, but he didn't respond. The walk through the dining room filled him with sounds of Ronnie's laughter, visions of her pretty little-girl dresses, and Robert Husting sitting at the head of the table. The third birthday, the day Ronnie had to grow up. The scene brought haunting sadness, and James felt the need to get out of the mansion. He exited as fast as he could.

Leslie was sitting in the kitchen reading the morning paper when Warren returned. She sipped on a coffee, but otherwise she seemed engrossed in a story. Warren avoided eye contact and skirted around the table toward the hallway leading to the family room.

"Wait. Warren, did you hear this news? About the Husting family?"

His heart sped up. His coat suddenly needed to come off. "What now?" The level of tension in his voice surprised him.

"That plane crash yesterday in California that everyone's making a big deal about. Was that the Husting you said you worked for?"

"I thought the plane was owned by the movie producer. What's his name?"

Leslie filled in the missing pieces. Warren struggled to remain nonchalant.

"Not sure if those people were related to Robert. Did it say so there?"

The details were read aloud. Warren made his way to the hall coat closet, listening to every word. "Well, I guess so. Can't say I remember those names."

"I made a pot of coffee to get through the morning chores. Want some?"

"Not now. Thanks."

"Did you get what you were looking for at the hardware store?"

"Not exactly. I think I can take care of it with what we have." *Whatever that is.*

Warren made his way to the basement to shuffle some boxes around. An hour later he emerged with a string of extension cords and lights. "Leslie, I think we need to replace these."

Leslie looked at him with her head titled. "I thought you said ..."

"Yeah. Never mind. I'll go now and take care of it."

Warren left the house again. Leslie watched him drive away in the drizzle.

Sunday, December 12, 2010

Betty and James sat in the guesthouse. No Christmas tree. No decorations. It was a cold day in Wilmington. The snow was heavy and wet, and tree boughs bent near the windows. The couple huddled around the fireplace with a quilt. Both held a cup of hot coffee, serving as a hand warmer.

"What were we going to do when this estate sold, Betty?"

"What do you mean?"

"Where would we be living? What was your plan?"

Silence hung heavily. Betty didn't have the energy to go through all of this with James again. He asked the questions too often. She still hadn't given him all the details of her work with ABS. She couldn't reconcile in her own heart all that had transpired. James had been asking the questions over and over. Since he'd figured out what was going on just days earlier, he wanted to know what Betty was trying to accomplish and why he had been involved in creating two tragedies.

Yes, Alej was the love of her life and had led her down a path that turned ugly. In the end, no one knew her deeds except Alej, who directed them all. Except one. James had always sensed something about Robert's death, and he'd helped Betty arrange the car accident in Wilmington. He was part of the last act Betty had committed to get the estate back into her own hands with no threats from family. He helped her into that cottage, watched her lace cups with some special spices, and then helped her cover up the evidence after the accident.

Dwight and Nancy Bastien's ill fate was not created by Betty's own hands, but certainly by her heart and mind. Randy was an easy negotiation. Taking care of Robert Husting's illegitimate family was easy. Randy was hungry for anything to continue a drug habit. Moving in and out of Mexico, carrying drugs that did all the lethal deeds of ABS had made him wealthy enough. The added bonus of having a few of the players out of the way only made Randy's work more lucrative. Fewer pockets to line meant more profits for him.

The fact that Randy could crash a plane that killed everyone and walk away worried Betty. She struggled to figure that out. Clearly this man was a force to be reckoned with. She had no idea where this plotline would take her next. What she appreciated was the elimination of other takers of riches that were, in her thinking, rightfully hers. A little communication to get Randy on board was the easiest task she had. The Husting estate did not play into the game. She had every confidence that Randy really didn't care about the property. He was a California boy with eyes on the remainder of the ABS movie business.

"Betty, I can't go on like this. The weight of knowing I may have helped you kill Veronica is more than I can handle." The sleep James had lost over the past forty-eight hours was taking its toll on him.

Betty turned her head slowly to face James, who sat at the far end of the small couch. Their feet extended to the middle as they each leaned on opposite arms. The quilt stretched across the full length, and the small fire radiated heat on their faces. James was sullen. She could see the pull of guilt, fear, and worry in his eyes. He hadn't been eating well since that cold day when he first realized what was going on. Sunken cheeks accentuated his demeanor.

Betty just looked at him. She gave no hint of reaction, but her heart was beginning to beat a different rhythm. She felt her face flush, and it took a few deep breaths to control her words.

"James. We've had this conversation too many times."

"But I don't have answers. All I hear is that you did what was necessary to keep the estate in the family. What family, Betty? You've been trying to sell it! And you're doing away with the original family owners!"

"Think about little Sandy. What do you think Ronnie would

have done with that property? Do you think for one minute that she would have included Sandy in what was rightfully hers?"

"But you were selling it! How in the world would Sandy get the property? She isn't even around! Do you even know where to find her?"

"We have to stop this conversation now."

Betty got off the couch and moved to the little kitchen. *I should tell him that Sandy is the agent who's been showing the property to buyers.* She fussed with nothing.

James let out a heavy sigh. "I'm taking a walk."

He threw the quilt off the couch and left his coffee on the small table. Grabbing a coat and hat, he was out the back door.

Betty hung her head and watched the tears drop on the kitchen counter. *Ware, I need you.* The words were loud and clear in her mind. Someone, something, was telling her to contact her brother. Now. The words of caution in the book of Proverbs clambered through her mind, the verses she had to memorize as a child:

My son, if sinners entice thee, consent thou not.

. . .

My son, walk not thou in the way with them; refrain thy foot from their path: For their feet run to evil, and make haste to shed blood.[5]

She pulled herself up from her slump over the counter and grabbed a coat. Running out the back door with no mind to the snow on the ground, she slipped down the back steps. Her head hit the ground hard. Pain riddled her neck and shoulder. The ringing in her ears sounded like sirens. *No. Thunder. It's December. Tree limbs breaking. Crackling. Bang! Gunshot?*

She was spinning. The sounds subsided. A bit of crackling in one ear remained, but the loud fireworks ended.

Get up. If you can get up, you're okay. Betty could hear her

---

[5] Proverbs 1:10, 15–16 (KJV).

father telling her the tales and beliefs of American Indians. If you can get to your feet, you'll survive. She lifted her head, but the spinning was worse. *Breathe. Just breathe. Go slow. One thing at a time.*

Lying back again, she was able to move to her left side. Her head pounded and throbbed, but in this position the spinning subsided. The crackling noises ended. Her arm stayed pinned to her side under the weight of her body, but there was nothing to feel. She put her right hand on the ground in front of her chest and pushed up, curling her knees toward her stomach. Rotating to her knees and right hand, she managed to sit up, knees bent, one arm dangling. Then it hit her. *Paralysis. No feeling, no movement.* "God help me." The tears came. So did the snowfall.

Betty moved slowly but with every bit of determination she could muster. Scooting back to the steps, she put her body against the bottom rise, using the side handrail post as a crutch to lift herself up to her feet. Her left leg felt as if it had fallen asleep. Her left arm continued to dangle without feeling. Wiping tears and shuffling her feet to move into the backyard, Betty continued on her quest to find James. *Keep going. Find James.*

Her search took her directly to the pond on the back property where she'd always found him when he had things to think about and needed space. The walk was challenging, and the snow came down faster. At least three times, Betty stopped to lean against a tree, relieving the pain for a moment. She was driven to find James to tell him everything. Together they needed to contact Ware and tell him her whole story, including the fact that she was now the owner of the Husting estate, that Frederick Whatton was an alias for her former husband, Alejandro Basil Stanis, and that Sandy was well, selling real estate and living in his neighborhood with grandchildren he needed to know.

This is the right thing to do. James will agree. We can fix it all.

In the distance at the edge of the pond, Betty could see what looked like James lying on the ground. A lump rose in her throat, and the worst came to mind. *Heart attack.* "James! James! I'm coming," she yelled as loudly as possible. The body didn't move.

And it is the Lord's Day!

The red snow was running away from his head. The gun they kept in the guest cottage lay on the ground in front of him. Betty fell on the ground and vomited. The snow fell faster, covering the ugliness.

Tuesday, December 21, 2010

The Treallor household was full of joy, at least on the surface. Warren felt great anxiety about the upcoming events. The kids were home. Rob was spending time at the Channing home, which was nearby. He had a full-fledged relationship going with Kathryn. The nature of their friendship was not clear. There had been some tragedy at the Channings' at Thanksgiving, and since then they had been pretty close. Warren didn't know exactly what had happened, but he let Rob have his privacy on that issue. He seemed to need it.

The Christmas tree was decorated and filled the house with the scent of fresh pine. Both kids were home for almost a month, but they each had their own long list of friends to visit. They each arranged to work in a homeless shelter for mothers and children during the holiday week, just as they always did with Leslie and Warren. This year, though, Rob added to the usual family Christmas schedule.

"Dad, how would you feel about getting together with the Channings over Christmas this year?"

Warren was taken by surprise. As he poured hot chocolate for the family, Rob sprung the question without any warning. Warren didn't say a word. He just continued to help out and transferred the mugs to a tray bound for the family room.

"Dad. Did you hear me?"

"I think so."

"Yeah? You'd like to get together with them?"

"No."

"No?"

"I think I heard you, and I don't know how to respond."

Now Rob was confused. Warren gave him a smile and a nod before picking up the tray and leaving the kitchen. Rob just followed his father back to the family room.

Leslie and Adrienne sat reading. The fire was ablaze; the tree, sparkling. The tray of hot chocolate became the center of attention as each reached for their own personalized Christmas mug. Warren stared into his cup. The melting marshmallows reminded him of himself. Succumbing to the heat of the situation, his mind swirled with thoughts of being with Sandra and her family. Everything about her reminded him of Ronnie. Sweetness prevailed in those thoughts. The connection became clear to him eventually. Sandra knew something that he didn't. She had something in her background that haunted him. The fact that Sandra was out of touch with her own children, that she didn't even know Kathryn had a daughter until recently, made Warren's head spin. How could he just show up there for a Christmas get-together knowing all that he did? Besides, he felt there was a much deeper relationship there.

Is Lizzie Sandra? Is Sandra my little Sandy? Could it be? Is she actually willing to have me at her house for Christmas? It can't be possible. But she's the right age.

"Dad!"

Adrienne was trying to get Warren's attention. He just turned and looked at her with a wrinkle in his brow.

"Dad! Are you okay?"

Warren nodded. "Sure. Of course. Why?"

The rest of the family just looked at one another.

It was Leslie who rescued the moment. "Warren, you didn't respond to Rob or Adrienne's comments about the fire or the tree."

"Oh! Sorry!" Warren felt at a loss for words. He was letting his past take over again. "I was daydreaming about this hot chocolate. It's too pretty to drink!"

"Ohhhhhkay!" Adrienne started to chuckle. "You sure had me convinced you were deaf there for a few minutes!"

Warren found the humor and joined in the laughter.

But Rob came back with his question, this time to Leslie.

"So, Mom. What would you say about going to the Channings' house for Christmas? Kathryn asked me if we could all come there one night or even Christmas afternoon. It'd be great. What do you think? Dad didn't answer me."

Leslie looked at Warren and waited for a comment. None came.

"Well, Rob, it's not like they're close friends of ours or anything. I don't know if I even know Dr. Channing. I know of Kathryn and her older sister because of you. And I know Mrs. Channing is a busy real estate broker; she showed me and Dad a piece of property. Why would we go there?"

"What property?" Rob got really curious.

"Oh, just something Dad had to look at for his company. I went with him." Leslie realized she had just made a mistake. She and Warren had agreed not to include the kids in any of this past fall's conversations. Neither Warren nor Leslie was really ready to retire, and the purchase of that property in Delaware would be a way into the future. "So why would we go there?"

"Maybe for me and Kathryn?"

"Oh. So are you trying to tell us something?"

"Not really. We're really close though."

"Well, what do you think, Warren?"

"I think it would be fun to break some of our traditions a little bit!" Adrienne chimed in with her own ideas. "Plus, I think Rob and Kathryn can definitely keep the party going. They have lots of good stories to tell all of us. I vote yes."

"Warren, what do you say?" Leslie wanted to please her kids, but not without Warren's input.

"Well, how about if you get more details, Rob? Mom and I like to be with close family or good friends on holidays, and maybe the Channings feel the same way." Without waiting for a response, Warren stood up. "Anyone want more hot chocolate?" He headed back to the kitchen.

Rob turned to Leslie. "Is Dad okay?"

Leslie wondered the same thing. "He's had a lot on his mind at work over the past few months. Christmas break will be good for him."

In her mind, Leslie questioned her own response. She knew that Warren was struggling with something. He always had withheld something about his past, but lately that lack of openness was growing and presented itself much more frequently. She wondered if she was too trusting.

"He'll be fine. We should just go ahead and make plans. Get the details and let us know. I'm sure he'll agree. You know Dad; he loves to celebrate Christmas with church and food!"

They turned back to their books and mugs, and Rob pulled out a cell phone.

The wheelchair felt uncomfortable to Veronica. The seat sagged, and the side rests were too high for her bony arms. Sandra maneuvered the apparatus through the halls of the medical building. She and Michael had spent enough time fighting about the arrangements for Veronica. In the end, Michael won. Sandra now needed to make room for an invalid mother in her own world. Nothing was reconciled. Nothing felt right.

With every turn of a hallway corner, Veronica tipped to one side then the other. Sandra paid no mind. *Maybe she'll fall out.* By the time they reached the last stretch of the long hallway, Sandra decided to take a break. The abruptness of that decision caused Veronica to fall forward and slam back into the backrest. "Sandra! What are you doing?! Can't you be a little gentler with me?!"

"You heard the doctor. It's been a week since you got home. We don't have to be do doting on you so much anymore. He wants you to try walking on the walker! Why am I pushing you around? Besides, I just need a little break."

Ronnie heard the resentment in Sandy's voice. She understood. Theirs was not a good relationship at all. It had been close to forty years since the two of them were together. Until Thanksgiving weekend.

Ronnie had a new meaning for Thanksgiving. She didn't know just yet if she was actually thankful or not. Sandy and Michael were called to the hospital, but they couldn't come. Something about an emergency with some baby that Michael had to help at the hospital. And Sandy—well, she was indisposed. Two days later, Michael arrived when called. All she could remember of that time was falling in and out of sleep, trying to make sense of things she was hearing, and feeling that someone was calling her to love more deeply and to give up on her past life. Ronnie knew that she had been resurrected and would have an opportunity to make her life right.

Having spent all of one week in the Channing household, Ronnie recognized many problems, not the least of which was her daughter's fondness for Jack Daniel's. Living with Sandy was not a blessing for either of them. Ronnie's misgivings about how she had led her own life were reflected back at her every day in the way Sandra lived now. Ronnie knew she herself was the product of wealth and not love. At least she'd found ways to get through those difficult times, the years when she gave up Ware and chose Frederick Whatton for the status he offered.

The hollowness of Ronnie's decisions continued to eat at her heart just as it had when she decided to come back to Wilmington to find her real family. There was much to mend, but the car accident changed her plans. The reality of facing whatever was in store for her made Ronnie long for Betty, Ware, and James. Her rocks. But who knew where they were now? Sandra probably didn't even remember them. She was much too young when that life ended for good.

Ronnie sat quietly, trying to get a little more comfortable in the wheelchair. Finally, Sandra moved to the front of the chair. "So do you want to get out of this thing and walk to the car?"

Ronnie was shocked. She had walked about the house to get to the bathroom. The walker was still a comfort, and she was graduating to a cane readily. A long-distance walk wasn't far off, but not today. "Sandy, I realize you're frustrated. I'd love to walk to the car. I'd love to throw away the walker and cane. You would not love for me to fall. So I suggest we reconsider that offer."

The tables had turned. Sandra knew her mother was right.

"I'll get you to the entrance. You can sit there while I bring the car around then."

The two proceeded without additional conversation.

Michael pulled into the driveway of his large home. He anticipated some anxious moments ahead when everyone planned to meet back at the house around dinnertime.

Sandra had taken Veronica for a doctor's check-up before the Christmas break. It wouldn't surprise Michael at all to find the two of them bickering about something.

Angela was doing much better. Her seizure on Thanksgiving was traumatic for everyone. Michael had concerns about Angela's well-being. He recognized signs of prenatal drug use and wondered what Kathryn had been doing with her life during her pregnancy. At some time, he would have to talk with Kathryn about the medical implications he predicted. He asked the best pediatric neurologists to take on Angela's case when the seizure happened.

He learned a lesson by not loving his daughters enough. That mistake haunted Michael now when he held his granddaughter. Kathryn had been staying with her parents for the past month. Rachel was home for an extended holiday break. Michael was desperate to repair his relationship with both of them. Angela was bonding everyone together. Except maybe Sandra. Even Veronica was spending time with the girls. Veronica was a new person too. She was kind and loving. There was a peace about her that Michael would have never predicted based on Sandra's upbringing.

The driveway was freshly plowed, and snowbanks formed small white walls around the circular drive. The evergreen shrubs that lined the drive were snowcapped, and the front door donned an oversized Christmas wreath. A very large red velvet bow and glistening ornaments nestled in the wreath's lush greens added a touch of joy. None of that came from Sandra. It was all Kathryn, a wonderful young woman Michael never really knew. His eyes filled up at the thought of all he had missed. The radio quietly played Christmas music, surrounding him with melancholy.

Rachel met her father at the back door. "You'll love it!"

Michael smiled spontaneously. His good looks came into full radiance, and Rachel recognized her father as a handsome man for the first time. He seemed to be present fully. His mind was obviously in the moment and not on a case at the hospital. "What will I love? What can be any better than having you and Kathryn and Angela here?"

He leaned over and kissed his daughter on the cheek as he hung his keys on the hook, then he put his coat and scarf in the closet. She grabbed his hand and led him into the family room.

A small but beautiful Christmas tree stood in the corner. It was decorated with white lights, red glass balls, and a white angel on the top. Angela was cradled in Kathryn's arms as the young mother sang a beautiful lullaby. The dim room gave way to the magic of the tree and the moment. Michael scanned the room. Off in a corner rocking chair sat Veronica. She had a lap quilt thrown over her knees. Her hands were folded in her lap. But her eyes stayed locked on Kathryn and Angela.

Michael put his arm around Rachel's shoulder. "Where's your mother?"

"In her study."

"I think we need her here to complete the picture, don't you?"

"Yeah. I'll go get her."

Rachel retreated to find her mother. Michael waited patiently, not wanting to upset the moment. He found his way to the couch, sat back, and kicked off his shoes. Everything else could wait. The upsetting scene he anticipated on his drive home abated. This moment needed to be savored for as long as possible.

Kathryn smiled at Michael. Angela was sound asleep. Ronnie watched from a distance, a light smile and a glow of warmth on her face.

Rachel returned. No Sandra.

She plopped down next to her dad. "Mom's nursing Jack in the study."

Kathryn nodded slightly. Michael let his head fall back against the couch as he let out a sigh. Ronnie surprised everyone. "Her loss. This is the best moment I can remember in many, many years." The sisters laughed out loud. Michael raised his head and smiled broadly.

"Veronica, might you like a cocktail before dinner? I think the doctor would approve."

"Thank you, yes. Scotch. Your best. Straight up. It's cold outside."

Christmas Eve 2010

Guests were scheduled to arrive at 3:00 p.m. Plans included a light buffet dinner of finger foods, a form of gift exchange arranged by Kathryn and Rachel that provided "a little something for everyone," and church. Of course church. Kathryn was well aware that Rob and his family would never miss the Christmas Eve worship service at their home parish, right on the waterfront in Greenwich. Faith, worship, and service were the pillars of that family. That foundation was what made Kathryn love Rob the way she did. In her time back in the greater Stamford area, she had come to know what she needed in her life. It wasn't the likes of Marcus. It was the love of the Treallor family and the caring warmth that Rob showed to everyone, not just to her.

The buffet table was set with all the family's best service pieces. Ronnie made sure that the cherished silver, china, and crystal pieces were pulled from their showcases and put to use. She found a renewed energy from her grandchildren and great-granddaughter. Her thankfulness for surviving a very long coma, having been tossed away as dead and resurfacing nearly unscathed, brought her new life. This tragedy was the second awakening for her. The first had come while she was living in California with Frederick, that night when she lost all her bearings, stumbled to the house during a party, and later left. Something very strange came over her. She knew that a life of superficial glamour was not the answer to her lifelong desires and yearnings. This family, though—this feeling was so very different.

I should have seen this life years ago. God was working a miracle. Ronnie just didn't see it that way yet. *Modern medicine and the fate of the universe. Thank you, DuLoche doctors! Amen, Lord in heaven.*

Michael had a heart-to-heart talk with Sandra—finally. When Veronica made the comment that it was Sandra's loss to have missed the family night a few days earlier, he decided it was time to resurrect the flame he once felt to save themselves from one another. He had convinced her to limit her drinking to times when she was in the presence of a family member, preferably only with him. Sandra agreed to try that, and together they removed the bottle of whiskey from her study. The scene could have been prettier, but it happened. All drinking glasses were returned to the family room bar. The decanters were emptied and washed, and not even a drop of sherry was available. Veronica and her granddaughters did the work behind the scenes by arranging all the glassware to be a pretty display of crystal. One missing piece would be noticed, and Sandra knew that.

Michael felt a sense of accomplishment with this development, but he still didn't know exactly how to handle the letter, the one Veronica had had in her purse at the time of the accident. *What does she remember?*

Something was drawing Michael to have a come-to-Jesus meeting with his mother-in-law. Even in the midst of this lovely holiday, the nagging was not going to stop until he figured out the relationship between Ware Treallor and Veronica Husting. With Ware and the Treallor family expected to arrive soon, the matter was pressing.

Rachel put the finishing touches on two centerpieces that adorned the buffet table. Kathryn followed behind her, carrying Angela in her arms. She handed Rachel two long red candles. "You have to add these. There's no way it's Christmas without candles." Rachel rolled her eyes. "Really, Kathryn. You have become quite the little Martha."

Kathryn smiled with pride and kissed Angela on the forehead. "Some things just change you, I guess."

Rachel adored her sister. Even more, she adored what her sister had become. With the kind of parenting the two of them had had, it was a miracle that Kathryn could be this nurturing.

As if reading her mind, Kathryn turned and smiled at Rachel. "I know. It's a miracle, isn't it?"

Rachel gave her sister a hug and moved away before she could become too emotional.

"Girls. Come here, please."

It was Veronica, calling from the family room. She was seated in the armchair next to the fireplace with her cane propped next to her for peace of mind. The two arrived quickly.

"Hi, Grandma!" Kathryn was the first to respond.

"Grandma." Veronica paused. "I can't believe it. I'm too young for that, even if I'm not feeling young these days!" She chuckled.

"Think again. Angela is your *great*-grandchild." Rachel didn't mean to sound quite as sarcastic as she did.

"And isn't it wonderful?" Kathryn recovered the moment.

"It is. It is indeed. I wasn't planning to talk about my age or our growing family. I have other, more important things to talk about."

Angela had fallen asleep in Kathryn's arms. It was the perfect time to put her down for an afternoon nap.

"Go put her down, but don't be gone long. I'll wait to say anything until you return." Veronica clearly had something important to say, and Rachel was now very attentive. She got comfortable on the couch and waited for Kathryn's return.

Warren and Leslie worked together to wrap the last of the presents they had bought for Adrienne and Rob. Each had their own list of wants for school, and most of it included technology of some kind. Warren had no problem with those requests. Leslie added her own picks to the gift lists, and together they created a balanced spread of practical and whimsical items. At the same time, there was always the gift of outreach. They knew the evening included time at the Channing home, but there would also be time at the shelter tomorrow. That was a high priority.

They put the gifts under the Christmas tree and stood back to admire the beauty and wonder of the season. Leslie reached for Warren's arm. He responded by wrapping it around her shoulders.

"What's eating at you, Warren?"

"Is it that obvious?"

"Yes."

"Leslie, I've never had these conflicting feelings before. But since I saw the old Husting estate for sale, I've been struggling with my past."

Leslie was careful not to jump in too soon. Her years of working with troubled people in the shelter had taught her how to respond to this type of confession. She knew she just had to wait and listen.

So she did just that. She waited, but nothing else came. Instead, Warren gave her a quick tug on the shoulders, dropped his arm, and moved away.

"The tree is beautiful, isn't it?" He kept the conversation safe.

Leslie didn't want to push. "Yes. Thanks for helping with it."

"Where's Rob?" Warren walked out of the family room in his quest to find his son, leaving Leslie bewildered.

Adrienne caught her mother's facial expression when she came in from the kitchen. "What's up, Mom?"

"Nothing. Nothing, really. Dad was just wondering where Rob is, and I've not seen him since noon. Did he get back from the errands he was running?"

"Sure. He's in his room wrapping some surprise package to take to the Treallors' house tonight. I think he found those German cookies that everyone likes."

"That's sweet of him. Typical Rob!"

Adrienne plopped on the couch with her latest book and started to read. Leslie moved about, tidying up the room, but she was focused more on Warren's comments about his past. It was not a surprise to her that something from his past was bubbling up. She had been waiting for this event literally for years. Her suspicions that Warren had always withheld something from her had just been confirmed.

——— ⌒⌒ ———

Betty made the turn off the turnpike at the Wilbur Cross Parkway. She followed the directions exactly as Sandra had mapped them out for her.

The 2003 Cavalier was doing fine in the weather. She was still comfortable driving long distances, even though she hadn't done much of it over the past ten years. James had always been around to handle things like this. Now she was on her own.

One week ago, she never would have thought herself capable of this strength. But God was watching over her. He knew that she needed to deliver the truth to the Treallor and Channing families, even if it was a sure death sentence for her. More than anything, she needed to confess everything to Ronnie and Ware. She needed them to know her sins. Only Sandra had an inkling of what was ahead. Betty struggled with how much she would confess. She needed direction. *Thy word is a lamp unto my feet, and a light unto my path.*[6]

Sandra had learned that Betty was now the real owner of the Husting estate. Her research into the property led her to Frederick Whatton, her stepfather. From there, she uncovered the real owner just by being around the property enough. On one occasion, Betty was walking across the backyard, skirting her way around the collapsed pool, just as Sandra exited the back door off the kitchen. The two nearly collided. There were a couple of

---

[6] Psalms 119:105 (KJV).

uncomfortable moments in that encounter, but in the end part of the truth was revealed.

Betty had no feasible explanation of why she lived on the property in the guesthouse. Being the caretaker made no sense. The property was well maintained by ABS employees. Being a tenant made less sense since none of the paperwork in the realty office indicated that rental income currently being collected. Consequently, Betty was trapped into telling Sandra that she did, in fact, have a financial interest in the property and was working with Mr. Stanis to sell the estate. Her explanation was that Alejandro Stanis was willing to give her a part of the proceeds if she just watched the comings and goings on the property and reported anything unusual to him. Betty didn't divulge in any way her true connection to Alejandro Basil Stanis, a.k.a. Frederick Whatton. She did divulge that Frederick Whatton and Alejandro were one in the same.

Betty knew that Sandra didn't deserve the hurt that certainly defined the future. From Betty's perspective, maybe what was ahead was a truth that would set everyone free. Especially her, even if she ended up in a jail cell. Betty knew that if she lost courage, she could be out of the country before the law caught up with her. Alej would help her.

Her travel toward Sandra and Veronica created anxiety. The trip itself was uneventful; the anticipation was exhausting. Just one week earlier, Betty would never have considered this reunion a possibility.

James's death took every ounce of her emotion and wit. Her own fall and pinched nerve came as a harsh reality that age was catching up with her. The coroner who arrived at the ugly scene when she placed a 9-1-1 call recognized her physical struggle and moved her to a local urgent care unit for a workup. No broken bones. Time and a sling brought her back to functioning fairly well. She packed the sling for precautionary reasons, but with specific exercises and anti-inflammatories, Betty had recovered remarkably well. Within about ten days, she was able to function well enough to make the trip.

James's funeral was well attended by the family he had in Wilmington. She never knew just how kind and loving they all could be. While they wanted to dote on her and offered their spare rooms for her to stay, Betty couldn't see herself there with them. Perhaps guilt was in the way.

The goal was in sight: bring everyone back together again at the Husting estate, where they belonged—mother, father, daughter, and granddaughters. Alejandro would have to open his arms to her again when he learned that Ronnie was with her real love, Ware. Maybe Alej could save Betty; she didn't really need to confess anything. Betty and Alej could escape to Mexico, where he'd always promised a happily-ever-after. *But I have to get this off my chest. God wants me to.*

She rounded the hilly bend. The sight ahead of her was breathtakingly beautiful. Betty could see a lovely home on a hillside. The snow made a surreal picture of the landscape as it glistened in the sun, which was already low in the sky. The roads were shiny. The winding drive looked like a typical Rockwell scene from some forgotten New England town. Luminaries lined the walkway, inviting her to step through the fictional scenery into the reality of a reunion from hell.

❧☙

Michael looked around his house with pride. The girls were remarkable, and so was Veronica. Every detail showed the warmth and love of a family reunited. Sandra kept her end of the bargain: no drinking if Michael was not present. The table offered a festive buffet spread, created to avoid seating assignments that could negatively affect the ambiance. The physical surroundings fed his need for closeness, something Michael never had felt in this home until now. Having adult children brought feelings of disappointment in how he had led his life. He knew he had missed out on a beautiful part of life—being a dad. A granddaughter added a sting to that hurt, and now he wanted to make things right.

The doorbell rang. He checked his watch. *Quite early.*

"I'll get it," he called to no one. *Where are they?*

The bell rang again. He moved a little faster, bumping into Sandra, who flew down the stairs.

"You go ahead and relax. I've got it."

Michael didn't expect this energy from her. But he accepted it and moved into the family room. He found Veronica sitting on the couch with a magazine in her lap, sipping a cup of tea. His daughters were huddled near the Christmas tree with Angela cradled in Rachel's arms while a doting mother looked on.

"Seems like people are arriving early." Michael wanted to strike up a conversation with his mother-in-law.

"Maybe. Not likely, though. Sandra must have something she's expecting."

"We'll see. I can't imagine anyone just stopping by on Christmas, so maybe …"

"Well!" Sandra stood at the family room door. "Good afternoon, everyone. I want to introduce to you Elizabeth Zane Stanis."

Warren and Leslie climbed into the front of the Jeep. Rob and Adrienne settled in the back. A few packages sat on their laps. Leslie held a platter of veggies and dip, arranged to reflect the red and green of the season and beautifully displayed. Rob chatted while everyone else nodded.

"So I expect that it's just us tonight. The Channings don't usually do much for any of the holidays. I guess having Kathryn there with her baby has made things a little different this year. And I know her older sister, Rachel, will be home too. I doubt she has any boyfriend or anything like that. So just us and them. It'll be great." Rob was on a roll.

A few uh-huhs were muttered in response.

Warren made no pretense about being skeptical of this arrangement. He hoped to have a quick bite and be on the road to church early enough to get a pew and not a chair off to the side. Christmas Eve was not a time for pretenses. Something about the whole plan felt forced to him, and he didn't know why. Nonbelievers were no problem. He served them all the time; the great commission was his guiding principle. But this felt very different. *Sandra Channing, the real estate agent. Sandra Channing, Lizzie, Sandy?*

Rob and Adrienne made small talk in the back seat. Leslie directed Warren through a couple of turns. The roads were beautiful, lined with glistening snow on the trees and shiny surfaces left by the warm sun that had beaten down on the snowfall earlier in the day.

Warren glanced in the rearview mirror. The reflection spoke to him. "Ware, you need to take the upcoming meeting very cautiously."

"Robert?!"

"What, Dad?" Rob responded with a bit of angst in his voice. It was not a typical occasion for Warren to call Rob by his full name.

"You'll be where you belong very soon. Remember your roots."

"What do you mean?" Warren responded first to Robert Husting, ignoring his son.

"I didn't say anything. What do you need?" Rob's confusion was clear.

Warren shook his head. Leslie was looking straight at him.

Adrienne didn't notice anything unusual; she was busy looking at the snowy scenery.

Leslie broke the moment. "Warren, did you mean to call Rob?"

He's following me again. Why?

"I thought he said something." Warren tried to cover himself.

"I didn't say a word, Dad."

"It's nothing." *Robert. Why? What?*

Soon enough, they pulled into the Channing driveway.

"Oh, the luminaries are just beautiful," Leslie spoke quietly.

"Yeah." Rob tried to downplay the overstated scene. "It will be even prettier when the sun sets completely. I bet this was Kathryn's idea."

The Treallor family made their way to the door to an unexpected greeting.

———— ✑✑ ————

Betty looked at the Channing family. She moved her gaze from face to face, looking for a familiar pair of eyes to lock with her own. Kathryn, Rachel, Michael. A baby. No recognition. Until she landed on Veronica.

Veronica's eyes narrowed. Her forehead squeezed together as she tried to make sense of what she'd heard. *Betty?*

Michael's expression was a direct replica of Veronica's. He, too, tried to figure things out. *Elizabeth. Is this the Betty that Sandra remembered? The one who raised Veronica?*

"Who's that?" Rachel hoped Kathryn knew more than she did. It was Kathryn who'd spent a great deal of time on the family tree project.

"No idea, love." Kathryn turned to Rachel, opened her eyes wide with brows up, smiled with closed mouth, and swerved her eyes back and forth.

"Mother. And she's not even nursing Jack today!" The two sniggered softly.

A quick glance around the room revealed that no one knew what to say next.

Betty locked eyes with Veronica. Both became teary. Veronica grabbed her cane to stand, but Betty was already upon her. The two embraced, gaining physical strength in one another's arms.

They swayed, cried, laughed, smiled, hugged, and got lost in some emotion that no one else was able to identify. Clearly theirs was a special relationship that had not been a part of any mother–daughter team in the household.

"My Ronnie. My Ronnie. You are so beautiful."

Veronica cried all the harder.

Kathryn and Rachel were in awe at the love that was palpable. It was Kathryn who broke the tension of the entire Channing family. She stood up and walked to Sandra. Reaching out, she hugged her mother. "Isn't it nice to have family?"

Sandra looked up at Kathryn, who stood a few inches taller than she. This emotion was a stranger to Sandra. She had protected herself from feeling anything near the display of love she was witnessing now. With natural responses kicked into gear, she hugged Kathryn in return. Burying her face in Kathryn's shoulder, she allowed a few tears to flow. Kathryn timed her next move perfectly, giving her mother just enough time to emote and recover.

"Come on over here with Rachel and Angela. They could use a hug too."

Sandra followed her daughter. Rachel stood and handed Angela off to Sandra. For the first time, Sandra cradled her granddaughter. A photographer would have been in heavenly bliss capturing the emotions of the room. Tears mingled with laughter.

Michael watched with trepidation, challenged to make sense of the moment. He walked out of the room without making a fuss.

This time when the doorbell rang, no one actually heard it. On the third try, the Treallor family received an unusual greeting. There stood Dr. Michael Channing, clutching an envelope in his right hand as he opened the door with his left. A stern eye greeted Warren, who reached out for a solid handshake.

Michael found himself clumsily seeking to stuff the envelope in his pants pocket to return the gesture. It was Rob who cleared the space.

"Hi, I'm Rob. Kathryn's friend? We've met once or twice, I think."

Michael shook his head and poured on his professional charm. "Of course! Of course! You're the Treallors! Welcome to our home. Come right in."

The false welcome dimmed the moment for Rob, in turn increasing the level of concern Warren felt about this whole idea of spending time with the Channing family. After some awkward introductions without a common connection in the room, Rob decided to move farther into the house. A complete dichotomy existed between the foyer and the family room.

Veronica and Betty sat in the far corner around the café table that usually served as a place to rest a drink or for two people to sit and have a quiet conversation. Sandra was in the rocking chair with Angela, and Kathryn and Rachel were arm in arm in front of a bay window that overlooked the luminaries, which were glowing behind them as they admired the scene.

Rob immediately made his way to Kathryn, who walked toward the entryway. She reached out and hugged him. "Rob, this couldn't be a better reunion of family. Mom invited a dear person from her childhood. I had no idea!"

Warren followed Rob with Leslie at his side, who was still holding a tray of veggies. Adrienne stepped in with Michael Channing right behind. Michael stepped around the three as they approached the family room. "Oh, let me take this tray to the kitchen for you. The ladies of the house are quite occupied. I'll be right back." He moved away, allowing Kathryn to greet the Treallors.

"Hi, Mr. Treallor! I'm so glad you're all here." Her genuine appreciation for the Treallor family radiated in her smile.

Warren cleared his throat, almost afraid to test his voice. "Hello, Kathryn." Audible stress punctuated his words.

"Hi, Kathryn!" Leslie picked up the slack. "It's so nice of you and Rob to arrange for all of us to be together tonight. I'm looking forward to seeing your mother again."

Warren fought back Robert's words. *Caution. Use caution.*

"Come in, come in. Everyone is just catching up in the family room. Let me take your coats."

Warren stepped into a fog. Like a beacon calling him out, his senses pulled him directly to Betty and Veronica in the far corner at a cozy table for two. *O God, help me!* Perspiration dotted his brow, and all color drained from his face. Leslie grabbed his elbow. "Warren!"

He made it to the couch and fell back.

"Please get some water, someone!" Leslie took control.

Betty turned from her position. "Ware!" She went directly to him. Ronnie sat stunned. She never queried who these friends were whom Kathryn had invited to this gathering.

Adrienne took a glass from Rachel and handed it to her dad. Leslie was at his side.

Betty made her way to her brother. "Ware. Ware, it's okay. I'm here with you. Breathe."

Ware closed his eyes and shook his head slowly.

"Sip the water. Keep your eyes open." Betty did the coaching.

Caution. Approach this cautiously. Ware was falling back into himself—his real self.

Leslie stepped away, tapping Adrienne on the shoulder. Rob followed them.

"Rob, do you think we should just leave?" Adrienne's voice was soft.

"No. I think something's going on for Dad, and we need to let him work through this. I don't know who that lady is. Do you, Mom?"

Leslie shook her head.

"Kathryn said her mother invited a dear person from her past. I have no idea."

Rob approached Kathryn and learned that this person, Elizabeth Zane Stanis, was actually Betty Treallor Stanis. Rob queried the relationship to his own family. He didn't know any other Treallors. Kathryn could not answer. She had no idea what the family relationship might be. She only gathered that somehow Betty was connected to her grandmother. She had overheard Betty tell Veronica that she was really a Treallor.

She warned Rob: "I did do some family research as a gift to my mother. Some of the family tree is a little sketchy, but I think maybe this person was part of her upbringing somehow."

Not knowing how to handle the information, Rob approached his mother and sister. He took them into the kitchen to explain what he had learned.

Ware sat staring at Betty. She had one hand on his knee; she wiped his brow with a paper napkin.

Caution. Be cautious.

"Betty?" he whispered. "Betty. Betty." Then the tears flowed.

She reached around him and hugged him, crying again for the second time in less than an hour. This was not like her. *Oh Lord, bring me through this.*

Ware sat with his eyes closed. *He leadeth me beside the still waters,*[7] *and now the storm is here. Caution.*

"Betty. How? Why are you here?"

---

[7] Psalms 23:2 (KJV).

"Oh, dear Ware. We have so much to talk about." She paused, sniffing and wiping the tears away. "Not here. Not now."

Warren became self-conscious of the moment. "Yeah. Later."

He looked around and noticed the room had cleared, with the exception of one person. Veronica was watching from her perch at the café table. She hadn't moved.

Their eyes locked. Betty noticed the exchange and removed herself, looking for the bathroom as a place to gather herself together.

Ronnie stood cautiously, smoothing her skirt.

"I thought you were dead."

Ronnie looked at the floor. "That's some greeting." Her eyes misted.

"No. Not like that. I didn't mean it like that."

"Ware. I'm sorry."

"Don't be. We did crazy things back then."

"No. I did crazy things. I'm so sorry." She caught her breath, pinched her lips together, and couldn't hold back. The sobs burst forth as Ware sprang from the couch. They embraced in a way that only two lovers can understand.

Another moment for Ronnie. A new moment for Ware. *Caution.*

Leslie stood watching; Adrienne looked over her shoulder. "Oh my God." The words were faint. Adrienne felt a lump in her throat. She took her mother's arm and led her back to the kitchen.

Rob went directly to Kathryn and put his arm around her shoulder. Silence was in order. They watched a love story unfold as Kathryn's grandmother Husting became a puddle of tears in the arms of Rob's father, Warren (Ware) Treallor. The two suddenly knew the connections. No words were necessary. She turned and whispered in his ear: "I do love you. But something tells me there is a family connection that is much closer than we would have ever known."

Rob lowered his eyes and removed his arm from her shoulders. He nodded slowly and stepped away.

"My family tree may have just become complete."

After what felt like an eternity, Michael stepped in. "Pardon me, but, Veronica, may I speak with you? Privately, please."

Veronica stepped away from Warren, who put his face up to the ceiling, reached up to dry his eyes before facing anyone standing behind him, then turned slowly around. He caught the backs of Veronica and Michael as they left the room. There stood Rob; Kathryn holding Angela; Rachel; Betty; and Sandra.

"Kids, I'm sorry. Can you please give me a minute with Betty and Sandra?"

The three looked from face to face and left the room without speaking.

"Lizzie?" Warren asked gingerly. "Is it really you? Sandy?"

"Yes. It is."

"You are really the daughter of Veronica Husting Simarillo?"

"Yes. I am."

"But." Ware didn't know where else to go with his questions, so he turned to Betty. "How? Where have you been forever?"

Betty smiled. "I've been around. Enough to keep an eye on your real family, Ware."

Now it was Sandra's turn to be confused. "What do you mean by that, Betty?"

"Well." Betty paused to get her thoughts straight. *Don't blow it. Ware needs space.* "You know, the Husting family was like our, his, family. We all worked and lived together. We missed one another. Right, Ware?"

"Yeah." Warren moved to the couch and fell into the cushions. *Use caution.*

Veronica returned with a stern look on her face. Michael entered the room right behind her and took his place next to Sandra.

Everyone waited to find out what was coming next. But the pregnant air hung heavy. No one spoke.

"So who would like a beverage? There's some hot cider in the kitchen and some sodas in the bar, and I do have a bottle of wine that we can open. What will it be? We should get started on that buffet that's waiting for us!" Sandra moved the celebration of Christmas into gear.

She played the gracious hostess. Rachel aided her, and Adrienne followed their lead. The mingling got started. There was small talk, no talk, head nods, and excuse-me's as people found their way back to the buffet table or off to the bathroom for private space. All in all, it was a tense, dreadful hour that passed. The food was tasty, and the music playing in the background was a complete contradiction to the tenor of the room. Through the bay window, the once delightful luminaries were burning down, and the front yard lost its festive appeal.

A tinkling on the side of a glass brought the room to attention.

It was Veronica. All eyes were on her. The beauty that Ware had seen in her forty-plus years ago had not faded. Her high cheekbones were accentuated by the way her hair hung just below her eye on one side. The sides were pulled neatly into a French twist, and small strands curled around her neck. Faint scars from the accident were well concealed. Diamonds studded her earlobes, and a tasteful string of gold beads ran around her neck. A high-collared black sweater came to a perfect V in the front, where a glimpse of black lace lingerie was visible. She held a water goblet high. "I propose a toast to the start of newly invigorated relationships. May each of you have a wonderful Christmas!" A few replies were murmured, and everyone found a glass that provided something to sip, be it water, ginger ale, or wine.

Veronica continued, "I would like to suggest that we all gather around the Christmas tree and let Kathryn, my delightful granddaughter, unveil a little surprise that she has prepared for her mother. Kathryn? Are you ready?"

Michael became very uneasy. He didn't know what to say or how to stop the impending train wreck.

Kathryn saw her father's discomfort and signaled to him with an inquisitive facial expression.

Michael responded with a tight-lipped face and a minor shrug of the shoulders.

"Dad? Would you like to introduce this gift? You did help me."

"Well!" Michael's voice was higher pitched than normal. Color rose in his cheeks. "Sure. Why not?" There was a hint of sarcasm, maybe even anger, that crept out.

He explained Kathryn's idea of creating a family tree. He talked of the research she had done to give the Husting family a sketch of their lineage and the addition of Angela to the family. He made light of the fact that he supported Kathryn, saying that really it was all her work.

At that, Kathryn unrolled a large sheet of paper. She credited Rachel with having helped her space out blocks and help with printing nameplates that were attached to portions of a large tree. Branches were creatively intertwined, colors were added for effect, and room remained for new additions to the family over time. She explained the websites she'd used to dig deeper and the pieces of the puzzle that her father was able to fill in.

Sandra, the recipient of the family tree, was awed by the product. "You did this? But how did you? You didn't ask me questions. Are you sure you have it right?" Her eyes scanned the large graphic. "Where is your grandfather Husting on this thing?"

So many questions. Rachel stepped back and watched her once-wayward sister walk her mother through the branches of her family. She had the history of the Husting estate in perfect alignment with the multiple generations of owners. It was Kathryn who turned to the assembled room to fill in one open question.

"There is still one piece of the puzzle! We couldn't locate my mother's birth certificate. But we know that Grandma was married to Quentin Simarillo. There's just a couple of gaps there. Maybe we could ..."

"Excuse me, girls." It was Veronica. She eyed everyone in the room, but her gaze lingered on Leslie. And then Rob. She looked at Kathryn again.

"Well, this will be harder than I thought. But it's time."

Michael knew what was coming. He moved to Sandra's side and put his arm around his wife.

Veronica continued, now visibly unsure of herself. She avoided Ware's eyes.

"As you probably all know, I suffered a very serious car accident just outside the entrance to the Husting estate."

Betty looked down and squeezed her hands together. Her legs went weak, and her whole body began sweating. Afraid she might do something crazy like fall to the floor, she moved quickly and sat at the café table, her hand supporting her head, which hung down. She closed her eyes tightly and clenched her teeth. *Oh Lord, spare me this moment. Spare me, please. And Ware.*

Rob knew that something was not quite right. He found his way to Leslie and let his support be known. Adrienne worked her way beside them.

"Well," Veronica continued, "when I finally recovered from a coma, it was Michael who convinced Sandra to take me in. Sandra, my lovely daughter whom I may not have treated as well as I should have over the years. My daughter who didn't want anything to do with me. And I understand why. I was chasing riches, not *life*. That car accident brought me to my senses. We're working on things together."

Michael cleared his throat loudly. "It's good to have you in our household, Veronica."

The family clapped. Betty kept her head down. Rob, Leslie,

and Adrienne looked as if they were missing some private secret. Warren held back a smile, but his joy at Veronica's well-being tugged at his heart. *My love, you are indeed well. And gorgeous.* His hand slipped along his pants pocket just enough to confirm that the diamond ring was indeed there. It was always there on important days.

Michael looked at Warren Treallor. He put the puzzle together. Veronica and Warren. Not Veronica and Quentin. *Sandra's real parents. In this room together.*

Veronica smoothly responded, "Thank you, Michael. You barely know me, but we're getting there. I admire that you opened your home to me."

Sandra didn't know where else this little presentation might go, so she stepped in to stop the potentially embarrassing moments that she saw coming. "This gift is so beautiful, so unexpected! Thank you very much, all of you, for putting your part into the family tree creation. We can get it framed and hang it in the family room. That seems appropriate to me!" She was shaking visibly. Michael saw the signs of an alcoholic struggling with sobriety.

Ware shifted his eyes. *Where's my family?* Self-conscious about the chasm he may have created, he shifted in his seat. Betty gathered herself and stood up. Ware followed her lead. The two moved to Veronica. "It's time we have a long talk, Ronnie. Ware and I have some things to share with you."

Ronnie shook her head. "No. You don't. I know you're siblings. I know you kept that from everyone at the Husting estate. Let's not go too far with family secrets that don't need to be shared, shall we?"

Veronica made her way to Sandra, pulling Ware along by the arm. "Sandra, your husband has been very diligent in protecting my secret for a long time. He was with me on that awful night of the accident. He kept an envelope in his possession and never betrayed anyone by opening it."

She paused, expecting Michael to jump in and add to her story. He didn't. He only looked at his shoes. "That envelope was labeled for Ware Treallor, and I had it my purse. I was trying to figure out how to leave it in a mailbox or at the Husting estate. I was aware that Ware was touring the estate with you. I saw him there. I also saw Betty on the property."

Shifting from one foot to the other, Ware displayed his impatience. *Use caution.*

Veronica slipped her hand into the side pocket of her sweater and pulled out a piece of folded paper. It was Sandra's birth certificate, signed by Ware Treallor. She handed it to Sandra.

The sheet of paper was shaking in Sandra's hand. Her eyes wouldn't focus.

"See there. It is signed by the father of the baby—your father."

Sandra just stared. She looked up at Michael. "What does this mean? Quentin Simarillo was my father. I don't know him—never met him. But that was my mother's husband!" Looking at Veronica, she asked, "What are you telling me—us—Mother?"

Veronica could be very smooth in any situation. Age and experience gave her a confidence she'd lacked in her younger years, the years when she needed Ware to get through the crises in her life. "The truth. It's time. The name signed there is accurate."

Warren looked wide-eyed at Veronica, then at Sandra. "Wait a minute. Are you actually using this time to say that Sandra is mine, my daughter? After all these years?"

Veronica sensed her poor timing but stood fast. "Yes. I am. Christmas. A season for love and giving. I am giving you one another. Father and daughter. Just as Sandra gave you your sister. Openly and without hesitation. I'm coming clean with you, Ware."

Warren didn't know how to respond. His first inclination was to hug Sandra, to tell her he knew something was there and that he'd kept asking himself if it were possible that she was the Sandy he knew, the one he'd created but did not have permission to father. There were too many emotions, thoughts, consequences, and possibilities and too much fear running through his veins. *Use caution.*

Instead of reacting with any of the emotions and first impulses he felt, Ware sought out Leslie, Rob, and Adrienne.

They were gone. *My family.* His head swung back around when he realized they were nowhere in the room.

Before Ware could think of an alternative course, Sandra was beside him. "So, Warren. We've had many opportunities to interact. Did you know you were my father?" Her words were curt and painful to hear. "All this time and you've been playing me. Thinking what? That you would find a way back to the Husting estate and own a piece of property you have no business owning?"

Michael turned directly toward Sandra. He knew she was speaking through a need for a drink, but he couldn't be that compassionate. "What are you getting at? Did you two know one another? Is this your client? Why didn't you tell me?"

"Why do you care?" Sandra now attacked her husband without a blush of the congeniality that she'd shown just hours before this party started. "My business is my business. I sell houses all the time!"

"But not to a man whose son is befriending our daughter! A man who is apparently very familiar with your mother's life, your life, and your family home!"

"And how was I to know that?!"

Sandra stormed away. The only sound was the slamming of the study door.

"Thank God we removed all the Jack Daniel's from that room," Michael spoke out loud, unashamed. Rachel headed after her mother.

Kathryn touched her father's arm before heading out of the

family room. "It's time for me to put Angela down." Michael nodded before dropping into the armchair.

Betty, Ronnie, Ware, and Michael were left in the family room.

"Drinks, anyone?" Michael was offering.

"I'll pass if you don't mind. I need to find my family."

"Of course." Michael stayed seated; it was Veronica who walked with Warren to the hall closet to retrieve his coat.

"You have no idea how many regrets I have, Ware."

"You're the same wonderful, impetuous, impulsive woman I've always loved, Ronnie. I made a promise to you. It might still stand, but I need some time to think."

He held her elbow and placed a soft kiss on her cheek. "Merry Christmas," he whispered.

Ronnie fought the tears and watched Ware walk out the front door. Betty peered on from the end of the hallway.

Ware stepped out into a dark evening; snow was falling heavily. Flashes of the Appalachian Trail ran through his mind. The walk home would be long and cold.

Chapter
TWENTY-SEVEN
January 2011: Secrets Unleashed

The Christmas season had unboxed too many pieces of information all at one time. There was no time for anyone to think, to reflect, to make sense of what was happening in the lives of several families. Some of that information only created questions, questions that were better left unanswered if people were going to continue living a free life. Ware Treallor was among those people who had more questions than he really wanted to ask. Particularly he had questions for his sister, Betty.

Seeing Betty on Christmas Eve at the Channings' home was overwhelming. He didn't know how to begin processing the things that had happened in her life. She confessed that she had been married for many years and that she'd never told anyone, not even him. Yes, he had been part of a scheme to keep the Hustings from knowing that he and she were brother and sister. That was merely so that they both could keep their jobs. The Hustings did not employ members of the same family. It seemed innocent enough. When Robert hired Ware, Betty was already working there. Ware had no idea that he would meet her there. He was all of eighteen years old and foolish. He saw no harm in covering up their relationship when Betty told him to do so. Betty left their home when he was only seven years old, and he thought of her as his big sister, translating to "she can tell me what to do."

The more difficult part of seeing Betty was learning just how conniving she had been with everyone's life, including his own. Betty had manipulated everyone. Ware felt totally betrayed by her. Ronnie was the one most hurt by Betty's misdeeds. That beautiful estate that Robert owned should have been left to Ronnie. Ware never understood why Robert had left the proceeds of the sale to him. The after-death contact that Robert was making with Ware in recent years now had new meaning. Robert had wanted Ware to get the estate back to Ronnie somehow. The younger Ronnie was frivolous in Robert's eyes. She never cared much about the important things in life. Ware could see the change in Ronnie's priorities. When they were young, she had been just the opposite of Ware, and that definitely was a draw for him. Now Ronnie had earned Robert's respect. Ware understood what Robert expected of him. He had to take care of Ronnie for life.

Betty's marriage to someone who conducted less-than-legal and certainly immoral business activities left Ware baffled and disgusted. He didn't understand how Betty could possess such an evil side. They'd grown up in the same wholesome, Christ-centered home. She admitted to him that Alej had some undisclosed business ventures in Mexico. Ware knew enough to conclude that Alej was probably involved in something very dangerous. *What does Alej really do? Why does he use an alias? Did Betty know that he had two lives? Did she know that he married Ronnie?!* Those were questions Ware did not want answered.

Through all of these conflicting feelings about Betty, Warren was battling his love for Ronnie. He had promised Ronnie that he would always be there for her when she was ready, and now she was ready. He didn't know if he could keep that promise.

Leslie walked into the kitchen to find Ware holding a steaming cup of coffee and just staring out into the backyard. Neither of them had approached the necessary conversation. The kids were both back at school now, and the house was too quiet. They had managed to keep things at the surface level while Rob and Adrienne were around.

"What's on the docket today?" Leslie tried to break the ice.

"Don't know. Headed to the office."

She fussed at the kitchen sink, looked in the fridge, and eventually poured herself a cup of coffee. "Do you think you want to talk about anything, Warren?"

"Yes. No. I don't know. I'm exhausted." *How can I even begin to tell her everything?*

"Let's take it slow, but let's start somewhere. Can we agree to that?"

Warren turned to look directly at his wife. "I'm not sure I can."

Leslie knew that she and the kids had made a huge mistake when they left Warren at the Channings' on Christmas Eve. He walked the four miles home in the cold. The odd thing was that no one talked about it after that evening. When Warren reached their home, he took a hot shower and changed into warm clothes, and then they left for church. They made it to the midnight service, but without their usual Christmas joy. Leslie felt terrible about her actions, but at the time, all she could do was escape. Since that night, she had lived with guilt about her quick decision, guilt that was building into constant anxiety.

Christmas Day was quiet. The family remained mindful of the purpose of all they were doing that day. As usual, they participated in serving a Christmas dinner at the homeless shelter. They avoided speaking of the events of the prior evening. Warren was worried about Rob, who had enough challenges figuring out exactly what to do with his life. Now he had his father's bad example to think about, and he'd lost any chance of a romantic relationship with Kathryn. Leslie was just worried with no particular target for her stress.

Kathryn and Rob had been moving forward in a very meaningful relationship. They were taking things slowly and treating one another with complete respect. Warren wondered just how romantic the two may have been at any time in the past. He was burdened with remorse over the damage he may have done by never following his heart and tracking down Sandra, his biological daughter. Instead, his own son ended up in a relationship with a young woman who was a close relative: Kathryn, Warren's own granddaughter.

Leslie tried again. "C'mon. Let's sit in the family room for a minute."

Warren followed her, each carrying their coffee as if it were something to protect them from facing themselves. They sat in their typical places on the couch, facing the black hole of the fireplace. Again, Leslie broke the silence.

"Warren, there has never been anything we haven't handled together. Let's not make this a first."

What have we ever had to handle? Rob wanting to leave school? Big deal.

"I love you, and there isn't much that can change that."

Not even Ronnie? Or Sandra? Or the fact that I'm a great-grandfather?

"Just tell me what you're feeling. We can start there."

Warren took a deep breath, looked up at the ceiling, and blew all the air out of his lungs with puffed cheeks. His shoulders dropped. Leslie reached over and rubbed his arm. "You know, I might not be as ignorant to what's been going on as you might think."

That was more than Warren wanted to hear. "What you are you talking about? What's been 'going on'? Are you accusing me of something that wasn't happening?"

Leslie had hit a hot button. She waited a minute, hoping Warren would say more. When he did not, she continued: "No, I don't think anything has been happening technically. But I've always wondered if there was something about your time in Wilmington that you didn't want to share with me. I know something difficult happened when you worked for the Hustings. I had no idea that Veronica was a part of your past. But it just makes sense to me."

Warren didn't know what to say. *Does she know that I still carry an engagement ring around?* "What makes sense to you? That Veronica was my first true love?" There was a new tone in Warren's voice that Leslie had never heard. Venom.

Leslie's eyes filled. She tried to respond without emotion, but she failed. Instead, she just cried.

Warren sat still. He couldn't find it in himself to comfort her. *Why didn't I just follow my heart?*

"I just need to have some time alone, Leslie. Please."

Leslie nodded. She didn't know what she was agreeing to, but she knew there was no sense in trying to push for details right now.

Warren left the room.

Leslie heard the Jeep roar out of the driveway. She did nothing to stop her tears.

Ronnie sat in her room at Sandra and Michael's house. She had convinced them to allow Kathryn and Angela to move in permanently, and Michael was with Kathryn now. They were moving her things out of her tiny apartment in Baltimore. Rachel was back at school. That left Sandra and Ronnie in the huge home alone.

So far, Sandra had stayed true to her agreement. She only had a single glass of wine, nothing stronger, and only if Michael was around her. Tonight would be the acid test. It would be just the two of them, mother and daughter. Ronnie wanted more than anything for Sandra to be whole and to heal from her addiction. But she also knew that might require a long program with strong family support.

It was Ronnie's sharing of Sandra's birth certificate that had sent everything into a tailspin. It may have been possible to manage Betty's revelation and all that she had shared with the family, but adding Sandra's biological father to the mix was toxic. Ronnie could see why. With Kathryn and Rob Treallor so entangled, anyone would be worried. In her heart, Ronnie knew God was saving them from a terrible tragedy. She so much as told Sandra so, but that message landed flat. Sandra had no soul for such things, just as Ronnie had had no soul for such things when she was younger. *Mother and daughter, oh so alike.*

As Ronnie sat thinking about what to do next, Sandra tapped on her door. Ronnie answered, "Yes?"

"It's me, Mother. May I come in?"

Ronnie straightened up. "Certainly."

Sandra walked in slowly, her hands folded in front of her. She moved around the end of the bed and sat on the far edge, facing Ronnie, who sat in the easy chair near the window. She just looked at her mother tenderly. Ronnie wasn't sure what to expect. This behavior was not common for Sandra.

"What is it, Sandra? What do you need to tell me?"

"A lot ... and nothing. I guess mostly I have questions that I'm not sure I want answered."

"Tell me the most pressing issue, and let's decide if answers will be helpful. How does that sound?"

Sandra just thought about that for a long second. "How did you get so wise?"

Ronnie just laughed. "Time does wonderful things to our minds, Sandra. Patience, some higher order maybe. Oh, and perhaps a coma. That clearly had some effect!"

The two found a way to break the ice with little bits of humor. Sandra proceeded to tell Ronnie that she'd never understood why Ronnie was so cold to her. She asked about the years at the Husting estate. She was too little to remember much, but she knew something awful must have happened in those years. Seeing Ronnie now in her older age was a contradiction of everything that Sandra had made her out to be. She just needed answers about her childhood and why she'd felt so compelled to be out of her mother's life completely at a young age.

Ronnie was astounded to be faced with these harsh realities, but she paused long enough to gather the strength and poise she needed to square things with her lovely daughter. Not a word left her lips until she had murmured a few pleading words to seek guidance from a divine being. *Oh Lord, show me the love and grace that your disciples preach on TV. Help me know what I need to say, and be here to pick me up when I stumble in the aftermath. Amen.*

The conversation went on for at least an hour. Ronnie gave Sandra the answers she wanted about Quentin Simarillo and Warren/Ware Treallor. She confessed her own shortcomings and her inability to follow her heart. By the time the full story unfolded, Sandra seemed to understand the greed that drove Veronica Emma-Mae Husting Simarillo Whatton. It filled a void in Ronnie's life. Sandra didn't exactly profess her own shortcomings, but Ronnie surmised that Sandra was a carbon copy of her. They talked about how money and material things are wonderful and can bring joy. But Ronnie added her new understanding about love. Sandra was beginning to feel things for Angela. Kathryn showed Sandra what mother–daughter love could be like.

"I hate what we've all been through, Mother. And I do blame you for much of it."

"I know you do, as you should. I only hope you can forgive me and together we can make up for the years we've lost. Angela gives us all a fresh start."

Sandra actually wiped a tear from her eye. "Damn, I need some whiskey."

Ronnie stood up. "This is the time you need to take a walk. Let's go."

That command took Sandra by surprise. Her mother was still using a cane to get around, but she bounded out of her chair and went to the closet to get walking shoes so they could make their way out the front door.

The cold air was actually refreshing. They walked on the driveway, around the house to the back, several times. By the time they quit and walked back through the front door, they were arm in arm with matching smiles and rosy cheeks.

Rob was in his dorm room. It was late, and he couldn't sleep. His mind was racing with everything he'd left at home—his parents, Kathryn, and Angela. Everyone he thought he loved had become, in some way, a contradiction of what he admired. He struggled with what he would say to his father more than to anyone else. The thoughts that ran through his mind only brought anxiety and left no space for rest.

By one o'clock, he gave up and dialed Warren's cell.

"Rob! What's wrong, Son?"

There was a long silence. Warren waited for what seemed much too long a time.

"Dad, I don't know what to say to you, but I need to hear your voice."

"You're probably so upset with me that you don't know where to go with your thoughts or your questions. Am I right?"

"Yeah."

"I've been there. A long time ago."

"What did you do?"

"I found a hiking group and put myself in the wilderness

along the Appalachian Trail for about a month. It gave me lots of time to think. It's a long story."

"Wow."

Another long silence.

"Jeez, Dad. There's so much about you I don't know. I thought I knew you really well. And now, all of a sudden, since Christmas, all these little secrets are coming out. What else is there?"

Warren felt a wall going up. *Don't shut him out now.* "Not much. But maybe I can explain a few things."

"Not sure I want to know."

"Can't say I blame you."

Warren rubbed his head. He was sitting in his easy chair by the family room fireplace. He didn't have the desire to go up to bed. He and Leslie were still finding it difficult to talk about the most recent discoveries. *God, please don't push my son away from me. I know I deserve it, but let me help him get through his trials. Maybe I have something to offer him.*

"What should I do about Kathryn, Dad? This is so sick."

Warren's blood pressure must have dropped. He felt as if he was wilting, falling backward. His ears started to ring. Instinctually, he leaned forward quickly and put his head between his knees.

"Dad, are you there?"

"Yes. I'm here. I'm having a bit of anxiety myself, Rob. I have to be honest."

"Can you come up here and meet with me?"

That's all it took. Warren ended the call, got himself steadied, and prepared for the drive. He woke Leslie to announce that he was on his way to meet Rob in Boston. If he left now with light overnight traffic, he could make it to Rob in less than three hours. They would have an early breakfast together. He grabbed a bottle of water from the fridge on the way to the Jeep.

Kathryn snuggled Angela in a booth at a roadside diner. Michael sat across from her, the beaming father and grandfather. They had been driving for about three hours, and Angela needed a feeding. Michael was patient. He knew the demands of motherhood and saw that Kathryn was glowing in her new role. The worries he had about Angela's development were still his alone. Angela should have been crawling around or at least trying to. There were no indications that she was ready to try. Michael was sure that soon enough Kathryn would pick up on the need to give Angela special attention of some kind. In the meantime, he was keeping an eye on his special granddaughter.

The task of moving Kathryn out of her small apartment may have been easy, but it depressed Michael to think of how she had been living. The tiny flat was one room with one wall of kitchenette. The tiny bathroom had no tub for bathing Angela, so the sink served double duty. Kathryn kept the place clean and tidy. He marveled at her stamina and will. That would be behind them soon. In another hour, they would be in Greenwich, in their lovely home, with a safe and easy lifestyle for Kathryn until she could get herself back on her feet.

"Dad, what is Mom going to do about Mr. Treallor?"

"What is there to do?"

"Well, she could be kind to him. He *is* her father. And she doesn't know Quentin Simarillo, her supposed father. You'd think she'd be happy to know the truth." There was a note of disappointment in her voice.

Michael shook his head. He was thinking of all the damage, mourning the loss Kathryn must have been feeling herself. "You really are remarkable, you know?"

Kathryn pinched her eyebrows in response. "Mom's the one we have to think about, not me."

"What about your feelings for Rob?"

Michael could see her eyes misting. Kathryn was trying to be strong. It wasn't that she didn't love Rob. Something about watching her mother learn of her own biological father made Kathryn rethink her disposition toward Marcus, the father of her baby. When her grandmother talked about love in front of the family on Christmas Eve, Kathryn felt a pull on her heart. She needed her own daughter to know her father. "Maybe I love him, but not in a way that would have made sense in the long run. Angela has a dad. I loved him, I thought. That part of me has to be figured out. Maybe she needs her real father in her life, right? I mean, look what happened to Mom—and, in the end, to me and Rob!"

Michael could only agree. His daughter was truly a beautiful young woman. He only hoped that she would not be misguided on this path that could lead back to an abusive husband and father.

"God will guide me, Dad. I'm depending on it. And I think Rob will help me. We love each other that way—in God's love."

Michael didn't respond. *Maybe she can help me. Maybe there's something to her beliefs that can help Sandra.*

Leslie lay on her bed, wide awake. It was only 4:00 a.m. By now, Warren was close to Boston, possibly there. She didn't want to call him. *What would I say?*

Her thoughts crept around, finding horror lurking in the dark corners of her mind. Life had been uncomplicated for Leslie. She lived a life of service, plain and simple. Her faith in God directed all her decisions. She wondered how she could have been so far off base with Warren. He was a quiet, unassuming man who valued the same things in life as she did. They worked side by side in the homeless shelter, he helping them set up a computer system to make their daily life easier, she serving as a nurse on staff. Together they found joy in the way homeless clients warmed to the friendly atmosphere of their temporary home. She never felt the years that separated her from Warren; their hearts were the same. They spent hours with their children, laughing and nurturing them to be such wonderful young adults. *How did I miss the clues that he loved someone else?*

The ring of the phone made Leslie jump, pulling her out of her dismal thoughts. The caller ID, "UWISC," banged on her chest: *University of Wisconsin.* Adrienne needed her. With a pounding heart and shaking hands, she answered the call. The message was a blur.

Her first reaction was to call Warren. *Why? He's with Rob.*

Shock made it impossible to think straight. After a quick shower and throwing on some fresh clothes, Leslie had gathered her wits enough to make a plan. Instead of trying to find a flight to Madison, she called Adrienne's cell. No answer. Adrienne had been taken to the university health center after some kind of accident, but she was being transported to the hospital. Leslie wasn't exactly sure what was wrong. There was something about her leg and a loss of blood.

She sat on the bed and cried. There was nothing to do. She could only wait. When she thought enough time had passed, Leslie dialed the health clinic number from the caller ID. A nurse answered and was able to provide more details.

Adrienne had been walking across campus and slipped on ice. In the fall, she cut her leg on the edge of a metal railing. The cut was clean, but there was a fair amount of bleeding. Adrienne had been taken to a nearby hospital for stitches.

Now Leslie was ready to talk with Warren. She dialed his cell. No answer. She sent a text to Rob. He responded immediately. Leslie communicated with Warren through Rob. The broken relationships made Adrienne's mishap seem immense, but ten stitches weren't really a big deal.

Rachel Channing generally enjoyed her studies at Amherst College. There was always a challenging project to tackle, and her classmates were interesting. As a liberal arts major, she had no idea where she would go after graduation. Her heart was not into this process after everything that had unfolded during Christmas. Her mother and father seemed to be turning a corner of some kind. She didn't want to even guess where that might be leading them, but they seemed to be more connected somehow. Kathryn was a breath of fresh air, even with her newfound religious focus. That baby was just beautiful. And having her grandmother in her life! There were no words to describe all of these crazy changes.

It was time to be making plans for the future, but all Rachel wanted to do was go home. Something was pulling her to be there to help Kathryn, and her parents, sort things out. She wanted to learn more about Veronica Husting and the estate. She wanted to know her grandfather Mr. Treallor.

Rachel knew that the spring semester could be rough, and she understood that discipline was needed now more than ever. She was hunkered down with her textbook open on her lap. She lived in a small apartment off campus with three other young women. They kept different schedules, but in the evenings everyone was there. Each was in her own area of the apartment, studying with a headset on. Rachel was no different. Tonight, the music didn't help her concentrate. It only distracted her.

There had been so many family mysteries opened at Christmas that Rachel couldn't focus on anything. She called home, and Veronica answered the phone.

"Grandmother, it's Rachel."

"Good evening, Rachel. Is everything okay?"

"I think so. I think I'm homesick, though."

"Homesick?! How can that be? How long have you been away at college?"

"I know. But things are different now."

"You're right. They are very different. For me too."

"Grandmother, I want to come home and be with you, and Kathryn and Angela, and Mom and Dad."

"I have no problem with that, but I'm not so sure how your parents will feel."

No one said anything more. Rachel knew her wishes would be dismissed. She would just have to wait until spring break. She said good night to Veronica and hung up. Tears ran down her cheeks. She brushed them away and returned to her studies.

Veronica did the same, returning to her bed.

Betty was safely in Mexico with Alej. It wasn't difficult for her to let him know just how dangerous it would be for him to turn her down. If Betty ended up in prison, she vowed to take him with her. After all, she explained, they were meant to be together. Her love for Alej was real. Unfortunately, so was her infatuation with his evil business. For all the beliefs in a higher order she espoused, there was something compelling about the rush she always felt from doing evil deeds. Warren would never approve. He would also never understand. She recognized the dichotomy in her beliefs and in her soul.

Alej took Betty back willingly. His love for Veronica had been a passing fancy, even if it did last for many years. Once he realized that she loved his money more than she loved him, she started to bore him. He had no tolerance for her frailty, which had developed over time. There was no room for the weak in his world. Betty was hearty and exciting. They reunited easily.

When they were safely out of the country, Alej demanded that Betty tell him exactly what happened when Veronica returned to Delaware. Betty never revealed that she was responsible for Ronnie's accident and ultimately for her coma. She only told him stories of everyone reuniting in a wonderful Christmas Eve dinner. Her account made Alej believe that Veronica had run back into Ware's arms and that they rode off together into the sunset, leaving a trail of broken hearts. Betty knew Alej would never try to follow up. The estate would be sold to Ware, unbeknownst to Alej. Sandra would handle the sale very confidentially. Betty was sure of that fact; she'd padded the broker fees for assurance.

The ranch in Mexico was beautiful. The hacienda was a sprawling building. Betty, in her old age, would have been happy just to settle down and enjoy the place. Instead, it became a bed-and-breakfast for long-term guests. She had the role of hostess. Alej worked with her, and they entertained the bigwigs of the movie business. Life was good.

Ware looked at Rob over breakfast. He didn't know how to begin answering his son's questions. *Lord, guide my words.* He took a deep breath and started talking. Rob listened with no judgment. Ware cried when he told the story of his Ronnie leaving him for the money and riches that she saw in Frederick Whatton. Rob was interested in hearing how Ware had pulled himself out of a deep hole, how the trek in the wilderness brought his love for Jesus back to life, and how he'd pulled himself up by the bootstraps and lived a full life with Rob's mother, Leslie, and his sister, Adrienne. What Warren didn't tell Rob was that he'd never had the strength to completely give up on his promise to Ronnie. He was still trying to figure that one out.

Rob understood. He could see that his father was sincere.

Ware left right after breakfast and headed back to Stamford. More than ever before, he was keenly aware of his own weakness. Rob was mature and dealing with these flaws in the family lineage. Ware was proud of Rob. He was also ashamed of himself. The drive home offered him time to reconcile things, to make a plan for his next steps. Two beautiful women, each very different from the other, both whom he loved. *Lord, Robert, God. Someone up there! Tell me what to do—guide every step of my path. Please. Amen.*

Veronica Emma-Mae Husting Simarillo Whatton was staring into the backyard, sipping tea, and daydreaming. She was envisioning her own young Sandra playing in that yard in a snowsuit, making snow angels, tossing handfuls of snow into the air—things she didn't remember ever doing herself, things she never did with Sandra. She drew the tea to her lips, but instead of sipping, she breathed in its steam. The scene before her blurred. Steam, tears. All of it blended together.

A heavy heart pinched her chest. *What do I do, God? Are you there? Tell me.*

Chapter
TWENTY-EIGHT
September 2015: Coming Home

The tent was in place, the tables were set, and the roses, pink and yellow, were being placed around the grounds of the Husting estate. Roses were spectacular in Ronnie's eyes, even after all these years. The fragrance filled every corner of the grounds just as she remembered.

All the arrangements were coming together beautifully. Wedding guests were arriving. With perfectly coifed hair, nails beautifully manicured, and makeup complete, Ronnie felt like a princess. She knew that her true prince was waiting.

This time, the wedding was a moment of love, commitment, and joy. Who wouldn't be filled with expectation and romantic dreams?

Looking out her bedroom suite window, she could see all the people who were important to her upbringing, growth, decline, and reestablishment. There were new faces as well, people who had pulled her up when she had fallen the furthest from grace.

Betty and the entire Channing family sat together. Ronnie's daughter, Sandra, and her son-in-law, Michael, were doing well together. They had worked through many of their problems, and Sandra had agreed to a treatment plan. Ronnie felt some responsibility for Sandra's alcoholism, but God was helping her to help Sandra.

The granddaughters were in attendance. Rachel sat next to her mother, and Kathryn sat next to Rob Treallor. Angela wore a garden dress that replicated the pink and yellow surroundings. She was growing into a delightful little girl. Seeing her daughter, granddaughters, and great-granddaughter together in one place empowered Ronnie to be strong and confident. These new feelings exhilarated her.

This time, the wedding was hers and Ware's. Together, they'd planned every detail. It had taken several years, but Ware was able to purchase and restore the Husting estate. He had no need for the likes of dirty money from Alejandro Basil Stanis, a.k.a. Frederick Whatton, movie magnate.

Betty, on the other hand, fell back to the love of her life, Alej.

There were many secrets about Betty that Ronnie and Ware decided to leave uncovered. It was better that way. Ronnie simply pursued a clean divorce from Frederick Whatton to keep things legal. She never fought for any of Frederick's riches. Life had changed dramatically. Heart and home guided her now, and it was a greater power that drew her to a knowledge that her choices were right.

Ware chose not to dig into Betty's past. He may need to know more about his sister someday, but he chose to leave the uncovered sins of the past well buried for now. Ronnie wondered if perhaps he knew more than he let on. Betty definitely shied away from some conversations and never wanted to give a full accounting of her time. She kept her plans quiet, and she was very vague about her knowledge of James's death and the plane crash that took the lives of Ronnie's half-sister and her mother, and some distant cousin and his wife. Ronnie sensed that some things were not completely on the up-and-up in Betty's life.

Ronnie agreed with Ware, and some things were going to remain unknown to her. By choice. Someday, perhaps, she would try to connect with the pilot of that plane, Randy Bastien, but certainly not in the near future.

Now Ronnie was ready to begin a new late-in-life storybook romance with her God-chosen husband. She was ready to become Mrs. Warren Treallor.

———❧❧———

Ware had lived through heartbreaks, and he had broken hearts along the way. Today he felt redeemed. God had taken care of his family and his poor decisions and had righted the ship. God had turned his family to open their arms and their hearts to Ronnie. It was God, in Ware's belief, who opened Leslie's eyes and insisted that Ware and Ronnie pursue what was right. She loved Ware and their children deeply. She honored the fact that Ware had never cheated on her, and she understood without reservation that there had always been a deep sacrifice in his commitment to her. Leslie wanted nothing more than for him to be healthy and happy. She interpreted his light-headed spells, moments of disorientation, and need to escape the moments that were close and intimate as signs of discontent. Ware accepted Leslie's suggestion for counseling to help them through the stages of separation and loss that come with divorce. Leslie became Ware's hero. She was much happier now that those skeletons had been released from the closet.

The challenging thing for Ware was the disappointment that his children felt. He had broken their hearts. As adults, though, they were amazingly astute about such things. Both had chosen to join him and Leslie in family counseling. Both realized that Ware had not betrayed anyone. They all knew that Ware acted on the love he felt for Leslie when he thought his true love was gone forever. Rob was particularly supportive.

Rob had fallen in love with Kathryn. She never did pursue a divorce from Marcus Belton. Rob helped her track him down. He led the conversations about what had happened over the years. Marcus did not receive Kathryn in their first meetings. Together, Rob and Kathryn visited Saint Mary of the Immaculate Conception Center for Women in Baltimore. The priest who ministered to women in the center helped them to resolve their own challenges and to locate Marcus. Together they prayed for Marcus, for his addictions, and for his knowledge of God's love. They believed a miracle would happen. It would be a matter of time. Kathryn had witnessed the damage of unresolved relationships in her mother's life. She wouldn't press Marcus into anything.

Ware knew how Rob felt. Unfortunately, in Rob's case, the discovery that he and Kathryn shared family blood made reconciliation of these circumstances much more critical. Ware shed enough tears for himself and for his son, and Rob knew of his father's remorse. They developed a strong adult bond during the unraveling of their lives.

Adrienne struggled to make sense of any commitment her parents claimed to one another. It was Leslie who reached out to her as mother-to-daughter advisor. At one point, Leslie believed she had let her family down by releasing Warren to Ronnie. Adrienne was devastated but remained in a good relationship with both her parents, for which Ware credited Leslie. There was no denying that Leslie was selfless. Through all the challenges and changes they navigated, Leslie's faith remained strong. She held fast to her conviction to serve God first and her family second. Her work at the shelter continued as her ministry. Nothing would change her passion for that work.

Ware stood under the tent, waiting for Ronnie to walk down the aisle created between two sections of folding chairs. He was dressed in a suit, nothing particularly special. His gaze scanned the setting. *Very Betty. Very Ronnie. Simple and elegant. Oh, the incredible years I lived here as hired staff.* The scent of roses filled his nostrils, and the colors of pink and yellow flooded him with nostalgia.

He walked to the backyard and opened the gate to the pool house. *The beginning. So many years. Tears.* The reflection in the pool caught his eye. "God's with you, Ware. Thank you."

"Robert?"

"Yeah. It's me. I'm with you today."

"How?"

"In spirit. Tell my daughter I approve and that I love her."

Ware stared at the reflection. *Peace.*

"Thank you, Robert."

"Tell her I'm happy."

We're home, finally.

———— ❦ ————

A toast to Mr. and Mrs. Warren Treallor started the festivities. Ronnie's tea-length dress was simple. Her hair was pinned up in her signature French twist. Her ears sparkled, and her wedding finger held the beautiful single-stone diamond ring that had lived in Ware's pocket for fifty years.

"Welcome home, Ronnie."

Ronnie touched a red fingernail to Ware's lips and closed her eyes in thankful prayer. "Do you believe there is a heaven, Ware?"

Discussion Questions

1. How do you characterize Veronica Emma-Mae Husting in her young adult years? What are the driving forces in her life? What does she seek, and where?

2. What do you think Warren's motives are in his pursuit of Veronica? How does his motive change, and why?

3. How do you think Veronica's half-sister, Margaret Leeder, influences Veronica's own thinking and goals in life?

4. What was Robert Husting's motivation for leaving the sale of the Husting estate to Warren Treallor? What was his plan, and how well did his plan work?

5. Warren Treallor and Betty Zane Treallor Stanis are half-siblings raised with the same fundamental ideology of good and evil. Discuss the reasons you think these siblings are so different.

6. What role does James play in helping the reader develop an understanding of Betty?

7. Does good win over evil? Explain.

8. The Channing family lives a privileged lifestyle with two daughters who had every opportunity to be successful. Rachel follows the expected path in life, but Kathryn finds her own way. What dynamics in the Channing family may have led to these differences in the sisters' approaches to life?

9. What behaviors does Sandra Simarillo Channing display that reflect her attitude toward her own upbringing? How does she address the ultimate test to accept her past?

10. At what point in the novel do you think Veronica better understands her life and her priorities? What are the indications that she is developing a new perspective?

11. Warren and Leslie Treallor seem to be the perfect couple. What is it that keeps Warren from telling Leslie about his past? What breaks his resolve to stay true to Leslie?

12. Rob Treallor is named after Veronica's father, Robert Husting. If your spouse chose to name one of your children after a former lover's parent, how would you respond? Discuss.

13. What is your reaction to the way that Leslie Treallor released Warren after years of marriage and still remained his friend? Is this a sacrifice that you could make in order for someone you love to be happy?

14. When Robert Husting visits Ware in spirit form, what is he trying to accomplish, and why?

15. If you could have dinner with one character from the novel, who would it be, and what conversation would you have?

CPSIA information can be obtained
at www.ICGtesting.com
Printed in the USA
FFHW021853011019
55346918-61071FF